NOT
BY
BREAD
ALONE

By VLADIMIR DUDINTSEV

NOT BY BREAD ALONE

Translated from the Russian by
DR. EDITH BONE

E. P. DUTTON & CO., INC. – NEW YORK
1957

First published in the U.S.S.R. under the title:

НЕ ХЛЕБОМ ЕДИНЫМ

Library of Congress Catalog Card Number: 57-11252

PUBLISHER'S NOTE

FOR too long the world has missed the authentic voice of Russian humanity. This voice was clearest and strongest in the novels of the last century, but recently has scarcely been heard at all. It is easy to see why *Not By Bread Alone* has caused a political sensation, for in it the voice of Russian humanity has spoken once again, in all its former strength and honesty and, moreover, it has spoken with the accents of a *novelist*. Dudintsev's work is rich in all those qualities which raised the classic Russian novel to heights of influence and achievement—in narrative, in character, in satire and seriousness of purpose. *Not By Bread Alone* will inevitably occupy a place of historical importance, but it will live more enduringly as a novel which illuminates a universal human predicament.

Soviet readers, discussing Dudintsev's book before authority pronounced against it, used one word more frequently than any other: "truthful." This was a tribute not only to Dudintsev's boldness in discussing unpleasant features of Soviet society, but to his integrity as a writer. There were Moscow students who shouted that the whole of Soviet fiction was a lie, with the exception of this one book. Soviet literature under Stalin, as the writers themselves have since admitted, grew tame, platitudinous, and dishonest. Its gaze was averted from life and fixed on a distorted picture created to appease and gratify a suspicious and vainglorious tyrant. After Stalin's death, some writers began to seek relief from the strain of circumspection and the tedium of forced complacency. The critic Pomerantsev scandalized officialdom by pleading for "sincerity" in literature. In spite of the uncertainties of official policy toward literature some work was published which could not have appeared in Stalin's time. But it was not until after the Twentieth Party Congress in February, 1956, that Soviet literature seemed to be passing from the "thaw" to a new spring. Dudintsev's novel is the outstanding work of this important period in Soviet literature.

In the late autumn of 1956, *Not By Bread Alone,* as it was being published in the magazine *Novy Mir,* became the subject of furious controversy and was discussed at crowded and turbulent public meetings. Prominent writers praised its merciless realism, its implacability, its humanity, its respect for ordinary people, its wealth of ideas, its loyalty to the true Bolshevik literary tradition, its "deep faith in the strength of our peoples and our society." A little later, certain lesser writers accused Dudintsev of "trying to blacken and pull to pieces all that the Soviet people has created." Toward the end of the year the Soviet Press was printing only unfavorable criticism. The organs of the Communist Party and the Writers' Union have delivered a verdict which will put an end to open controversy: Dudintsev, they say, is a talented writer and meant well, but he has drawn a distorted and pessimistic picture of Soviet reality, given his affections to an unworthy hero, and ignored the forces which in fact preserve the Leninist ideal incorruptible and ensure its ultimate triumph.

No one has attempted to deny that events such as those described took place. On the other hand, authority is not at present prepared to endorse publicly such a dark picture of Soviet reality under Stalin. Dudintsev, says one Soviet critic, has given the impression that the Drozdovs were a "mass phenomenon," whereas the Party insists that even in the worst days of the "personality cult" the "cadres of the Soviet State" as a whole were sound. Further, Dudintsev has, from the official point of view, dealt unsatisfactorily with a most awkward problem: the problem of what to say about the Party itself in Stalin's last years. It would have weakened and falsified his story if he had shown the Party in its conventional role, as the guardian of the public conscience, the supreme judge sitting above the bureaucrats and righting the wrongs which they commit, the *deus ex machina* who delivers the righteous man from his powerful enemies. Instead, he excludes the Party as an organization from his novel. His silence might be understood as a mute contradiction of the official declaration that even in Stalin's last years the Party as a whole remained true to itself and generally efficient. Lopatkin and his friends are the "real Communists," but they are so few, and often helpless against the unscrupulous bureaucrats, most of whom must themselves belong to the Party. Is there not here a heretical suggestion that grace resides in individuals and not in organizations? Lopatkin has another literary ancestor, besides the nineteenth-century progressive intellectual. He is strongly reminiscent of those austere Communists who in earlier Soviet fiction sacrificed their comforts, their personal happiness, their health, sometimes their lives to the "building of communism." They held power and fought against the "survivals of capitalism" in the minds and behavior of the masses. Their spiritual descendant is powerless, and his struggle is against their political heirs. It can easily be understood why official Soviet literary criticism, which is used to regarding every novel as a political generalization, has refused to accept Lopatkin as a hero of the times. Finally, some of the political observations scattered throughout the novel are uncomfortably close to the sort of demagogic utterances which the Party found it necessary to discourage last year, especially when unrest among the young intellectuals, disturbed and overexcited by the Twentieth Congress, was aggravated by events in Hungary and Poland.

Dudintsev's present position is uncertain. To the surprise of all who read the authoritative denunciations of *Not By Bread Alone* it was published in a single-volume Soviet edition of 30,000 copies in May, 1957. At the same time, Dudintsev, together with a group of Moscow writers, has been under great pressure to make a public admission of his mistakes. Whatever the immediate future holds for him, we believe that his countrymen will be proud of his book in years to come and that Dudintsev will sooner or later take his

7

place among the most interesting Russian writers of the Soviet period.

* * * * * *

At one time we were informed that Mr. Dudintsev wished to make changes in the American edition of *Not By Bread Alone*. We replied that we would publish the book as it originally appeared in *Novy Mir,* but if the author cared to write a preface explaining his attitude we would consider including it. Mr. Dudintsev has written such a preface, and it follows this note.

PREFACE

In the course of the years during which I worked at this novel, the futile question, "Was I not washing dirty linen in public?" never once occurred to me. Carried away by the work, I did not allow myself to be diverted toward unnecessary speculations that the dirty linen that was being washed (with the object of making it cleaner) might be made use of by somebody. I took no precautions in this respect. No inhibiting considerations stayed my hand.

True, I knew that in the West things were regarded in a different light from the one we meet with every day in our Soviet way of life.

But I measured everything by my own standards. This is what I thought: if, for instance, after reading the books of many highly gifted Western novelists I did not sit down and write political indictments of their regimes and governments; if, although not accepting certain ideas expressed by Western authors, I nevertheless found no hatred in my soul for the people discussed in these books; if my eyes were open to perceive the evil—sometimes painted in vivid colors in such a book—but also the good which the author champions; then, I assumed, the literary West would pay me back with the same measure of objectivity, would understand in the same way what I reject and would notice in the same way (at least notice!) what it is in the name of which I live and labor.

We Soviet people jealously guard the basic principles of our life, that uplift of the soul and that purity of new human relations which spring up in us from our early years. And with all the force of which a dedicated man suddenly torn from a beloved activity is capable, we repudiate those who bring disillusionment, introversion, and selfish calculation into our ranks, we pour out on them all our anger, and however tough such seasoned timeservers may be, we shall force them to surrender.

It was these feelings that the Soviet readers saw in my book. These feelings are in no way related to that little smoke of hope which may perhaps rise in the heart of some Russian landowner grown old in exile when he reads a propagandist article about my book.

We speak boldly and honestly about our deficiencies and our difficulties, because they are the birth pangs of a new world in which there is no injustice, a world the principles of which are being confirmed and marching to victory in my country.

In my book I freely raised a question which seems to me very important. The decisions of the twentieth congress confirmed me in the consciousness that I was right. I do not deny that the relations between the characters in my novel are dramatized in a certain way which derives from real life: as in every large family we have feast days and also work days saturated with acute and varied situations. But a family, the members of which all know one another well, always finds the right solution to its conflicts. We are not afraid of grave, forthright, purifying discussion and are quite capable of showing the door to those of us who might wish to oppose to the common good their own narrow personal interests.

I know that many of my readers abroad could have had a sound appreciation of all this, if they had understood what it was all about, if they had known it and were not biased. How could we get them to understand? Perhaps the foreign press might help in this.

But I have here in front of me a few foreign "respectable" newspapers and journals. And I see that in my novel, intended chiefly for "internal consumption," certain journalists—unfriendly "experts on Russia"—at once saw only the passages that interested them, the passages I did not cover up with a shield of qualifying clauses. They began to play up these passages with that professional "tact" which had already been commented on by Balzac.

Passed through their merciless filter, my novel unnaturally split

10

into two parts. The part containing the positive thoughts of the author was discarded by my biased critics—they had no use for it. The negative facts, the "dirt" which I washed out when I cleaned some dirty linen—those were taken as weapons, as proof of conclusions prepared long in advance.

When I read these articles, I was horror-stricken. I thought: "Have I not caused my people unexpected harm when I wanted to do it a service?" As a front-line soldier, still carrying in my body some metal from the recent war, I am well aware of the significance of the printed word, particularly of the kind of word which rouses hostile feelings toward whole nations, toward millions of people. Stinging newspaper lines are not so harmless; they are plaited into a long fuse which leads to the powder vaults of war. Among the journalists concerned with politics there are some soldiers in mufti. Making use of the fact that the question of their behavior is as yet not debated in the commissions of the United Nations, they are the first to violate frontiers and begin an exchange of shots many years before the first real shot is fired.

When I took in my hands a few newspapers with these horrible articles by "experts on Russia," I felt as though my novel, a peaceable ship in foreign waters, had been seized by pirates and was flying the skull and crossbones.

But fortunately I saw other newspapers, too, many other reviews by more modest people who made no claim to a monopolistic "expert" quality; reviews which perhaps contained a stricter criticism of the literary deficiencies of my novel, but nevertheless talking not of "bombshells," not of "dynamite," not of "assault," but of a work of art with all its intricate contradictions and peculiarities, rooted in the personality, philosophy, and life experience of the author.

I want to hope that contemporary lovers of the artistic word in the West possess a sufficiently solid immunity to strident headlines dictated by the events of the day. Therefore I will not start a fruitless argument with the "experts on Russia." I present my book to the new reader, counting on his unbiased judgment. Of course, as the author, I would like the reader to go with me and, if only for

11

an hour, to enter trustingly into our life and share the feelings of my countrymen, feelings in which there is hatred of evil, too, but of which the principal is a great love of humanity and faith in the inevitable victory of the forces of reason and justice.

Moscow.

PART
1

I

A<small>T</small> high noon a train was pulling into the railway station of Muzga. Snowdrifts had formed high ridges on both sides of the track and were piled up against the walls of the station building, right up to the sign showing the name of the station, "Muzga." The snow-covered tops of the coaches floated past and came to a standstill. There was a bustle on the platform and then three men in felt boots and identical sheepskin jackets ran toward the end of the train, to the last coach, which was the sleeper from Moscow. They clambered into the coach, came into view again, and passed down case after case, all in gray covers. . . . Suddenly a wind of curiosity seemed to blow across the platform; there was a faint murmur and then all ran in the same direction, and gathered in a dense crowd near the Pullman from Moscow.

"Who is it?"

"Drozdov. He'll get out in a minute. . . ."

"Here he is. . . ."

Hardly anyone succeeded in catching a glimpse of the new arrival, because he whom they called Drozdov was of very small stature. But in contrast everyone could see the soft fur hat, and under it, the face of his companion—a beautiful gray-eyed woman, a full head taller than Drozdov.

The crowd moved back to the station building and melted away unsatisfied. Only a few, who had been quick enough in circling the station building, could see two troikas dash away into the distance with a squealing of sledge runners, away to the white, snowy edge of the steppe from which black smoke rose and billowed lopsidedly, covering one half of the sky with a dirty gray veil. There, beyond the distant snowline, it seemed as though a naval squadron were passing beyond a horizon that was the sea. The smoke came from a gigantic industrial plant built here during the war, sprawling over several miles, with buildings, shops, storage sheds, and railway lines. In those first postwar years the *kombinat* did not figure on any map or in any geography book.

The general manager of the *kombinat*, Leonid Ivanovich Drozdov, or simply, Drozdov, as everyone called him in these parts, was returning from Moscow after having been summoned there by the Ministry. He had been accompanied on this journey by his young wife, from whom he had not parted for a single day since their marriage. Now they had come back, both well pleased—she with her shopping in Moscow and he with the way his affairs were going. A departmental head, who was his friend, had given him to understand that he might quite soon expect a transfer to Moscow, and this had long been Drozdov's desire.

Two other managers whom Drozdov knew well differed from him on this point. They held that it was better to be the hub of the wheel in a factory than a mere spoke, even if it were in Moscow. Drozdov knew, but did not mind, that his material position as a departmental head would be somewhat less favorable than at present. He accepted the reduction in salary the change would entail; he had quite made up his mind about that. Nor did the prospect of less freedom worry him. "I shall always be myself," he told himself. The difficulties that would arise in a job of a wider scope held no terrors for him—on the contrary, they attracted him. He even had a theory about it. He thought a man should never shirk growing pains, should always strive to rise higher and always feel slightly less than sufficient. A man's job should always be a little beyond his powers. It was in such a situation, continually tensed, that men developed most quickly. And as soon as one began to be equal to the job, as soon as one had been praised once or twice—the thing to do was to move up into a region of fresh difficulties and then reach out once more, again seeking to keep up with the others.

"Yes, I built up this *kombinat*. What of it?" he thought, narrow-

16

ing his eyes at the noise made by the sledge runners. "We didn't do too badly during the war; we got a few banners and decorations. And now we are still keeping at top level. I'm fifty-two now. . . . Three, four, five. . . . Say thirteen more years to go. . . . That's quite a reasonable backlog. Quite reasonable. One can make a devil with horns in that time."

The *kombinat,* like a great city gradually unfolding itself, seemed to advance toward him and hem in the steppe from the right and left. Five tall brick chimneys stood in the center, in a row, all of the same height and all five emitting a cloud of black smoke. Below it one could see many lesser clouds—gray, reddish, or poison-ously yellow. On one side stood the dark cooling tower of the evap-orators, from which steep billows of vapor rose, gleaming a par-ticularly pure white amid the black clouds. The whistles of the factory switch engines were already audible. The road was flanked on both sides by uniform small two-flat houses of white brick with steep slate roofs—houses built under the social-welfare scheme. Drozdov came out of his reverie, rose in his seat, and prodded the driver with his finger.

"Let's walk, Nadia! Will you? Heavenly weather, isn't it!"

The sledge stopped. Drozdov's wife gathered up the soft folds of her coat, bought six days before in Moscow, and stepped out on to the clean, not very deep, and dazzlingly bright snow.

"What wonderful snow!" she said in her gay, youthful voice.

Drozdov lingered behind for a moment. He tore a hole in a large cardboard box, pulled out some bright-colored, very large oranges and distributed them in his various pockets. Then he waved to the driver and roughly stripping the peel off an orange, hurried to join his wife. Calmly she accepted the peeled sections of fruit and they walked on, enjoying the sunny winter day. Drozdov was short. He wore a shiny chocolate-brown leather coat with a collar of marbled karakul and a gray karakul cap to match. His wife was tall, with a look of perpetual sorrow lurking in her gray eyes and no color in her cheeks; but her lips were a bright rose, and she had a large velvety birthmark on her cheek. She was wearing a cap and a coat of light chestnut-colored silky fur; a broad-shouldered, expensive coat, which sat on her somewhat lopsidedly. She lagged behind continually, and Drozdov waited for her, each time holding a freshly peeled orange in his hand.

Nadia was pregnant. Drozdov, walking in front, screwed up his eyes and wrinkled his yellow dry-skinned forehead in the attempt to conceal a joyful smile. People passed the time of day with them, stepped off the path into the snowdrifts and stared at them, both while face to face with them and after they had passed. Leonid Ivanovich gave each passer-by a look out of his tired, happy black eyes. He knew what these people would say later, behind his back, as they stepped from the snowdrift onto the path again: "He's thrown one wife over—she was getting old. Now he's got himself a young slip of a girl—and he is quite off his head about her!" "Suppose I *am* off my head!" he thought. "Must one put up a show and live with a wife one never cared for and avoid meeting the woman one loves? Isn't it simpler to do as I did?" He looked back at his wife and she smiled at him from under her little bonnet. "Particularly as our Shura says; Leonid Ivanovich was born to have two wives. He's got two bumps on the top of his head." He laughed as he recalled this and glanced again at his wife. "She is young!" he thought with pleasure. People's stares did not trouble him. He felt no embarrassment at reaching only to her shoulder. True, Nadia always stooped slightly when she was walking with him, in order to appear less tall. This was already getting to be a habit with her.

They walked along like this, approaching and receding from each other, taking up the entire street, and nodding to or exchanging greetings with friends. Now and then school children went past with satchels and portfolios. The older ones stood aside and, interrupting each other, chanted: "Good morning, Nadezhda Sergeyevna!" Nadia taught geography in the school. When the Drozdovs had passed, after a moment's pause, the children made a rush for the orange peel trodden into the snow. With whoops of merriment and wonder they grabbed and pocketed the bright, scented marvels—

18

no one had ever seen anything like orange peel in this steppe region which until quite lately had been at the back of beyond.

The Drozdovs lived close by, on Stalin Avenue. This was a wide road; its houses were also of the two-flat type, but had sheet-iron roofs and large windows. In Muzga it was said that the "top brass" of the combine lived in these houses. Drozdov's house differed in no way from those of his neighbors, except that he was the sole occupant; both flats had been converted into one.

Drozdov entered the lobby after his wife, stamped his feet, and cleared his throat. The servant, Shura, a sturdy village girl, looked through the crack of the door and immediately opened it wide.

"Oh my, a new fur coat! Welcome, Leonid Ivanovich! Nadezhda Sergeyevna, you must stand us one, to drink to your new coat! What is this fur? How soft it is!"

"It's a foreign fur," Drozdov said impressively, narrowing his eyes as he helped his wife to take off her coat. According to her custom, Nadia stooped a little as she stood before him. "It's a fur from overseas; they call it mink."

At these words Shura burst out laughing.

"Enough of that! Here, take it and hang it up—in the wardrobe."

Nadia took out her hatpins and went to her room, swaying as she walked. Drozdov, in his black suit, divested of his overcoat, looked thin. He had yellowish protruding ears. He hummed something indistinctly, rubbed his hands, and walked across the house, down a long passage, toward the kitchen.

"Mama!" he cried cheerfully. "Can't you see we have arrived!"

"I see, I see!" his mother's masculine voice answered from the kitchen. "Aren't you a bit early?"

"Mother!" Leonid Ivanovich stopped at the door. His somewhat ironical gaze took in everything: the strings of onions hanging on the walls, the Russian stove and next to it the gas cooker with its cylinder of compressed gas, and near the door a low tub of sour cream half-covered with a cloth. "Mother!" He closed his eyes and stood a few seconds, then he slowly opened them—with him this

19

was a sign of restrained annoyance. "Mother! What have you done with my Glazkov?"

"I sent him to Slobodchikov for some cream. Nadia needs fresh things. And now he is resting. The man was at the wheel forty-eight hours, after all."

"That's all right." Drozdov's gaze once more embraced the kitchen and came to rest on the tub with the sour cream. He kept his eyes shut for a long time and then, slowly opening them, said in a shrill, boyish voice: "All the same, don't order the machine out without my permission. I shall leave orders at the garage——"

"Order away!" said the old woman, not looking at her son. "Go on! Give orders! Show that you are the master!"

Drozdov returned to the passage and went to the telephone.

"I want the dispatcher. . . . Well, break the connection. . . " He sniffed sleepily into the receiver—this was another of his habits. "Alexander Alekseyich? . . . Here? This is Drozdov. Yes. . . . Thank you. How are things with you? Y-yes. . . . Has the fourth machine been fixed? . . . And the furnaces?" Drozdov's voice took on a threatening note. "It whistles? How d'you mean—whistles? What's that? My respected comrade, suppose I was away, not ten, but twenty days, would the machine whistle for twenty days? It must be working, not in four days, but by the day after tomorrow. . . . All right, don't let's argue. . . . Yes, I'm coming down straight away. . . . Hell! . . ." said Leonid Ivanovich, and hung up.

But he calmed down and told Shura to tell all telephone callers that he was not in.

"Aren't we getting anything to eat?" he shouted in the direction of the kitchen.

Three hours later he left the house carrying a large leather folder. At the gate a gray-green car was waiting. Drozdov seated himself beside the youthful driver Glazkov, and frowned; in an instant he appeared a different man. The car turned and twisted among the houses and stopped at a two-story high building, with large square windows. Still frowning, Drozdov climbed the steps, pushed open the glass door, and dragged slowly up the stairs and along the passage, nodding as he passed to those he met. Everyone knew that the chief had arrived and a few people were already waiting in his anteroom. Drozdov entered his office, a spacious, high-ceilinged room with a large russet carpet crossed diagonally by a green runner. He was followed by his secretary, a woman with little make-up, wearing a tight skirt and a thin white blouse.

"Who is outside?" Drozdov asked, smoothing the hair on his temples and running his fingers over the double bump of his bald crown. He did have two bumps on the top of his head—a good omen!

"It's the inventor. About those pipes."

"Yes, yes. I remember. He can wait. Let Ganichev and Samsonov come in."

The secretary went out, and Drozdov walked around his enormous desk. On it stood a glittering inkstand cast of Kaslinsk iron made out of the insignia of hetman's power. There were two maces, a massive seal, the hetman's flag, and some other heavy and significant-looking objects. Drozdov walked around this table and dropped into the armchair. Drawing his head between his shoulders and clenching both his hands together into a single huge pale fist, he let them rest on the table in a gesture of expectation. But something seemed to cross his mind. He quickly changed his posture, picked up the receiver, moved some levers on a black appliance which looked like a large typewriter, and spoke in a sleepy voice to the workshop where the fourth machine was not working properly. At this moment Ganichev, chief engineer of the *kombinat,* and Samsonov, secretary of the party bureau, came in. Ganichev was very tall, stout, and clean-shaven. Over his blue suit he wore a work jacket of thin brown cotton. Samsonov, who was the same height as the general manager, wore an old army uniform without shoulder straps, and boots. Both men sat down in front of the managerial desk.

"Well," Drozdov said. "Here we are, comrades. What's the news?"

21

"There is always some news or other, worse luck!" Samsonov said. Ganichev gave him an uncomprehending look.

"This is the news *I* have brought." Drozdov opened the folder and showed a sheet of drawing paper covered with graphs and columns of figures. "In future our reports will be made in accordance with this schedule. I will pin it up straight away where everyone can see it." Drozdov took a few drawing pins out of the hetman's headgear, frowned and, in his creaking boots, walked to a yellow board on the wall. "I'll pin it up like this"—he rose on tiptoe—"so that everyone can see."

"Excuse me, Leonid Ivanovich." The giant Ganichev hurried to him. "Permit me. I am a bit taller, if I may say so."

"In such a case Napoleon would have said"—Samsonov threw himself back in his chair—"you, Ganichev, are not higher—only longer."

He laughed loudly. Ganichev seemed not to hear, but Drozdov turned toward Samsonov, closed his eyes, and then slowly opened them. This was intended to express a controlled anger, but the amused glint in Drozdov's black eyes did not escape Samsonov. The general manager had enjoyed his quip.

"Comrade Samsonov"—he raised his head and drew his brows severely together, laughing with his eyes only—"Comrade Samsonov, historical parallels are dangerous. Mind your step!"

An hour later Ganichev left. Drozdov, sitting comfortably at his desk, again clenched both hands into a single great fist and looked at Samsonov with raised eyebrows.

"What was that you said about Napoleon?"

Samsonov readily repeated it.

"Leonid Ivanovich!" He laughed. "May I tell you another funny thing?"

"Let's hear it."

"It's about that chap Maxiutenko, who has such a large family. Do you know what he got himself into? Auntie Glasha caught him in the drawing office with that girl from the planning department, that little Vera! During the midday break. Imagine! They had even locked themselves in!"

"Does his wife know?"

"No one knows as yet. I am still trying to decide what to do. I don't feel like making a fuss; after all, he has three children. And there's the wife. One feels sorry for her when one sees her. She is a good woman."

"A good woman, you say?"

"Yes, really good. That's just it!"

"I must scare him!" Drozdov pressed a button on the wall behind him. "He must be given a bit of a fright."

The secretary came in.

"Call Maxiutenko to me."

"But that inventor . . ."

"I know. Let him wait."

"Then I'm off." Samsonov got up.

"By rights it is you who ought to deal with such matters, with moral pressure." Drozdov gave him a sharp, amused glance. "All right, all right, go."

A minute later Maxiutenko, a bald, fair man with a high complexion, reddish eyebrows, and moist feminine lips, stood before the general manager.

"Ah! there you are! What are you staring at? Sit down, Comrade Maxiutenko. . . . Tell me, how are you getting on with the pipe-casting machine? The Ministry will have my blood about it one of these days. Are you ever going to get that machine finished?"

Maxiutenko came to life. He spoke hurriedly:

"Leonid Ivanovich, everything the designers could do they have done. The improvements which were sent us have been passed on to the technical side."

"Is that true?" Drozdov closed his eyes, as if tired, passed a finger over his dry, yellowish forehead, and asked, without opening his eyes: "What's this mess you have got yourself into again—with that little Vera?"

Maxiutenko said nothing. Drozdov breathed deeply and evenly,

23

with closed eyes, as if asleep. Then he half-opened his eyes, gave the pale, sweating designer a sorrowful look, and closed them again.

"You, as a member of the Party, ought to know that you won't get any medals for a business like this," he went on, as though in his sleep. "I thought, indeed I was convinced, that you would feel at least a spark of gratitude toward the man who twice"—here Drozdov opened angry eyes—"*twice* got you out of a tight spot. Now listen, Maxiutenko." He came out from behind the desk and paced up and down on the carpet, not in a straight line but along an intricate curve, turning alternately, right and left. "There is something definitely wrong with you, young man. I would say you tend to misbehave yourself. I don't suppose your wife knows anything about it, does she?"

"No, she doesn't." Maxiutenko spoke in a whisper, wiping his forehead with his handkerchief.

"And your wife is a very good woman. Now, what am I to do with you, you Don Juan! Be careful, for you only have one bump and not two on the top of your head. If you had two bumps, like me, here, look. One, two, you might have a second wife. And mind —a wife! A lawful wife! But look at what you are doing! And what shall I do with you? I have had an official report. Take a sheet of paper and write me an explanation. Sit down here and write. Here's some paper and a pen."

Half an hour later Drozdov, sitting at his desk, his large horn-rimmed spectacles on his nose, was reading Maxiutenko's explanation.

"You are evading the issue, young man! You are keeping something back." He took off his spectacles, gave the designer a look of commiseration, and walked to the safe standing in one corner of the room. "I shall put it in there. If you get into a scrape again, I'll make the whole lot public. Look, here are your old sins. Here is another of your apologies. Remember when you were drunk and lost the letter? Here it is, see! Go, and don't forget: Drozdov has taken you in hand. He'll see you through!"

Maxiutenko went out and the secretary came in again.

24

"Leonid Ivanovich, that inventor . . ."

"Is he still waiting? Well, let him come in."

Instead of the inventor it was Samsonov who entered.

"Well, how did it go?"

"He blushed, as usual. Sit down here, I am seeing the inventor.
, . . Please come in." This he was saying to a tall, lean man standing in the doorway. "This way, please."

Samsonov sat down in an armchair and looked at the floor. The
inventor crossed the carpet with an even step and remained standing at the desk. He was wearing a military tunic, darned at the
elbows, military breeches with frayed pale pink piping, and tidily
patched shoes instead of boots. Everything was carefully cleaned
and pressed. The inventor held himself straight, raising his head
a little, and Drozdov noted at once the peculiar dignity of his whole
bearing which is so attractive in a spare, soldierly figure. The man's
fair hair, long uncut, separating into two great locks, framed a high
forehead, cleft deeply by a single sharply defined furrow. The inventor was clean-shaven. For an instant one sunken cheek twitched
in a nervous smile, but he quickly compressed his lips, and gazed
mildly with his tired gray eyes at the general manager.

That mild gaze troubled Drozdov somewhat, and he lowered
his own. The fact was that three years before the inventor had submitted to the inventions bureau of the *kombinat* a project of a
machine for the centrifugal casting of iron drainpipes. The documents had been forwarded to the Ministry, some correspondence
had ensued, and ever since, whenever Drozdov went to Moscow,
this very quiet, reserved, and to all appearances very persistent man,
came to see him, and asked him to hand a letter to the Minister,
and somehow push this business. The present, most recent trip to
Moscow had also been the occasion for a letter. But Drozdov, having taken the letter, as he had always done, this time had not put it
in the Minister's own hands, as the inventor had requested, but had
given it to one of the young men sitting in the Minister's waiting
room—his first assistant. Drozdov had no idea whether this letter had
reached the man to whom it was addressed, and he had not ventured

to ask the Minister about it. Nor had he asked the assistant, because of the elusive insolence with which that young man conducted himself toward visitors, taking a long time over answering questions, and even turning his back on his interlocutor.

That was how the case had stood. But about six months before another obstacle had arisen: the Ministry had sent down the plans and specifications for another centrifugal machine proposed by a group of scientists and designers headed by a well-known scientist, Professor Avdiyev. Instructions had been given to build this machine at once. By now, the work was already well in hand, standing irrevocably in the way of Lopatkin's machine. Drozdov felt a little to blame. In the days when, for certain reasons, he had been in particularly close touch with the school in Muzga—where Nadia was a teacher—in those days, wishing to show the generosity of his nature, he had lightly promised the inventor to push his project. But in these three years he had done nothing at all. And now that this project of Professor Avdiyev had cropped up—Avdiyev who had for many years been regarded as an authority on centrifugal casting —Lopatkin's project was irretrievably done for. On Avdiyev's side were knowledge and experience and an established organization, it had attracted attention, and—as a departmental head of a friend of Drozdov had expressed it—it "opened up perspectives." Experience told Drozdov that one should never, even unintentionally, get in the way of influential people engaged in some project which "opened up perspectives." Besides, it would be downright foolish to observe a quixotic neutrality in this matter at a time when the Ministry's instructions demanding that the Avdiyev machine be produced with the least possible delay were reason enough for him, Drozdov, to take sides with the Avdiyev group. Of course Drozdov would long ago have informed Lopatkin of all that had already been decided in secret, had it not been for those sorrowful and confiding eyes, which made him feel uncomfortable and forget all his little tricks. Hence it cost him a very great effort to say what at last he now had to.

"Sit down," he said, getting a little pale. "Samsonov, let me intro-

26

duce Comrade Lopatkin; Dmitri Alexeyevich, if I am not mistaken?"

The inventor shook hands with Samsonov. Then he sat down and there was a long silence.

"What can I say to you?" Drozdov covered his face with his hands and remained so for some time. Then he took his hands from his face, rubbed them together, and locked them into one large fist, while he gazed at the inventor as though working something out in his mind. "Hm, yes. Well, complete rejection. There it is, my dear fellow, no one supports you."

Lopatkin made a gesture with his hands, as if to say: "It's all my fault," and got up to go. This was all he had come to find out. But Drozdov again said: "Er—ye-es——" He had not finished what he had to say.

"I have read your complaints made to Shutikov." His tone as he mentioned the deputy minister was casual. "Yes, I read them. Very witty. You had a little to say about me, too. Oh, it's quite all right!" Drozdov smiled. "My feelings are not hurt. You are acting quite properly. The trouble is, you have one weak spot—you have no substantial grounds for complaint. I am under no obligation to promote your machine. Our *kombinat* is not meant to produce pipes. The drainpipes we are making are needed only for the Ministry's own housing projects. They are only a drop in the ocean. You ought to have submitted the whole thing to the proper department and not to us. That was your biggest mistake, Comrade Lopatkin."

The inventor said nothing, only clasped his hands over his massive knee. His hands were large and bony, with thickened joints on slender fingers.

"Your second mistake consists"—Drozdov wearily closed his eyes —"consists in being an individual on his own. The lone wolf is out of date. Our new machines are the fruit of collective thought. You will scarcely succeed in anything, no one will want to work with or for you. I have come to this conclusion after a thorough study of all the circumstances"—here he smiled sorrowfully—"of the question."

27

"Yes, yes, I understand. . . ." The inventor smiled, too, but his smile was sweeter: he understood the state of mind of the general manager and was anxious to relieve him first of all of the painful necessity of saying unpleasant things to a visitor. "You must excuse me, please. . . ." He stood up with a resigned gesture. "To tell the truth, I got into this business by accident. Although I am a single individual, I am not doing this for myself. . . . Thank you. Good-by." He gave a slight bow and walked to the door with firm, resolute steps.

"A broken man," Drozdov remarked. "He wasn't strong enough. He proved weak. Such men are broken by life."

"I suppose so," Samsonov agreed.

"Did you know that he was the physics master in our school? The one where Nadia teaches. So you see what a business it is! He's a university graduate."

"What if he is? Universities aren't . . ."

"Oh, but his was Moscow university. You may not know it, but he is a genuine inventor. Has a patent, too. Certificates. When his authorship was acknowledged, Moscow immediately asked him to go there and work on the project. And there is a law about inventors: if you are summoned to work out your idea, you leave your old job and you get the same pay at your new one. So he went off to Moscow—ha-ha!"—Drozdov laughed so that he shook in his chair—"so off he went! And this is the second year he has been out of a job. They engaged another physics master here, and when he got there they gave him the sack. There had been no funds allocated. Now it's clear who was behind it all. It was Vassili Zakharych Avdiyev. He himself has been tinkering with the same sort of thing for a long time. So ever since this one . . ."

"You should explain that to him. How can he pit himself against doctors," added Samsonov, "and professors!"

"Of course not. But somehow I like him. He must be helped. Throw him a little coal perhaps." Drozdov picked up the receiver. "I want Balashkin—Porfiri Ignatyevich, is that you? Listen: send some coal to this chap, this Lomonosov of ours, Lopatkin, on East

28

Street. Yes, that's the man. How much? Half a ton should be enough, I think! And a little firewood—about half a cubic meter. So-o, is that how it is! Well, I can't be bothered with such things. I can't be bothered. It's your job. It's you who are the fuel god. . . . Write it off. In any case, let him have it today. See to it."

sume. To that end, I beg . . ." Here his face . . . "If you should be caught,
I don't . . . And I little care, do about that, a rouble wire. So in a
. . . her father . . . Well, I can't be reckoned with. At midnight, I said,
the robber! It's you, bag, I'd you who are in their right . . . . Who
of the . . . In any case, by this have it ready. See? In . . .

2

NEXT day Nadia had to go to work. An hour before the lessons for the second shift were due to start, she put on her coat, cap, and green fur mittens, stood awhile in front of her mirror, and when she left the house even tried to run along the snowy path to the gate, so brightly did the snow shine under the dark-blue sky and so happy did she feel. But she did not run all the way to the gate; she changed to the heavy, somewhat rolling walk which had already become a habit. She emerged into the street, gradually the snow lost its brightness for her, she forgot her new coat, and the happy smile faded from her face, which grew almost sad. Nadia was thinking hard.

She had come to Muzga three years before, immediately after graduating from the training college. In the very first year she had become acquainted with the man whom everyone referred to simply as "Drozdov." Nadia had been amazed at the time at his small stature, which she found difficult to reconcile with his reputation for an unusual capacity to rule and command. In the teachers' lounge she had listened with lively interest to anecdotes about him. These anecdotes were always told in a low voice, with respect, but also with a certain hostility. One such anecdote was this: Drozdov had driven with his little car to a fuel store. He had stopped the car in the yard and watched for some time how customers were proceeding from the gates to the office, wading in high boots through a large puddle of spring thaw water, and floundering in the deep mud that reached to the knees. Then Drozdov had ordered his driver to drive into the same puddle, and opening the car door, gaily shouted for Balashkin, the manager of the fuel yard. This part of the anecdote was told with particular relish: Balashkin was not popular in Muzga. Drozdov had called him, and in front of everybody had asked him to come closer to the car. There had been nothing Balashkin could do. He had come closer, just as he was, in his yellow shoes, and had stood in the puddle for half an hour, listening to Drozdov's unhurried instructions about taking an inventory of the fuel stocks. As a result, next day a high wooden sidewalk had been built into Balashkin's fuel yard.

Nadia enjoyed Jack London's novels, and thought that Drozdov somewhat resembled the gold prospector in *Burning Daylight*. She had come here, to Siberia, with the secret hope of meeting that sort of hero, a man capable of welding together the strength of thousands of men—manual workers and technicians—men capricious, ruthless, difficult to please and quick to take offense. She had first met Drozdov when an excursion had visited the *kombinat*. Three days later this little man with the brittle boyish voice was already taking her for troika drives at night across the steppe, glittering with frost crystals in the moonlight. A month later she had gone to live with him in his house, freshly redecorated for the occasion. True, the marriage had been unofficial—Drozdov's lawful wife lived in another town. "She left me, but it was I who was to blame," Drozdov explained. "I got carried away by my work and she—she wanted a personal life." His wife would not give him a divorce. But that was only a temporary difficulty. A few months passed, and in a new passport Nadia was already described by a new name: Drozdov.

Two years had gone by since then. Thinking of this, Nadia sighed. It was a deep sigh and quite unexpected. Nadia asked herself in alarm: why the sigh? For a long time now she had been noticing, when she looked in her mirror, that her eyes were strangely thoughtful, and widened as though by fear. For two years now sudden, frightening questions had been coming into her head and she had not been able to answer them until her husband had got home. Drozdov would listen to her with a smile and reassure her with a clear answer that solved all difficulties.

31

During his very first conversation with his wife—it was on the fourth or fifth day after their unofficial marriage—Drozdov refuted everything she had been taught from her infancy, and she had received from him, with fear and delight, a new, boldly simplified conception of life.

"My dear," he had said wearily, sitting down beside her on the divan. Now they both appeared to be of the same stature. "My dear, this is what it all amounts to: everything you say is nineteenth century. It's all literature. I must tell you that I understand nothing of it, and don't mind that I don't. That's how it is. But this is what I can tell you in answer to the question about my tactless—as you were pleased to call it—treatment of my subordinates. My dearest spouse," he went on facetiously, "people must be clothed and fed. Therefore we, the toilers and moilers, look at the world this way: the land gives bread and the snow gives harvest. If soot pours from a chimney, that is a loss and at the same time a reminder: there is an order of the Ministry about the reduction of losses and we wear out the seats of our pants day after day trying to achieve this. A man standing before me is either a good or bad builder of Communism, a good or bad worker. I have the right to think of him so, because I cannot think of myself in any other fashion either. I live only as a worker, at home or at work. I am nothing but a worker. I get rung up at night when I am simply a sleeping man, and reminded that I am a worker! We are engaged in a race with the capitalist world. First one must build the house and then one can hang up the pictures. Have you ever seen one of those sturdy carpenters who smell of honest sweat, and who build houses? I am such a carpenter. The whole truth is in my hands. I will build the house and then you will begin to hang up little pictures and little ornaments on the walls, and I shall be forgotten. Or, rather, we shall both be forgotten, for you are my dearest better half and will share my fate. That is how it will be." He put his hand on her shoulder. "Are you satisfied with this explanation?"

Nadia remained silent and Drozdov, looking at her askance and quizzically out of his black eyes, said, in sharper, more decisive tones:

"I belong to the producers of material values. The main spiritual value in our time is the ability to work well, to create the greatest possible quantity of necessary things. We are working for the basis."

At night, on returning from work, he would sometimes take the *Short Course of the History of the Party* to bed with him and, putting on a pair of large spectacles, would read, always the fourth chapter, the philosophical one. And Nadia would also read. They lay side by side in the square wooden bed, with a bedside cupboard and a reading lamp on each side. Having found the right place in the book, Leonid Ivanovich would take off his spectacles.

"You said that I was always going to extremes. There can be no extremes for those who work to strengthen the material basis. Because it is matter that comes first. The more I strengthen it, the material basis, the firmer our state will be. You won't find that in Turgenev, my dear."

"But you've got things mixed up. It is not the things themselves which make up the material basis but the relationships between people in connection with things," Nadia once said to him a bit timidly. She had given the subject much thought but had never felt quite at home in it.

Drozdov reread the page dealing with the basis and said again:

"I strengthen the basis. I produce things in connection with which people will enter into relationships. Let there only be things, then we needn't worry about there not being people enough to enter into relations in connection with them!"

He ruled men firmly, with a slight note of irony. He decided intricate problems in an instant, and the affairs of the enterprise under his management ran evenly on a slightly upward course. The Ministry always mentioned Drozdov in its instructions as an example to others. Nadia had for a long time been looking at the world through his eyes—she looked at it perhaps with some alarm, but could not help herself: she could not think of anything independently.

So lost in thought that she was aware of nothing around her, Nadia walked to the school over the snow that crunched under her boots like starch, and her breath was blown away by the frosty wind as if it were a flimsy scarf.

On crossing Stalin Avenue and East Street—the longest street of the settlement—Nadia caught sight of Lopatkin, former schoolmaster. He was wearing a military cap with ear flaps and an old black overcoat. He was coming straight toward Nadia, his collar turned up and his hands in his pockets. For the whole of the last year Nadia had no longer exchanged greetings with him, mainly because she had at one time been much attracted by him. Or, to put it plainly, she had been in love with him and now she could not forgive herself for having been so silly. Also, because she was sorry for the character and was afraid she might hurt his feelings by her compassion. If she gave him a greeting and appeared sorry for him, he might make a scene! Nadia, pale, and with head down and eyes averted, passed him, hoping with all her might that he would not greet her and would not stop. Lopatkin seemed to have understood her—he creaked steadily over the snow in his patched black shoes, stumbled clumsily as he stood aside for her to pass, and vanished like a bad dream.

There had been a time when he was a normal human being. Nadia recalled that he had taught not only physics but mathematics, too. And now he was pestering Leonid Ivanovich with his ridiculous and ill-conceived project. He was constantly writing letters to everyone, to members of the academy, to ministers, and even to the government! The war must have touched his head as it had of so many others. What had Leonid Ivanovich said about him? . . . Oh, yes, he had said that they had nothing else to worry about in Moscow than to read the letters of these men from Mars.

Nadia sighed, and her thoughts again returned to the familiar pattern. There was her husband; obviously that was how things went: there might be one thing you didn't like in a man, another thing you didn't understand, and a third thing that was just splen-

34

did. Man was a contradictory creature by his very nature. Drozdov himself had told Nadia this. And it was true.

Only last summer, when they had all gone on an excursion into the country, how nice he had been to everyone! He had played volleyball, ridden on somebody's bicycle, reminisced about his youth. Then he had started a competition for making sandals out of birchbark. All had given up, but he had deftly manipulated the wire and plaited a pair of tiny sandals out of birchbark. There they were, still hanging above the table in her room. He was so very kind and simple when, coming home from work, he put on a pair of striped pajamas and busied himself with his fishing tackle, soldering hooks, and whittling gadgets for pike fishing. If only he would not sing! Drozdov utterly lacked an ear for music, and when he started singing his favorite song in the kitchen—a song that one could recognize only by its words—it seemed to her that he must have had a few drinks too many somewhere.

"Ye-es." Nadia sighed and, brushing aside all memories, climbed the steps leading up to the school.

There were still twenty minutes left till the beginning of classes, and the three oilcloth-covered settees and the chairs in the teachers' room were all occupied. The Russian teacher, an old spinster, was correcting exercise books at a small table, surrounded by books and school satchels. Another old lady, the biology teacher, was looking through exercise books in a corner of one of the oilcloth settees, and her satchels and books lay in heaps beside her on the floor. Two young smiling junior teachers were also sitting there. They were wearing a little make-up and their hair was curled. Both wore identical blue woollen blouses with short sleeves which left their arms bare almost to the shoulder. The third old lady, Angiya Timofeyevna, the mathematics teacher, sat down next to them and treated them to a lecture about these sleeves.

On another settee the good-looking young chemistry teacher and two teachers of German, both of them with varnished fingernails, were sitting side by side. The talk here was about stockings with black heels which were just coming into fashion, and which no one here had seen as yet. In the farthest corner of the settee sat the only man in the school, Sergei Sergeyevich, the history teacher, who ostentatiously unfolded his newspaper and screened himself with it from his neighbors.

On the third settee there was an unoccupied place. Here a friend of Nadia, Valentina Pavlovna, teacher of English, had established herself with her exercise books. She was snub-nosed, with a jolly upward slant to her eyebrows and gay little curls combed onto her wide, bulging forehead. This forehead made her face unattractive—it seemed made out of two different halves: the upper and the lower. But Valentina Pavlovna was unaware of her misfortune. She was always cheerful, she hobnobbed with the youngsters, and her light, happy laughter could often be heard in the teachers' room. No one would have imagined that she had an unhappy husband who was in love with her and whom she had deserted, taking their daughter with her, because she herself had fallen in love with another man, although this other man did not care for her, and did not even know of her love.

Seeing Nadia, Valentina Pavlovna silently shifted her seat on the settee. Nadia sat down and they immediately put their heads together and began to talk under their breath, like conspirators.

"Well, how is it? Does it kick?" Valentina Pavlovna asked.

"All the time. A real hooligan!"

"What month are you in?"

"The fifth. Nowadays all sorts of things make me feel sick. The other day my mother-in-law showed me some material for baby linen, and I suddenly felt sick because of it! And what about you? Any news?"

"The same as ever," Valentina Pavlovna said, and for an instant her merry, trusting eyes were darkened by the distant shadow of a sorrow.

Meanwhile the mathematics teacher, having done with the two ladies of fashion, at last turned her attention elsewhere.

"Welcome, Nadezhda Sergeyevna," she said. "You, too, were hauled over the coals last night. At the staff meeting."

36

"What for?"

"Why did you . . . Rimma Ganicheva does well in all subjects; you alone gave her a 'D' for geography."

She said this in a stern voice, but everyone in the teachers' room knew Agniya Timofeyevna and her idea of a joke.

"And who hauled me over the coals?" Nadia asked, smiling.

"The headmistress. And she was right: if Ganicheva gets a 'C' for biology, she ought to get no less than 'C' for geography, too."

Nadia straightened and bit her lip.

"You see, Valya, it's always like that. . . . Remember I said so? The headmistress always picks on me and always through third persons."

"Nadezhda Sergeyevna is backed up by her husband," said the Russian teacher, taking off her glasses. "I was quite plainly told: give Solomykin a 'Three.' It is not the pupil who is to blame, but your own deficient work. And do you know what that boy wrote in his composition? In four consecutive words he made five mistakes. About Turgenev! In the ninth grade!"

"There are no bad pupils, only bad teachers," said the Russian teacher in a deep voice, and everyone laughed.

"Oh, I would argue with her, I wouldn't give way just like that!" Valentina Pavlovna whispered audibly. "Our Russian teacher is as meek as a lamb."

"As if you yourself, Valya, had never given way!"

"True, at times one gets tired of fighting and shrugs one's shoulders: all right, have your 'Three.' And what is the result? All this is done not for any good that comes of it, but simply for the report. But what is needed is knowledge and not good marks: the scraps of paper we issue here do nothing but harm. On the strength of such a scrap of paper a man is given a job, when in fact he is merely one of these Solomykins, dragged up by his ears; and such a one may even come to be a physician! Or the head of a department! Worst of all is to hear a man talking ungrammatically who has been put over you, and so is able to order you about."

Valentina Pavlovna added something more and laughed, but

Nadia suddenly froze. Looking down and seeing nothing, she lost herself in thought. She remembered how one day Drozdov had sent her a note from the general manager's office which began with the word "Enshure" written in large letters and wrongly spelled. Later Nadia had tactfully spoken to her husband about this: she was afraid that he might write such a note to someone else. But he had answered pointedly: "Spelling—is just spelling." But Nadia had quickly interrupted him and changed the subject, sensing that the next thing he would say would be: "—and nothing more."

"I walk about in Moscow and read the signs: 'Orders on clothing accepted,' or 'Materials Supplies Basis.' In gold on marble! And the people who write such things are all pupils of ours. All Solomykins! And I think, Nadia . . . What is the matter? Are you ill?"

"It's nothing. I was just thinking. I always start thinking when you get talking. You know, I am quite incapable of putting up a fight. I can't even think properly!"

"And why should you fight? You are as safe with Drozdov as behind a wall. Why did you give Ganicheva a 'D'?"

"For prompting and for having a crib. I always reduce the mark if I notice such things. Without mercy. Listen, Valya, have you seen *him* today?"

Valentina Pavlovna shook her head: no, she had not seen him.

"And yesterday?"

"I saw him. At a distance"—Valentina Pavlovna spoke in a whisper—"I sometimes go to see him. But not often."

"I wish you would let me get a glimpse of him somehow. You really love him?"

Valentina Pavlovna nodded yes, it was serious.

"Is he good-looking?"

"What do looks matter? You remember the beauty of Hélène in *War and Peace?* Beauty is a relative matter."

Having said this, Valentina Pavlovna caught herself and glanced at Nadia to see whether she, a beauty, was not offended. Did she not regard all this philosophy as the self-defense of the plain woman? But Nadia was listening with wide-open eyes, and Valentina Pavlovna sighed with relief.

"It is not beauty that matters here, Nadia. You know that at one time I was an active member of the komsomol, and I sometimes feel that *that* has remained in me—for my whole life. When I first met this man . . . By the way, love did not enter at all into our first meeting; for me, it began with the desire to help him. As in the good old komsomol times."

"But how did you come to love him? Suddenly? At first sight? Valyushka, come! Tell me!"

"No. Not suddenly at all. Not at first sight. You know, to fall in love takes more than just seeing a person. There must be some kind of clash. Some kind of conflict is needed for character to show itself. And we did have a clash. But I was the only one to feel it."

"Didn't he?"

"No. He didn't. For him I am someone strange and incomprehensible. Just as my husband is for me. If I meet him, I turn scarlet although at thirty I'm no longer young! Ah, Nadia, you don't know what it's like! If only one look of his could tell me what—what *I* cannot even hide! . . . For a minute of that kind I would sacrifice everything. He notices me, remembering me, but not as I do him. I think of him in a different way." Valentina Pavlovna bowed her head, then raised it, and Nadia saw tears in her clear, trusting eyes. "You know, he is a man of very high principles. He is bold. He is clever. He impresses everyone he meets. He is a real hero, the kind I dreamt of when I was a little girl. If only I had met him sooner! I would have followed him to the ends of the earth! I would not have hesitated an instant! I was better than I am now."

"Darling!" Nadia pressed her hand against the settee and touched her shoulder. "You are still better than all the others!"

In the passage outside a bell began to ring thinly. The teachers leisurely collected their books and journals and left the teachers' room.

"Enough gossiping!" the old mathematics teacher said in her

deep voice which combined geniality with gruffness. With a sigh the two friends stood up.

"We'll talk another time, shall we?" Nadia said, looking at her friend with eyes in which pleasure and sadness mingled. "Would you like to? Shall we talk again?"

"I don't know why it should interest you so much. Why pretend? You know what love is, just as well as I do."

Nadia suddenly felt as if her expression was strange, and false! She said: "Of course I have known love!" and then added: "Do be kind, Valentinochka, I am so confused, I can't understand myself at all."

At the foot of the stairs they parted with a tender handshake and a smile and Nadia entered Class Seven B with the same odd, distracted smile. She exchanged greetings with her pupils, sat down at the table, and all her incomprehensible misgivings receded into the background.

From the second row Rimma Ganichev stared at her, frowning. Her dark eyes were set unpleasantly wide apart, toward the temples, and reminded one of a pair of binoculars. Nadia's gaze came to rest on her class helper, Sima Sianova, a pale, thin girl with a worried expression, and she smiled at her. Nadia had long felt a strangely maternal tenderness and solicitude toward Sianova.

"Now, how well have you learned the lesson?" Nadia looked at the blackboard. Yes, naturally, her helper had been busy—she had hung up the maps, had wiped the blackboard clean, and had drawn on it the outline of the northern and central region of the European part of the U.S.S.R. "Ah, yes, very good. Splendid!" Nadezhda Sergeyevna said in her classroom voice. The lesson began.

She called three pupils up to the maps, and having asked each of them a question, glanced at Sima. This quiet, obedient child was very nervous at being sent to the blackboard, and always got a "C" for geography. Nadia decided that she must deal with this fear in her best helper, though suddenly she herself felt a little frightened.

"Sima!" she called, as if she had just thought of it, wearily covering her eyes with her hand.

The girl stood up, dropped her book, and, without noticing that she had done so, stumbling with fear, walked to the blackboard.

"You have shown the northern region of the European part. Now put in the rivers of the north, and mark the areas of useful minerals. Don't be afraid," she added, more gently.

"I am not afraid, Nadezhda Sergeyevna. Here is the Pechora." Sima, smiling faintly, began to draw a thick line for the Pechora, starting with the Dvina cape.

Nadia felt an anxious pang. The class was whispering. Sianova stopped, and her face lost its color. Then she quickly wiped off the Pechora and, instead, confidently drew the branching Dvina. She rapped the chalk against the board and looked around. Everyone nodded vigorously. Nadia looked down at the class book. Having finished with the Dvina, Sima drew the Pechora, the Mezen, and the Onega. When she had traced all the windings of the Onega, she looked around again and the pupils in the first row, looking furtively at the teacher, nodded cautiously. "I'm not going to notice," Nadia decided. Under Sima's small hand, the rivers Narva, Kola, and Tuloma quickly and correctly appeared on the board—it was already more than she had been asked for. "But she knows it all. She only lacks courage," Nadia thought, as she listened to another pupil's answers. She glanced at the outline of the northern region of the European part and saw that the deposits of apatite and bauxite were already shown. Only Ukhta was missing. "I'll give her a "B," Nadia thought. "Perhaps after this 'B' a new life may start for her."

"Well," she asked. "What's the matter?"

Sima's animated face fell suddenly.

"I forgot something," she admitted, and put down the chalk. "And I can't remember it at all."

"Sit down. I am giving you a 'B.' And now all together, we'll try and remember what you forgot."

But at once Nadia saw Ganicheva's hand raised.

"Look! Rimma will tell us straight away!"

Ganicheva stood up, glanced to right and left, and then, looking fixedly in one direction, began to speak, raising an eyebrow at each word.

"You, Nadezhda Sergeyevna, gave me a 'D' when I was prompted. But Sima was prompted the whole time. And I'll tell you by whom: Parisova, Slautin, Vialtsev . . ."

"We didn't!" several of the children cried at once.

"But you nodded! You did, I saw it! And when she did the Pechora, Khanapetova at once hissed, and then Sima rubbed it out. So there! . . ." And without finishing the sentence, Ganicheva sat down, her large, wide-spaced eyes shining with vindictive satisfaction.

"Sima will clear up our doubts at once," Nadia said. Sima stood up. "Your mark depends on your answer, Sima. If you were prompted, I shall give you a 'D.'"

"Yes, I was prompted," Sima said almost inaudibly.

"We didn't prompt!" The whole class was in an uproar. "We nodded! Nadezhda Sergeyevna! We only nodded!"

"Yes, they nodded," Sima said, even more softly.

"Very well. I shall give you a 'C.'" Nadia sighed and looked hard at the Ganichev girl. "I am giving you a 'C.' But remember, children, to tell the truth out of spite is just as bad as to conceal it. People who want revenge are the most likely to tell lies; though now you can see that sometimes they also tell the truth. If what Ganicheva wanted was to improve Sima's work, she ought to have spoken to her first. And you yourselves are just as bad. You nodded. Why did you do it?"

When the lesson was over, several pupils from the class stopped Nadia near the teachers' room; they were all subdued and serious and asked her to give Sima a "B" after all.

"It's hard for her to do her lessons," said dark-haired little Khanapetova, the chief prompter. "They are a large family and very poor. She has a lot of housework to do, too. We help her all we can."

42

"Help her by all means, but not by prompting in class," Nadia said in the tone of one used to exercising authority; then she looked thoughtfully out of the window and asked: "Where does she live?"

"On East Street, right at the top."

"I must go and see for myself," she thought, not suspecting that she would encounter the great turning point of her life there, in the Sianov family's little home.

3

NADIA would have liked to visit the Sianovs the next day, but was unable to do so; since Drozdov, who was in high spirits these days, had taken it into his head to have a party, or, as he himself put it, to "have a blowout," Nadia guessed that he had received more precise and confidential information from Moscow about his new appointment, something far more important than he had yet told her. That was why he was almost beside himself with good humor, and had finally hit upon the idea of giving a "leaden anniversary party," for it was exactly two years since they had registered their marriage in the local registry.

Drozdov fixed the day at once and sent out the invitations. A dressmaker came and began to make a blue cashmere dress for Mrs. Drozdov—a specially ample dress, to which Drozdov gave a different name every day; an old woman, Shura's aunt, arrived from the neighboring village and started work in the kitchen.

Nadia wanted to invite some of her own friends, and told her husband. Drozdov asked, "Whom?" and she gave the names of a few teachers—Valentina Pavlovna's among them.

"Yes, yes!" Drozdov said; he closed his eyes and rubbed his hand hard across his face, almost as though he wanted to wipe away his nose and lips. "I shouldn't, if I were you. Why?" He peered at her through his fingers out of one eye. "Because they are . . . How shall I put it? . . . They are the slaves of things. They will see the objects which surround us and identify us with them. They, for instance, have no grandfather clocks. For this reason they will always project their envy on to quite unsuspecting people. As it was with Mozart

44

and Salieri. Sooner or later, through no fault of your own, you will be separated from them. Take that as the answer to your question. I should not invite schoolteachers if I were you. Of course you can ask them if you like, but that will only speed up the process of isolation."

Nadia, after thinking it over, invited to her "leaden wedding" only one of all her schoolteacher friends, Valentina Pavlovna.

On the evening of the party she prepared to welcome her guests. She had been thinking all this time of her husband's words about isolation, and was already trying to find a place for herself in the comfortless existence which his high and responsible position had forced upon him.

The usual guests began to arrive. The first to appear was the director of the Coal Trust: a burly fellow in a leather coat lined with dog fur, and a new felt cloak. After him came the Ganichevs, husband and wife, the wife heavily made up and wearing a black German lace dress. Mrs. Ganichev immediately filled the room with the overpowering perfume of some sort of unknown scent. She was very like her daughter Rimma. Nadia knew that she had another daughter, Jeanne, who had gone to Moscow and was studying chemistry. It was said that while still at school, during her last year, she had had some sort of romantic affair with Lopatkin, the physics teacher.

The Ganichevs were followed by Guliayev, secretary of the district party committee, a swarthy Kuban Cossack, with an aquiline nose, dressed in military uniform. The next to arrive was the chairman of the district Soviet executive committee, elderly and stout; he, too, was in military dress. After him the manager of the State farm burst into the room, covered from head to foot with snow and wearing two fur coats, one on top of the other; he had crossed the steppe in a sleigh. Soon after him came Valentina Pavlovna. She took off her furs, appeared in the drawing room for a few minutes, then joined Nadia in the hall. By this time Nadia was welcoming the district prosecutor and his wife.

The men had already filled the room with cigarette smoke, and

Nadia was feeling slightly sick. She was receiving another guest with a smile, Miss Kanayev, the loud-voiced manageress of the local retail trade administration. She smiled, but when Miss Kanayev lighted a cigarette close to her, she shivered violently.

"I simply can't," she whispered in Valentina Pavlovna's ear.

"What month?" Miss Kanayev asked, taking her by the shoulders and breathing tobacco smoke into her face. "Oh—I see! Well, why stand here? Go and sit on the sofa."

But Nadia heroically remained where she was.

In the drawing room, meanwhile, there was gay, disjointed talk.

"Well, Leonid, my boy, so we are to drink to your departure today, you say?" This was the manager of the State farm.

"Yes." Inevitably, at such moments, Drozdov closed his eyes. "Yes, we must part, with manly courage, and glass in hand. As befits the stern men of Siberia. . . ."

"Don't forget our Muzga! There's nowhere like it on earth."

"Oh, the memory of Muzga will go with Drozdov to Moscow in any case," Miss Kanayev said. "He isn't alone—there are two of them!"

"Three!" cried the director of the Coal Trust. He had obviously had a few already somewhere else.

"How nice! Now my Jeanne will have company. We're all Siberians together, after all!" Mrs. Ganichev put her word in.

"How is she getting on there?"

"She's finishing her second year at the university."

"Leonid! Leonid!" a gay, insistent voice called from the other end of the room. "Before you go, you ought to get a move on and fix things about that grader! For us to remember you by! So that we could get in our autumn supplies by road!"

"Ganichev will do all that," Drozdov answered with a laugh, "when he succeeds to the throne!"

Valentina Pavlovna was standing next to Nadia and watching the guests through the wide-open door.

"Come to us! Join our little circle!" Mrs. Ganichev called out to her, squirming in a way that was intended to express friendliness.

She had just been telling the other women about Austria, where she had spent a whole year with her husband.

"Well, and how did you find it after our Siberia?" Drozdov interrupted her flow of talk, going to the door without waiting for an answer.

"Oh, there's no comparison!" Mrs. Ganichev squealed, gesturing with her hands. "I would never have come back from there if I had had my way."

Valentina Pavlovna said nothing, merely letting her calmly observant gaze rest on Mrs. Ganichev.

Outside, in the hall, Drozdov summoned Ganichev with a wink of his eye. Ganichev jumped up and they stood together by the wall, the small man and the tall one.

"Well?" Drozdov asked under his breath, frowning.

"He said that he was very doubtful."

"Here! Tell me plainly: what has he dug up?"

"He wants to stop the work on the Avdiyev machine."

"I am told nothing," Drozdov drawled. "Here's a fine state of affairs! Has he the right to do it?"

"He advises us not to be in a hurry."

"I don't know anything!" Drozdov frowned again, fidgeting with his knee. "Avdiyev and the Minister will give him what-for. They'll veto him!"

He turned briskly on his heel, as if to go.

"Who is it you are talking about? Has something happened?" Nadia asked softly.

"What could happen to us?" He smiled at her warmly. "Perhaps Chernomor will elope with the bride? No, it's the factory; it's always the factory!" he added solemnly. "Our factory is not some little hole-in-the-corner workshop, you know."

Nadia was unable to play the part of hostess to the end. When, at a signal from Drozdov, the guests went into the dining room, after the first few toasts, she passed her glass with the remainder of the cherry brandy in it to her husband (in order that he might finish it, since the toast had been for their happiness), then excused herself, and left the room. She lay down on the divan in her own room and Valentina Pavlovna came at once and sat down beside her, looking at her with a sad, attentive gaze.

"Nadia! Why, there was not a single friend of yours at the party. Nor of Drozdov's either!"

"It's quite true," Nadia said, and was frightened by her own words. "No one—except you."

"I don't count."

They were silent for a long time. Nadia lay without moving, staring at her friend's severe, plain profile.

"Why was that?" Valentina Pavlovna asked.

At this moment the door leading from the dining room to the hall opened, and Mrs. Ganichev's high-pitched voice could be heard:

"Good heavens! Who would have thought it at the time? By the way, my Jeanne wrote to me that he had not justified the hopes . . ."

"Who? The inventor, eh?" Drozdov asked, laughing, and then the door was closed.

"About whom were they talking?" Valentina Pavlovna asked quickly.

"About our Lopatkin."

Again there was a silence. Valentina Pavlovna suddenly took Nadia's hand.

"Are you annoyed with me? For heaven's sake, don't be angry! It's simply that I didn't expect— This isn't a party, it's an official reception, on the district scale— 'Those present were . . . etc., etc., etc.' All V.I.P.s! Why were none of the rank-and-file here today? Ordinary people, like Dr. Orekhov, for instance? Doesn't she often come to see you on ordinary days? And Agniya Timofeyevna, who is so fond of you. Wasn't she invited either?"

Nadia did not answer and Valentina Pavlovna, after a glance at her pale face, covered with gray blotches, asked no more questions.

From the next room came the sound of an inharmonious, somewhat hoarse chorus—the guests were trying to start a singsong. But the song somehow failed to get going. Then there was a clapping of hands.

"Comrades!" It was Miss Kanayev's voice. "An element of organization must be introduced into this matter! Let the bridegroom sing the principal part, and the chorus will join in. Come on, Drozdov!"

And Drozdov began to sing his one-and-only song in his vibrating, colorless voice. Nadia blushed. As usual, the song could only be recognized by the words. But the chorus, with an effort keeping its volume under control, came in with a will, and put things right.

Valentina Pavlovna put her arm around Nadia's shoulders.

"Never mind, never mind! . . . What is this? Is it yours?" Valentina Pavlovna was looking at the cottage piano, whose polish reflected their two figures. "Do you play?"

"Not properly speaking, but I sometimes just—follow my thoughts with it."

"Do follow your thoughts now, then, please do."

"They would hear me." Nadia looked at the wall. "And they might come in and want me to play. I feel that they have already taken plenty upon themselves, in there. I'd rather leave it until tomorrow, perhaps."

"And who is this?" Valentina Pavlovna stood up and took a photograph in a brown wooden frame from the wall. It showed a young peasant in a peaked cap, a black coat, and new boots. He was sitting, stiff and remote, with his knees wide apart and his elbows sticking out. A lock of hair had escaped from under his cap, as though by accident, and on the lapel of his coat Valentina Pavlovna noticed a badge edged with silk ribbon.

"Is it he?" Valentina whispered with respect.

Nadia nodded.

"Did he take part in the civil war, then?"

"No. In those days everyone wore ribbons."

"When was that?"

"In twenty or nineteen. He was working as a carpenter then. He put up very handsome cottages. He has photos of them somewhere.

No, Valya, he is not as bad as you think." Nadia looked at Valentina Pavlovna and her gray eyes seemed lighter and larger, because of the tears that were rising in them.

"Nadia, my dear, what are you talking about? You seem to be arguing against yourself, not against me. Of course he is not bad! At least, I hardly know him. But I should rather imagine that he is kind and humane and all that. I was only thinking: why . . . ?"

"He is not bad," Nadia continued obstinately. "He works a great deal. He has simply forgotten about himself. He thinks only of his work. That is all!"

"So you love him?"

"Well, I married him, didn't I? He is my husband!" Nadia said angrily, sniffing and beginning to fold and unfold her handkerchief.

The guests left late. Drozdov saw them to their cars, standing in the porch, then loudly banged the door, and, humming to himself, walked briskly into Nadia's room.

"Well, comrade pedagogue?" He sat down beside her. The vodka he had drunk had made him rather pale, but his movements were well under control and his speech was as sober as ever, with the same touch of characteristic irony. "What is the matter, madam? Are you sick?"

"I wanted to ask you, Lenya: why have you no friends?"

"What do you mean, no friends? Who were all those people then? And what a mess they've made in the dining room, simply frightful!"

"I mean real friends."

"Real ones? So that's what you want. Look here, Nadia, I told you once before, remember? We can't have friends here. A friend must be independent; but the people here are all dependent on me in one way or another. Some envy me, some fear me, others keep their eyes open, others again are seeking their own advantage. . . . Isolation, my dear. Complete isolation. And the higher we rise, you and I, the more complete will this isolation be. Indeed one can only have friends in childhood. I should very, very much like to have friends. That is why I put all my hopes in you."

He stood up and paced up and down, not straight ahead, but in a zigzag, with sudden turns and twists and stops.

"They all drank our health. But do you think they are friends? They are not. The secretary always looks at me out of narrowed eyes. There is something in me he doesn't like. Drozdov's firm hand is not to his taste. Sometimes I don't act acccording to the book and that annoys him. You see—he left early. He took himself off soon after you went. Who else is there? Ganichev? He seems all right. Yes, *seems* so. But he is my successor. When I go, he will get my job and he knows it. So he is waiting for me to get out, so he can step into my shoes, and the sooner the better."

"So Guliayev left early?" Nadia said thoughtfully.

"He is young and a conciliator." Drozdov guessed her thoughts and again began to speak of Guliayev. "One can't stay away from Drozdov's party if one is invited. It might be dangerous to offend Drozdov. But as to fighting Drozdov—he is too scared to do that. He could not win if he did. His district is a poor one. And the whole economic basis"—he smiled. "Excuse me, economic base is in the hands of that fellow Drozdov. So he sits on the fence. He came, but he left early 'on business.'"

"Who was it you were talking about with Ganichev in the hall?"

"That chap who came from Moscow, a certain Galitsky. Doctor of science. We are producing a machine here, and he says its underlying principle is out of date. The day after he arrived he said only that he would help with the assembly. Three days later I asked him what they thought of the machine. 'Seems all right.' Two days later we met again; he looked quite ill. All tousled, pale—wouldn't look one in the eye. Naturally! After all, he represents the customer. He muttered something and took himself off. And now he has spoken out!"

Drozdov looked at the floor, blinked, then threw back his head with a determined gesture.

"So that is how it goes, my dear. Who are to be our friends? We, you and I, are no longer students. We are serious people, many-faceted people. And there will be more and more facets. Simple keys will no longer unlock us. And the way out of all this? The answer is: we must close our ranks. Once we have come so close to one another." As he said this, Drozdov put his arms round his wife, then leaned back and looked at her from a distance. "You're lovely. Lovely!"

Only a few words—and everything fell into place. But was it really everything? Nadia looked at her husband, but she saw him as though through a mist. Truly they were many-faceted, both of them. Especially he. He had so many facets that one could even get lost among them all!

4

A DAY later, coming straight from school, Nadia walked along
East Street to pay a visit to the Sianovs. The street, a good two
miles long, was flanked by small earthen-walled dugouts. In
this part of the world such houses were called "dugouts." A double
row of yellowish electric lights climbed constantly higher, until it
was lost in darkness on the ridge of the immense hill towering
above the settlement, which sparkled with its endless snows in the
daytime. Nadia took a long time to climb it, sitting down from time
to time to rest on the seats placed in front of almost every "dug-
out," and then walking on again. At last she reached the summit
of the slope and found the little mud hut that bore the number
167. The house was half-buried in the earth and was surrounded by
posts hung with barbed wire. She knocked at the tiny frosted window, through which a dim light shone and which was on a level
with her knees. Somewhere beyond the hut a plank door banged,
the snow crunched under footsteps, and Nadia was confronted by
a bony woman, dressed in blue gingham, with an apron tied round
her and sleeves rolled up to her elbows.

"We are the Sianovs," she said. "Come this way." She led Nadia
behind the hut and beyond a narrow, high haystack. "Here it is. Be
careful, don't fall!" she said, and opened a low door under the haystack. Nadia entered. The place was filled with the warm, damp
smell of a stable, and in the gloom she could distinguish the brown-
and-white flanks and placid face of the cow slowly turning toward
her. She could hear the tinny sound of the streams of milk hitting the
sides of the pail; the cow was being milked, and Nadia felt, rather

53

than saw, that the milker was Sima Sianov, her pupil. A moment later the girl's thin form appeared from behind the cow.

"Good evening." Sima Sianov looked quite different here, and her face wore an expression of welcome befitting her position as hostess. Her mother opened a second door and Nadia stepped into a warm low-ceilinged room. At once she saw five children sitting at a table, each with a hot potato in its hand. And the potatoes were white and mealy as only one's *own* potatoes can be! Five youthful heads turned toward Nadia.

"Good evening, children! I have come to see how you are getting on," she said, unbuttoning her coat and sitting down on a stool in the middle of the room.

"You are welcome," Mrs. Sianov said, raising her feverish black eyes to Nadia's face. She was at a loss what to do or what to say next. "We are managing, as everyone does. The trouble is, I've felt a bit sick lately. Can't walk properly. And there's something wrong with me, some female trouble. Only it's such a long way to the hospital . . . So this is our housewife now!" She pointed to Sima, who was crossing the room quickly with the milk pail.

"I have come about something," Nadia said, "but there's no chance just now, I can see."

"What was it?" A voice came from behind a sheet which Nadia had thought was hanging on the wall. But now it was revealed as the curtain to a door that led into another room. "What is it?" The questioner now stepped out from behind the curtain, an elderly, rawboned, baldish man in a white undershirt that contrasted vividly with his huge, dark, work-worn hands. "Good evening," he said pleasantly, beginning to button up the neck of his shirt. "Mrs. Drozdov, isn't it?"

"I came to inquire whether it wasn't possible to give Sima less work to do in the house? . . . But now, I see . . ."

"Yes. Sorry. This is how things are with us." The man put his hand on the red-gold head of one of the little ones. "I myself go out to work and do a bit of overtime on top of it. Our housewife can't do much. She is ailing, our housewife is. So our Sima has

54

to stand in for her. But won't you take off your coat? Let me help you. And let's go in here, where there is more light."

He drew back the sheet and Nadia, bending her head, stepped through into a narrow, cleanly whitewashed, windowless room. The bright light of a lamp hanging at eye level made her narrow her eyes. She turned, and gave a scarcely audible gasp. Lopatkin, one leg crossed over the other, was sitting on a narrow bed right in front of her, eating a potato. He, too, was wearing a white shirt, and it seemed to Nadia that he was very thin. On a small table at his elbow stood a clay bowl with peeled and obviously very hot potatoes. A little heap of grayish salt lay on a scrap of newspaper.

Lopatkin started when he saw Nadia, and his face showed many things: first, that he was embarrassed at sitting there in front of her in his shirt sleeves, eating potatoes and dipping them into gray salt from a piece of newspaper, and, at that, potatoes which were not even his own. It also showed that he himself was well aware of what she must be thinking of all this. But he merely started slightly and then stood up, bowed to Nadia, and dipped the potato in the salt.

"Please take a seat," Sianov said, and Nadia obediently sat down on a chair. "This is our permanent lodger, Dmitri Alexeyevich Lopatkin. I think you are acquainted."

"Yes, we are," Lopatkin quietly confirmed, breaking the potato in two.

Nadia looked around and saw a drawing board leaning against the wall beyond the table. A sheet of drawing paper was attached to it on which was the outline of a machine of some sort. And above the table, exactly opposite Nadia, a photograph the size of a postcard was hanging on the wall. In the picture a young girl with half-open pouting lips looked down at Nadia. She looked very like Rimma Ganichev, except that her eyes were not so far apart, and Rimma's threatening expression was not there. "Jeanne," Nadia thought, and glanced at Lopatkin with curiosity.

Sianov stood close to Nadia, frowned, and scratched his unshaven cheek. He smelt strongly of home-grown tobacco.

"But what are we about!" he exclaimed suddenly. "Wouldn't you like to taste our potatoes? They are very good today—quite a treat! Agatha, a plate!"

"Never mind the plate," Nadia said, and took a hot white potato, silvered with glints of starch, from the bowl. She knew that she had expected this invitation.

"So much the better. We can have a chat over the potatoes. Permit me, I can sit here." He sat down near Nadia on a stump of pine, took a potato, and was about to dip it in the salt, when he checked himself: "Sima, give me a knife, my dear."

There was a silence.

"Well, comrades . . . Nadezhda Sergeyevna, isn't it?" Sianov began. "We find our whole family foregathered, so to speak. Our whole team," he added, glancing at Lopatkin.

"Yes, I can see now . . ." Nadia began, when Lopatkin, who appeared to be admiring the potato in his hand, blurted out:

"We'll release Sima."

Again there was a silence. Lopatkin calmly ate his potato and helped himself to another one.

"Is that your work?" Nadia asked, pointing to the drawing board.

"Yes, it's mine," he answered quietly.

Nadia, too, finished her potato, helped herself to another, and while she was blowing on it, glanced several times at Lopatkin. The collar of his shirt was undone, showing his powerful neck. His face was calm, as though he were alone in the room, resting after a spell of hard work. His long, lusterless hair looked somehow dead, as if it, too, were tired. Once he glanced at Nadia with his kindly gray eyes and she felt suddenly that something warm and virginal, something that she had fought against in the past, stirred in her for an instant. But he turned his eyes away and looked at a potato just as kindly. In order not to let the conversation flag, Nadia addressed him once again.

"Excuse me." She gave him a pleading look, but blushed and

56

checked herself. "I just wanted to ask . . . If you don't mind, do please tell me what your invention is."

"I have no invention," he answered. "Quite seriously, there is no invention at all."

"Wait a minute, Dmitri Alexeyevich," Sianov intervened. "You are puzzling the lady. You see, there is a sort of invention and then, again, there isn't. But on the whole, the thing is useful, and has prospects. That is—for the future."

"I'll tell you all about it in a minute." Lopatkin pushed away the bowl of potatoes. "May I smoke? Uncle Pete and I would each like just one."

He put his large, bony hand into the pocket of his jacket which was hanging on the wall and dug out a handful of home-grown tobacco. Nadia felt an involuntary admiration for the angular power of his arms and shoulders, for his masculine good looks which were already beginning to droop under the strain of his relentless day, and-night work at the drawing board.

When he had rolled a cigarette, Lopatkin lighted a match and drew the smoke in greedily, closing his eyes every now and then as he did so.

"I'll tell you all about it, Nadezhda Sergeyevna. I have always had a great respect for you. I understand you, and I feel I can tell you everything. You will understand. Besides, I don't want you to share the general opinion that I am crazy."

He drew in a mouthful of smoke again, frowned, and knocking the ash off his cigarette with a quick, nervous gesture, went on:

"It's a long story, but I hope I shall be able to cut it short. Up to thirty-seven I worked in a motorcar factory. This preface is necessary, if you are to understand everything that has happened to me. I worked in the chief mechanic's crew; I was a highly skilled engineer myself. Our job was the maintenance of the main conveyor—it's a job that has a lot of angles. I had a friend, another engineer, and he worked on the same conveyor. His name was Ivan Zotych. This Ivan Zotych had to take six nuts for one wheel of the car and six for the other. The spokes of the wheel were fitted by another workman—Ivan Zotych only handled the nuts. As the car came to him, he had to stick the nuts on where they belonged. An electric wrench hung beside his hand, and he screwed all the nuts tight in one instant with that electric wrench.

"He was a careful, sober fellow. Always arrived on time, at seven-thirty. Watching him, I understood the essence and the power lying in the modern division of labor. It should be developed to a point where the least possible time is taken up by subsidiary operations, by the necessity of thinking what to do, and so on."

"But, excuse me," Nadia interrupted him, blushing, "you are depriving the workman of the power of thinking. So in time he would stop thinking altogether. We are trying to end the division between manual and intellectual work, and now you . . ."

Lopatkin gazed at her intently, then looked away and smiled almost imperceptibly.

"Nadezhda Sergeyevna, you never used to talk like this! I am glad to see that you have learned quite a lot in certain directions. It is impossible not to be aware of the value there is in somebody's firm guidance."

Nadia blushed more than ever.

"To go on," Lopatkin said quietly. "The division of labor should make operations so simple that anyone could carry them out without any special training. This would give us the greatest possible productivity of labor. As for the workman you are worrying about— *let* him think! Why shouldn't he? But not about where he put his hammer the day before; he ought to be thinking creatively, for instance about the complete elimination of manual labor and the transition to complete automation. Let him study the ultimate mysteries of his trade. Let him turn into a savant. If that comes about, we shall really have ended the division you mentioned. But if we are going to think about the hammer which cannot be found, then we shall never end this division. Tell me, is there anything opposed to common sense in this argument?"

"No. I agree with you completely."

"All right. Then we can go on from there. Dmitri Lopatkin, the engineer, graduated in physics and mathematics, and after being wounded in the war, came to Muzga to teach physics. He took his class on an excursion to the foundry of the *kombinat* and suddenly noticed that they were turning out drainpipes, which are even more of a mass-production item than automobiles. But here the production was the same old hand job as in the time of Demidov in the last century; they made an earthen form and poured the iron into it by hand, out of a jug. It's all quite simple, Nadezhda Sergeyevna! I took the experience acquired in the motorcar industry and transferred it to the production of drainpipes. Any man who had ever seen a conveyor—Ivan Zotych, for example—could have done the same! But of course only if he felt strongly about such backwardness! So I constructed a casting machine to the best of my ability and subordinated all its parts to the proper laws—the law of the best possible use of machine time (which means that the machine's working tool should produce pipes all the time without stopping), and to the law of the economic use of production space. I'm sorry, I am talking a bit drily! I have developed a sort of shop jargon!"

"Never mind. I can understand."

"Well, I designed a machine and submitted the drawing to the Bureau of Inventions. It's true that I thought it was hardly conceivable that in those scientific institutes they should not have understood such a simple thing long ago, but I submitted my project all the same, just in case, and eight months later I got this."

Lopatkin bent down quickly and pulled out from under the bed a plywood chest full of bundles of papers. He opened a folder and held out to Nadia a greenish-blue document, typewritten on thick, shiny paper, sewn with a silk cord and sealed with a red seal.

"Here, see for yourself!" Nadia noticed that Lopatkin's hand was shaking. "You can convince yourself, Nadezhda Sergeyevna, that the invention was made, considered, and acknowledged to be useful and original. But you must not attach too much importance to this. Handsome as it is, it is still only a scrap of paper, and it should be valued only as such. With your permission, I'll have another smoke."

With kindly solicitude, Sianov handed him a scrap of newspaper. Lopatkin silently tore off one corner, rolled himself a cigarette, lit it lopsidedly, and blowing out the flame, drew the smoke in deeply twice.

"Where was I? . . . Oh, yes. Well—I got this scrap of paper and every day, morning, noon, and night, I gloated over it. I got all worked up, imagining I was being useful! I had been told that a machine was needed! And so it went on for several months. But that wasn't what I had racked my brains for. I began to write complaints. First one, then another, and another. . . . After six months— oh, rapture!—I was summoned to Moscow. *Resign employment at once; you will build your machine in such-and-such an experimental workshop.* Can you imagine my excitement? Uncle Peter here, and I, we danced with joy, almost tore the hut apart! I threw up my physics job, perhaps you remember? And off I went. For two months I was given the runaround at the Ministry. For two months I got paid, but I saw virtually no machine building. In the third month I got a call from the Deputy Minister, a certain Shutikov, who says to me very amiably: *'There's nothing we can do. Our budget has been cut. It's out of our hands now. Perhaps some time next year. . .'* Imagine it! *Perhaps! And so they went about their business, repeating: may God be his judge!* That's how it happened, Nadezhda Sergeyevna! And so I came to be Uncle Pete's permanent lodger."

"Why didn't you go back to your job?"

"I'm sorry. Let's proceed in proper sequence. How had it happened? It turned out that my machine had been sent for an expert opinion to a certain Professor Avdiyev. There is this important personage in Moscow. And the professor said it was no good. Without bothering about proof, he declared: *'It is impossible to get pipes by means of a machine without a long casting channel.'* He is a celebrity, his words are precious, and he is sparing with them. *'Channelless casting is a myth,'* so that's that. And once it is pronounced a myth, the Minister won't touch it. Because Avdiyev is an authority! He holds the chair of foundry technique! *'Avdiyev and other Soviet research workers!'* A Columbus!"

"Listen, Dmitri Alexeyevich!" Nadia interrupted him, blushing scarlet. "Even I . . . I mean . . . Professor Avdiyev . . . but he really is a great scientist!"

"There is something more to it: this scientist, shortly before I got my testimonial, also submitted a machine for pipe casting."

"Do you mean to say that he? . . . that your? . . ." Nadia asked in a dry voice.

"Oh no! Not that! He has his own design, of course, and a very original one too!" Lopatkin finished his cigarette, half-stretched out his hand to make another, but stopped halfway. "No that's enough! I have smoked my ration today. I didn't mean to say anything. You ask: why I didn't take a job? The reason was: because I had to write every day to argue that Columbus was wrong. You are smiling again. You have been told that Avdiyev is infallible, and so you smile. Your smile is for Avdiyev and he uses it."

Though he spoke in this way Nadia had no time to take offense, since she no longer had any control over her expression. "How idiotic I must look!" she thought in confusion.

"And I declare that pipes not only can, but must, be cast without a channel!" Lopatkin continued obstinately, without looking at Nadia. "And I have to prove it, that is why I cannot take a job. Besides, I am working out a new variant and that means 1,400 components and 12,000 dimensions all tied up with one another. Of course it is difficult for one person to do it by himself. It could either be done by a team of designers, or else by a lunatic such as I. Uncle Pete is my only helper. And he, too, is a bit off his rocker."

"But don't you even get bread ration cards?"

"Even without bread cards, we don't seem to be getting any thinner," Sianov said from behind Nadia. "What we need is a ration card for drawing paper."

"I don't understand." Nadia raised her shoulders. "You could apply to the management of the *kombinat.*"

When she stopped speaking, Nadia became aware of a strange silence. Lopatkin and Sianov exchanged a scarcely perceptible smile.

"I'll tell you, Nadezhda . . . Sergeyevna, isn't it? Well, this is how it is, Nadezhda Sergeyevna, we, too, Dmitri and I—there was much we didn't understand. But when the roast cock, to put it bluntly, pecked us—if you'll pardon the expression—on our behinds, we understood everything. And not only did we understand—we also learned how to act. Of course, before we understood, we had been to ask Comrade Drozdov for drawing paper. In our innocence. He refused, of course. And he was right; one can't waste the state-owned drawing paper on all sorts of unanticipated extravagances. True, he did give us two sheets at first—the same amount as for the wall newspaper. But that was all. However, for all that, we are not going without drawing paper."

"And our ink is genuine Chinese!" Lopatkin said, with an unexpected smile.

"No, we are not going without drawing paper," Sianov continued thoughtfully. "We even hope to win through in the end. It's true, no one believes us. . . . Everyone is busy with the program."

"One needs a head on one's shoulders to understand, and some sort of heart in one's breast to believe!" Sianov's wife all of a sudden said angrily, from the next room.

"You are not speaking about us, Agatha?"

"You know well enough about whom! Sit still, Aniki. Afraid to call a spade a spade, are you? Well, I'll tell you straight. . . ." And Sianov's wife burst into the room, her dark eyes blazing feverishly, waving her arms, which were white and bared to the elbow, and putting her hands on her hips. "If the state and the Academy of Science have approved it, it's the duty of everyone to help as much as he can. That is, if he is conscientious, like my Peter here." She jerked her chin toward Sianov, then stopped, and looked at Nadia silently, for a long time, gradually regaining her calm. Then she left the room and, beyond the curtain, rattled the pots and pans, and shouted to the children: "To bed with the whole pack of you!"

"She's got spirit," Sianov said good-humoredly.

Nadia went home. She did not go alone. Lopatkin, almost invisible in the darkness, walked beside her, the collar of his light overcoat turned up, his hands in his pockets. He was thoughtful, and it seemed to Nadia the whole time that she was aware of his thoughts. At this moment it was as though he was made of iron. Perhaps he was thinking of the long, hard road ahead for him with his invention. "No, he is not crazy!" Nadia thought. "There is still the same power that I once sensed in him. A tremendous force. Before, it was dormant, not yet brought to bear on anything, but looking out from his eyes, like a new, untried weapon. And now that testimonial, with its ribbon, has made this quiet man show his steel. Of course Avdiyev is to blame as well. He may be very important, but he ought to have been more explicit. It needs serious proof to a man like Lopatkin if he is wrong, or he will never give up. It's not an easy matter."

At the corner of East Street and Stalin Avenue they came to a stop.

"Now you will get home all right. Good-by!" Lopatkin said abruptly, turning on his heel and disappearing into the darkness, the dry, sharp snow crunching under his tread.

When she reached home, Nadia sat for a long time alone at the large dining table. Her gaze was fixed on the brightness of the nickel-plated sugar bowl. She was waiting for her husband; she had stored up many questions today to put to Drozdov. The servant girl came and went noiselessly, bringing and then removing cream, homemade cake, salt cucumbers, and pickled cabbage—things for which her young mistress had recently acquired a great liking.

Later on Nadia went to her own room, and without switching on the chandelier in the center, played Chopin for a whole hour in semi-darkness, beginning and leaving off again at random, and repeating over and over again a few particularly melancholy and wistful passages. Her husband did not come. In the drawing room the clock struck eleven. Drozdov had nicknamed this clock "wood snipe" because of its unusual tone. Remembering this, Nadia smiled.

63

At that moment the telephone rang shrilly in the hall. She hurried to it, picked up the receiver, and heard Drozdov's sleepy voice:

"Nadia? I shan't be home tonight. The machine is still whistling. If necessary, you can ring me at the workshop. How are you feeling? All right? Is it true? Well, then, go to bed right away, and sleep. Good night."

Nadia sighed and trailed disconsolately to the bedroom. "That is the answer to all my questions," she thought. "But then he would tear himself to pieces to justify himself!" Of late Drozdov had often remained at work into the small hours, and if he got home earlier, he had fallen straight into bed, refused any food, and moaned softly in his sleep. "One needs to have a heart in one's breast!" In her mind she mimicked Agatha Sianov, smiling wryly, as though defending her husband. "No heart could stand up to this strain! Grumbling as they did! Let them try *this* sort of thing—five nights, one after the other!"

She lay down in the square wooden bed but could not sleep for a long time, and sometimes sighed in alarm as she felt the movements of the child in her womb.

In the morning, when she opened her eyes, she saw her husband's head on the pillow beside her. Drozdov was asleep, his face buried in the pillow, like a child's in its mother's breast. Only that this child was gray at the temples, and had a tired yellow face with a high forehead.

Nadia dressed and went out, closing the door behind her soundlessly. She drank her tea in the dining room, and the "cuckoo clock" had already croaked eleven o'clock when Drozdov came out in his bedroom slippers, without any socks, wearing military breeches with suspenders, smiling and fresh after his wash.

"Strong for me, please!" he said, sitting down beside Nadia.

"I have asked you before." She gazed at him with mournful gray eyes. "Why do you overdo things so? Is it really necessary?"

"It's almost the end, Nadia. The finish. The last lap!"

"I don't understand."

"Before I leave, I must bring off something that will leave

64

Ganichev so far behind that he will never catch up. That will be Drozdov's parting shot!"

"Why do you say things like that?" Tears glistened in Nadia's eyes. "You know you are far better than you make yourself out to be!"

"I am what I am!"

Drozdov got up and went to the sideboard standing between the two windows. He looked at himself in the mirror from under his brows as if about to butt at his reflection, touched his temples, threw back his head, and pushing his hand into his belt, said:

"Here I am. Standing face to face with myself. Now I will add to my portrait by a description of my innermost being." He closed his eyes, then slowly opened them again. "I see many deficiencies in this man; they are remnants of the past. This is a man of the time of transition. There are some slight traces of what used to be called 'ambition.' And I myself can't understand how one can live without it. But the men of the future will understand. I want to do better than Ganichev. And I want no one to have anything but a good opinion of my work. I am pleased when I get promotion or any well-deserved rewards. These are testimonials to my good qualities. I am glad to go to Moscow, too, and I am quite sure I shall do well there. There are many weak spots in me, because I love life. Touch me where you like, you will always find a living, tender, sensitive spot. That's why I need armor, like a snail. This armor is my strong will, which is not a bad thing for a man to possess. It holds him in check. And I shan't overstep my limits. Of course I shan't tell anyone that I want to fire a farewell salute. Only a wife may know that sort of thing. As you see, I am still young, and human passions are not unknown to me. For me, of course, there is no road to Communism. I am already too much encrusted; enclosed in a shell, a coat of armor. But as a builder of Communism I am useful, indeed first-rate. That is where this man fits in."

He took one more look at himself, turned slowly toward the table, and raising his eyebrows began to sip his tea noisily. "Or would you prefer me to behave in the Christian style?" he asked, and smiled suddenly at Nadia, as one smiles at a little child. "Would you? Perhaps you would like me to make a mess of my job and get nothing but reproofs? Well, I won't. Let some knight errant do that, some Don Carlos."

"But why all this?" His reasoning had again confused Nadia. "Why can't you just quite simply do your work? You have a plan and you have your duty, haven't you?"

"It isn't possible 'quite simply to do one's work.'" Drozdov closed his eyes and answered Nadia's questions with assurance. "No one works 'just simply.' There is always a personal factor involved that eludes the grasp."

Once again Drozdov appeared to have explained everything satisfactorily to Nadia. She could think of no more questions to ask her husband. But when she went back to her room after breakfast, her brows were knitted. She was struggling, as it were, to think of one more decisive question, but her mind stubbornly withheld it from her.

5

NADIA spent the following days thinking deeply. She was in a strange position. She felt an irresistible urge to discover, at all costs, some argument in defense of the man whose force she had at first quietly, even enthusiastically, accepted. In the Sianov cottage she had found out much that was new to her, and Drozdov, though he had easily answered the questions that had so worried her, had not reassured her for all that. He would have done better not to answer at all, for she had almost found the answer for herself: it was that her husband was busy at the works night after night; like all creative people he did not spare himself, he did not get enough sleep, he was tired, he couldn't be expected to keep an eye on everything.

He would have done better not to answer at all!

She was expecting the correct, the perfect answer. In school, to whomever she spoke, she expressed exaggerated praise or pity for her husband, and expected them to agree. But they at once realized that she was lying and looked at her curiously; what could have provoked such unexpected fervor? She quarreled with Valentina Pavlovna, who said somewhat ironically: "I don't think Drozdov was as tired as all that!" True, they soon made it up, but neither the quarrel with Valentina Pavlovna nor their reconciliation lightened Nadia's horizon.

And then something unexpected and awkward happened.

One day, at the end of January, Nadia went to school as usual, climbed the stairs to the teachers' room, and saw the scene that was familiar to her in every detail. Each teacher was sitting in her accustomed place.

As usual, Nadia sat down on the settee beside Valentina Pavlovna. But before she could begin talking to her about their eternal
subject, true love, the secretary, who was sitting at a table at the
far end of the teachers' room, announced with an air of triumph:

"Citizens, do you know who is coming here today? None other
than Dmitri Alexeyevich Lopatkin! There has been some progress
in his affairs, and he is coming to get some information."

The announcement evoked different reactions from each teacher.
Old Agniya Timofeyevna beamed and nodded approvingly. The
young teachers of the junior classes exchanged glances and giggled.
The word "inventor" seemed strange to them, and, besides, they
knew Lopatkin to be a crank: he had no girl friend and did not
come to dances.

But Nadia suddenly said in a loud voice:

"Poor fellow, I was at his house not long ago. One senses immediately that he is a failure and is quite unhinged. You know how
it is in such cases: everyone else is wrong, he alone is right. A very
depressing state of affairs. Everyone is attacking him—the scientists,
the officials."

What had prompted her to say this? Perhaps the same impulse
that had led earlier to the quarrel with Valentina Pavlovna. Nadia
spoke loudly and without conviction, waiting for someone to interrupt her and to say something favorable about Lopatkin so that all
her doubts should be resolved. At the same time the baby began to
move in her womb.

But no one said a word. On the contrary, there was a complete
silence. Everyone was listening.

"You understand: I was surprised and even interested by this:
our Leonardo da Vinci lives in the house of a working man, a
certain Sianov, the father of a young girl in our class—7b. He is
getting no ration cards for bread, he has lost weight, he smokes, and
sits at his drawing board from morning to night. One thousand four
hundred components—just imagine! Twelve thousand measure-
ments! And the important point is: it all counts for nothing, because he is not a specialist." She laughed forcedly and again felt

uneasy. Still no one had interrupted her. "It seems to me that it would have been possible to do all he did without all this tragic to-do!" she continued. "Surely one can teach physics, at least not refuse bread and quietly, that's the point, quietly work on a . . ."

Someone stepped painfully hard on her foot. She cut herself short and saw Valentina Pavlovna's flushed forehead and face distorted with shame and rage. Her palms grew damp. She looked around and felt that she was growing pale: in the doorway, calmly waiting, with his eyes on the ground, stood Lopatkin. After waiting a little longer, and realizing that Nadia had ended her long tirade, he walked with a firm step to the secretary's desk, smiling and nodding to the teachers he knew.

Nadia collapsed against the back of the settee, gave several deep sighs, and silently stretched out her hand toward Valentina Pavlovna. She was feeling very ill—a strange wave of heat flooded her body, and invisible primus stoves seemed to be humming louder and louder all round her and closing in on her.

"Comrades, go to your lessons," someone said. "And you, Valentina Pavlovna, call the doctor. You know which one: Andrei Illiodorovich."

Someone lifted Nadia's feet up on to the settee. Someone in a white overall asked: "Have you a pain here?" and touched her belly. "Yes," Nadia said. The same voice asked: "And here?" and the hand touched her loins. "Yes, yes, it's hurting! In different places sometimes here, and sometimes there," Nadia said, beginning to cry; she was so frightened. "Drozdov has sent a car," someone said. Soon Nadia was lifted on to a stretcher, covered with her soft fur coat, carried out into the street, and driven away in Drozdov's little car.

In the hospital she was carefully undressed almost without being aware of it and taken into a passage crowded with beds standing close together against the wall on both sides. A tall man in a white gown and white cap walked past her and stopping a woman in a white gown, whispered: "Haven't you cleared it yet? Do so at once!" "Why can't she be in with all the others?" the woman asked loudly.

"What's that? Don't you know your orders?" the man said in a frightened, angry whisper, grabbing the woman by the arm and pushing her into the nearest ward.

Soon two female orderlies with a young nurse in charge carried Nadia along the passage; she was aware of sick women's eyes gazing at her from every side. One of the orderlies opened a door with her foot, Nadia was carried into a ward and laid on a large bed whose springs creaked softly under her weight. The nurse adjusted the sheets and gave instructions to the orderlies in a loud voice. Presumably she was the head nurse. Her eyes glanced over the ward and she went out, saying over her shoulder: "There is a bell, just in case . . ." Then it was quiet. Nadia turned her head, and saw silk curtains and a window through which the winter dusk showed blue. The door opened and two doctors came in: the tall man and a woman. The electric switch clicked and a bright light came on. The doctors spoke to each other in low voices near the door and then approached Nadia. They looked worried. The examination began.

"Does it hurt here?" the male doctor asked in a loud voice, as though speaking to a deaf person.

"Yes. And here, too. And here," Nadia answered.

"Well, for the time being we won't touch it," he said under his breath to the woman doctor. "We can give her a stimulant. Better not give it intramuscularly, but in tablets. Have we got any?" Talking in this fashion, they slowly walked to the door.

"Tell me, are these the pains?" Nadia asked in alarm.

"Weak ones," said the doctor, "which may stop again."

"If you lie very quiet," the woman doctor added.

An hour later, when it was already dark, Nadia was handed a note:

Nadia, my dear, don't worry, lie still. Tomorrow morning we are coming to see you. Valentina.

Nadia lay with wide-open eyes, staring at the ceiling and thinking. The pains became stronger and then weaker by turns. "What on earth got into me?" she asked herself. "Why did I suddenly begin saying things I didn't mean at all? And where did the words come from?" But she immediately pulled herself up. "At least I needn't lie to myself. All the things I said were Leonid's ideas, what he always says." Yes, she had unconsciously been trying to test this point of view. "But why was I so terrified? Why do I feel guilty toward Lopatkin?"

She rang the bell, and a few seconds later the door of the ward opened softly and the same head nurse came in. Her belt was drawn tight, she was young but with the hard eye of one accustomed to authority.

"Please tell me," Nadia asked, intimidated by her, "at what time tomorrow will visitors be admitted?"

"From nine in the morning. But to you they can come earlier."

Next morning Nadia was awakened by a slight but persistent rustling in the ward, like a mouse. Opening her eyes, she smiled. Yesterday's pains had stopped, and *he* was moving from time to time in her belly. The rustling in the ward continued. Turning her head, Nadia saw a little old orderly who was polishing the floor with a cloth wound around a broom. The orderly looked under the bed, stuck her nose into the bedside cupboard, and even opened, one after the other, the drawers of a little red table that stood in a corner.

Nadia watched her with interest. Having examined all the drawers of the little table, the old woman looked around, and her eyes met Nadia's.

"Don't worry. I'm not touching anything that belongs to you. One of the women left a comb behind. That's what I'm looking for. Where could it have got to?"

"But why did she leave it behind?"

"The women were all put out into the passage, in a great hurry. The ward had to be cleared for you!"

"But why all this trouble for me?" Nadia asked incredulously.

"The ward was not meant for them. They were only kept here for a time. Until one of the higher-ups was brought in."

71

"And why isn't the ward for them?"

"That's the orders."

"But why such orders?" Nadia asked quietly, speaking almost mechanically.

"Why! Why! How should I know why? Why, indeed!"

Nadia hesitated, then pressed the bell. She glanced at the clock and immediately slid her feet off the bed on to the floor. It was twenty minutes to nine. Valentina Pavlovna and the other teachers were due to arrive at any minute.

"Give me a dressing gown, quick!" Nadia said, then, shrugging her shoulders, she ran out into the passage in her short white hospital shift.

"What is it? Come back, quick!" she heard the frightened old orderly whisper.

"I'm not going anywhere. I want the medical superintendent. At once!" she said in a tone of command to the head nurse who had come running and who was now flying as fast as she could along the narrow passage between the two rows of beds.

Pale faces rose one after the other in those beds. Nadia was standing near the door of her ward. Angry patches of crimson appeared on her face, spread to her forehead, and then to her neck. Again she felt a wave of heat rising in her chest and head, she was overcome by weakness, and sat down on the edge of the nearest bed.

"What do you want?" a pale-faced woman with unkempt hair asked her, sitting up in the bed. "Are you daft, jumping out like that?"

Nadia did not reply. Two figures in white coveralls had appeared at the end of the passage. The doctors hurried toward her, and the one in front, the tall one, raised his arms in protest while he was still at a distance.

"What am I to do with you, Nadezhda Sergeyevna? What is wrong? Your husband is telephoning every minute to ask how you are. What am I to tell him?"

"I want to . . ."

72

"Let's go first and lie down in the ward, and then you can tell me all about it."

Nadia beckoned him with a feeble hand. He bent down, his face reddening as he did so, and turned his ear to her.

"I shall not go anywhere . . ." Nadia was feeling very unwell, and closed her eyes. The primus cookers were again buzzing in her ears. "I'm not going anywhere," she whispered, "until you have them all brought back."

The doctor did not understand. He straightened up.

"She wants them to be brought back," the old orderly explained. "Them what you . . ."

"Oh! I see!" The medical superintendent looked hard at Nadia and then pointed with a wide, decisive gesture from the passage to the ward. At once the head nurse and two orderlies rushed to the far end of the passage, lifted up a bed with the patient lying in it, and carried it into Nadia's ward.

"It will all be done in one minute," the medical superintendent said affably to Nadia. "Our mistake. You must excuse us. Perhaps now you can go back, while we . . ."

"Will you give me your word that everyone will be brought back?"

"Good Lord, there's no question about it. And now, allow me . . ."

The doctors took Nadia's arms and led her carefully back to the ward, to her bed. Nadia lay down. The woman doctor took her hand and at once turned to the head nurse.

"Bring a thermometer." She gave a significant glance at the medical superintendent, who gazed back at her with the same fixed look and then took Nadia's hand.

"Any pain?"

"O-oh! Yes!" Nadia whispered feebly, without opening her eyes.

"Yes, looks like it," the medical superintendent said, looking at the woman in the white overall. He tiptoed to the door, opened it wide, and Nadia heard him say sharply: "Hurry up there! Get a move on!"

The orderlies brought in a second bed. Nadia lay with closed eyes and suddenly heard the voice of the head nurse saying:

"Lidka, shift that bed a bit. These wives of chiefs are worse than the chiefs themselves. Take this one, for instance. One can never guess what they'll want next."

Nadia opened her eyes wide. The head nurse, catching her eye, at once smiled sweetly and bent over her.

"What is it, my dear? How are you feeling now?"

Nadia bit her lip and turned away.

Four or five people in white overalls were already standing in the doorway—the teachers, with Valentina Pavlovna at their head. Valentina came forward, took Nadia's hand, and sat down on the edge of her bed. There were tears in her eyes. She said nothing, only pressed Nadia's hand.

"My dear," she said at last. "Dear Nadezhda Sergeyevna! We all love you very much! So the time of trial has come for you, too, my poor dear. Never mind. Just lie quietly, please, don't make us all anxious, don't run about in the passage. Lopatkin sends you his regards. He asked me to give you this letter. My dear, we all understand perfectly, all of us."

The medical superintendent came in and asked the visitors to cut their visit short because of the patient's serious condition. The teachers left at once, nodding and smiling at Nadia. She waited a few minutes and then opened the letter. It was short—a single page from an exercise book, with wide spaces between the lines.

Lopatkin wrote:

Dear Nadezhda Sergeyevna, I quite understand your position and I want to tell you that I do not blame you for anything. You are very honest and straightforward, and you have faith in people. That is why you so easily submit to authority. I appreciate Comrade Drozdov's exceptional gift of leadership, although, as it often happens, we differ greatly in our outlook on life. It seems to me that you do not share his views entirely, and that is what led to this whole incident. I think your spirit is alien to compromise and is

74

beginning to grow restless. That is good. I press your hand and beg
you to forgive me for having been the involuntary cause of your
suffering. D. Lopatkin.

Nadia reread the letter several times, and when she heard her husband's footsteps outside the door, hid it under her pillow.

Drozdov was in a white gown that reached to the floor—it was obviously one of the medical superintendent's own. He stopped in the doorway, and Nadia heard a woman's voice say:

"Comrade Drozdov, Nadezhda Sergeyevna's condition compels us to . . ."

Drozdov glanced quickly around the ward but did not see Nadia. He smiled in obedience to the doctor's orders and backed out. Two days later, in the morning, he came again, but this time he was wearing a small overall, a woman's. He saw Nadia, sat down beside her, took her hand, and frowning with mock sternness, said:

"Quite the little heroine, aren't you!"

Listening to him, Nadia silently contemplated his bald yellow forehead, his strong white teeth, and tried to penetrate to the soul of this man, whom she never had, and still did not, understand. But she saw only his shrewd, affectionate, somewhat ironical dark eyes. "Why don't you say what you mean?" she thought. "What is the meaning of this praise? Why 'heroine'?"

"Yes," said Drozdov, and smiled. "An uprising, eh?" He looked around, laughed, and shook his head. "Put things to rights, haven't you? But now you must see that you get well."

"You know," Nadia said in a weak voice, "before the war, when I was a little girl, I was in hospital. In Leningrad. But there it wasn't . . ."

"Well, and now you are in hospital in Muzga!" Drozdov said amiably, apparently failing to perceive her meaning. He said nothing for a while, only smiled, trying to think of something cheerful to say, and then: "Muzga, as you see, treats you with more consideration!"

No, he had no intention of troubling her with serious conversation today. He had made up his mind to divert her with amusing bits of news.

"Do you know that drunken baboon Maxiutenko is being transferred. To a branch of the Projects Institute. I racked my brains to find out what it could be for. It turned out that it is as an expert on iron pipes. It was he who designed Avdiyev's machine, so now they are getting him to do the other as well. The fellow certainly has gone a step up. But if I am not there to look after him, he'll go to the dogs quickly enough."

"The Avdiyev machine you said?" Nadia asked involuntarily. "But that doctor of science, that newcomer, said it was no good. Perhaps the other one is Lopatkin's machine?" And Nadia raised her quiet gray eyes to Drozdov's face.

"You think so? Quite possible, Shutikov and all the others have gone quite crazy; all they talk about is pipes. It's true, that Galitsky did tell me that Avdiyev's machine would never get beyond the experimental prototype. It could well be that at the center they have found this out and have changed their minds."

"Yes," Nadia said, and again Drozdov failed to perceive the special tone in which she spoke.

"Are you tired?" he asked, and his eyes grew moist and tender.

"No." Nadia smiled, but her thoughts were not with him.

"Now, look, don't start anything again. Your uprising was only a partial success, as one might say. Tomorrow perhaps Mrs. Ganichev may be brought here and all your protégées will be chucked out into the passage again. It is neither I nor you who have arranged things in this way. These are privileges which, in a given phase, are distributed according to the quantity and quality of the work done. Equalitarianism is something harmful. I, for instance, do not use hospitals at all. My job won't allow me to. If I am ill, I stay on my feet. If people like me once lie down, they never get up again!" Having said this, Drozdov closed his eyes in an impressive way, then playfully opened one, and laughed. "And if someone like you is sick, being nice to look at, she must have special comforts. You are my special darling. A precious flower. But when Mrs.

76

Ganichev lies here—she will certainly run them all off their feet."

And so, without having noticed anything unusual in his wife's tone and expression, Drozdov said good-by to her, once more cast a glance around the room, smiled, and took himself off. He had scarcely left before Nadia had again put her hand under the pillow. As her eyes followed him to the door, she drew out Lopatkin's letter . . . *having been the involuntary cause of your suffering* . . . she read, and at once saw before her the spare frame and broad, bony hands of the man who concealed his disappointments so well, his lusterless hair, his sunken cheeks, and, under the brows, the hollow eyes, so full of manly, tolerant warmth.

A fortnight later she was discharged from the hospital. Drozdov was informed of this by telephone. He came home from work late, as usual, and was surprised not to find his wife in the bedroom.

"She is in her own room," Shura told him. "I made up the folding bed for her. I wanted to put a feather bed there, but she wouldn't let me. Doctor's orders, she said."

6

I N April Nadia gave birth to a son. This event seemed to lift her
out of a rut and to give a new turn to her character. She
seemed to forget all her friends, and met both Valentina Pavlovna and her husband with the same preoccupied, almost estranged
look. In her own room—scrubbed, aired, and white with sheets and
diapers everywhere—she was quite different, but there, also, not the
same as she had been before. Wrapped carelessly in a dressing gown,
with her hair uncombed, she was radiant with a secret maternal
rapture. For hours on end she walked, sat, and again walked by her
sleeping baby. She changed his diapers, kissed and anointed with
vaseline the pink folds of his tiny body, or demanded hot water to
prepare a fresh solution of boracic acid in place of the one that
had been prepared only two hours before. Having read in a book
that the human hair might be a source of infection, she at once
asked for a pair of scissors, and sitting at her mirror and humming
to herself she ruthlessly and clumsily cut off her long hair and hid
the remainder under a white headcloth. And all this she did smil-
ingly, her cheeks flushed with happiness.

Drozdov had ordered a baby carriage for his son from the machine shop of the *kombinat*. It was made in three days—a tiny stream-
lined carriage gleaming with nickel and blue enamel—and brought
to Nadia's room. On the twentieth of May "Mrs. Drozdov, in person," as they said in the settlement, put on her belted gray gabardine
coat, pushed the carriage into the street, and walked along the still
damp but already firm path, the carriage running easily along in
front of her. Nadia gave it a slight push from time to time, never

taking her eyes from the semi-transparent celluloid hood through which the tiny face of the sleeping baby could be seen.

Nadia pushed the carriage to the crossroads and turned into East Street. She moved slowly along the endless street, thirstily breathing the cold spring air, and recognizing the spring scents—here the smell of fresh-turned earth, there the odor of decaying planks. Warmed by the spring sun, she seemed to be sleeping with her eyes open. Then she awakened and saw Valentina Pavlovna coming toward her across the street and smiling. She was carrying a roll of drawing paper, clutching it awkwardly to her. This roll attracted Nadia's attention. It reminded her of something, aroused some memory in her, and, as she greeted her friend, she felt as though the amazing but correct solution to some riddle was forming in her mind.

"Oh, do let me look!" Valentina Pavlovna threw the heavy roll of paper into Nadia's hand and bent over the carriage. "Good God, how wonderful!" she whispered. "And how soundly we are sleeping! And what a pretty doll we are! How pink our cheeks are!"

"And where are we going?" Nadia asked, playfully following Valentina's tone.

"Oh, never mind. Just around here somewhere." Valentina Pavlovna's prominent forehead reddened slightly.

"On a mission of charity?" Nadia asked quietly, giving back the drawing paper.

"Well, yes." Valentina Pavlovna grew even redder and added lightly, "I got him this drawing paper."

"How is he doing?"

"He is doing drawings of a new model."

Nadia said nothing. To guess is one thing, but such an open admission was more than she had expected.

"Valia . . ."

Valentina Pavlovna blushed crimson.

"So you have been caught out, haven't you?" Nadia whispered, kissing her hot pink ear.

Valentina Pavlovna did not answer. They walked on silently for a long time.

"He knows nothing of that—of what you said—that time in the teachers' room, you remember?" Nadia asked.

"And he must never know," Valentina Pavlovna whispered.

"Would you like me to tell him? Or to arrange something so that he finds out? Shall I?"

"There is nothing to be done. Please understand that. And I ask you, very seriously, just to forget all about it. If he got to know, I should never be able to go there any more."

"Do you mean it?"

Again both of them were silent for a time, deep in thought.

"Is he at his drawing board again? What is this model?"

"It's the last one!" Valentina Pavlovna said proudly. "He has had a directive from the Ministry. It said that he was to design the old model, but he was just completing the new one, so it will be that one that goes into production."

"Goes into production? Is that certain?"

"I saw the Ministry's directive myself."

"Can he possibly be genuine?"

"I never doubted it for an instant." Valentina Pavlovna narrowed her eyes and stared grimly at some invisible enemy. "In my opinion even the man who once, long ago, was the first to make himself a pair of bird's wings and jump from a belfry was 'genuine' also. The common herd laughed at him, of course. The common herd in the kindness of its heart allows such—fliers to exist, but only on one condition: that they should meet with no failures. It laughs at failures."

"What is it you are trying to say?" Nadia slowed her pace. Her lips trembled and tears glistened in her eyes. "Valentina!" she exclaimed.

"Lopatkin did not crash. His wings proved genuine. But if you saw how violently his nose bled at times—when he gets too excited —a man who in his day was the champion sprinter of his university!

Dear Nadia, don't be offended, but I have been shielding him for more than two years from ridicule and suspicion."

"Valentina! So he has not forgiven me, after all!"

"You mustn't say that. You mustn't. It's as though you were only concerned about yourself. Of course he forgave you. Of course. But it was hard on him. Oh, Nadia, if you could see how he broods when he is alone. How he rereads that directive over and over again! You would have understood a great deal. Why am I telling you this? I need not have told you about the Ministry's directive. Or, again, the Ministry might not have issued such an order. Or his wings might have proved weak; there might have been some mistake in the calculations perhaps. What then? Would you have been convinced that he was not 'genuine' and have looked down on him with a sense of superiority? Just now, without thinking, you said: 'Can he possibly be genuine?' I always wonder who it was who taught you not to have faith in people. Where did you get that feeling of superiority? Nadia, my dear, isn't it better to start by having faith and not to begin doubting till later, when one has sufficient proof?"

Late that night, coming back from work, Drozdov heard beyond the wall of Nadia's room the steady creaking of the baby's cradle and Shura's soft, monotonous singing. He went into his wife's room. Nadia was lying on the divan in the soft half-light, gazing at the lamp, which was shaded by a multicolored cloth. Shura was rocking the cradle and singing a lullaby in a low, thin voice.

Nadia, without looking at her husband, pointed to a place on the divan. Drozdov sat down obediently.

"What is the news?" Nadia asked.

"As from tomorrow Ganichev is king of the *kombinat*. He has taken over."

"Has the telegram come?"

"Yes, it has. I am leaving for Moscow in a week. There's a flat already available. I am leaving you behind for the time being. When I have arranged everything there, I'll send for you. Don't be afraid, you will have an escort. He will see you safely to Moscow."

He said no more but lay down on the divan to rest. Shura went on rocking the cradle and singing her lullaby.

"Another bit of news!" Drozdov said, coming to life again. "That Lopatkin! He has made it! They rang me up today from the design branch. They wanted Maxiutenko, and at the same time inquired about Lopatkin."

"I know. He is just finishing a new model."

"Oh! A new model, you say?" Drozdov got up and began walking up and down the room. He always paced to and fro when any new idea seized him. And Nadia caught herself watching his every movement closely. "A new model, you say?" Drozdov asked, again stopped, glanced at the child's cradle, and sat down. "And how do *you* know that?"

"I was told." Almost imperceptibly Nadia smiled. "Tell me one thing." Her voice sounded sleepy and she did not look at him. "Tell me, Comrade Drozdov: can you take criticism?"

"It depends on the kind of criticism," Drozdov said, and laughed.

"I am not a Party member, but now I am going to criticize you," Nadia said, and stopped.

"Well, go on! Criticize!" Drozdov said after a short pause.

"I don't think you will hear such criticism in your factory. I would like to know why you felt an urge to sneer at this inventor. To talk about him behind his back! No, don't interrupt me! To say such things about him! And to whom? To me, a member of the collective in which he himself once worked! Do you respect any human being at all—except yourself?"

During this unexpected tirade Drozdov tried constantly to interrupt Nadia's outburst. Closing his eyes, he kept interjecting: "Nadia!" "Nadia!"

"Listen, Nadia," he said at last. "I understand what you mean. Listen! First of all I did not sneer at Lopatkin, I only said what I thought and then only to you, my own wife. I did not force my point of view on you in any way. I once knew a factory director who boarded, lodged, and clothed a crazy inventor for several years. They were designing a perpetual-motion machine together. Our

82

Minister likes to quote this as an example. That is what influenced my point of view to some extent."

"Oh, the Minister!" Nadia said ironically.

"No, not the Minister. At the present moment we have a whole series of new circumstances which have changed . . ."

"Do you imagine you have answered me?" Nadia asked softly.

Drozdov raised his hands in a gesture of dismay.

"Remember? You called him—"

"My dear Nadia. Stop a minute! I'm not arguing with you. Perhaps I *did* show a little weakness in giving way to a momentary impulse. But it was only a reaction to his own failings. All these—creators have a very highly developed sense of their own importance."

"How do you know? Did he tell you?"

"Whenever he came to see me, he always held his head like this." Drozdov threw his head up angrily in a way Lopatkin had never done.

"And how ought he to have held his head in front of you? Like this?" Nadia bent hers with exaggerated humility to her husband, making him frown.

"I don't believe in the existence of so-called 'superior beings.' Together with the conception 'genius,' there necessarily exists alongside it the idea of the 'common herd.' " Drozdov had hit on what seemed to him a brilliant idea; he jumped to his feet and began to pace up and down, looking very pleased with himself. "I am a descendant of the common herd. I have a hereditary aversion to all these—these—irreplaceables!"

He stopped in front of Nadia. She was silent; she could not find the necessary words, although she felt, as always, that he was somehow not quite right.

"Look," she said at last, "you say that you are a descendant of the common herd. The common herd is not necessarily the same thing as the poor. On the contrary, the poor think a great deal and speculate about their own fate, or even about the destiny of mankind. And, by the way"—here Nadia smiled—"in this process of

83

reasoning, such poor men sometimes have made discoveries of genius. The common herd is something quite different, don't you think?"

Drozdov did not reply.

"It is in truth something dark and terrible," Nadia went on thoughtfully. "It is the worst of all, always striving to seize as much as possible and always crooked. And once it gets hold of something, it at once grows fat and bloated with a snout instead of a face."

Drozdov looked at her sharply, sat down, and held his head in his yellow hands.

"And from those whom you call 'superior beings' and I call simple 'honest men' you can take everything away—you can make beggars of them, and yet they will still light the way for others! You have found a good place to look for conceit! In Lopatkin, who is himself destitute, and yet—all he thinks of is how he can help the little daughter of Sianov—a mechanic who works in your factory. Oh!" Nadia cried suddenly, covering her face with her hands and beginning to sway from side to side. "Oh, Lord, what have I done!"

"Nadia! What's the matter?" Drozdov was increasingly concerned.

"You know, I cut him dead for a whole year! Once we met on a narrow path and I turned my head away! And he understood, and was sorry for me—sorry! And he, too, pretended not to have seen, or not to have recognized me!"

Drozdov laughed uncertainly and put his hand on Nadia's shoulder.

"Well, you were guilty of bad manners. But where do I come in?"

"You can't see where you come in?" Nadia asked quietly, and Drozdov shrugged his shoulders.

"If at least you did not make excuses!" Nadia began again, glancing at her husband. "I shouldn't know how to face him now, if I were to meet him! Good Lord, you even begrudged him a sheet of paper! No, not begrudged; it was worse than that. You couldn't be bothered to move so much as a finger. You could not give the man even a scrap of paper!"

"Well, my dear, such is the fate of the individualist! If he had been a member of a collective, he would have had paper. But who would pay attention to him, to a lone hand?"

"So you are in the right?" Nadia interrupted him. "So no one would pay any attention? No one at all? Then what did he make his drawings on?"

Drozdov shrugged his shoulders once more and said nothing.

"What I can see—from this whole conversation," Nadia said softly, sighing, "is that some people have the peculiarity of thinking in feelings. I may not know a man, I may not have any *cut-and-dried* information about him, and yet I can decide at first glance that I like him! That he is attractive! That I want to be in his company! That I trust him! I can even guess if he is finding life difficult. Have you ever felt anything like this happen to you?"

"What you say is right, of course."

"There you are! So it's right. It seems that I can always beat you in a question of feelings, although you may prove to me logically that it's you who are right. Sometimes you even prove . . . yes . . ." she gazed thoughtfully at the wall on which hung a photograph of Drozdov as a young man. "You were better then."

"Carry on! Carry on!" Drozdov said, getting up quickly and again pacing to and fro.

"If there were an audience here," Nadia said, "if there were three hundred people or so, your eloquence would win them. You could convince them, but you could not even look me in the face. But there *is* no audience and you *are* looking me in the face. And I can see that you haven't a leg to stand on. Tell me, Lenya, what was it you were thinking about just now?"

"When?"

"Just now. About five minutes ago. Why did you get up and start walking about just as you are now?"

"Nadia! This is impossible! Why this cross-examination? Yes, I was thinking about something. About the Avdiyev machine."

"What about it?"

"Nothing much. Technical difficulties."

"And what else did you think of? When you jumped up and started walking?"

"I've told you. There was nothing else."

"So there was nothing else? All right. Go and take a nap."

Drozdov kissed his wife's cheek, expelled his breath with a faint sound, and went to the bedroom.

Next day preparation for the move began in the Drozdovs' house. A truck from the *kombinat* brought well-made packing cases of white lumber. Drozdov's mother and Shura began at once to pack the crockery. Three days later, when everything was ready, a small engine shunted an empty freight car to the loading ramp of the *kombinat*. Workmen, supervised by old Mrs. Drozdov, loaded all the packing cases and some of the furniture into the truck, which was then closed and sealed up.

Soon Drozdov left for Moscow. Shura was sent back to her village, and Nadia was left in the half-empty house alone with her mother-in-law and her little son. She had not been teaching for a long time, but now, out of boredom, she began going to the teachers' room every day to say her good-bys, and, with her baby on her knees, she watched, with a forlorn smile, the former active life going on without her.

A fortnight later there was nothing left to watch in the school. The examinations were over, the school was empty, and even Nadia's friend, Valentina Pavlovna, had gone with her little daughter to stay with relatives in the Ukraine. Sometimes Mrs. Ganichev would call on Nadia, and in her fat painted face Nadia read: "What! Still here?" Mrs. Ganichev walked through the empty rooms and said to old Mrs. Drozdov: "I shall put the wardrobe here, and the sideboard there!"

At the end of June Nadia at last got a letter from Drozdov, in which he described their new three-room flat on Sand Street. Later a telegram came that said: *Come.*

Ganichev at once sent to Nadia a young technician, Volodia, by name, who for the occasion had been given some mission to Moscow to the technical directorate of the Ministry. Volodia brought tickets for the Moscow coach and quickly packed the remaining things. There were still four hours before they had to leave, and Nadia went out for a walk, leaving the baby with the old woman. There was a sense of oppression in her breast, an unfamiliar feeling which was neither fear nor heartache. As she went out into the street and looked about her, the feeling became stronger. It was this that drew her back to the school; once again she opened the door, walked through the deserted, echoing second floor, and still felt no relief. The dull pain only increased.

Then she turned into East Street. The wind blew clouds of dust downhill into her face. She drew her scarf over her head, and climbed quickly uphill in the teeth of the dust-laden squalls of wind. She reached the top. Here the wind was fiercer, a steppe wind from Siberia. And there was number 167. By day it looked even more ramshackle; it was not even whitewashed. Nadia stepped over the barbed wire, went around the little shed on which there was now no hayrick, and opened the door. The cow had gone—probably it had been driven out with the herd. Nadia opened the second door, and the first sight that met her eyes were the five children sitting at the table. There was a stranger with them, dressed in a light-gray gabardine overcoat. He had managed to squeeze himself in between the table and the tiny window and was sitting there in a twisted position, stretching out one long leg to the side, with his felt hat on his lap. He was drawing something for the children, his hair ruffled, one black lock hanging into his eyes. The children, as though at a word of command, all turned their blond heads and rapt gaze in Nadia's direction, and for a moment exposed to view a sheet of paper lying on the table. On it the stranger had almost finished the picture of a wolf with a coat that bristled rather like a broom.

The stranger half rose, bowed to Nadia, and scrutinized her with watchful, narrowed eyes. His bony, thick-lipped face still wore the rapacious and craftily wolfish expression he had drawn on the paper. Nadia was so taken aback that she forgot even to return his greeting.

"Who's there?" the voice of Mrs. Sianov asked from the other, smaller room.

"It's me," Nadia said, realizing already that Lopatkin was not there. "I've come to say good-by."

"Oh, it's you, is it? Well, come in." A bright electric bulb was switched on in the other room. "Do come in, will you? I've been taken bad, I have."

Nadia looked uncertainly at the stranger and then quickly entered the other room. Mrs. Sianov was lying in Lopatkin's bed. Nadia took it all in at a single glance: the drawing board was gone, and what was more to the point, the snapshot of Jeanne Ganichev had disappeared, too.

"Where is he?" she asked hurriedly, with a sweep of her hand implying everything—the portrait, the drawing board, and Lopatkin himself.

"He's gone to the regional capital. He helped to put in the potatoes, and then he was off. You've heard, I s'pose, about his business. Well, he's gone there, to the branch office. To design the machine."

"Will he be coming back?"

"Of course. He's left all his things here, under the bed. He'll be coming back all right. In the autumn or perhaps before."

"Then I'll leave a letter."

"How far away is that branch?" The stranger reminded them of his presence. His voice was a slow, drawling bass.

"About a day and a half, at least," Mrs. Sianov said.

"Oh!" said the stranger. "Too bad that I missed him."

"I am going away and would like to leave a few words for him," Nadia whispered hurriedly. "Could you find me a scrap of paper?"

"Genka!" Mrs. Sianov shouted, with an effort heaving herself half out of bed. "Come here. Open that box, there's an exercise book in it. And bring the ink and the pen."

Genka brought the things, and Nadia sat down at the table and began to write rapidly.

"So you say it's all been arranged for him?" the stranger's voice was saying doubtfully in the quiet beyond the flimsy wall. "H'm. So he's gone. Tell me, Agafia Timofeyevna, hasn't he perhaps left any little drawings behind? I'd like to see them."

"And what might you want with them? Did you come specially to see him?"

"Well, it's like this, you see," the stranger drawled, appearing in the doorway of the smaller room; he was very tall and was forced to bend his head, which made it appear as though he were supporting the roofbeam on his shoulders. He looked at Mrs. Sianov out of serious black eyes and said: "I have come from Moscow to test a machine here—a machine intended for the same purpose."

Nadia turned quickly around and leaned forward, concealing her letter.

"Was it you who came to us during the winter? Are you Galitsky?"

"I am!" He transferred the gaze of his black eyes to her and drew his thick black brows together. They gazed at each other for a while with silent interest.

"So the machine is good, after all?" Nadia asked at last.

"You must ask the workmen. They are plain-spoken chaps. They'll tell you all about it."

"They cursed it and cursed it, but nevertheless they built it."

The stranger sighed and gave Nadia an undefinable look. "I have my own point of view about this machine, you see, which I shall finally clarify while I am here. And because of that I would like to put off this conversation a little. In a month, when everything has been definitely cleared up, I shall be glad to . . ."

"I am leaving for Moscow today."

"That doesn't matter. You'll hear about it even in Moscow. The ripples from this business will spread as far as Moscow."

"Will they?"

"Perhaps not. But that makes no difference. Your husband will tell you. He is no less concerned in this affair than I am."

And apparently not noticing the color flooding Nadia's face,

Galitsky turned to Mrs. Sianov and said, stressing his point with his outstretched finger:

"It is very important for me to find out the principle on which Comrade Lopatkin's machine is based, because if I were to come to an unfavorable conclusion about it, I would have to be able to suggest something else."

"My husband will soon be back from work—you had better talk to him," said Mrs. Sianov. "Perhaps there may be some drawings somewhere."

Nadia wrote a letter, folded it into a triangle, addressed it in large letters to COMRADE LOPATKIN, and left it on the table, the address side downward. She said good-by to Mrs. Sianov and the children, gave Galitsky a lively glance and a nod, and went out into the street. The wind blew her rapidly forward and down toward the black smoke screen of the *kombinat*.

The car was at the door of her house, and Volodia and the old woman, in their traveling clothes, were waiting for her, seated on the luggage. The Ganichevs were sitting on two of the trunks—they had come to say good-by.

Nadia threw her coat over her shoulders. Mrs. Ganichev gave her a wet, noisy kiss, and said: "Thank God! We were already imagining that you had decided to stay behind. Our regards to Moscow." Volodia managed to carry three suitcases at once, Ganichev took one, and the driver another, the old woman carefully picked up the baby, wrapped in a green blanket, and they went out to the car. And soon Nadia was driving along the familiar road, going away from this place forever and leaving everything irretrievably behind. She looked back and saw for the last time the smoke-curtained *kombinat*, behind it the hill covered with yellow feather grass, and scattered over it the little clay cottages of East Street. She looked back again and again at the cottages with a vague and oppressive sense of being orphaned. It all disappeared slowly behind her right shoulder, and receded forever into the past.

7

D MITRI ALEXEYEVICH LOPATKIN had in his time been one of those very healthy, very strong men whose most distinctive characteristic is their good nature. He had never had an enemy, and there were no dark spots on his conscience with the exception of a permanent sense of guilt toward his mother, who had quietly passed away in the town of Murom before the war, without having been able to see her only son once more before she died. The son had been too busy at the time with his studies at the university and his work in the factory, and had put off the visit to his mother from winter to summer, from summer to autumn, and had not even written to her very often, although he had sent her money. Having received a short letter from the neighbors, Lopatkin went to Murom, sat for a while in his mother's empty room, sought out in the cemetery the simple grave with its iron marker and with his own surname on the tablet, and took off his cap. He did not obviously mourn his mother, but his friends noticed that he grew somewhat quieter, and that this quietness remained with him permanently.

When the war started, he was called up as a private in the infantry, but was soon promoted to command first a squad, and then, at the beginning of forty-two, a platoon. He was discharged in the same year, the war having left him with several roughly-healed scars which looked as though they had been inflicted with an ax.

In the army he learned to smoke, to talk without gesturing, to listen patiently and in silence, and to make decisions quickly. There was also another characteristic which developed in him: to think of his men first and of himself last. The hungry Leningrad front

91

brought out this quality in many men and Lopatkin had received his last wound there, near Lake Ladoga. From the war he also brought back a decoration: an Order of the Red Star.

When Lopatkin came to teach in the ten-year school of Muzga, he was twenty-seven years old. And if at that time, at first sight, the teachers' room put him at no more than twenty-five, three years later, he had begun to look considerably over thirty; the hundreds of small sheets of paper and dozens of large ones on which he set out the details of his machine had all left their mark on him. He kept all these details in his head, saw them when he closed his eyes, altered them, combined them with one another in his mind, and also made them work. But his hopes and disappointments influenced him even more than all these other constituents, components, and the drawings put together. These hopes and disappointments were brought to him by a young post woman in envelopes marked with the black or colored rubber stamps of the various ministries, directorates, and committees. In the course of two years Lopatkin learned to conduct correspondences, file papers, decipher their hidden meaning, and collate the answers received from various offices and persons. In each document he perceived a human face. When a brief opinion first arrived from Professor Avdiyev, a false and ruthless face seemed to stare at him from the paper. No one had discerned that falsity except Lopatkin, but to him it was as clear as day. Avdiyev was evading the issue: he pretended not to discern any underlying idea in Lopatkin's design, and only criticized the imperfections of its execution, in which Lopatkin was in fact somewhat weak. The professor insisted that "the machine was complicated and clumsy." Shortly after this came a lengthy opinion by another expert, Tepikin. He, too, said, as though of his own accord: "The machine is complicated and clumsy." And Lopatkin saw the face of the "young scientist working out problems set him by Professor Avdiyev." Six months later a letter signed by Deputy Minister Shutikov was delivered at the little house in East Street. It contained the same by now familiar formula: "The machine is complicated and clumsy." But the face of this paper was different: it

92

was the honest face of an obedient civil servant, who had copied the formula from Tepikin, and was glad to find a reason for winding up a tiresome affair, and submitting the document for signature to the Deputy Minister. He had even put his name in one corner of the paper. This little goblin in the Ministry was, as it were, the sentry at the gate, through which Avdiyev's phrase penetrated into the offices, and turned into the wisdom of the powers that be.

During these years Lopatkin learned to regard with suspicion papers that were adroitly worded and beautifully typed. But he did not learn to stop hoping and expecting, and these constantly recurring flashes of hope gave his features the hard, obstinate traits of a martyr.

Uncle Pete Sianov, the master of the little house in which Lopatkin had lived ever since the year 1943, worked as an engineer in the machine shop of the *kombinat*. From the very first steps Lopatkin had taken toward the realization of his invention, Uncle Pete had enlisted himself as his supporter. At first he had politely inquired as to the purpose of some component; later he had tried to help, but nothing had come of it—he had been unable to conceive the machine's existence in three-dimensional space. After that he began to bring little models of steel and brass made by him in the factory, and the work began to progress considerably faster. Sianov was enthusiastic about Lopatkin's machine. Secretly amazed at the tenacity of his lodger, he began to feed the hungry but proud inventor on the sly. He brought him his dinner, putting it on the little table when Lopatkin was not looking, and quickly effacing himself as though he were engaged in taming a wounded wild bird.

So Lopatkin became a part of the family. True he made up his mind there and then to carry out in the Sianov house all that could be done with hammer, ax, or spade. But he soon felt that that was not enough and began to take on pupils, to coach dull pupils, to instil in them interest in the exact sciences, and cure them of laziness. His clients increased and his financial problems gradually receded into the background.

In the morning, after he had chopped enough wood and cleaned up the yard, Lopatkin went out for a walk. In an hour he had covered the whole settlement downhill and uphill, at a brisk, even pace, and then sat down at his drawing board. During his walks Lopatkin sometimes met one or the other of his former pupils; on occasions he stopped, shook hands, and asked how they were getting on—he remembered all their names. The children, not able as yet to hide their feelings, would stare at him goggle-eyed; some with respect—for was he not an inventor?—others with open scorn—for was he not a crank?

That would not have mattered so much, but Lopatkin sometimes encountered adults, in particular that "Mrs. Drozdov herself." Ever since Lopatkin had returned from Moscow she had stopped greeting him; had passed him with an animated face and a friendly glance directed at the region of his buttons. She appeared happy, beautiful, and thoughtfully tender. "Such parasitic, strongly-scented flowers, pale, convolvulus blossoms, grow from some unknown soil to blight us," Lopatkin thought, following her with his eyes. "And they despise us, and no one can open their eyes, no one can restrain them, for they are stupid."

"Yes, that is just what she is like," Lopatkin whispered, filled with hatred of her.

Yet at the same time, he did not act according to the dictates of his pride and vanity. He stood aside courteously for her, and even crossed to the other side of the street and pretended to be entirely immersed in his own thoughts.

Then he learned that she was pregnant. Her face became blotched and yellow, and her walk slow. She moved with difficulty, and the prospect of becoming a mother evidently frightened her. Lopatkin at once forgave her everything. True, this was not wholly unconnected with certain circumstances of which Lopatkin had gradually become aware during the preceding winter.

Valentina Pavlovna, the English teacher, a thirty-year-old, a lively woman who was constantly blushing, often came to visit the Sianov home. Her face was hopelessly disfigured by a high, protruding pink forehead. This blemish would have been less noticeable if

Valentina Pavlovna had only been able to conquer the habit of constantly blushing, seemingly without reason.

But in any case, Lopatkin was little concerned with anyone's physical beauty. Mrs. Sianov, for instance, found something unpleasant in the glance of the young woman with eyes too far apart, whose portrait was pinned on the wall of Lopatkin's room, although Lopatkin saw something different in those eyes, something resembling sympathy or affectionate approval. And he felt a strong impulse to look into them.

With Valentina Pavlovna, Lopatkin always appeared calm and detached, making an effort not to notice her awkward movements, her inappropriate words, and constant blushes. He was always glad when she came: Valentina Pavlovna somehow formed a tie between him and the world outside, acting as a sort of gay and lively newsreel for him. Besides, she believed that Lopatkin's pipe-casting machine was not a mere figment of his brain. She, too, believed that this machine would finally prove itself. And once he knew that her faith was sincere, it became possible for him to accept her contribution to a longed-for objective: the rolls of excellent drawing paper which she obtained from some unknown source.

Valentina Pavlovna spent hours sitting in Lopatkin's little room while he drafted a new model of his machine, or ruminated over an unfinished drawing. She silently gazed over his shoulder past his shaggy, too-long hair, at the corner of his bushy reddish eyebrow, which was now raised in surprise, now lowered in anger, depending on how the work was going. Or she would suddenly begin to chatter about goings-on in the settlement or the school

And from all this chatter another face would gradually emerge to gaze mournfully at Lopatkin: the face of "Mrs. Drozdov herself." It looked as if this once-happy member of the Young Communist League, daughter of a simple financial accountant, had been mistaken in her choice of a husband, had been made a captive, and had not begun to realize this until it was too late.

"Do you know how she argues now?" Valentina Pavlovna related. "No one has ever argued with me like it before. She puts forward some proposition and waits for me to refute it. And she is delighted when I smash it to smithereens. But if I say nothing and think it over, she is annoyed, and goes for me tooth and nail! It's amazing!"

"Yes, it is!" Lopatkin was remembering Nadia's recent visit to the Sianovs.

Valentina Pavlovna came one morning, silently stood a roll of drawing paper in a corner, sat down on a stool, and unbuttoned her blue-gray coat with the blue-fox collar.

Lopatkin was mixing India ink in a little saucer. He glanced at the roll of paper in the corner and said half in joke, half in earnest:

"Look out, Valentina Pavlovna, or I shall be falling in love with you. You are giving me more than life."

Valentina Pavlovna laughed, blushed, and hid her face in her coat collar.

"I am serious." Lopatkin smiled at her. "In order to stay alive, one needs bread. But however hungry I might be, I should always be ready to exchange my bread for a spark of belief. When I was in hospital, we were all wounded men there from the Leningrad front. And something had happened to some of them—they had starved too long out there, and I saw them now drying bread crusts on the radiator and hiding them when they were dry in a pillow slip. I am a little like that, only with me it's in connection with people who believe in my cause. And it's the same with drawing paper. I'm saying this so that you will understand. A mere 'thank you' is not enough. I shall always remember these days and always be on the lookout for an opportunity to . . ."

"Dmitri Alexeyevich, stop it!" Valentina Pavlovna turned toward him a face that was both happy and offended. "You have almost hurt my feelings. I am content with very little; do you imagine I don't understand? I have faith in you!" she almost shouted. "Do you hear? So it's all right. You need the drawing paper—and I am happy!"

She checked herself suddenly, blushed, and added:

"I know that the state needs this machine, and that it is the duty of all honest people to help you."

Neither of them said any more after this.

While this conversation was going on Lopatkin glanced quickly and involuntarily at her several times. He drove away the constantly recurring suspicion, which, while it flattered his vanity, frightened him by its depth and seriousness. His conscience told him to stop guessing, to see and hear nothing, or this new and affectionate friendship might be destroyed.

So he rattled his saucer, cleared his throat, coughed, and finally switched on the radio—it was a broadcast for children—in order not to be obliged to notice feelings which had almost reached the point of open demonstration. He could not have reciprocated these feelings. He did not want to repulse this advance, and hastened to deal with the situation by diplomatic procedure. It must be confessed that in this he was successful. Valentina Pavlovna got up, as though she had awakened from a trance, and turned the radio on louder. Then, following some obscure train of thought, she began looking at the portrait of Jeanne Ganichev stuck up on the wall.

"Does Jeanne still not write?" she asked.

Lopatkin had not yet had time to answer when a woman's voice was heard from outside, a door banged, and Mrs. Sianov came in out of the cold in a fur coat, her head tied in a scarf, and threw two letters on the table.

"There's your correspondence for you—I forgot it yesterday. Carried it about in my pocket. Soon we'll have to make silage out of those letters of yours."

With a steady and practiced hand Lopatkin tore open the first envelope, which bore the imprint of the Ministry. For an instant a pain seemed to shoot through his temples as he read the words: *It is not considered possible.* . . . Then he threw the handsome document under the table. For a moment an expression of weariness appeared in his eyes, it was as if he froze up, and his lips curved in a sneer; but all this quickly passed. He picked the paper up off the floor, read it calmly through, smoothed it out, pulled out a drawer, and filed

97

it in a folder which already contained many such handsome documents. Then he threw the folder back into the drawer, sighed deeply, and looked up at the likeness of Jeanne. "It looks as if there were to be no end to our parting," he thought to himself, easily penetrating the superficial hardness of her gaze, and coming to rest in warm, affectionate depths whose existence was known to him alone. He had already forgotten that there was anyone else in the room—his constant guest.

"Yes, it's the devil!" he said, and stretched out his hand for the second envelope.

It was a letter from *her!* Valentina Pavlovna realized this at once and took her leave, tittering pitifully, as though alone in an empty room, and went away quickly, not stopping even to button up her coat.

Now it was quiet in the room. Lopatkin read the letter, and began to stroke his hair, his cheek, his shoulders, without noticing what he was doing. The loud voice in the letter—something like a radio announcer's—which told him of the unexpected rupture, seemed to sound in his ears.

Dmitri!

I have reread all your letters. You always write that your affairs are going well, that they are improving, that your machine is already being built, that "suitable provision" has already been made, that Professor X, member of the Academy, is praising you, and Dr. XX is extolling you to the skies. I was flattered to read all this, and I even boasted of it to my friends. I also wrote letters to Muzga. They were all answered, and it turns out that you were lying to me. I shall not repeat what my friends wrote, but I have no use for deceit. I don't want to be the heroine of a tragedy in verse. And, in any case, it's all so depressing, all somehow so wrong. Please write me the whole truth, give me the opportunity of deciding my future as ordinary adults do. Between the outlook on life of a young girl and that of a grown-up young woman there is a difference that one begins to understand with the years. I have not enough strength, I feel I shall have to resign my future Edison to another, more courageous woman. . . .

Having read the letter, Lopatkin raised his eyebrows, looked at Jeanne's likeness, and reddened. The chair creaked as he stood up, snatched a sheet of paper out of the drawer, and began to write very fast, his pen scratching loudly over the paper.

Very well, my dear, I will write you the whole truth. I see that the time has come for us to square accounts. I must offer you my apologies. I thoughtlessly lured you on to the doubtful path of being the friend of an inventor, without so much as knowing whether I was an inventor at all or merely a crank. I am glad that your eyes were opened in time and that you can thus escape a terrible fate. My affairs are at present going worse than ever, I have used up nearly all my matches, and not one of them would light. They only smoked. And in the past I at least had a full box of them. Yet I still look with the same hope as always to the last match. You can regard this as a lie, but allow me to assert that I shall soon be celebrating a victory. Our machines will be at work in the factories, and Uncle Pete and I will be looking at them with pleasure and inventing new ones, because we like doing this sort of work. I shall soon calmly try to strike my last match. Perhaps it will light. Of course it is a pity that you will not be with us in waiting for the flame to spring up. But this "soon" is soon only for me. I am used to delays—I may take several years to strike this match. And who knows when it will come alight? So please forget everything that you and I talked about, because that was all words and even involved a certain risk. And that is not the right thing for you. Remember only the mathematics and the physics, but not too well, because these sciences are bad for people who are afraid to take a risk. I wish you a speedy recovery from all the trouble I have caused. But Moscow is very good at healing shallow wounds.
                                                  Good-by,
                                                    D. Lopatkin.

Lopatkin stuck down the flap of the envelope, threw his coat over his shoulders, and hurried out into the street without a hat. A post-box nailed to a wooden post creaked in the wind. The letter dropped into its iron depths with a dull thud. Lopatkin had turned back in the direction of his house when he saw the post woman hurrying toward him up the hill. In her hand was a large envelope, and on it the familiar blue seal of the Ministry.

"A greeting from Moscow," the post woman said, handing him the letter as she passed, crossing the road.

Numb with cold and covered in snow, Lopatkin rushed to his room and tore open the envelope with the bitter smile curving his lips. Yet another handsome document! But—what was this?

The Ministry has once more examined. . . . The decision has been taken to produce a prototype. . . . The head of the projects branch has been given instructions . . . attach you to the designs office for the time required and put at your disposal the required number of assistants. . . . The requisite financial means have been assigned. . . .

"Hell!" Lopatkin said. He threw the paper down on the table, then took it up, and read it again from the first word to the last. "It's enough to drive a man crazy. What the devil are they up to now?"

Again he took up the paper and looked closely at the signature. It was like a fine, straight green seam made with a sewing machine, with a thread hanging down at each end of the seam. It was from the Deputy Minister!

He considered the question: what to do about the letter to Jeanne? Then he shrugged his shoulders. Let it go!

"Of course, how could any man not go crazy with all this!" he said to himself. He threw off his overcoat, lay down on the bed, and at once fell asleep.

That evening there was a little celebration in the Sianov household. Uncle Pete obtained a bottle of steppe vodka, as yellow as

100

kerosene. A mixed salad was made of salt cucumbers, potatoes, and sour cabbage, and dressed with genuine cottonseed oil. The friends ate, drank, and laughed to their hearts' content. They kept counting on their fingers how often such letters had come before, and how many bottles had been drunk on those occasions. It turned out that in two years there had been only four encouraging letters and three bottles drunk. Once they had gone without vodka.

Lopatkin laughed louder at this than all the others and his laugh was more bitter. And, as on previous occasions, by the evening he was running a high temperature.

"That's because you are not used to drinking spirits," said Uncle Pete, looking intently into Lopatkin's eyes. "You've got fever. It's no use trying to resist a fever."

And putting his arms around Lopatkin solicitously, he took him off to bed. But Uncle Pete was wrong. This was not a fever; it was hope.

By morning it should have left Lopatkin, who had grown even leaner during the last twenty-four hours. But a new letter had come from Moscow—a copy of the decree transferring "Engineer Maxiutenko to the projecting and designing bureau of the branch office of the State Institute of Projecting Foundry Equipment . . . to assist in the realization of the projected casting machine devised by Engineer Lopatkin."

"Oh, so now they have made me an engineer!" Lopatkin said to himself.

The next thing was a messenger girl from the management of the *kombinat* who knocked at the door and handed Lopatkin a note from Drozdov, written in brown pencil on a sheet of paper with the director's heading: *Comrade Lopatkin! Please come to my office to discuss your business at 12.00–27/1/47.*

Lopatkin hurriedly got ready for this call. He looked at his shoes and cleaned them, sticking the patches down with collodium. Then, while the iron was heating, he shaved, cut the frayed edges of his sleeves and trouser legs close with a pair of scissors, and sticking a thimble on his finger, oversewed the shorn edges with thread.

101

Finally, having sprinkled his tunic and breeches with water, he pressed them through a towel, producing a knife edge on his breeches from hip to ankle.

Having put his clothes in order, he dressed and went out. On the way he looked in at the school, and asked the secretary for a testimonial "from the former place of employment," which would, of course, immediately come in useful at the project and design office. The testimonial was at once made out but the rubber stamp was found to be locked up. This trifle was to prove the first link in the chain of events that ended in bringing Nadia to a hospital bed; Lopatkin promised to call back for the testimonial and went away, to return later.

He hurried to the interview with Drozdov. The secretary stood up when he entered the reception room, but did not announce him, merely opening the door to the general manager's office and asking Lopatkin to enter. So he was expected!

As he had done the last time he had been here, he crossed the carpet in a straight line and came to a stop between two armchairs, in front of an enormous dark-red table behind which sat a small, bald, bristling man with a thin yellow face. Drozdov gave him a friendly look out of lively dark eyes. His head was drawn between his shoulders, and both hands, clasped into a single large fist, lay on the green tablecloth.

"Well," Drozdov said, standing up and shaking hands with Lopatkin, then motioned him to one of the armchairs and sat down again, assuming his habitual posture so accurately that it seemed as though he had never left it. He closed his eyes, for a while said nothing, then archly opened one eye, raised the eyebrow nearest Lopatkin and said: "So you are to be congratulated, eh?"

"Not yet, I think."

"You mean to say . . . !" Drozdov grinned and closed his eyes. "He means to tell us that he is modest!"

At that Drozdov squinted over his shoulder, and Lopatkin, following his glance, saw at the far end of the room, sitting in an armchair, a baldish man in officer's uniform but without shoulder straps

—the same man who had been with Drozdov on the last occasion and whose name was Samsonov.

"We know that, Comrade Inventor," Drozdov went on good-humoredly with a sly grimace. "Modest, that's what you are! I suppose you had a little celebration over this; but you didn't invite me to it, eh?"

"It was the fourth celebration, Leonid Ivanovich. Perhaps there will have to be as many more."

"Come, come, man! This is a fit of alarm and despondency! Dostoevski stuff! We'll soon dispel all that. Now tell me, Comrade Lopatkin." Drozdov drew a desk calendar closer, and took a sharply pointed pencil from the hetman's iron hat. "I am expecting a telephone call today from the Branch Projects Office. Maxiutenko is being transferred there from here. To assist in the realization of the projected casting machine devised by Engineer Lopatkin. Do you know that name?" He gave Lopatkin an amiable sidelong glance. "What I want to know, Comrade Engineer, is: when are you going there?"

"I'll go . . . First I have to finish something. It will take another three months."

"Three? That's all right with me. But will it be all right for you? Maxiutenko is working on the Avdiyev machine here. Aren't you afraid . . . ?"

"I know. Let him work."

"The inventor has a generous mind," Drozdov remarked to Samsonov.

"And in three months we'll start on mine," Lopatkin said quietly, "provided this Deputy Minister doesn't change his mind."

"Shutikov? No, he won't change his mind. He's gone crazy over your machine. It's all he talks about. His hobbyhorse. So it will be in May? Well, we'll make it that. I don't think there is anything more."

Lopatkin stood up, wishing to take his leave, but Drozdov seemed not to notice his outstretched hand.

"Sit down, sit down, what's your hurry?" He laughed jovially.

"What's your hurry? I can't imagine," he said to Samsonov, and the other stirred in his chair and threw one leg across the other. "I can't make it out!" Drozdov said, and took up the telephone receiver. "Hallo! I want Fabrichkovski," he said into the receiver, and his face darkened. "Comrade Fabrichkovski? An inventor will be coming to see you presently . . . today. No jokes, please, they are out of place. I am just telling you, Lopatkin, the inventor, will be coming to see you. I want you to dress him up. . . . Yes. From me. . . . These financial observations. . . . What d'you mean—there is no money? We are not so poor as all that. Can't the *kombinat* manage to equip one inventor? . . . No, tell me, can it? . . . Well then, dress him. Dress him properly. I want him to go about looking like a Minister. Have a suit made for him, just like yours. Or give him your own. And your ears, too, if need be. . . . That's better, now I can hear a man talking, not a boy. That's all."

Slamming the receiver back onto its cradle, Drozdov gaily slapped the table with his palm.

"You walk downstairs and to the left—there you'll find our supply hell. Ask for Fabrichkovski. They'll pounce on you at once and before you can bat an eyelid you'll be dressed in the latest Fabrichkovskian fashion. Well, all the best. . . ." Drozdov stood up and gave Lopatkin a firm handshake. "Go on, make your machine, take our technique a step further. Don't forget us. Come to us if you want anything. We'll give you a hand."

Lopatkin thanked Drozdov, and bowed to Samsonov, who returned the greeting by taking one leg off the other. Lopatkin left the room quickly, bowed to the secretary without stopping, and ran down the stairs. He put his coat on, opened the glass door, and found himself outside, on the trodden snow. Here he stopped for a moment, looked down at his overcoat, at his breeches, and frowned. Why hadn't he gone to see Fabrichkovski, why hadn't he accepted Drozdov's rich gift? Had he not accepted drawing paper and India ink from Valentina Pavlovna? The answer was simple: Valentina Pavlovna believed in him, but this fellow—his eyes told a different tale—even now.

104

Remembering the testimonial, he went back to the school and appeared in the door of the teachers' room just as Nadia had begun her loud discourse on the ill-starred Leonardo of Muzga. What Lopatkin noticed first was that her words sounded strangely loud in the silence, like an echo in an empty room: the teachers had recognized Lopatkin and all sat dazed with surprise. Then he saw Nadia's face, her eyes appealing for support. She was tormenting herself, it seemed, with words that were foreign to her, with an irony that was foreign to her, with a foreign tone of voice. Lopatkin wanted to draw back, to hide, but at that moment her dark glance met his, she gave a little cry, said no more, and turned very pale.

He could not forget that moment either on the following day or even after a month. He remembered it again on that last day of May, when, having completed his new model, he unbent his back with an effort, and at last, a happy man, went for a walk on East Street.

At the foot of the hill, not far from the administration of the *kombinat,* a little gray-green car shot past Lopatkin. It went by at a great speed, then, after braking suddenly, stopped. Drozdov opened the door and put a foot in a highly polished boot onto the ground.

"Hail, inventor!" he said gaily, giving Lopatkin a sharp glance.

Lopatkin went closer and shook the general manager's small yellow hand.

"Still here?" Drozdov asked, still looking at him sharply.

"I shall be going soon; everything is ready."

"Good. What about the clothes? Fabrichkovski was expecting you."

"I was busy, Leonid Ivanovich. Every minute counted. You know what the likes of us are."

"Yes, you've done a thorough job."

Drozdov understood perfectly well that this was merely a polite refusal of his gift. He also realized that he had made a mistake in offering Lopatkin a suit of clothes. In order not to lose face, though at heart he was annoyed, he said jocularly:

"I get it! You fellows are above such things. Pleasures are alien, sufferings alien, too! Well, have it your own way!"

He shook hands with Lopatkin, turned to the driver, and slammed the car door. Through the celluloid side curtain Lopatkin for an instant saw his eyes. Yes, it seemed that Drozdov had made an attempt that had proved unsuccessful: he had wanted to make friends with the inventor, just in case . . . And now he was frowning as he peered at this incomprehensible crank, this "superior being." And the "being" reacted with a similar probing and distrustful look.

8

ONE day at midday in the middle of June, Lopatkin was walking unhurriedly along the wooden pavement of a wide street in the district capital, which was untended and bright with luxuriant green growth. It was Sixth Siberian Street, completely overgrown with bright young grass that contrasted vividly with the white goats that were grazing here and there. The young leaves were rustling and quivering on giant poplars, twisted out of shape by the wind. Lopatkin breathed their pungent scent, that reminded one of the happiest moments in life. He felt that during these years his body had lost its former strength; the scent of sap seemed to be urging him to make friends with the poplars, and to draw vigor and quiet indifference from them.

Lopatkin was enjoying his freedom. He possessed nothing except one case which he had left in the cloakroom of the collective farm. He could do as he pleased—he could take a steamer up the Obi to the Polar circle, or up the Irtysh to Lake Zaisan, and there, between heaven and green earth, find himself a job, lashing rafts together, or putting out the buoy lights at dawn, or counting the morning clouds. Or he could stay where he was. Here, in the garden of number 141, the elderly resident was crawling about in the raspberry bushes, carefully trimming away the dry shoots. The whole place was in apple-pie order, the trunks of the apple trees had been whitewashed, the young plants were planted out, little paper bags protected the tomatoes, at the back of the vegetable garden there was a small shed where light was reflected from the glass frames, and everything was carefully laid out in beds with paths between them.

107

These were all possibilities, this was freedom, but Lopatkin's feet carried him along all this while, clattering on the planks of the wooden pavement. He had his road planned out and it led to number 177.

Here it was. At the back of the yard stood a long two-story building of gray concrete with large square windows and a long flower bed extending from the entrance to the gates. An old watchman stopped Lopatkin at the gate. He interrupted his tea drinking, telephoned to someone, giving the name "Engineer Lopatkin," and finally wrote out a pass, valid only for a single occasion. Lopatkin entered the house through a cool entrance hall. When his eyes had adjusted themselves to the half-light, he saw that there were posters, a blackboard for announcements, and a large wall newspaper, with the title *Constructor*, pinned on the wall. One third of this wall newspaper was taken up by a column called "Who dreams what," cartoons and poems, and in one corner there was the drawing of a postbox.

Lopatkin turned into a passage on the left. Here rolls of paper had been dumped straight onto the floor, there was a strong smell of ammonia, worried young women in black overalls were rushing about, and from a large room, lighted by a bright violet light, the hum of electric appliances could be heard. Lopatkin realized that this was where blueprints were being made, and that a stranger had no business here. He quickly returned to the hall, and having stood about for a while, went off to explore the passage opposite. He opened one of the numerous doors and saw a large, well-lit room filled with tables. On every table was a drawing board with a yellowish stencil on it. At the tables sat young girl tracers. They all stopped working to stare at Lopatkin. There was a smell here like nail polish. In one corner a sewing machine chattered tediously— it was here that the tracings were trimmed, and the floor was littered with bright thumb tacks trodden into the wood.

Lopatkin, having quietly examined this room, asked where he could find the director of the branch. The head of the copying office, an elderly woman, came out and showed him the way along the passage.

"Up there," she said, pointing to a staircase. "On the second floor, to the left. That's all right, young man."

The upstairs passage was carpeted with a red-and-green runner, and Lopatkin walked along it feeling somewhat intimidated. A familiar, pleasurable, overwhelming feeling made his breath come short and drove him to hurry. This had all happened to him once before, when for the first time he had received a letter with the Ministry's seal on it. He carefully read the signs containing the names of the departments: department of electricity supply, of tooling and equipment, of accessories—and came to a sudden stop at a door. There was no sign on it, but it was covered with brown oilcloth, and Lopatkin knew at once that it was the director's door. He opened it quietly and handed the secretary the letter from the Deputy Minister. The secretary took the letter and began to read it with compressed lips, while Lopatkin, holding his breath, looked around the room with apparent calm. H'm, yes, there was another door covered with oilcloth, and on it the inscription "Chief Engineer." But where was the director? Aha, there was a second door, too, like the other, and on it the same sort of nameplate, except that its inscription was shorter and more impressive: "Director."

"Leave the letter with me. The director is out at present. Come back tomorrow morning."

Next morning, when Lopatkin presented himself at the office, the secretary stood up.

"The director has passed your papers on to Comrade Uriupin. To the section for special equipment. Come, I'll show you the way."

Lopatkin stood aside to let her pass. She walked in front of him along the passage, her hands pressed closely against her thighs. A door opened; beyond it was a brightly lighted workshop full of machines. But they were not simple machines, but drawing boards on special iron stands, with levers, counterweights, and handles. Cloaks and raincoats hung from the handles, and coatless young men, in linen blouses or silk tennis shirts, looked out from behind the drawing boards. Here and there older men could be seen, in shirts, with neckties and studs. Here, too, the floor was bright with thumb tacks trodden into the wood.

Behind a glass partition stood one more iron stand with a drawing board, and, farther off, a writing desk. At the desk Uriupin, the head of the section, a thinnish, swarthy man with a head of thick hair shot with premature gray, lifted one mobile eyebrow, then bent forward and froze in an attitude of expectancy. His coat hung behind him on the back of the chair. The sleeves of his silk shirt were rolled up. His dark, bony hands lay on a sheet of drawing paper.

"Comrade Lopatkin," the secretary announced, giving the chief an almost imperceptible intimate smile and left the room, still pressing her hands closely against her thighs.

"Sit down," Uriupin said in a steely voice, indicating a chair with his hand, which had a very large black watch strapped on the wrist.

Then he frowned, banged on the partition with his fist several times, listened, scowled, and shouted:

"Arakhovski!"

A very tall, elderly designer came at the call, looking straight ahead with a fixed gaze. He had black hair, carefully smoothed and parted. He was wearing a much-washed faded shirt with studs, and a necktie. He sat down on the chair next to Lopatkin's, still looking straight ahead at the chief. Lopatkin dug into his pocket, fished out a nut, and began to press it forcibly against his finger without being aware that he was doing so.

"Let me introduce you," said the section chief, setting his hands wide apart on the table. "This is Comrade Lopatkin, originator of a project."

"Oh, an originator. Delighted," Arakhovski hissed, turning in his chair toward Lopatkin and revealing the bare pink gums of an old man. From that instant Lopatkin felt Arakhovski's fixed gaze resting on him, though it turned away now and again.

"Well, we have looked into this—er—your proposition," the chief said, suddenly raising his voice. "We have looked into it, you understand. And we could not make it out at all! Excuse me, I am no

110

specialist, for me this is a closed book. Here, for instance." He pulled out a drawer in the desk and took out a folder of drawings—the beloved, familiar drawings made long ago by Lopatkin on Valentina Pavlovna's drawing paper. "Here, for instance, this gear —what is it for?"

"It's the gear of the casting mechanism," Lopatkin said, turning the nut over and over in his hand. "And this is the mixture regulator."

"H'm," Uriupin said.

"Excuse me," Arakhovski interposed, examining his cufflinks with a worried air. "We have not really become acquainted yet. I would be interested to know what the originator's special qualifications are. Tell me, are you a college-trained engineer? Or a foundryman?"

"I am a graduate in physics and mathematics," Lopatkin answered.

Uriupin was immensely pleased with this reply. He smiled all over his tight-skinned face, showing his teeth. "That is, that in respect of the project in hand your knowledge is more of a general kind?" There was a note of triumph in Uriupin's voice. "We have time enough, so I'll tell you a little story. After all, I was an inventor once myself. Oh yes, I was a serious rival of yours!"

He paused, as though harking back with pleasure to his youth as an inventor.

"Once I invented a mole trap. I am not being sarcastic. I found the mole's hole, cut out a piece of sod, and set up an ordinary mousetrap there, with a trip thread. The mole would trip over the thread and so work the trap. . . . Yes, well, I put the sod back over it all and went to look at it next day! Damn it all, no mole! I thought it over and made ten different traps, based on all sorts of different principles. And didn't catch a single mole! And the beast, it filled every trap with earth, every single one. Sealed them up from both sides! But listen, that wasn't the whole story. What did that mole do? A mole crawling along his passages always cleans them, and so pushes a little mound of earth along in front of him. It was that

111

earth that got into my trap. And so the mole stopped up all my traps. It was his mark of approval, so to speak. And what an expert he was! My elastic trap he spotted because of the smell of rubber, and he stopped that up, too, the rascal! Smelled it from afar. But d'you think I gave up? Oh no. I made a seine for him out of strong steel wire, with pointed ends, like this, you know, so that the mole should crawl in and not be able to crawl out again. And he was caught, but . . . But! Imagine this! A mole has very powerful forepaws: he simply broke my steel seine and escaped through one side. And of course stopped it up. As if he was saying: 'You silly ass, you work from paper to construction. Get experience first, study me, and then start inventing.' So I gave it up!"

Uriupin laughed, gasping for breath. Arakhovski bared his gums in a smile, and crossed his legs so that Lopatkin could see his brown cotton socks.

"Altogether it's incomprehensible. I don't get it. I don't want to say that the idea may not be ingenious." As he said this, Arakhovski bent his head, showing the parting in his hair, and twiddled one of his shirt studs.

"A living thought! If at least there were one living thought in it!"

"Here, what's that? Is my head your foot perhaps? Is it?" a young and very self-confident voice said loudly behind Lopatkin's back.

He turned around quickly and met the ironical and hostile gaze of a young man in his early twenties. He was wearing a blue tennis shirt, with a small sports badge on the chest. His tawny hair stood up in whorls. Behind him several young engineers were standing, staring at Lopatkin with curiosity. But the tousled one turned sideways toward Lopatkin and slapped the muscles of one arm with the other hand.

The section chief raised his head as though to say: "Shut up, you!"

"What is this, Anatoli Ivanovich? Don't I see by the back of his head that they've sent us another originator?" the tousled engineer with the sports badge retorted. "They don't put it in the plan, but they send them all the same." Now he was addressing Lopatkin.

"You wouldn't understand, of course. You are the *entrepreneur*. You organize the business—and someone else has to do the spade work. But this is not the Avdiyevian Congo."

The chief raised his head even more severely.

But the tousled youngster was not to be suppressed. "When you have Avdiyev's gray hairs, I mean his *learned* gray hairs, then perhaps you will have servants of your own."

"Ah, by the way," Uriupin remarked, as though he had not heard what the young engineer had said. "By the way, do you know Professor Avdiyev's machine? It's already in the testing stage. In my opinion it ought to work."

"Mine will work also," Lopatkin said.

"But will it even go into the workshop? Excuse me, I mean it seriously, didn't you fiddle a bit on the drawings? And why do we need two? Do you really think yours is a better one?"

"Most probably."

"Every inventor thinks his own machine is best. But I tell you plainly—I am no supporter of your particular . . ."

"I am very sorry," Lopatkin said calmly, tossing the nut on his palm. "I hoped to find supporters here. It seems that some comrades have not understood the crucial point. This is something new."

"Oh, we are not afraid of novelty," Uriupin interposed. "We leap at novelty."

"Yes, they say the better is the enemy of the good!" the young engineer added ironically. "The trouble is, we don't seem to see any 'better.' I have heard one or two things about Professor Avdiyev's machine."

"Allow me to finish." Lopatkin, looking down, put the nut in his pocket. "You have said many unpleasant things to me, and I have not yet answered, so in a way I owe you something. Especially you," he said, turning to the young engineer. "But I think you will pardon me if I do not pay this debt. You know, by profession I am a schoolmaster. I never imagined that the devil would drive me to give the Ministry advice about something that is outside my scope. I am sorry to have taken you from your proper job. It seems I am

113

always interfering with people's plans. But at present I am not even able to give it up."

Lopatkin was about to prove his point by the document signed by the Deputy Minister, but realized in time that Uriupin was one of those little bosses who did not like to be shown the limits of their power.

"I should like to get down to business," he said quietly. "If necessary, I can give you detailed explanations. I have models with me. The comrades will understand them. Perhaps they may even find a supporter or two." He smiled.

"Have you priority for this?" Uriupin asked abruptly, after a short silence.

"Yes, I have priority," Lopatkin answered mildly.

There was a long, significant silence.

"Then why waste time?" the chief said. "Comrade Arakhovski, you take this matter in hand, figure out what can be made of it."

He put his hands on the table as though about to stand up, and added in his steely, alert voice:

"I am giving you the best specialist in mechanics and mathematics. He is our pride, our Lagrange."

"Is it to be complete?"

"That will depend upon you and upon him."

Arakhovski, tall and stooping, silently took the folder of drawings from the table and conducted Lopatkin through the maze of drawing tables to a far corner of the room. There he had a small table and a drawing board on a stand. He sat down, put on his pince-nez, unrolled the first sheet, the general view of the machine, frowned, snorted, and sniffed voraciously, as it were, at the drawing. He sat for a long time over the drawing, sniffing to himself, then laughed, baring his pink gums, and threw down his slide rule onto the drawing.

"How long did it take you?"

"Six months."

"So I see. You put in all the details. And all the dimensions. Didn't you know that there was no need to do all that? This, and this, and all this mess here?" He prodded at several spots in the drawing with his finger. "In technical work there are certain accepted norms, standard components or whole assemblies out of which one can put together a machine. Put it together. Get that? And you went to all this trouble! You even put in the threads of the bolts! What you say, Kolia? Hi! D'you hear?" He raised his voice, addressing himself to someone at the other end of the room. "The schoolmaster has made quite a tidy job of his little machine!"

"Arakhovski's current passion!" the ironical voice of the tousled young engineer came back. "Some sort of humming top, I bet."

"No humming top, it's a real machine. And if I were you, comrade footballer, I'd come and take a look."

The young engineer threaded his way through the drawing boards, came up to Arakhovski's corner, leaned on his shoulder, and together they began to examine the drawing.

"You saw this?" Arakhovski tapped the drawing with his pencil. "Well? And you said there was no live idea in it!"

"I know damn little about casting machines," said Kolia, straightening up and still not looking at Lopatkin. "I see only that reducers have been stuck in both where they are wanted and where they are not. And that is a sure sign . . ."

He did not finish. Three dull thuds came from the distant partition and the chief's shrill voice called: "Comrade Arakhovski!" Arakhovski immediately stood up, and looking straight ahead of him, walked along, maneuvering himself between the drawing boards.

He came back after a few moments, put his coat on, and threw the pencil and slide rule into the drawer of his table.

"You will have to take a rest, Comrade—er—Lopatkin. I have to go to the factory. Meanwhile, get your economic affairs into order. We can meet again tomorrow afternoon."

They worked together in this way all next week; every day for about two hours. By the end of the week Arakhovski had become more and more taciturn, and Lopatkin noticed that he was again keeping his eyes averted.

115

Then the moment came, when, having checked all his calculations over once more, the old man took off his pince-nez and hissed, with averted eyes:

"Let's go and see Uriupin."

The head of the section was sitting at his table as usual, and seemed to have been waiting for them, his dark hands spread flat on the drawing. He was wearing a silk singlet, the color of stale meat, with scarcely perceptible gray stripes in it. His bony sunburned face was twisted into a condescending but impatient grimace.

Arakhovski silently took a seat opposite him. The other chair was taken by Lopatkin. He, too, said nothing. Uriupin lazily stretched out his hand and took the folder Arakhovski held out. He tapped his huge watch with a fingernail, raised it to his ear, then opened the folder and took out the drawing, the general view.

"Well, what is your opinion?" he asked.

"It seems to work out all right."

"With you everything seems to work out all right." The chief glanced at the drawing. "Well, all right . . . let's see . . . you could have Yegor Vassilyevich . . . Let him cook up a general view."

"Anatoli Ivanych! Have you forgotten? I've got that giraffe on my hands."

"What giraffe?"

"That mill. I am busy from morning to night."

"True. We are already exceeding our estimates. Then who is to take this on? You must excuse us, Comrade Lopatkin, we have our own business worries. Such as that mill. It was not planned, we worked it out according to the draft design. Like your machine. We submitted it. They sent it back. They themselves had given us the wrong technical specifications. And now we have to remake it. But where is the time for all this to come from?"

"Yes," Lopatkin agreed. "It's really . . ."

"And the men? Where are they to come from? There aren't any. And no money either."

"Yes," said Lopatkin. "Yes. I see."

116

The chief was thinking. His mobile eyebrow twitched as he looked Lopatkin straight in the eye and said:

"I shall have to take your machine."

There was a long silence. A cool wind, redolent with the scent of flowering poplars, blew in at the open window, fanning their faces pleasantly. Arakhovski, his back curved like a bent bow, frowned, and looked straight ahead of him with apparent indifference. Lopatkin tried to guess whether it was a good or a bad sign that the chief himself had undertaken to direct the work on the project. Uriupin himself, meanwhile, was looking at him with the hard gaze of an opponent about to strike a blow.

"So that is decided!" Uriupin said. "Comrade Arakhovski, send Yegor Vassilyevich to me, and that new fellow, Maxiutenko."

Without so much as a glance at Lopatkin, Arakhovski went off, looking as though he had quarreled with everyone present. Lopatkin followed him with his eyes, quite taken aback. Hardly had he gone, when Maxiutenko appeared, smiling all over his face. He was a fair-haired man, foppishly dressed in a pale mauve full-cut silk shirt tucked into blue breeches and with sleeves held up by rubber bands around the elbows. He had popped out from behind a drawing board, as though he had been sitting there all the time waiting for his cue.

"Comrade Maxiutenko," the chief said severely, "this is the originator, Comrade Lopatkin, and this is his project. You already know about it. Jot down an elevation of the machine for me. If you have any questions, bring them to me. I shall be in charge of the business. Ah, and here is Yegor Vassilyevich. We'll give Yegor Vassilyevich the gear."

Yegor Vassilyevich, a gray little man with a paunch, dressed in a dark-blue sateen tunic, gave the originator a cursory glance and reached for the drawings, but drew his hand back at once, for the chief had picked up the folder and handed it to Maxiutenko with a flourish.

"Maxiutenko will show you the whole thing. You are appointed to his group, Yegor Vassilyevich. It's a responsible job, but knowing you, I shall not talk about quality. However, we need speed as well. I don't think speed will do you any harm either."

Four drawing boards on stands—which were here called "drawing combines"—and a writing desk, were set up in a far corner of the room for the group assigned to Lopatkin's project. Two taciturn young draughtsmen glanced quickly at Lopatkin and then at each other, and sharpened their pencils. Yegor Vassilyevich, frowning and sniffing, threw himself back in his chair in front of his drawing board. They were quite ready to start work; they were piece workers —their earnings depended on the number of drawings they made.

Maxiutenko for his part adopted a lofty pose at his "combine"; he rested his foot on the high rail under the table, put his elbow on his knee, and stuck his empty pipe between his teeth. This was because the most important job had been entrusted to him. And also because in the same department was an engineer with thick plaits twisted into a bun on the nape of her neck and another engineer with luxuriant fair hair that reached her shoulders.

So the first day of basic work began. Much was done that day, and Lopatkin realized that his project was not by any means so clumsy technically as it had been said to be. A few days later he hinted as much to Maxiutenko:

"I notice that we are having no objections from the chief designer."

"Why should we?" Maxiutenko lifted his foot from the rail, took out his rubber tobacco pouch, filled his pipe, and stuck it between his teeth. "What is there to argue about? It's a good machine. He said so himself. And Arakhovski said so, too. So why argue?"

"And yet Comrade Uriupin told me when we first met . . ."

"He tried to discourage you, didn't he? He always does that. That's as it should be. The originator must be morally prepared for working with us, so that he will listen and not make difficulties." He tittered, shifted the pipe in his mouth, took out a box of matches, and left the room; he often went out to have a smoke.

Once or twice a day the chief came up to Maxiutenko's table and gave instructions, tapping the board with his fingers and shouting in a loud voice:

"Take that away! Take away that bolt! D'you hear? Take it away! What are you thinking of? Take it away at once; it spoils the whole caboodle!"

"Shout away!" Lopatkin thought. Now he was enjoying everything, even this imperious shouting, and Maxiutenko's melodramatic posturing, and the silent energy of the draughtsmen who produced masterly drawings of the details, sheet after sheet.

The outline of the machine was gradually taking shape on Maxiutenko's drawing board. And for some unknown reason Kolia, the tousled young engineer with the sports badge, came to look at it nearly every day. Sometimes Arakhovski came also, and looked at the drawings without saying a word, only, as it were, sniffing at them.

Then, suddenly, a conflict arose. Early in August, when the work on the general view was finished, Maxiutenko one day pinned on his board a sheet that showed the main shaft and bearings of the machine, and, having filled his pipe, went out to the porch to "meditate." At that very moment the section head approached Maxiutenko's drawing board. He had recently been giving the machine a lot of attention, had summoned Maxiutenko to his office behind the partition, and when he passed Lopatkin, would nudge him with his elbow and say: "Aha, our originator!" Standing at the drawing board, he often handled the pencil himself.

Now he approached the stand, sat down on the chair, wrinkled his forehead, and contemplated the drawing with compressed lips. He closed his eyes tightly, as though to drive away some apparition, then stared out of the window, drumming on his knees with his fingers. Presently Maxiutenko came back, smacking his rather too-red lips with satisfaction and bringing with him the acrid smell of pipe smoke. The chief said something and Maxiutenko shrugged his shoulders. Then both cast a rapid glance at the drawing. At that moment the tousled and forthright Kolia stopped beside them, his hands in his pockets. He looked at Lopatkin and gave an angry laugh.

"Look here, Maxiutenko!" Maxiutenko turned with a start at the sudden harsh sound. "Why must you invent the bicycle over again?"

"Bicycle? What bicycle?"

"This one! And you an experienced engineer! Why clutter up the design with these two reducers?"

"What's that?" Maxiutenko and the chief spoke almost in unison.

"If you put a reducer here, it must have a higher ratio. But what d'you want it for? We have a perfectly normal assembly, which Comrade Uriupin has already used on two machines. You have, haven't you, Comrade Uriupin? Then why all the fuss?" Kolia was now addressing Lopatkin. "Where will the machine be used? In a foundry. Compressed air is available in every foundry. So all that is needed is a common, ordinary air-pressure contrivance. Go to the records office and they'll give you a complete, ready-made design!"

"What you say is—hm—not quite in accordance with—er'm . . ." Uriupin had begun, and then stopped, searching for the right word. "Two or three such decisions, suggested to the originator—and 'quantity would change into quality.' A new idea would result, for which approval would have to be sought, there would be a lot of correspondence . . ."

"And in the end, if the machine didn't work, the originator would put the blame on us, for having departed from the original design!" Maxiutenko said, and looked at Uriupin.

"It's for the originator to say," said Kolia and walked toward his own seat. But he stopped again in the middle of the room and added, looking back: "The only thing is that air pressure isn't an idea, though it salvages the idea, it's true, while reducers and worm gear would ruin it." He walked on, disappeared between the drawing boards, and only his deep, grumbling voice could be heard: "and you know it well enough! So why wait? At the first test that shaft would break and no mistake about it. Tim, you saw, what they . . ."

Uriupin raised his head and listened, eying his department sternly. None of the men looked at him, all were silent, all were bending over their drawing boards and appearing to study their constructional tasks intently. Only from the boards behind which Kolia had disappeared his youthful bass could still be heard:

"I've been going over there and watching for four days now. . . . 'Let's go and have a look at what they are cooking up,' I said to myself. And what *are* they cooking up . . . ?"

"Comrade Lopatkin," Uriupin said when Kolia had finished speaking, bending his head on one side and knitting his brows, "if one thinks it over, this air-pressure business is tempting, isn't it? What do you feel about it?"

At these words Maxiutenko put his foot on the rail of his combine, set his elbow on his knee, and began to suck his empty pipe. A gentle summer breeze ruffled the blond down on his bald patch. Lopatkin walked over to him, and looked at the sheet of paper on which Maxiutenko had indicated the gears of the reducer by a very fine dotted line. Lopatkin's tired face revealed all his feelings clearly —they were simple, not hedged around with a cold caution, and not battered out of shape by duels. Lopatkin had faith in his experienced designers, and felt surprise that they should have passed over so obvious a thing as air pressure, especially as there now proved to be a standard design—in other words, that this assembly had already been worked out and was being used ready-made, in the same way, for instance, as a water tap. He had only just realized all this, and he stared at Uriupin in surprise. Uriupin had by this time smoothed out all the wrinkles in his falsely youthful face under the graying hair and was smiling, showing his steel teeth. He could read the thoughts of "this schoolmaster." But Lopatkin did not fail to notice the wolfish glint in the chief's cheerful eyes.

"I have thought a great deal about this, Comrade Lopatkin," Uriupin said, eying the drawing doubtfully from a distance, and almost appearing to yawn as he spoke. "It could be tried. True, cylinders will have to be put in in four places. Comrade Maxiutenko, let's knock up something, just to see how it works out . . ."

Having said this, he went up to the board, put one hand on his hip, and with the other drew a few pencil lines, so faint as to be almost imperceptible, straight on to the reducer in the drawing.

"That's about how it should be. Now you can carry on with it, Comrade Maxiutenko."

Then he prodded Lopatkin jovially in the ribs, stuck the pencil in the pocket of his blouse in a jocular fashion, and unhurriedly threaded his way between the drawing boards to his cubbyhole, stopping now and then at one or another of the drawing boards.

Maxiutenko pinned a fresh sheet of drawing paper on his board, filled his pipe, and went out to the porch to meditate. Lopatkin was thoughtful, too. He sat for a few minutes at Maxiutenko's combine, passing his fingers over his forehead. His suspicions had been aroused, but he saw no real danger. He wanted to smoke, and taking out his pouch, rolled himself a thick cigarette out of newspaper and his home-grown tobacco, licked the paper, went out into the passage, and lit up. He choked on the acrid smoke, but drew it in deeply again and again, then went downstairs and out on to the porch. His eyes fell on Maxiutenko's bald head. He was sitting on the steps, and drawing something with a pencil on the concrete parapet of the porch. His pipe was wheezing and he was so deeply immersed in something that he did not notice Lopatkin. Lopatkin stood still for a moment, then went closer and looked over Maxiutenko's shoulder. He saw on the rough gray concrete a pencil sketch of a circle and in it six smaller circles, placed symmetrically. The whole thing resembled the drum of a revolver.

"Ah, so this is our designer's real laboratory!" Lopatkin said with a laugh.

He himself was quite unaware that he had hit the nail on the head, and was very surprised when Maxiutenko, caught in the act, flushed a dark red, covered the drawing with his hand, and hastily began rubbing it out.

"Why spoil it? What makes you blush like a young lady?" Lopatkin squatted down beside Maxiutenko. "Surely you can allow the originator to see it!"

"Oh, it's just a bad habit I have!" Maxiutenko, still very red, took out his handkerchief and wiped his forehead. "I can't think properly when other people are by." He crossed out his drawing with his pencil, and stood up. "I just can't, you see? Devilish nuisance."

"And what was it you were drawing?"

"Oh, I was thinking of a piston . . . for the air-pressure device . . . it's in the plan . . ." He took out his rubber tobacco pouch, filled his pipe, began to smoke, and regained his composure.

"Comrade Maxiutenko," Lopatkin suddenly remembered, "why not use the setup Kolia mentioned?"

"Of course. I said so at once. But this wretched head of mine goes its own way." Maxiutenko threw a sidelong glance toward a dark spot in the concrete, spat on it, and rubbed it out with his foot. "I'll do that. I shall have to go to the records office and look up that design."

He shifted the pipe between his moist scarlet lips, plunged his finger into the ash, and took himself off, elbows akimbo. Lopatkin could hear him in the lobby, and felt reassured. He could see that the man was working at the project with his whole heart in it, not as a mere routine job.

Maxiutenko did, in fact, bring a blueprint of the air-pressure device from the records, and began to "dash off"—that is, to draw on sheets of paper—the moving parts of the machine, and "write into" them a cylinder and piston. Lopatkin was with him and by the time the day was nearly over they had between them dashed off two variants, and had given the calculators the basic figures for the computing of the loads on piston and cylinder.

The day had brought perceptible progress, and Lopatkin left the office in a cheerful frame of mind. The pleasant quiet of early evening lay over the street. A crescent moon floated in the blue sky like a feather on smooth water. A herd of cattle was raising a cloud of dust. Whips cracked and the cows came ambling along the roadway and spreading over the pavements, looking into the open gates. To get out of their way, Lopatkin had to get off the path and squeeze himself into a hedge. As he waited, the warm smell of milk floated to him with the dust, and he heard the lisping, good-humored voice of Arakhovski saying:

"So they won't give way to the inventor? What do you say to that?"

Lopatkin laughed. Arakhovski, dressed in a Russian linen blouse embroidered at neck and wrists, with his coat over one shoulder and a brief case in his hand, was approaching him.

"So you are laughing, you humane man!" he said with the same good humor, putting his hands on his hips, and surveying the herd with a philosopher's eye. "And yet this is no accident—it is a significant phenomenon. If My Lord Wolf were standing on this pavement instead of you, it would be quite another matter! And that is the trouble."

Then they were silent, each pursuing his own thoughts. When the herd had passed, they walked slowly along the street.

"Well, Comrade inventor," Arakhovski said. "Do you know that you have chosen a most crooked and dangerous path?"

"I have almost come to the end of it now. It's two years since I . . ."

"To the end of it? My dear fellow!"

"You don't know . . ." Lopatkin interposed.

"I know everything! Listen to what I say. Listen, you will be none the worse for it. Whether you believe me or not is your business. But you have not come to the end of even a tenth of the things fortune has in store for you. If you want me to, I can help you to take at least one step forward. But of course only if you would like me to."

"Of course I would!"

"So, you want me to? Then listen! You know nothing about designing. You know nothing about mechanical details. You don't know the language of technical drawings. Don't laugh, but listen to what I am telling you. Your knowledge is sufficient to formulate an

124

idea, but not enough to create a design. And for working with Uriupin, your knowledge is completely inadequate. Why, they have already played you a lousy trick, old man, and all you did was smile and say: 'Thank you!' Good job that Kolia was there and saved you. Because he is a young man, and talks first and thinks afterward. I, too, want to save you, but more solidly, more radically. To start with, I'll give you three books of about three hundred pages each, make you study up on them, and then examine you on them. When you have digested them, you may be able to spot some of the spokes they will be putting in your wheel. Then there will be fewer breakages on the way."

"Thanks in advance, Kirill Methodievich."

"No need for thanks. It's Sunday tomorrow, isn't it? Come and see me tomorrow, toward evening." Arakhovski stopped and gave Lopatkin his hand.

"Pardon me, but where do you live?"

"In this little house here that we are in front of."

Lopatkin looked and saw the familiar number, 141. It was now quite smothered in green creepers. The little shed was no longer visible. The vegetable garden overflowed with green, the yellow faces of the sunflowers all gazed in the same direction, toward the sun, which was setting beyond the house. The red currant bushes were sprinkled with green and brown berries, and pale little apples hung on dwarf apple trees. At the far end of the garden a hammock showed white between two birch trees.

"I saw you here," Lopatkin said, "on the first day, just after I got here."

"It's possible. I dig here every day. This is my garden of *Epicurus*, as one might say. See the hammock there? There is a small table as well." Arakhovski laughed and raised one finger: "Tomorrow at seven, please."

Next day, when the coming of evening had emptied the street, Lopatkin pulled at the wire ring on the tall slatted gate of Number 141. He pulled, and somewhere in the depths of the yard there was the dying note of something striking on a resonant copper bowl.

A long-legged reddish-chocolate-colored setter came running to the fence with a friendly bark, wagging its tail. A slow-moving elderly woman opened the gate and showed Lopatkin in. Arakhovski was in the vegetable garden, reclining spread-eagled in the hammock. The neck of his shirt was unbuttoned, he was a different man here from the one in the office; here he was a proud and hospitable host who had the look of a hero and did not avert his eyes. On a little table beside the hammock an open book lay spine upward. "Newton: *The Mathematical Principles of Natural Philosophy*," Lopatkin read, and conceived a profound respect for the owner of the book.

"Sit in the hammock, there's room enough," Arakhovski said. "Maria Nikolayevna!" he shouted, turning round.

"All right, all right!" came the answer from the house.

Lopatkin sat down in the hammock and was aware that the man sitting beside him was a muscular heavyweight.

"Kirill Methodievich, how old are you?" he asked.

"Just guess! How much would you say?"

"About forty-eight?"

"Wrong!" Arakhovski laughed aloud, revealing his gums. "Try something higher. What about sixty?"

"That's not possible!"

"Well, it is. Why? Don't I look it?" He laughed again. "It's because I don't spend my time inventing things," he trumpeted in Lopatkin's ear.

"No! no! What sort of inventor do I seem? Your pointed remarks don't affect me."

"Don't affect you, you say?" Arakhovski looked impatiently toward the house, but Maria Nikolayevna was already bringing a tray with a bottle and plates.

"Coming, coming," she said, setting the tray down on the little table.

"Let's have a drink, Dmitri—what's your name—Alexeyevich. By the way, that's a good Russian name!" Arakhovski poured out

126

drinks from the bottle. "You are in luck; it's genuine stuff, this, got a voucher yesterday. So here's to our friendship!"

Arakhovski emptied his glass and said nothing more. His eyelids reddened; he impaled a piece of cucumber on his fork, and began to chew it dexterously on one side of his toothless mouth.

"So you say you are no inventor? Then what the hell did I bring you here for? No, no! Every man is an inventor who is creating something new in his own sphere. Inventors can be anywhere, in science, or in technique. Don't belittle yourself, you're a perfectly genuine inventor."

He spoke the last words with special emphasis, looking Lopatkin straight in the eye.

"Take it from me: you have chosen a difficult path. Technics is king. This king is followed by a suite: the guardians, and passers-on, and popularizers of knowledge. Most of them are professors, who teach us, but who create nothing themselves. Around them one may find inventors also. Only they don't wear gala dress and most of what they get are kicks. And you, too, Dmitri Alexeyevich, must prepare for kicks if you join this outfit. I can see your future in your face. Your idea is very important, but your future is dismal. You'll realize this, when you have studied the material I am going to give you."

Arakhovski poured out some more vodka, and drank without clinking glasses. Having drunk, he laughed bitterly and shook his head.

"Yes, I, too, was an originator. I, too, have such a thing—blue, with a ribbon and seal. A certificate of invention."

"May I ask what you invented, if it isn't a secret?"

"I invented something, Dmitri Alexeyevich; I could scarcely believe it myself. It was a machine for piercing rock, in mining. In rock, you understand. I even had a working model of it that I put up against a brick wall, and it went through it in front of the respected public like a knife through butter."

"And then?"

"There are certain walls, Comrade inventor, which no machine

127

on earth can pierce!" Arakhovski poured himself out another drink, drank it, and began to turn a piece of cucumber round in his mouth. "They talked with me, Dmitri Alexeyevich, they said: 'Go to the cash desk, take what they give you—and shut up!' I didn't shut up, and so they very politely broke my back. You, too, will hear such talk one day. Smooth, educated, polite candid talk."

"I know."

"You can't know everything."

"I can guess. And I am still taking it on."

"What are you thinking of doing? How do you expect to overcome the kind of capitalism that exists in Uriupin's heart?"

"We'll manage somehow. Does such a thing as 'the people' exist, or doesn't it?"

"What is 'the people'? 'The people' is you, and me, and all of us. You and I have spotted one enemy, because we have come into close contact with him. But the other enemies, on other sectors, we don't spot. There for the likes of us all professors are archangels and prophets."

"But why should we concern ourselves with other sectors? Let's stick to our own. If I exist, it means that other people like me exist, too. There's Kolia, for instance. And yourself."

"And who told you that I am like you? Perhaps I am a wolf? Perhaps I may get up and eat you right away."

"I'm not afraid of that kind of wolf!" Lopatkin smiled. But Arakhovski raised a warning finger.

"Fine words, but all moonshine! In life everything is grimmer and bleaker. Go to our Ministry, or to the Central Scientific Institute of Foundry Research, to our Avdiyev, and there on the shelves you will find confirmation of what I am saying. Dozens and hundreds of little coffins, and all of inventors, like you. Ninety-five per cent of them are rubbish, just duds, and a coffin is where they belong. But five per cent is pure radium, and yet it will lie there until the archangel blows the last trump. The followers of His Majesty Science are masters of the burial business."

"Yes, but what are you, then?" Lopatkin asked.

"I? Just an old badger. A defeated one. At one time I, like you, rushed out of my den and into the thick of it. But now I am a crippled badger. What saves me is simply my protective coloring. On the principle of 'open your eyes and shut your mouth,' I shut my mouth and sit in a corner—hee! hee!—as far as possible from the rough and tumble." He fell silent, and sat for a while sighing and shaking his head. "No," he said suddenly. "Of course I am not like that at all, because I have never lost faith. I saw you—and my hopes flared up again. Kolia isn't like that either. True, he is still un-fledged, but already Uriupin is afraid of him. We had a chief here before, who was one of the best. They removed him and sent us this gray wolf."

"Uriupin?"

"Yes. You don't know him yet. He's a big bad wolf! Lupus! He was appointed and my hopes died down. Then I saw you—and I began hoping again. Remember what Briussov wrote: 'We shall carry our lighted torches into the catacombs, the deserts, the caves.' But he's wrong. Once the torches are lit, we can no longer carry them away. So tell me: what shall we do with them, these lighted torches? I am already extinguishing thought—I have found a means: I invent new gadgets for fishing tackle. I'm a fisherman, after all. Or I think out some trifle for my gardening with the same fervor. First-rate! I get quite enthusiastic—and so the time passes. You see how hopeless it is: a thinker cannot give up thinking!"

"Hear what I have to say, Kirill Methodievich," Lopatkin said, laying his fist on the table. "I hold out my hand to you! D'you understand? Live in hope still!"

"What an idealist you are!" Arakhovski smiled a tired, sorrowful smile, and his eyes looked somewhere away into the dark distance. "As I look at you, I . . . Oh, what an idealist!" He shook his head.

"Kirill Methodievich, I swear to you that it will be as I say!"

"Swear, swear! Thank you for even that much. And meanwhile, if you really are that sort, I'll help you all I can. I want to impress certain theses upon you. Find time somehow to come here."

"Kirill Methodievich, let's drink to those lighted torches!"

"How am I to understand that?"

"In this way: that they cannot be carried away to deserts or to caves; that they cannot be put out! That they are inextinguishable! That they will go on burning, to people's delight!"

"And to the agony of some! Well, have it your own way. Let's drink!"

Arakhovski drank, gulped, broke off a piece of bread, smelled it, and looked impishly at Lopatkin.

"Such an idealistic toast should be accompanied by the smelling not of a piece of bread, but of a bread-ration card—hee! hee!—for white-collar workers!"

9

A RAKHOVSKI gave Lopatkin three books: *The Use of Air Pressure and Hydraulic Pressure in the Construction of Machinery, Calculation in Mechanical Engineering,* and *Machine Components.* Lopatkin recalled the habits of his student days, and sat down to the books as though preparing for an examination. A fortnight later, when Maxiutenko had finished with the air-pressure mechanism, had passed it on to the detail draughtsmen, and was himself engaged on a fair drawing of the elevation, Lopatkin went up to him and said:

"Comrade Maxiutenko, I have looked over your solution and cannot accept it as satisfactory."

"What solution?" Maxiutenko turned round with a start.

"Of this air-pressure assembly here. You have put in four cylinders—that is too complicated; one can manage with two. I made a sketch of it at home today."

"And where have you been up till now? You were here, weren't you?"

"I have been reading some books. I read one—and suddenly saw it all. Before that I didn't know some of the simplest things. But you, as a designer, must agree that . . ."

"I don't know." Maxiutenko stared out of the window with blank eyes, and slowly reddened. Suddenly he jumped to his feet, and meandered between the drawing tables, to Uriupin's den.

Soon the chief's steely voice was to be heard behind the partition: "What is it? *What* air pressure? *What* cylinders? Why *two*? *What* books?"

Presently they both came out, Uriupin first. Threading his way between the tables, he knocked against one or two of them, but never looked round. He strode up to Lopatkin as though to demand satisfaction for some insult.

"What's all this between you?" he asked, addressing himself to Maxiutenko with a sweep of his hand.

"It's all my fault," Lopatkin said. "I made the mess."

He appeared not to notice Uriupin's irritation, pushed a chair toward him, sat down himself, and unrolled his drawing.

"It seems to me that Comrade Maxiutenko has complicated the construction—he has put in two cylinders too many. The point is that these two cylinders would work only to half capacity if we balance the two arms. . . ."

"But, Comrade originator!" Uriupin protested, with controlled irritation. "Comrade Lopatkin! If we go on like this, there never will be an end to the changes! And who is to pay for it, I'd like to know?"

There was a silence.

"Leave it as it is!" Uriupin commanded abruptly, and stood up in order to make a quick and effective exit.

"I will not sign the project," Lopatkin said quietly to his back.

"But, man, can't you understand!" Uriupin snapped, turning round. He bent over and slapped his flat, dry palm down on the drawing pinned to Yegor Vassilyevich's drawing board, so that all the old man's beautifully sharpened pencils were scattered, and bounced to the floor. "Understand!" the chief shouted, slapping his hand down once again. "This is money, this is time, this is a plan!"

"That concerns only yourself and Comrade Maxiutenko," Lopatkin said, looking at him coldly. "The point is beyond dispute. If it is clear even to me, then to you it ought to be even clearer. I have no objection to calling in an arbitrator, and if he can prove to me that my solution is a work of genius far beyond the capacity and knowledge of any average designer, I will withdraw it."

This was the voice of a different, a new kind of man, and Uriupin said no more. Maxiutenko, too, was silent; but the detail draughtsmen raised their heads, and looked first at Lopatkin and then at each other.

"A dispute?" said the tousled Kolia, making his way to them and looking toward Arakhovski's corner with a quizzical smile. "What's it all about?"

"Is this a correct solution?" Dmitri handed Kolia the sheet with his own sketch.

Kolia glanced at the drawing, laid it on the table, and studied it intently.

"The solution is correct, and, it seems to me, the best possible one," he said, looking with narrowed eyes first at Lopatkin then at Uriupin.

"And this one?" Lopatkin asked, unfolding Maxiutenko's draft.

"This? Did *you* do this?" Kolia asked, looking at Maxiutenko.

"What is this?" Lopatkin asked again.

"This? Botchery!"

"Nikolai, really! Your expressions! . . ." said Uriupin, screwing up his face sourly. "We are not on the football field now."

"Then I'll put it differently: No score. You must play it over, Comrades. Play it over!" With that, Kolia went off to his table laughing, and there he sang once more, in a melodious tenor voice: "Repla-a-ay!"

And the design had to be "replayed." In September Lopatkin discovered two more clumsy contrivances, and one very crude mathematical miscalculation, as a result of which the whole project had to be remodeled over again.

But in spite of everything a day came when the project—one hundred and sixty sheets, one thousand four hundred details, twelve thousand dimensions—was submitted to the originator for his signature, and Lopatkin, having warily scrutinized every sheet, signed his name on each. After this the sheets were sent to the tracing department on the first floor. A few days later transparent tracings perforated on a sewing machine were sent from there to Lopatkin, for his signature. He signed, and the tracings went downstairs again

133

to the blueprint department, where there was a tremulous violet light and a smell of ammonia.

There had been more than one snowfall, the streets were damp and cold, the mud was already sticking to and hardening on the wooden pavement, and it was the last gray day of October, when Lopatkin was finally handed his project—a clearly printed "author's copy" bound in a folder. Uriupin shook his hand so vigorously that he himself teetered up and down with the force of it. Maxiutenko, too, gave him his heavy, flabby paw. Then both technicians and Yegor Vassilyevich came up to him, shook his hand hurriedly, withdrew, and talking quietly among themselves, prepared to go home, for the working day was over.

"Our next meeting will be in Moscow," Uriupin said brightly. "I have fixed up an official mission for you."

Lopatkin thanked him, made a bow that was intended for all of them, and went out. He had rushed along the entire length of Sixth Siberian Street, hardly noticing where he was going, before he realized that he had left his copy of the project behind. "Tcha!" he made a gesture of annoyance, and turned back. It was already dark. He walked fast—the office would soon be closed.

But there was a light burning still in the office, and the door was open. Lopatkin went into the room that contained only drawing combines, walked around the partition, and at once saw Maxiutenko's bald patch and Uriupin's coarse brush—the gray fur of a wolf. Heads close together, they were examining a small drawing. Maxiutenko was the first to hear the sound of Lopatkin's approach. He looked up, caught sight of Lopatkin, and stood petrified, growing red. Then Uriupin looked up, and furrowing his forehead into a multitude of wrinkles, gazed at Lopatkin, his eyes narrowing evilly.

"I left the project behind," Lopatkin said, picking up the folder which lay on a chair, and turning to go. He averted his eyes deliberately from the designers and their drawing—he did not wish to probe their secrets.

As he left the cubbyhole he heard his own name called, and stopped.

"Shall we tell him, Comrade Maxiutenko?" Uriupin asked. Maxiutenko grew even redder. "Yes, we'll tell him," Uriupin decided, and smiled at Lopatkin. "Comrade Lopatkin, come a bit closer."

Lopatkin returned, and took in everything at a glance. On the section chief's table lay the sketch of a machine for the centrifugal casting of tubes. And in the sketch he saw the familiar circle with six smaller circles inside it, like the cartridge nests in the drum of a revolver. The drum stared at him with its six eyes, but Lopatkin was not disconcerted, he stared back without flinching. But he felt, with annoyance, that his ears were beginning to burn.

"Comrade Lopatkin," Uriupin began, in the indifferent tone of a tourist's guide. "We have here . . . well—that is Comrade Maxiutenko's and my attempt to do you out of your job!" He tittered, threw Lopatkin a rapid glance, and reddened very slightly. "No, you mustn't think we did it to damage your . . . our . . . er . . . our joint. No, it occurred to us quite recently, with Comrade Maxiutenko, having nothing better to do. We suddenly found that there was something in the idea." He laughed again.

"Why talk about it?" Lopatkin stepped up to the table. "Let me see the sketch instead. Aha!"

For a long time he turned the sketch this way and that. Uriupin said nothing, only watched him with eager curiosity. Maxiutenko, his head lowered, was drawing a circle and in it six smaller circles on the table. Lopatkin drummed thoughtfully on the sketch with his fingers, and finally raised his tired but smiling eyes to Uriupin's face. He was not able even to glance at Maxiutenko.

"I think, Comrade Uriupin, that you have taken a wrong turn here. You will get no priority for this machine part because it is Picard's machine. This machine gives an uneven cooling of the tubes, results in a whitening, and hence in brittleness of the casting. Picard built a special annealing furnace and treated the cast-iron tubes in it to cure the whitening. You would have done better to consult me first, as this is something I am a past master in. So, then, this is simply Picard! And the drum is no novelty, either—it is merely a slightly altered version of the feeder of my own machine. The notion is the same, but the constructive solution is inferior. In my machine one can regulate the temperature of the molds by varying their numbers. Your drum ties you down—you must of necessity have exactly six molds, neither more nor less."

At these words Maxiutenko's bald patch grew pinker and pinker, and Uriupin wrinkled his nose in a discouraged fashion. Never before had Lopatkin seen him like this.

"I suppose I might have put it more tactfully," he said. "But I spoke simply as a live reference book. We had better leave feelings out of it."

"Quite true!" Uriupin laughed, but his eyes stabbed through Lopatkin. "Well, all right. Thanks for your frankness. Until we meet again!"

On his way back Lopatkin looked in on Arakhovski to say good-by. Arakhovski showed him into a large room feebly lighted by a lamp with a large shade of faded orange-colored silk. They sat down at the table facing each other. Lopatkin felt Arakhovski's sharp, amused glance resting on him. The old man was sitting in semi-darkness, and his lips moved as he prepared to tease his guest.

"Uriupin and Maxiutenko have made a tube-casting machine," Lopatkin said.

"You don't say so!" Arakhovski bent forward eagerly. "Come on! Tell me more!"

"There is nothing more to tell. The working parts are stolen from Picard, the feeder from me, though somewhat simplified, it's true. They have just been discussing it with me."

"Discussing it? Just like Uriupin, though. He is a bold chap. And what did I tell you? Your idea, Dmitri Alexeyevich, will breed imitators to the very end. Oh, yes, before I forget, take the January to March issue of *Metal* and look through it. If I am not mistaken, some Volovich or Korovich—can't remember exactly—has written about your machine. I am not sure, but have a look. I seem to remember that there *was* such an article."

There was a silence. Arakhovski moved back into the shadow,

136

not taking his eyes off Lopatkin. Lopatkin sat in silence, thinking: "What threat may result for me out of all this?"

"You will become a designer," Arakhovski said slowly at last, with obvious satisfaction. "You're not the first. In the design departments you will find plenty of former inventors like myself—men who extinguish their ideas, who abort the fruits of their minds. Who, in any event, don't believe in the possibility of invention. But you—you won't go back to schoolmastering; you'll become a designer of machines. Am I a real oracle or not?"

"We shall see."

"Now listen to my farewell advice. When you get to the State Institute for Projecting Foundry Equipment and the discussion of your project begins, don't squeal when you meet with injustice. Don't protest aloud in indignation. Above all, don't forget that your project is satisfactory. I have looked over every sheet. But—don't let's have any of these sarcastic smiles with arms crossed on your chest," he boomed in a bass voice, shaking an admonitory finger. "Take action only when you are certain, only on a dead certainty—and do it quite silently. Bore into the business like a drill. If you begin to shout and throw your weight about, you will only be like the traditional inventor, and you will make it easier for them to fight you."

He paused, his lips again curving in a quizzical smile.

"Take into account," he said after a short silence, "take into account that the Central Scientific Institute of Foundry Research is full of expert gravediggers. That is worth making a note of. Here's a pencil and some paper. The lecturer who wrote about your machine is one of them. And this machine, it appears, is to be produced by them. Put that down—about the metal quarterly, and when you get to Moscow, look it up in the library. Put this down as well: in the C.S.I.F.R. Avdiyev is prince. And in general it is his principle to squeeze everybody. He is a big shot also in the organization for the production of casting machines. Can you see what it all amounts to? He knows all about you and you will be greeted. But keep a mile away from these institutions—even good lads there

137

will be doing you down, because they believe in their idol; he has stuffed their heads with belief in his superiority. Try to make contact with the factory chaps. Understand?" Arakhovski shouted suddenly, stretching forward over the table. "Young man, you are going into battle against the monopoly of Vassili Zakharych Avdiyev, so make sure your powder is dry! And this comrade . . ." Arakhovski got up and disappeared into the semi-darkness ". . . will be your companion." He came back and put a book on the table. "It's Lagrange. A first-rate mathematician and mechanical engineer. I strongly advise you to make friends with this great man; he will be a substitute for old Kirill Methodievich! Write to me as often as you can. Somehow I believe in you."

Two days later Lopatkin traveled to Muzga in a cold, half-empty train. His coach creaked, jolted, often came to a stop, and started again. After twenty-four hours of this Lopatkin stood on the rain-washed platform of the Muzga railway station. Having waited at the station for several hours, he climbed into the back of the *kombinat* lorry, and settled himself on a reel of thick wire. By the time it was growing dark he was wiping his feet at the door of the Sianov cottage.

With a smile, his lower lip caught between his teeth, he opened the damp-swollen door that was always sticking, and plunged into the pleasant warmth of the cottage and the smell of cabbage and of drying woollen socks. The children squealed with delight all together, and jumping from their beds and from the stove, threw themselves on "Uncle Dmitri." Nor were they mistaken: each got a home-made, brightly colored lollipop.

The last to welcome Lopatkin was Uncle Pete, though they had already greeted each other with looks of pleasure—and this had expressed the most important thing.

"Well, how are you getting on?" Pete asked.

Lopatkin silently held up the folder containing the project.

"So now you're for Moscow?"

"Yes. Moscow it is."

After dinner Lopatkin leisurely told them the story of how his

138

project had been worked out and redesigned many times. Putting a saucepan with roast potatoes on the table, Mrs. Sianov suddenly remembered something. Taking a letter folded in the shape of a triangle from the window sill, she gave it to Lopatkin. He unfolded the triangle, put it on the table beside the saucepan, and after finishing his story as he sipped a tea brewed from carrots, he began to read it.

Dear Dmitri Alexeyevich, he read in piecemeal fashion, at the same time answering Sianov's questions, *I am writing to you, perhaps for the last time, because we are leaving Muzga. But I cannot do otherwise than write. From now on I shall always feel guilty. . . .*

"There's no help for her, she will always be filled with remorse!" Lopatkin thought, interrupting his reading to take a gulp from his glass and to explain to Sianov that Uriupin was not only the chief designer of his group, but also the head of the section.

He read on:

I don't know whether what I am telling you will help you. I feel obliged to do all I can for you, although it is very little. But still. . . . You are no doubt aware that Avdiyev's machine is being made in our factory; anyhow, I am going to describe it to you. It can be taken apart, and the parts, which are tubes, are called molds. These tubes the workers fill by hand with forming sand, then the mold is put back into the machine and metal is poured into it. The workers are grumbling about it; they say they are losing their bonuses because of it. Because, as Galitsky, one of our specialists, has said, this machine is wasteful, both of machine time and of manual labor also. My husband considers Galitsky to be Avdiyev's right-hand man; he has come to the factory from C.S.I.F.R., and so we were all astonished when he said that this was not a machine at all, but merely an accessory for manual casting. Now here is the most important thing of all: in order to save Avdiyev's face, my husband has decided to keep the matter dark, and has canceled the official tests. Yet four of these machines are still under construction, and Ganichev is going to cast pipes with them. So it is he who will have

139

to carry the burden of writing off the losses in wages and metal, which are expected to amount to at least a million roubles. In the end there will be a tremendous catastrophe. I now know for certain that Avdiyev's machine was built out of the funds which had been assigned for yours. This was the work of Shutikov, the Deputy Minister, though he is hardly likely to tell you! Yet it is all exactly as I say.

"Well, I'll be darned!" Lopatkin said to himself, impaling a slice of potato on his fork. He did not go on reading the letter, but gave Sianov the folder containing the project, and began telling him about the sketch Maxiutenko had made on the concrete parapet of the porch.

Squinting at the letter with one eye, he read the remaining lines,

Dear Dmitri Alexeyevich, now that you have won through, I have changed my mind about a great many things and I understand a lot. I have a deep respect for you; I have never known anyone so steadfast and so admirably patient as You . . .

"Whew! She is even beginning to write about me in a capital letter!" Lopatkin smiled to himself.

. . . and I beg you not to bear me a grudge. I have been punished for my frivolity as it is. What I am already going through is quite enough. By the way, I have met Galitsky; he takes a great interest in you, and has been to see the Sianovs. I wish you all possible happiness. N. Drozdov.

"Well, that is what happened on the last day. . . ." Dmitri went on with his story as he folded up the letter. "I left the project in that fellow Uriupin's cubbyhole. When I went back for it . . ."

And he gave an account of his last meeting with Uriupin.

Next morning, as usual, Lopatkin rolled up the sleeves of his military undershirt and chopped wood by the little shed. While he was standing the logs up on end, first one way and then the other, and hitting them each a smart blow with the hatchet, he was think-

140

ing of what might be awaiting him in Moscow. He chopped the wood up into very small pieces of a convenient size for lighting the coals. An hour or two went by without his being aware of it. Then, all of a sudden, he felt that someone was staring at him from behind. He turned around; Valentina Pavlovna, in her gray-blue coat with the blue-fox collar, was standing in the street near one of the posts that supported the barbed wire.

Lopatkin threw the hatchet down on to a pile of wood and went out to her.

"Is it true?" she asked him, raising her eyes to his face with assumed unconcern.

"Is what true?" he asked with equal casualness, although he knew well enough what Valentina Pavlovna's question meant and what she wanted to say to him.

"You are leaving Muzga tomorrow. Is it true?"

"Yes."

She began to redden, and turned away, then looked at Lopatkin once more and pivoted childishly on her heel.

"For Moscow?" she finally said. "How splendid!"

"Not too bad! We are taking the offensive!"

"When are you leaving?"

"In the morning."

"Aren't you cold, in your shirt sleeves like that? Do you realize that we shall not see each other any more?"

Lopatkin said nothing. After a pause he appeared to remember something and announced joyfully:

"The project is completely ready! Did I tell you? Five fair copies, and everything just as it should be. And now I am going to put up a fight for it!"

"How one-sided all you men are," Valentina Pavlovna said. "You are all somehow so, so . . . unmusical!"

Again there was a silence. A snowflake floated slowly down between them through the frosty air. Valentina Pavlovna followed its course with unseeing eyes.

141

"Well, then," she sighed, "I suppose we had better say good-by. Will you write to me?"

"Valentina Pavlovna . . ."

"I insist! You *must* write to me! And now . . . bend down. I want to kiss you."

Bending down, he tried to answer her with a jocular chivalry, but she said:

"Please don't say anything. All words are lies. Don't speak!"

She kissed him several times, then turned her back upon him, and it seemed somehow as though she had shrunk. And so, walking fast, and without looking back at him again, she crossed the road.

PART
2

I

IN Moscow, in one of the many lanes off the Arbat, there is a four-story dark gray concrete building. All its square windows are exactly alike, and below, in the center of the ground floor, an entrance has been made in place of one of the windows. On black plates of thick glass screwed to both sides of this doorway the word "C.S.I.F.R." in large silver letters is visible from some distance off. As you get nearer, you can also read what is written in the smaller type, and learn that this massive dark-gray building houses the institute dealing with projects for foundry equipment.

The month was January, but the pavement was as clear of snow as in summer; water dripped now and then from a roof, and sparrows were twittering. Here, in the middle of Moscow, at noon, among the conglomeration of penetrating motorcar smells, were wafted slight, almost imperceptible currents of fragrant air like a foretaste of the still distant spring.

Lopatkin, with the folder containing his project held behind him, was walking slowly along the lane and gazing at the old and the new Moscow houses. He had already, of course, caught the delicate, distant scent of nature's premature awakening, and although it gladdened him it also put him on his guard, for was it not deceptive? Yet his soul welcomed every fresh gust of the lively breeze. Overhead, clouds, swelling like wind-blown sails, were moving rapidly across the blue sky. A large drop of water fell on his coat collar, splashing him, and he smiled. "Saviour Adoration Alley," he read out aloud to himself. "An old place, this. There must be a church somewhere near here, too." As he was thinking this, he caught sight of it: a tiny ancient church in old Moscow style. Small crooked trees with dry brown leaves still hanging pushed between the cracks in the peeling brick of its walls. The little cupolas had been stripped of their iron roofing, and pigeons were flitting to and fro among the rust-stained network of rafters.

It was one of those rare days when everything surrounding Lopatkin seemed to promise success. He had been living in Moscow for the past six weeks, and he had gone first thing every day for a walk to a telephone booth. He had dropped fifteen kopecks in the slot and for this modest sum had been able to talk to the secretary of the director of the Institute of Projects, who had said: "Ring up again in two days." Lopatkin had telephoned again in two days and had received this answer: "Your application is to be discussed on the twenty-third." He had telephoned on the twenty-third, only to be told: "The discussion has been postponed. Ring again later." But today when he had telephoned, the secretary had said: "The discussion has been fixed for one o'clock."

The first time he had a chance Lopatkin had visited the Lenin Library and had gone through a set of the periodical *Metal*. In the March issue he had found an article by Volovik, a graduate of technical science, all about a new machine for the centrifugal casting of pipes designed by the C.S.I.F.R. Volovik and his friends had somehow managed to see Lopatkin's drawings, no doubt while they were being reviewed. Combining Lopatkin's coreless mixer with a device from the Picard machine, they "had reached a satisfactory solution for a task which today faces a number of our departments." Dmitri smiled as he copied these "fruits of two years of research" into his notebook. Even here he had been lucky; Volovik had not understood or had been afraid to steal the main feature of Lopatkin's machine—interchangeable molds.

The expense account for his trip to Moscow had been used, but he did not mind, for he had received an unexpected stroke of luck. Soon after his arrival in Moscow from Muzga, food rationing had been abolished and a new currency introduced. All his savings, including those made on his expense account, were in a savings account, and now Dmitri received two thousand of the new currency.

146

With this he could continue to live in Moscow for another three months, even with the hotel bill and the daily fifteen kopecks for the telephone.

Recalling all this, Lopatkin held his head even higher and gazed at the lane brightened by the spring sun that was shining in January. All the houses seemed to answer back with a gay, understanding smile. Lopatkin chose a passer-by who looked as respectable as possible, and asked him the time. There were still forty-two minutes before the discussion of his project began. "After the discussion is over I'll buy myself a watch," Lopatkin decided. He crossed the road, pushed open the oak door, walked up a few steps to the lobby, left his overcoat and cap in the coatroom, straightened his coat, and ran lightly up the stairs to the second floor.

Here he was met by the sight of a gigantic wall newspaper whose title *The Designer* made him smile, as did the drawing of a letter box in one corner of the sheet.

The corridor on the second floor, covered by a soft carpet, indicated to Lopatkin the proximity of higher authority. And indeed he at once caught sight of a thick glass nameplate with the word "Director" written on it.

A little farther on was a small conference room with a brown notice board on the wall. Several people were sitting there, looking bored. In the passage, deep-voiced, energetic-looking men in gray gabardine uniforms with silver shoulder straps were promenading in groups. These were the engineers. A small body of men was gathered on the landing of the stairs near the entrance to the smoking room. A few immaculate black coats stood out conspicuously here and there among the uniforms. These were worn by the scientists who had no doubt been invited to take part in the discussion.

Lopatkin went to the smoking room. The uniforms and the black coats turned in his direction and made way for him. But apparently the impression he created was not very deep, for they all returned to their own animated and absorbing conversations. Dmitri entered the smoking room and would have pulled out his

147

hospital tobacco pouch, but remembered himself in time, and took out instead a pack of White Sea cigarettes, bought especially for the occasion.

"Ah, you are here already, Comrade Lopatkin!" It was Uriupin's voice coming from a far corner of the smoking room. The engineers at the door turned to stare at Lopatkin. "A greeting to the respected originator!" Uriupin went on in his resonant, steely voice, emerging from the blue-gray, smoky depths, looking sturdy and well dressed in a new uniform, but almost choked by a high-standing collar. "Glad to see you, my dear fellow! It will soon begin."

At this moment a gray-haired, frowning, and somewhat wrinkled engineer with the green stripes of a general down the sides of his trousers appeared at the door. Several of the men in uniforms and black coats hurried up to shake hands with him. Uriupin, as he stretched his hand out to the general, inclined his whole body as though he were about to fall forward. The general said a few words to him; Uriupin smiled, made a gesture with his hands, and accompanied the general to a low door which opened out of the smoking room and gave access to more private premises. At the door Uriupin turned, and his face assumed its usual hard expression. He stopped beside Lopatkin, lit a cigarette, took Lopatkin's arm, and moved a bit farther along—he wanted to be in a position to overlook the stairs.

A moment later the general, one hand in his pocket, walked across the smoking room to the exit with soft but resolute step. Uriupin looked after him with narrowed eyes, put his hand on his hip and said:

"A remarkable man! A patriot of the institute!"

"Do you mean the director?" Lopatkin asked.

"Ye-es. He has succeeded in establishing the authority of the institute at the Ministry. Naturally he did not exactly put himself in the background, but he has a very good nose for smelling what is required! There are no flies on *him!*"

Lopatkin said nothing and they smoked in silence. Uriupin was about to say something more, but instead he suddenly grasped Lopatkin's arm.

"Look! Quick! Over there! That's our great man. Academician Saratovtsev. In three years he will be eighty. Splendid, isn't he?"

A procession was moving slowly past the smoking room in a wide arc. On each side walked smiling, well-built engineers and handsome black-coated scientists, and in the middle a stout old general, rosy-cheeked and clean-shaven, except for a pair of fine upturned mustaches.

"A mastodon!" Uriupin commented, and for the first time Lopatkin saw a glow of enthusiasm in his eyes. "Do you know that he fought a duel with Wrangel himself, and left his mark on him, too! Everything he does, he does thoroughly. People say that if he had aimed a trifle lower, Wrangel would have been done for. And what a handsome old chap! What bearing! A mammoth! A chief justice!"

"So he's a justice!" objected a little unshaven man wearing the uniform of an engineer, who had approached them unobserved, with a deprecatory gesture. "You are off the beam there, Comrade Uriupin! The mathematical bump is well developed in him, I agree. But as for being a justice—he is a positive king of England, that's what he is! And leader of the Conservative party, too! His Excellency, Vassili Zakharych Avdiyev."

"Still shaking your fist at the sky?" another engineer, a lean, graying man with a massive gold ring on his finger, said derisively.

"What if I am! You, Krekhov, as the faithful old servant you are, would naturally rush to his defense! And yet, when one thinks of Avdiyev's latest machine . . ."

"Whatever certain discontented people may say, Avdiyev is a self-made man. Brainy. One must realize"—the engineer with the ring was addressing Lopatkin—"like Lomonosov, the man came into science with nothing! He threw his whole weight into it and pushed aside everything that stood in his way. Have you read his first thesis, written for his degree?" Krekhov's eyes glowed with admiration. "You must read it! You can get it from the library. I strongly recommend it."

"Is it as good as all that?" asked the unshaven man.

"Good isn't the word for it!" A third engineer broke excitedly into the conversation hissing: "Brilliant! Brilliant!"

"Ah, the tigers have come!" whispered the unshaven man, drawing closer to Dmitri.

Uriupin jerked himself away from the wall, left the smoking room hurriedly, and intercepted two solid personages dressed in black, carrying brief cases. He shook hands first with one then with the other, and laughed. But these two, as they talked to him, still kept their reserve and exchanged frequent glances, like accomplices.

"Avdiyev has not come—that is not a very good sign!" the unshaven engineer remarked to Lopatkin under his breath. "I believe you are the originator. I want to tell you, so that you will realize: if the project were going to be approved, Avdiyev would be here. He enjoys these occasions, the handshakings and all that. But when a project is going to be turned down, he uses his two doctors, Tepikin and Fundator. Caesar merely gives the orders: to let the tigers loose on the gladiators! And the tigers leap out! But please don't think, for heaven's sake, that this is only malice on my part. It is simply the experience of many years. Everything here is still done just as it was five or twenty years ago. Exactly the same! Without exception!"

"There is going to be a fight! Galitsky has come!" someone exclaimed loudly and gaily, and a young voice at once answered from the depths of the smoking room which was blue with tobacco smoke:

"A storm is brewing, but we shall fight. . . !"

Lopatkin looked to right and left of him, and asked the unshaven engineer: "Who are they talking about?"

"The one who has just come in. Galitsky. Don't you know him? He's a fallen angel. He left the Scientific Institute of Foundry Research not long ago. It was because of the Avdiyev machine—there was some disagreement between them, and Avdiyev doesn't like that sort of thing!"

Meanwhile both doctors bowed to Uriupin with an almost identical expression in their eyes, went into the smoking room, and took out their cigar cases. One of them was serious, with the pretty face of a plump brunette; his long black coat loosely molded his waist and his feminine curves.

"That's Fundator, doctor of science," the unshaven man said to Lopatkin. "In our office they call him 'the young Circassian maiden.' That one plays it all in a soft key, and in a scientific manner. He will be sorry for you, shed tears, and pronounce a heartfelt 'amen.' And the other, 'neither hither nor thither, Tepikin is in a dither.' " The engineer laughed. "Now *he* is a doctor. He will act as chorus. His line is usually 'one never knows.' Doubts are his stock in trade. So there you have your opponents. And that they *are* opponents you can be quite certain!"

A bell rang somewhere in a distant passage. "It's beginning!" Lopatkin thought, and impatiently jerked another cigarette out of the pack. It broke in his fingers; he threw it away and took out another. One after another the smokers threw their stubs into a large nickel-plated urn and went out into the passage. The two "tigers" came out also. They were not in any hurry. Fundator walked with a dignified air, his head held high; Tepikin shambled clumsily along. "Time to go!" Lopatkin thought, and hesitantly, nodding farewell to his companion, he went out calmly, and, as he imagined, wearing an expression of complete indifference. An engineer whom he did not know overtook him, gave him one glance, and said:

"Pull yourself together! Your face is completely white! Don't give them that satisfaction!"

The little conference room was almost empty. About twenty specialists had come to the session. Lopatkin knew none of them. But they obviously knew each other well. They lounged casually in their chairs, as though completely at home, exchanging greetings, whispering in their neighbors' ears, passing notes to one another. In front, by the chairman's table, a stenographer was laying out her papers. Somebody was busy shifting the chairs. Somebody else gave

Lopatkin a box of thumb tacks and said: "Come on, originator, get busy!" Whereupon he began pinning the sheets of his project up on the brown notice board and fastening them with thumb tacks to the wooden slats on the wall. When he had finished doing this, he looked around. Everyone was staring at the pale originator in his coat with the too-short sleeves. Someone was already sitting in the chairman's place—it was the director of the institute, a gray, wrinkled man in the uniform of an engineer, with a general's shoulder straps. Beyond him, in an easy chair, the academician, his eyelids lowered over his eyes, appeared to be dozing; only the sharply pointed ends of his mustache pointed briskly upward. Fundator was there, leaning back in his chair and holding a brand-new brief case on his lap. Half hidden behind his powerful figure, Tepikin was whispering something in his ear. Fundator was listening, his eyes turned toward the ceiling.

"Well, comrades, there is a motion that we should begin!" the general said in a level bass, looking at his wrist watch. "It is exactly ten minutes past one. I think it is time." He paused for a moment, then gave Dmitri a sidelong glance. "Are you ready?"

Dmitri stepped forward about to answer "Yes," but the general was no longer looking at him.

"Comrades, we have decided to take as our first item the discussion of the centrifugal machine. The matter is clear, it will not take up much time, nor will it tire our respected guests. I shall call upon the originator of the project, Engineer Lopatkin. If you please...."

Lopatkin picked up the pointer. He suddenly felt like a teacher again. He raised his head, his face cleared, and the *class* listened in silence.

"This machine is intended for casting iron pipes by the centrifugal method." With each word he uttered he felt more at ease and gained more confidence. "You are no doubt aware that we are suffering from an acute shortage of various kinds of pipes...."

The general tapped the table impatiently with his pencil and was about to open his mouth, but thought better of it and remained silent.

". . . and yet, however strange it may seem, these pipes, which ought to be coming like cigarettes out of automatic machines, are in many places still being cast by hand, or with machines which are essentially not machines but merely accessories to manual labor. Iron runs like water, yet we are making no use of this fact!"

"Excuse me." The general wrinkled his face in an expression of disapproval and sighed. "Pipes are in short supply, iron is fluid, steel is dense—after all, we are not children! We know all this already! Please come to the point of the project—its essential peculiarities."

"As you please. Our machine differs from other machines in two radical respects," Lopatkin went on. "In the first place, it is not a mere accessory, but a genuine machine, in which the working time is fully exploited. On all machines with which we are already familiar the auxiliary operations are carried out manually, and during this time the main device—that is, the casting machine proper—is at a standstill. On my machine all auxiliary operations are carried out by a special mechanism, working simultaneously with the casting machine, and not holding it up. This insures an increase in the productive capacity of the machine which at present is no less than five times what it was before. The second peculiarity of this machine is that it occupies only a fourth of the space required by existing devices, such as, for instance, the machine developed by the C.S.I.F.R., a description of which was published in the periodical *Metal*. This decrease in dimensions is achieved by the coreless casting of the metal. The C.S.I.F.R. employed the same feed device as my machine, but still retained its old dimensions. Then why employ coreless casting at all?"

The entire technical council laughed in unison. There was a movement and a shifting of chairs. Then silence again, this time a friendly silence.

"And so," Lopatkin continued, "we could build one factory in the place of four and still put the same number of machines into it as at present we plan for four factories. That would bring us a saving of . . ."

153

"Just put that actual advantage into our hand," the general said affably, "and as for calculating the saving, we can do that for ourselves!"

Dmitri did not answer him. Moving the pointer across the sheets of the project, he briefly explained how each part of the machine functioned. Then he picked up the chalk and passed to the calculations. He quickly filled the board with the basic calculations, maintaining that the machine would produce fifty pipes an hour; that each pipe would weigh a pound less; that only two workmen were needed to work the machine; and that all processes could be made completely automatic in the future. "The whole conception of this machine," he said, "includes the possibility of establishing an automatized plant operating without the participation of workers." He finished his report and stood aside.

"As for automation, we shall have to see about that!" the general remarked, looking at his watch. "Meanwhile, you have saved us all fifteen minutes! That is not bad for the time being. Well, are there any questions for the speaker?"

"I should like to ask the originator," Fundator drawled in a mellifluous voice, looking benevolently at Lopatkin. "Please tell us, Comrade—er—Lopatkin, what is it you have there, on top? The annealing chamber? As on Picard's machine?"

"That is the cooling conveyor. But it has no special heating. The newly cast pipes will be directed up there—and that will insure evenness of cooling and the removal of stresses."

After a pause, a few more apparently innocent and casual questions were asked. Then there was a special silence which no one ventured to break. No one spoke. Fundator stared at the ceiling. Tepikin appeared to have gone to sleep, resting his ingenuous face on Fundator's shoulder from behind—but no, on second glance he was whispering something in Fundator's ear. The general looked first out of the window at the clear blue sky, then at the drawings of the project, then at the ceiling. Finally he turned his pencil around and tapped the table with its butt end.

"Well, comrades . . . shall we give our verdict?" he asked, raising one gray eyebrow.

"Might I just . . . ?" Fundator seemed to awaken suddenly from a sleep; he stood up, holding a small sheet of paper in front of his eyes.

"Er—the work on which we have just received a report," he began with an appearance of naïveté, looking up at the ceiling. "The work which we . . . of which we have here heard so interesting"— here he bent forward—"and so detailed a report from the speaker, is very important and, I can also see, very effective. But at the same time it characterizes Comrade Lopatkin"—here he smiled at Lopatkin—"characterizes him, I would say, as an inventor who hopes to solve all problems through enthusiasm. I really feel somewhat embarrassed at having to say this, but Comrade Lopatkin has shown himself here to be completely bankrupt as regards theory—if he will pardon the indelicate expression! He has not enough theoretical knowledge and he wants to design a completely new machine by rule of thumb, by trial and error." Fundator put out his hand and grasped softly at the air. "Basing his technical decisions on hunches, that is to say, manifesting a total lack of a correct professional approach. But when his attention was called to this, as I am reliably informed, he refused to agree and rejected the necessity of more competent intervention, either from the research workers in C.S.I.F.R. or from . . ."

"Well, you see, Comrade Fundator," the general interrupted, "this was due to the fact that the idea in itself was very alluring, and certain comrades had faith in the creative faculties of the originator . . . and . . . well, of the workers in our projects branch. They simply took a chance."

"Then let them enjoy the results of their gamble!" Fundator said jokingly.

"I have not heard any real criticism of the project." Lopatkin's voice sounded stern. "Kindly criticize in detail, with the pointer and chalk in your hand."

"Quite right! Why not? Well, here is some criticism for you!"

Fundator went up to the drawings. "Here, you have introduced an annealing chamber. You yourself said it was in order to eliminate stresses. Which means that you are not convinced that such a technical solution will give you pipes without chilling. Or are you?"

"I have introduced the chamber in order to make use of the heat released by the cooling pipes and to make the process of their cooling independent of winter drafts. But even without this chamber there would be no chilling."

"Where are the calculations to confirm this conviction of yours?" Fundator raised his hands in a deprecatory manner and smiled at the almost-empty room. "The state does not make financial grants for acts of faith. Are you convinced? But ask our highly respected Peter Benedictovich Saratovtsev, and he will tell you that not only are there no calculations, but there is not even a theory which might lead us to make such calculations."

At these words the academician nodded impressively several times, without opening his eyes.

"And you say," Fundator went on, his round eyes wandering from face to face, "well, here is a concrete objection for you: we are not against such a machine, but we think that first of all we must find the theoretical premises for the creation of such a machine. Our institute has already taken certain steps in this direction, but Comrade Lopatkin does not recognize any argument or authority. Yes . . . then . . . about the resistance to wear and tear . . . of the molds. . . . Why! You, my dear fellow, have put forward nothing in support of your assertions! But—what's the good?"

Fundator turned around, showing off the perfect fit of his black suit, shrugged his shoulders, and went back to his chair. Now it was Tepikin's turn; he at once stood up and went forward.

"Having heard out to the end the ideas put forward by Comrade Lopatkin, I attempted, comrades, to find some rational kernel in *this* business. The housing shortage, the need for pipes—all this is correct. But now let's take this construction. Is it good or ought it to be *changed?* This again is a question of secondary importance and might even become redundant if we carefully check up on the

156

scientific justification of the given machine. What is the point? It is impossible not to agree with Comrade Fundator, who . . ."

Tepikin, drawing in the air with his finger, which was so white it looked as though it were frozen, talked for a long time in a dejected tone, throwing doubts on every part of the machine.

"Fifty pipes an hour?" he asked, taking out his handkerchief, blowing his nose, and answering himself with a laugh. "On paper it is always like that! As in Tolstoy's *War and Peace: 'Die erste Kolonne marschiert, die zweite Kolonne marschiert.'* But when it comes down to practice, bang! You get not fifty pipes, but only ten, and even those, if you give them the slightest tap, break into bits like clay pots, because of course chilling has taken place! And you know that well enough yourself, my respected originator!"

Finally Tepikin, raising a finger for each item, enumerated all the machine's doubtful features, demonstrating with a laugh that he had not enough fingers for the purpose, then he paused, suddenly turned serious, and said with feeling:

"Dear Comrade Lopatkin! For God's sake, don't misunderstand me! If the problem of pipe casting could be solved so simply, believe me we should have sung your praises long ago, and would somehow, with you, have got such a machine going with a bang. After all, it is not the gods who fire clay pots! And we, too, on my word of honor, are not eating our daily bread in idleness!" Here he laid his hand on his breast. "We, too, are just the very least bit patriotic, Comrade Lopatkin!"

Someone pushed a chair forward for Lopatkin. He sat down, and unconsciously began fingering the buttons on his coat. Tepikin scratched his head, seemed to remember something else he wished to say, but refrained with a gesture of resignation, and waddled back to his place behind Fundator.

"Permit me!" Lopatkin heard a slow, angry bass voice exclaim.

"Comrade Galitsky, Peter Andreyevich," said the general, glancing at the stenographer and turning his pencil around again.

"Where have I heard that name before?" Lopatkin asked himself.

157

This Galitsky proved to be a tall, slow, long-nosed man in a gray suit. His glance sought out Lopatkin's. He raised his black eyebrows almost to the top of his forehead, his black eyes and large nostrils widened with disapproval, so that it appeared as though he were looking at Lopatkin with four sharp pupils.

"Before I cross swords with Engineer Lopatkin," he growled, "I would like to address a few words of criticism to the respected representatives of C.S.I.F.R. Only a year ago the government built them a fine residence and this circumstance, as I now see"—here Galitsky coughed triumphantly—"has not been slow to have its effect on science. Scientists have ceased to be interested in the immediate practical issues of pipe production. They have become immersed in the deeper theoretical mysteries. What they are pursuing now is the bottom of the ocean, the bathysphere!"

Everyone laughed, and Fundator reddened slightly.

"And if," Galitsky exclaimed, and with a long finger appeared to be catching at something above his head, "*if* Comrade Fundator had looked at this matter from a practical angle, from the point of view of the tasks facing us today, and even tomorrow, he would have found much that was of value in Engineer Lopatkin's project. Tell me, which is better: a muzzle-loading musket or a machine gun? The machine gun, of course. And what Engineer Lopatkin is proposing to us is just that: a machine gun! He eliminates the gun crew which today is loading your matchlocks, comrades of the C.S.I.F.R.! He substitutes for them a machine gun's cartridge belt, and gives us an economical, quick-firing gun. Am I right, Comrade Lopatkin?"

Lopatkin, pleasantly surprised, nodded hastily.

"But don't rejoice too soon, originator, I haven't got round to you yet!" said Galitsky turning back to Fundator. "Let's continue. You talk about chilling; you talk about theory. But is it not obvious to all of us that what is suggested is a flexible device which affords the possibility of determining by experience the degree of temperature required in actual practice? Lopatkin can find it in this way by groping, much sooner than you can, comrade theoreticians!

158

Because the solution is here, within reach. He will give us pipes, and give you the basic data, and then you can write dissertations about it all!"

Everyone laughed. The general brightened up, relaxed, drew something with his pencil on a sheet of paper, and shook his head. When silence was restored, Galitsky turned his sharp black eyes toward Lopatkin, fiercely distending his nostrils, then strode up to him.

"There is, however, in your idea, comrade originator, one merciless 'but,' which is a result of your, as one might say, hermit way of life. It is absolutely essential for thoughts to be cross-fertilized with other thoughts, otherwise they degenerate. I am thinking now of your coreless feed device. It is effective, and Lecturer Volovik was not slow to 'remold it creatively.' He at once 'deviated from it,' or, to put it plainly, pinched it! But, comrades, he pinched an empty purse!"

At this there was laughter.

"And why was the purse empty? This is why!" Galitsky grabbed a piece of chalk, crouched over the board, and began to write down large letters and figures, the chalk rapping loudly on the board. "Ferrostatic pressure," he was saying, as he wrote, "the temperature of the metal obtained from the crucible . . . pouring time for the metal . . . speed of revolution. . . . Do you know what would result from your short channel and your slope for the mold? The metal would not run down to the end before it began to harden and so we would get an irregularly shaped pipe."

"No, we should not!" Lopatkin exclaimed in a shrill voice unlike his usual one.

Galitsky spread out his fingers as though exhorting him to calm.

"Well, well! So now you even shout at me! Keep cool, read the formula, and digest it! Your calculations are not linked with the scientific conceptions regarding the plasticity of metals. Just envisage the distance the iron travels as it revolves in your pipe. It would be at least eighty feet. Eighty feet, and losing heat all the

159

time! Even a schoolboy could tell you that! The metal in your machine would crystallize by the time it got about halfway through!"

"Permit me!" Lopatkin jumped up. "Permit me! I have just three comments!"

"Comrade Lopatkin," said the general, "we have our regular procedure . . ."

"Say what you want to!" Galitsky said.

"My first comment is," Lopatkin's voice was calmer now, "that I am not an engineer, I am a schoolmaster in a secondary school. In our school no one except myself has any ideas about centrifugal casting and so there was no one with whom I could 'cross-fertilize my thoughts,' as Comrade Galitsky demands!"

The gathering sighed audibly; then there was silence.

"I wish that you, at least, would understand me, Comrade Galitsky. Do you really think it right that anyone who stumbles on to a new idea and wants to give it to the nation—is it really right to denounce him as an anti-social element? To make jokes of this sort at his expense?"

While Lopatkin was speaking, Galitsky several times raised his burning black eyes thoughtfully to his face, but lowered them at once when they met the inventor's calm and weary gaze.

"I would have tried to 'cross-fertilize thoughts,' " Lopatkin went on with a scarcely perceptible irony. "I am continually aware of my deficiencies as a designer and metallurgist. But Professor Avdiyev had no such desire. He said it was all a 'fiction,' and that that was all there was to it."

"Why not? Of course it is a fiction." Fundator's careless drawl broke clearly into the silence.

"My second comment is," Lopatkin continued, "that in the Muzga plant to this day they are casting pipes by manual methods. Probably you all know this; you all know also that iron is of more fluid structure, and steel of denser. This fact induced me, a schoolmaster, to throw up my job and become an inventor, a step I now belatedly regret. And my third comment is this . . ."

Lopatkin went and stood beside Galitsky at the board, took the

160

chalk out of his hand, and began to write letters and figures, tapping the board noisily with the chalk.

"You break up the process into separate parts, forgetting that these separate parts have a mutual interaction. You forget the centrifugal force, you forget that heat losses in a heated metal mold will differ from those in a cold mold. And you forget the main thing also: that as the result of the slope and the rotary motion of the mold, the metal will be instantly distributed throughout the while length of the mold. And quite evenly, too! But I, on the contrary, can still reckon on there being time to spare for the pipe to form in a horizontal position!" Lopatkin rapped loudly on the board with the chalk and stepped back.

Galitsky stared at him in apparent astonishment, then leaned against the board, blinking, as he thought the matter over. One minute, then another, went by in silence. An animated murmur began to be heard in the room and grew imperceptibly louder. Here and there a hesitant clapping of hands was audible.

"Comrade Galitsky!" said the general, rapping the table with his pencil. "We are waiting!"

"Just a moment!" Galitsky, without taking his eyes from the board, made an absent-minded gesture, spattering his coat with chalk dust.

"I can't understand what there still is to think about! It's all as clear as daylight!" Fundator exclaimed.

"Mathematics have shown that even daylight is not so completely clear!" Galitsky objected, still looking at the board and tapping it with the chalk.

"Peter Benediktovich, wouldn't you care to . . . ?" Rising in his chair, the general addressed the academician.

"What is there to say, properly speaking?" The academician opened his eyes, the misty, pale-blue eyes of an old, old man. "The matter is clear. Truly as clear as daylight. If the machine is to be made, it means spending thirty thousand roubles on an experiment. But our job is not to experiment, it is to produce. I should recommend that the scientific dispute be referred to the proper institution. There, all experiments can be made on existing equipment. Nor should one underestimate the already available data. Personally, I am inclined to think that coreless casting is a fiction. Yes," he shook his head, "the usual attempt to solve an intricate problem at one stroke! That's all it is!"

"Permit me to add my comment." Fundator stood up. "In contradistinction to Galitsky, we, in the institute, took up a more serious and objective attitude in discussing this machine, and are prepared to defend our scientific positions without hesitation. Not wishing to prolong this in any case too long-drawn-out debate, I am submitting our theses, in which the advantages and drawbacks of Comrade—er—Lopatkin's machine are analyzed in detail to the technical council. . . ."

And he laid the theses, consisting of several typewritten sheets, on the table in front of the general.

"Comrade Fundator," Galitsky protested indignantly from beside the board, "adherence to principle does not consist in standing on the same spot all the time!"

"We have somewhat overstepped our schedule," said the general, looking through the theses Fundator had presented. "Does anyone else wish to speak? No? Then I think, comrade, that the conclusions are clear. The majority of comrades inclines to the view that it would not be expedient to build this machine. A mere raw idea cannot serve as a foundation for serious work. It is, however, already obvious that the problem of the centrifugal casting of pipes must be solved in one way or another. The efforts of both scientists and engineers must be directed toward this end. I assume that the Ministry will set us such a technical task in the near future. Are you in agreement with this decision?" he asked Lopatkin.

"*I* disagree!" Galitsky said firmly from his place by the board. "The machine is simple. It may have to be modified in some respects. The layout may have to be made more convenient. But the chief point is clear. The originator must be brought together with a competent designer and calculator, to produce the machine. The

162

arguments submitted by Comrade Lopatkin are sufficiently weighty to justify the necessity of experimental testing."

"Does anyone else disagree?" the general asked placidly. "No one? Then I declare the meeting suspended. Comrade Lopatkin. Lopatkin, do you hear? Are you interested in seeing the minutes? Then come to the secretariat one day soon and you will receive a copy."

Lopatkin went out into the passage and lit a cigarette. People were moving all around him, bumping into him from every side, but he stood still, wrapped in a cloud of smoke, sighing heavily now and then, and with each sigh drawing the smoke deeply into his lungs.

"Comrade, if you want to smoke, go to the smoking room," someone said, and his legs began to move, carrying him along of their own accord.

Uriupin, unnaturally gay, met him at the top of the stairs, exclaimed, "They *did* do it down after all, the devils!" and disappeared. Lopatkin walked downstairs. Near the cloakroom someone pushed a hand vigorously under his arm, gripping him by the elbow.

"Comrade Lopatkin," Galitsky's bass voice boomed in his ear. Lopatkin turned around sharply, ready to defend himself.

This man with the black eyes, steady gaze, thin nose, and thick lips, came close to him and examined him intently for a while.

"I should be glad if you would stop lumping me together with all those . . . with them . . . well, with your opponents," he said. "Certainly I permitted . . . it's true . . . I did allow certain expressions. One goes on talking simply through inertia, imagining that one is right. And then it turns out that . . . It is only now that I understand a simple fact. That one must not fall foul of Avdiyev and these others. . . . And not everyone would even wish to oppose them. It isn't your fault that you have conceived an original idea! And it is a good idea; it would be a pity to chuck it away. But all the same, you are wrong in one thing."

163

Lopatkin frowned slightly, his lips tightening a little as he looked at Galitsky.

"You are wrong in one thing!" Galitsky repeated with a laugh. "You are not simply a schoolmaster, you are also quite a fine engineer. And it is dangerous to argue with you!"

Galitsky seemed to be in a hurry. He put on his black overcoat and his shabby, reddish fur cap, gazing all the while at Lopatkin, then dashed to the exit, but stopped suddenly and wagged his finger at him.

"Improve your machine regardless of what anyone says! Work on it. We shall meet again."

2

WORK on it!" Lopatkin thought as he stepped out into the brightly lit street, sensing even more clearly, aware now of the fresh spring scents. Then all at once he remembered that he had only two thousand roubles and they would not last for more than four months. And what about paper? And a place to work in? "After the discussion I'll buy myself a watch," he recollected, an absent-minded and uncertain smile flitting across his face. His foot touched a piece of ice. "I must buy myself some boots," he thought suddenly, walking faster. He was accustomed to doing things instantly, without any hesitation.

He found a department store on the Arbat, and chose himself a pair of plain black leather shoes. The cash register hummed, clicked, and rang its little bell, and now Lopatkin found himself with three hundred roubles less in his pocket. He did not even try the shoes on; the velvet and nickel of the trying-on chair, placed in a conspicuous position, intimidated him.

He went back to his hotel, and walked up to his room on the sixth floor. There were five beds in the room. Lopatkin sat down on his own and changed his shoes, ate a slice of cheese with a large hunk of bread, put a lump of sugar in his mouth, and drank a glass of water out of the carafe. He was already beginning to economize.

Then he shaved in front of a little round mirror he had propped up on his pillow, dressed again, and went out to wander in the streets and think over his affairs. As he went downstairs, he looked around him, and seeing that there was no one about, put the parcel containing his old patched boots into a large and handsome urn intended for cigarette stubs.

Out in the street it was snowing—the short January spring was over. "I must buy galoshes," Lopatkin thought; "they save shoe leather." Twenty minutes later he was treading the slush in a pair of new galoshes, his stock of money now reduced by another forty roubles. He stopped at every notice board on the way and eagerly scanned the "labor wanted" advertisements. He saw no fewer than six demands for skilled factory workers, and felt greatly cheered. Single men were offered accommodation in hostels—it was just what he needed. After all, he had once worked in a motorcar factory.

"I won't give in!" he said quietly, his face darkening. "No, comrades!" He began walking faster. "Nothing doing! It won't come off—not this time! Now I shall go on fighting for another two months, and take a job in a factory. It will be my refuge!"

It turned out that, as usual, he was following the same familiar route that he had walked the day before. Because of this, he made a sharp turn and entered a side street, passed over several crossings, and again found himself at the familiar spot he had already visited more than once: it was Metrostroy Street. Lopatkin entered it exactly opposite the old five-story block where Jeanne lived. He stopped there, musing, and was about to stroll on along Metrostroy Street, but instead pulled himself up and turned quickly into a side street: what if she were to come out and he were to run into her? What could he say to her? To judge by externals, he did not look much of a victor at this moment.

Yet neither could he go without having seen her. In a month he had only twice succeeded in catching sight of her: on both occasions he had followed her at a distance to her own door, like a callow youth.

Dmitri looked down at himself, and saw that he was covered with snow. That was lucky! He turned his collar up higher, dug his hands in his pockets, drew his head in between his shoulders, and slowly walked along Metrostroy Street to Crimean Square; on both previous occasions she had been going home from the subway station there.

He walked up and down and then up again. All this time the

snow seemed to be growing even whiter and the sky darker—dusk was creeping out of the side streets. "Why am I here?" Dmitri thought, stopping short resolutely, and at that moment he saw Jeanne. She was coming toward him, in a black tightly belted coat, her hands in her pockets, her pretty head, wearing a little green knitted cap with ear flaps, bent forward. She was not alone. A young army captain in a new cap and a coat with glittering buttons was holding her arm and looking down sideways at her little cap.

"You understand?" Dmitri heard him saying in a staccato tenor. "Kolka was sitting here and Mishka here, and I was dealing. There wasn't a fourth, you see? And Kolka has no idea of the game. . . ."

They went by slowly, trying to keep in step. Jeanne's gaze slid calmly past Lopatkin, who at that moment resembled a snow-covered sentry.

"I shall give you a bad mark for drill," Jeanne said. "You can't keep step!"

Lopatkin followed them slowly, falling farther and farther behind, then he stopped. And the two in front fell into step at last, and quickened their pace with obvious pleasure. "No, I'll have one more look at you!" Lopatkin thought, crossing the road, overtaking them on the other side, then crossing back again, leaning against a shopwindow rail and contemplating the buttons and hair-dos inside with a surprising interest.

He heard the captain's voice again: "Kolka can't play at all, he has no idea, you see!" The captain even went so far as to slap the leg of his boot, and Jeanne laughed. "And I gave him a clear *bon chance!* And he didn't know! Quite helpless! You see how it was?"

Lopatkin turned, and his heart suddenly missed a beat. Jeanne was looking straight into his eyes. There, in the depths of hers, something seemed to stir. But no! She had not seen the snow-covered figure; between her and Lopatkin stood Kolka and the captain's highly polished boot. Her face looked the same as it had three years before: white, with protruding Mongolian cheekbones under dark, widely spaced eyes. She was smiling, one shoulder turned toward the captain, her eyes lowered slyly.

167

"What do you mean to imply by this? Am I Kolka and are you the *bon chance* that dropped into my lap and that I could not appreciate? And do you know what *bon chance* means in French? Well, I shan't tell you! Look it up in a foreign dictionary!"

"Ha-ha-ha!" A great laugh rose inside Lopatkin. "Good for her! That's the stuff! She has fixed him!"

Still standing motionless, his eyes followed them with a sharp, fixed gaze. Then he crossed the road and strolled to the Kropotkin Gate, looking around from time to time.

Suddenly he saw them both slow down uncertainly, or rather, Jeanne lagged behind, and the captain stopped. She was looking at the ground, as though trying to remember something while her companion waited at a short distance, his head bent sympathetically. Jeanne remembered whatever it was and walked quickly back, bumping against passers-by in her desperate haste. The shopwindow! She reached the painted guard rail, stood still, cast a hurried glance around her, and pressed her hand to her breast. She hurried into the shop, but came out again almost immediately. The captain came up to her with an inquiring expression on his face. "Wait here, I'll be back," she indicated by a gesture, then ran on toward Crimean Square. "Come what may!" Lopatkin thought, and had already turned around and was about to overtake and confront her unexpectedly, when at the same moment he thought: "What could I say to her? Wouldn't I have to invent something over again to deceive her with?" He hid quickly behind a pillar, and in the distance he saw Jeanne slowly coming back. She stopped by the shopwindow, touching the guard rail.

It was getting dark now. The windows were yellow with lights; the small red and yellow lamps of motorcars blinked as they streamed past. Lopatkin walked along the boulevard, toward the Arbat, past rows of benches occupied by representatives of Love, Repose, and Motherhood. He was thinking of the day when, correcting his pupils' work, he had made the first tentative sketch of his machine on the cover of one of the exercise books. He had merely made a rough sketch—and then had been carried away. That was how it had started! "Yes, I discovered my destiny!" he thought, smiling quietly as he shook his head and made a gesture with his hand. "I've let the genie out of the bottle, and now I can't get away from him! But why not cheat him? Arakhovski did! Why not go back to schoolmastering in some cozy corner and be a normal human being, like all other people, these sitting on the benches. Throw all the correspondence, all the drawings, all this 'individualism' into the fire! And Jeanne would come back to me—peace and quiet is all she wants. . . . What is it that prevents me?"

He went on, to the Nikitsky Gate, feeling as though the released genie were laughing hoarsely at his side and listening to his thoughts. "No, no, no!" the genie said. "Before, you might still have thrown the exercise book into the fire. Yes, before, perhaps, but not now, when you know that you hold a genuine discovery in your hand, for which all these, sitting on the benches here, will one day thank you. . . . Provided—ha! ha!—that it ever sees the light of day!"

Two days later Lopatkin received the minutes of the technical council's session and found in them all the phrases with which he was by now so familiar: ". . . in view of the intricacy and unwieldiness . . ." "not a paying proposition in comparison with the simpler machine constructed by Professor Avdiyev . . ." "a series of essential drawbacks" . . . and a great deal more in the same vein. The minutes ended with the words: "it was decided to consider it unsuitable . . ." after which came other no-less-familiar phrases.

Lopatkin by now knew the whole formula in advance; he had met with it more than once, it had already figured in the correspondence conducted from Muzga and so it now made no impression on him. He replied in the same vein; on the spot, in the waiting room of the director of the institute, writing with a practised hand a complaint addressed to the chief of the technical department of the Ministry. Putting the address of his hotel on the envelope, he handed the complaint in on the first floor of the twelve-story Ministry building, which occupies half of Pashutin Passage.

Next morning, at his hotel, he was called to the telephone. A placid female voice said: "Comrade Lopatkin? Comrade Lopatkin, Comrade Drozdov will see you this afternoon at five. Bring your passport with you, your pass will be ready." As he left the telephone, Lopatkin thought: "Which Drozdov? Can it be the same one? Come to think of it, *she* did write something about leaving Muzga."

At three o'clock Lopatkin shaved, cleaned his shoes, and out of old habit polished the buttons on his coat, using a special little brush and a button stick for the purpose. At half-past four he got off a bus at the permit office of the Ministry and stood contemplating the skirting of the ministerial building. It was of polished black stone with greenish crystals that glittered coldly below the polished surface. At five o'clock he found himself sitting on a settee in a pale cream waiting room, by a door padded with a soft brown material. Beside the door, on a nameplate of thick glass that was screwed to the wall, was lettered: "L. I. Drozdov, Chief of the Technical Department," in severe gold letters.

On one side a secretary, a young girl with a pink-and-white face, with downcast eyes, was lifting telephone receivers and answering in a low voice: "Leonid Ivanovich is engaged." Her thick whitish-yellow plaits, twisted into a knot at the back of her head, seemed to radiate light. "A Russian sunrise!" Lopatkin thought, smiling.

An electric signal buzzed behind the "Sunrise's" head. She stood up, paused for a moment looking down at her blouse and her hands, and then quietly entered the chief's office. She came back at once and said politely: "This way, please!"

The office of the chief of the technical department was smaller than the general manager of the *kombinat's* had been. But the chief himself was colder and more severe than the general manager. He was wearing a gray uniform with a colonel's shoulder straps. And he sat motionless at his gigantic writing desk, his head drawn in between his shoulders, his hands clenched in front of him into a single large yellow fist; and in his lean, shrewd, nervous face Lopatkin read: "You and I know each other! But acquaintanceship means nothing to a government official!" On a divan at one side a man

170

was lying, a man with a high forehead, gold-framed spectacles, and an expensive suit, the color of concrete. He gazed fixedly, with an expression of interest, at Lopatkin, and fidgeted with his pearl-white fingers as he lay on the divan. Shutikov! Lopatkin recognized him and bowed.

On a little table at Drozdov's elbow an electric signal buzzed faintly. The chief frowned, picked up the receiver, and waving Lopatkin to an easy chair with one hand, answered "Yes" in a sleepy voice.

Lopatkin sat down, as usual crossing his legs. Drozdov looked at him and closed his eyes, indicating that he had to listen to all kinds of nonsense over the telephone.

"Who else?" he shouted into the receiver. "Will Alexander Sergeyevich Pushkin do it instead of you? Now you start . . . ringing me. . . . What you are to do? Just do as I told you!"

He put the receiver down, came out from behind the desk, and stretched out his hand.

"Good afternoon. Welcome to Moscow! Let me present you! Comrade Shutikov, this is our inventor!"

Shutikov got up, his gold-framed glasses glittering, shook hands with an amiable, apologetic smile, remarking: "Comrade Lopatkin and I have already met!" and again lay down on the divan.

Drozdov opened a silver cigarette case and offered it first to Shutikov, then to Lopatkin. They both lighted up. Drozdov went back to his place, settled himself in the chair, closed his eyes, then slowly half-opened them again.

"Well, how goes it? More complaints, eh?"

"Yes, Comrade Drozdov, I have more complaints."

"Quite right, too. So you are not satisfied with the council's decision?"

"No, not in the least."

"Is it as bad as all that?" Drozdov directed a sidelong look toward Shutikov. "Aren't you being a bit hard to please?"

"I cannot agree to a single point."

171

"Not a single one? Yet the decision does contain certain supporting arguments."

"But other arguments were put forward as well at the technical council's meeting. One's in my favor."

"By whom? Galitsky? By one man only—a minority. Those scientists are a difficult lot. As soon as anything crops up, they take a vote. Democracy, that is."

As he said this Drozdov looked again in Shutikov's direction.

"The point is, Comrade Drozdov, that the meeting was not sufficiently representative," Lopatkin said. "If Academician Florensky had been invited, there would have been two votes in my favor."

"You don't know anything," Shutikov said, beaming benevolently. "No one has ever got those two ancients together at the same meeting. One of them always politely declines or falls ill as soon as he discovers that the other one has also been invited!"

"Very convenient!" Lopatkin remarked, turning toward Shutikov. "But one could name at least a dozen other scientists who have expressed a favorable opinion about my machine. Why were *they* not invited? Why only these sixteen?"

"I looked through the list of those who were invited. They were all names that carry authority."

"But the selection was blatantly discriminatory!"

"Come, come, my dear fellow!" Still smiling, Shutikov rose. "I really cannot carry on a serious conversation on this plane! The Central Institute is an authoritative body. We cannot simply disbelieve them, just like that. If collectively they say that the machine is no good, it is the conclusion that comes closest to the truth. Answer this comrade briefly, Comrade Drozdov, in the spirit I have just outlined. Give him an answer. And now, permit me . . ."

"Could *you* not possibly see me for a few minutes?" Lopatkin asked.

"By all means. Telephone to me. I am always willing to talk to you. But now allow me to wish you . . ."

Shutikov smiled his modest, apologetic smile, shook Lopatkin's hand limply, and left the room.

When the door had closed, Drozdov stretched himself, and bracing his feet against something, pushed himself away from the desk.

"There you are, man! There is our opinion! Have a cigarette! For all practical purposes that is the Ministry's opinion."

"We shall try to refute it, also," Lopatkin said, taking a cigarette from the case. His eyes encountered Drozdov's long, familiar, quizzical expression and he felt that he had missed some opportunity that Drozdov would never bring up of his own accord.

"In the present case," Drozdov said, "you will be licked. And you also have given a demonstration of what one might call political instability."

He emerged from behind the desk, his hands in his pockets, and his eyes on the toes of his boots, and began pacing to and fro.

"Look here, Comrade Lopatkin, if I were a writer, I should write a novel about you. Because you are a truly tragic figure embodying within yourself"—here Drozdov turned toward Lopatkin and stuck his hand into the breast of his coat with a jocular gesture —"a whole epoch, which by now is irretrievably past and gone. You are a hero, but a solitary one." Having said this, he was silent, walking about the carpet in crooked circles. "We can see through you as though you were made of glass, but you cannot understand us. For instance, you do not understand that we can do without your invention, even if it is a genuine, a great discovery. We can do without it and, just imagine—without even suffering any loss! Yes, Comrade Lopatkin, without suffering any loss, because of our accurate calculations and the planning which insures us a steady advance. Even if we admit that your invention is a work of genius. If statesmanlike calculations make it necessary to put on the agenda the task . . ."

"It has been a long time on the agenda!" Lopatkin remarked.

". . . which you are trying to fullfil by yourself," Drozdov went on. "Our designers' and technicians' collectives will find a solution. And this solution will be better than yours, because collective research always leads to the quickest and best solution of any problem. The collective is superior to any individual genius."

"You should speak more concretely. What about Professor Avdi-yev?" Lopatkin was beginning to say, but Drozdov did not listen; coming closer, he looked fixedly at Lopatkin out of his amused black eyes.

". . . and the result, Comrade Lopatkin, is something you cannot understand. We building ants . . ." As he pronounced this word, a cold monster of hatred stirred at the back of his ordinarily jolly eyes. "Yes, we building ants are necessary. . . ."

"One of those ants—" Lopatkin tried to interrupt him, but, raising his own voice, Drozdov did not allow him to finish.

". . . while you solitary geniuses with your tremendous ideas that stand on tenuous legs are not necessary. There is no capitalist here to buy your ideas, and the people have no use for primitive passions that jolt the economic routine. We shall reach the required decisions gradually, without panic, at the required time, even at the required hour!"

"And yet one of those ants," Lopatkin resumed evenly, holding himself in but feeling hate boiling up in him, "one of those ants has nevertheless crawled up a birch tree as high as it can and now presumes to think for all the rest, and to decide what the people have a use for and what they have not. I am an ant myself." Suddenly something broke loose in him . . . "But I don't crawl up a birch tree, I drag a caterpillar ten times my own weight into the antheap. So be good enough to . . ."

"To give you a formal answer in writing?" Drozdov sat down at his desk, and then said nothing more but rubbed his forehead with his yellow fingers, waiting. Then he added: "Or would you be satisfied with this . . . er'm . . . cordial talk?"

"Please write with all the formalities," Lopatkin said.

"So you want to put up a fight for your caterpillar?" Drozdov said frigidly. "Very well, very well! We'll fight!"

He rose formally and held out his hand to Lopatkin.

Two days later Lopatkin received a letter from the deputy chief of the technical department, with a flowing signature that was illegible. "Your complaint has been submitted to Deputy Minister

174

Shutikov, and has been rejected as presenting incorrectly the course and decision of the Technical Council of C.S.I.F.R."

Lopatkin had known in advance that this would be the answer, yet all the same when he read it, he grew pale, went out to the hotel lavatory, and smoked his home-grown Siberian tobacco in there for half an hour. Then he went back to his room, and scowling and muttering threats, wrote two letters—one an answer to Shutikov and the other a complaint addressed to the Ministry.

From that moment it was as though a new life began for him. Every morning, having trimmed the frayed sleeves of his tunic and cursed himself for the hundredth time for having refused the suit Drozdov had offered him in Muzga, he marched out to do battle, first carefully drawing up a plan of campaign. With long, nervous strides he almost ran across Moscow to be received by some committee, or commission, or directorate. Meanwhile his brain was not inactive; on the contrary, it was working vigorously, conjuring up for retribution now the smiling, amiable Shutikov clad in a golden halo, now Drozdov's complacently closing eyes, now the naïvely astonished effeminate Fundator. And Lopatkin destroyed them all in the wink of an eyelid. "What are they saying about me among themselves?" he brooded, whispering to himself: "Unfitted! Trash! Possesses no powers of penetration! Oh, how I would like to be one of them, just for one hour, to see what they are really thinking! Do they see or can they understand what it is that makes a man's eyes blaze? Do they know that I am right? But in that case—why, they would be criminals! And if not, they are fools! Then how is it they are sitting where they are, this Shutikov and this Drozdov?"

Sometimes Lopatkin stopped dead in the street, as though he had run into a wall. That was when sudden doubts arose in his mind. "Could it be that it is I who am wrong?" he thought, growing pale, his hand reaching into his pocket for his tobacco pouch. When he had lighted a cigarette, he walked slowly on, once more reviewing every aspect of his case. "But Academician Florinsky was in favor of my machine from the start. And there were other such opinions, too, after all. And Galitsky—he is a well-known, serious worker! They ought at least to build an experimental proto-type. That's what they ought to do! Then why don't they? Are they chary of spending public money?" As he thought of all this, Lopatkin would suddenly laugh out loud, astonishing the passers-by. He could not suppress this bitter laughter when he remembered Avdiyev's machine, which had been built, only to result in losses amounting to millions. It was not even a machine, but merely a primitive contraption—yet it had left not the slightest stain on the solid reputation of this "Columbus."

His thoughts were clearest during the night. He tossed and turned in bed and often, at midnight or around dawn, went out to have a smoke. He got used to writing down his thoughts, and at the end of each week he used the notes to compose one or two letters that contained caustic allusions to certain persons who had "transformed a public institution into a bureaucratic stronghold" or with exposures of the "mutual assistance between monopolists" which "is destroying every live idea born among the common peo-ple." Having written the address always of the same committees or newspaper offices on the envelopes, he would drop them in a letter box, whereupon his overheated brain would immediately suggest to him a better and more certain move, and a fresh letter.

As he flung his best, most logical arguments into the face of an imaginary Shutikov or Drozdov, Lopatkin stopped more and more often to draw a deep breath and, with surprise, to put his hand on his chest, over his heart, or on his back, on the shoulder blades. The clearer his thoughts were, the stronger a hitherto unknown but increasing pain pressed on his heart from behind.

He made an appointment to see a doctor at the polyclinic and one morning, feeling somewhat frightened, he entered the white surgery that smelt of valerian. At once, in a hurry, he tried to de-scribe in detail to the doctor all his pains. Two nurses turned to look at him and the doctor, an old woman with her hair dyed yel-low, said to him several times as she filled in his index card: "Don't excite yourself! Calm yourself, comrade!" She listened to his heart-beat and his lungs, then wrapped a strip of black material connected by rubber tubes with a manometer and a rubber ball around his bare arm. As she pumped air in the red fluid rose in the manometer tube, and then began to fall by soft jumps.

"Young ma-an," the doctor drawled, following the movement of the fluid with her eye, "your blood pressure is too high. You must take exercise and sleep; sleep and take exercise, and not worry! Eat fruit. On no account take meat or spirits. This sort of thing can end up very nastily, so watch your step!"

From that day on Lopatkin ordered himself to, and in fact did, manage to forget that he had invented anything. He now circled the city by a definite route twice a day, a walk of five kilometers each time. After his walk he swallowed some tablets and lay down to sleep, and if he found a letter waiting for him, he threw it unopened into the suitcase under the bed.

He continued this regime for about ten days, and the business of attending to his health might have dragged happily on for a month if something had not occurred that greatly affected his destiny. One morning he was walking his usual beat and looking at the day's newspapers stuck up on wooden notice boards. Everything was exactly as it had been the day before and all the newspaper articles still by-passed his conscious attention that had been so severely inhibited during his unexpected illness. He went from one paper to another, scrutinizing the houses he passed on the way, or reading signboards and smiling if he happened to notice such phrases as: "corsets, falsies, and half-falsies," since funny things are allowed in a sickroom. He was strolling along in this way unthinkingly following his new lazy habits, stopping occasionally to glance at a newspaper without actually reading anything, when suddenly he saw standing out against the undifferentiated background of print a banner headline: "Open the door to innovators!" It headed a long article that took up the entire feature space in the paper, and was signed by none other than Deputy Minister Shutikov!

Lopatkin was surprised. He smiled as he ran his eye over the article, exclaimed, "Well, well!" and shook his head. Then he began to read the article from the beginning, but after the first paragraph he frowned again and exclaimed in a threatening whisper: "The devil! That scoundrel! No, I can't let that pass!" Then he quickly crossed the street, bought a copy of the paper at a newsstand, and with long strides hurried back to his hotel, stopping every now and then to make a note of some useful idea.

Once in his room, he sat down at the table and spent the rest of the day, until late that night, writing a letter to the editor of the paper.

Why [he wrote] *has the enviable opportunity of summing up our technical achievements in the columns of your universally respected paper been afforded to Comrade Shutikov of all men? Perhaps he was commissioned to write the article in his capacity as chief of one of our great technical departments? But ask a thousand inventors, those for instance who have had dealings with Comrade Shutikov, and I am certain that 95 per cent of them would say that Comrade Shutikov had not helped them, but had only smothered their inventions. A past master of the smoke screen, he has deceived you, too, comrade editor. He writes: "During the past year alone more than four thousand inventions and labor-saving devices have been installed in the enterprises run by the Ministry." But ask him how many of these were inventions in the true sense of the word— that is, innovations that radically break with old procedures and so demand special attention on the part of the superior authority. If you put this question to him, you will see at once why he has lumped together under one heading both labor-saving devices and inventions: he is acting like the quartermaster who substitutes hardtack for meat, and then covers the operation by using the word "provisions." The author rightly points out the advantages of continuous production and centrifugal casting in his article. Yes, but as long ago as 1944 . . .*

Here followed twelve pages that accurately described Lopatkin's vicissitudes.

I gave up my job at his call [he wrote late that night], *and came to Moscow. And once here, I was rebuffed by him and the funds assigned to the construction of my machine were used by him to construct Avdiyev's machine, which will produce nothing but losses. Recently a tendentiously hand-picked committee rejected my project; I wrote six letters to Comrade Shutikov, describing in detail all these wrongdoings, but received no answer at all. Comrade Shutikov had promised to see me, but up to now I have made sixteen unsuccessful efforts to obtain this interview. I have neither been received nor connected by telephone.*

Lopatkin decided to take this letter to the newspaper office himself. After polishing his buttons and his shoes, he entered the pinkish-colored building of the newspaper combine at exactly two o'clock. Here he was at once surrounded by the peculiar smell of printing, like the smell in a kerosene store. He got into an elevator with two photo-reporters and a woman messenger carrying copies still wet from the press, and rode up to the fifth floor. The correspondence department was still closed. He asked the messenger when it would be open and received the incomprehensible answer: "When the flight is over."

He decided to wait, and wandered about the building at random, reading the inscriptions on the doors with interest. A passage led into a spacious room with oval columns and a picture window in place of one wall. Here heavy armchairs covered in stridently patterned violet velvet were ranged around a table for visitors. Lopatkin sat down in one of them. A minute later a gray-haired, emaciated old man with dirty white whiskers, dressed in a shapeless gray overcoat that was knitted out of thick thread like a stocking, came in quickly from the passage. He held a gray cap behind his back. Sizing up Lopatkin quickly through his spectacles, with shrewd, feverishly bright eyes, he turned with a scarcely perceptible shrug of one shoulder and sat down in the armchair next to him.

There was silence. Half an hour later Lopatkin gave a cursory glance at his neighbor. The old man was fidgeting nervously with the toe of his patched black boot. "Sabotage!" he whispered suddenly. "Some sort of evil aim!" He turned to Lopatkin.

"Have you ever been a literary man, comrade?"

"Why? Are you one?"

"Imagine it! The article was already set up in type," said the old man, not answering his question. "It is to be in that very issue! But the editor took it out!" He squirmed angrily and shook his head. "It all happened as Schubert says in the song: 'He took her with a smile and I gave way to tears.' Though of course you wouldn't understand. . . . Try thinking up something serious, any-thing—a machine, for instance. Submit it. It comes up for con-sideration. You see looks directed at you!" He shook his head and his voice sank to a deep bass: ". . . as though you were a rogue and a swindler! Then you will understand!"

"You are an inventor, I suppose?"

"No need to ask, my dear fellow! What have you got there—a letter? Let me see it."

He snatched the sheets of paper deftly out of Lopatkin's hand, and held them up to his spectacles.

"Quite clear! So you have a certificate of invention!" he said as he read. "So you are Lopatkin? Dmitri Alexeyevich?" His tone grew perceptibly warmer, changing with an astonishing rapidity. "You have written a sound letter, Dmitri . . . Dmitri Alexeyevich. If I were the chief"—here he laughed shortly—"I should immediately write on it: 'to be carried out at once.' But as it is I advise you to take my experience into account and not waste your efforts!"

"But listen! . . . I am not applying to the C.S.I.F.R., this is to a newspaper."

"My dear fellow! My *dear* fellow! Who in this office could decide which of you is in the right, you or your Shutikov? For the time being it is Shutikov—he is a personage endowed with the confidence of the state, and you the man in the street. Your affair is of a most specific nature. This is not a quarrel about who should have a cer-tain flat. In order to decide this question, the letter must be sent to be examined by those who know. And how many are there who *do* know? And where are they to be found? In that very C.S.I.F.R.! All you have done is to change the needle, Dmitri Alexeyevich—that is your name, isn't it?—but it is the same old record, a very old one indeed, and it will play the same old tune: 'Refuse, refuse, refuse! . . .' "

Lopatkin frowned.

"Don't be annoyed with *me!*" the old man said even more kindly, turning toward Lopatkin. "Judge for yourself: your letter comes into the hands of the chief of the correspondence department himself. He is a decent sort, he wants to help you. But the letter is incomprehensible to him: something about ferrostatic stress, something about the properties of cast iron. . . . This must be sent for approval. To whom? Here you warn that the C.S.I.F.R. people are monopolists. But who will undertake to look into it and, what is more to the point, who can prove it? And without authoritative proof, you can't get anywhere around here. Does Little Red Riding Hood know that a wolf is lying in Granny's bed? Just you try calling the venerable grandmother a wolf! Have you ever acted the part of a slanderer?"

"N-no."

"All this is according to rule. You produce something new, and this new thing is sent for an opinion to the old!"

"And why not to the new?"

"Because it is always the old women who bustle around newborn babies. And you—you are new!"

"I can understand all this in general, and I built no special hopes on this letter. But if, from your own experience, you could predict for me . . ."

At this moment the passage filled with hurrying, gesticulating people. Obviously the "flight" was over. The old man stood up.

"It is not difficult to predict, comrade. Let's meet again in half an hour. Here."

He walked quickly away, with a youthful step, and turned into the passage. Lopatkin waited for a bit, then got up, and with an air of casual indifference betook himself to the correspondence department. An elderly woman, who must have been the head of the department, asked him to sit down opposite her, listened attentively to his conclusions, and read the letter.

"We shall check up on this, comrade," she said thoughtfully, scrutinizing him with a remote expression. "For the time being I can say nothing. We'll write to you."

When he returned to his velvet armchair, the old man with the spectacles was already there, biting his knuckles, deep in thought.

"Wherever one goes, it's as if the devil had been there first!" he whispered, looking sideways. "Throw him out on his ear—that's what they say! No interview!"

The old man got up and they walked silently along the passage.

"At one time I applied the wrong tactics," the old man began, on the stairs. "I made rows, forced my way into offices. Now I know better, but now it's too late—I am known everywhere as being a bit touched! Just remember that! Oh yes, you wanted to know what to expect. Listen, this is your road: you will run to and fro bestirring yourself, and getting there in the end, and your invention will be spirited abroad!" He whispered the last few words, a mysterious gleam coming into his eye.

"Well, now! That's the last thing I am afraid of! Nonsense!"

"You'd better not say that!" The old man brought his whiskers close to Lopatkin's ear. "You are talking to a man who underrated economic espionage, and suffered for it!"

"You don't say!" As he spoke, Lopatkin involuntarily took a closer look at his new acquaintance, at the shapeless overcoat that resembled a knitted sweater, the gray face, runny nose, and yellowish gray whiskers. "Actually suffered? Tell me about it, please."

The old man motioned to him with a glance: "Let's go out into the street." They went down the stairs in silence, passed through the mirrored labyrinth of the lobby, and once out in the street, this strange specimen of a man thrust his arm through Lopatkin's.

"I won't ask you for identity papers!" he said, taking a fleeting look all round him. "I have studied your face. It is a splendid passport for an inventor, in which everything is registered, including the length of his experience. So I'll tell you something: all my life I have been under the observation of foreign intelligence agents. Though they proceeded very crudely, they managed to steal one of my best inventions. The others I successfully preserved."

"So you are not a literary man?"

"Surely you can see what sort of literary man I am! I tried writing reviews of the technical journals for this paper. I almost became a literary man, but the editor got wise to me in time and sent my stuff to be checked by our friends. Yes. Well, first of all, let's make each other's acquaintance now that we have got as far as this. My name is Busko, Professor Busko, Evgeni Ustinovich."

Lopatkin, looking forward to an interesting conversation, rolled a cigarette, and held out his pouch to the professor, in order to seal their acquaintance with a smoke. But they had just come to a stand around which some drunks were lounging. The old man excused himself, approached the little window, counted some money out into his palm, waited for a moment, then pushed the money across the counter and quickly tossed off a drink.

"I have chased around too much, you know! Everything inside here is cold and wheezy!" he said, putting his hand on his chest and coming back to Lopatkin. "Now, where shall we start? Ah, yes —well—my specialty is fire."

With that he began a long circumstantial story. And their conversation was as unhurried as their leisurely pace through the city on their first walk together.

By six o'clock in the evening, when Lopatkin had already heard a third part of his companion's history—how twenty-five years earlier he had discovered a powder that instantaneously put out any flame, how this invention had been rejected by one consultant and expert after another, and how finally fire extinguishers containing this same powder had appeared in foreign countries—at six o'clock the companions found themselves trudging along a narrow, dark street, Liakhov Street, opening off Sivtsev Vrazhek Lane. Lopatkin might almost have imagined that their legs, which are apt to choose their own route during conversations between scientists or thinkers, had

183

brought them here of their own accord. But after they had passed a few houses, Professor Busko, calmer after telling the story of his sufferings, suddenly stopped, pointed toward a two-storied dilapidated house that was squeezed between two enormous gray-stone buildings, and said:

"This house was built before the great fire of Moscow. Although it is made of wood, it was not burned down. And it will certainly not be burned down now," the old man laughed, "because I am living in it."

3

LIAKHOV LANE was built up on both sides. Some of the houses were gigantic buildings, some little wooden cottages, with whitewash over the wood. Quietly and stubbornly the old Moscow lived on, side by side with the new, at the gates of which stood glittering motorcars—the Moscow of steel, reinforced concrete, covered by plaster and faced with polished shining granite. Dmitri and the professor came to a tall house with several dozen obelisks on its roof and over the entrances. On its side wall Lopatkin saw an enormous poster with the inscription: "Household Goods Insured." There was also the picture of a couple, a respectably dressed man and woman, sitting rather diffidently on divans to right and left of an open record player, with a radio on one side of them and a wardrobe with a mirror on the other.

"They are listening to Klavdia Shulzhonko!" Busko said with a laugh, taking his guest's arm. "They have been sitting at that record player for years. There is a couple exactly like them in our flat."

The old man conducted Dmitri through a high arch into a courtyard, and now they were in old Moscow, among rambling wings, barns, and sheds with dovecotes on them. After several more turns they again caught sight of the same ancient patrician house, its columns and stone steps sunken in the ground. They walked up to the second floor, and while the old man fumbled for the keys in his pocket, Dmitri gazed pensively at the high carved door, on which were almost a dozen bell buttons. "Ring for Petukhov only," "Sinitsky," "Zavish and Tymiansky only," "Bakradze," he saw inscribed on scraps of paper stuck under the buttons. "Newspapers for Petukhov" was written on the iron mailbox.

185

At last the old man opened the door, and Lopatkin, looking about him, entered a long, dim passage with a very high ceiling. This high, smoke-stained ceiling was all that was left of the patrician apartments. Everything here was divided into small and yet smaller rooms. Old Moscow was sick, and the inhabitants who overcrowded it—even those who loved old things—dreamed openly of new individual apartments, even if their ceilings were low.

"By the way, my first invention was concerned with this sort of thing," the old man said, guessing Lopatkin's thoughts; "it had to do with bricks and ceramics."

"And mine, too, incidentally." Lopatkin sighed. "Yes, mine also has something to do with housing—it concerns pipes."

"Have you noticed the ceiling?" the professor said. "It's old-style stuccowork."

While Lopatkin tried to discern this stuccowork, the professor snatched something deftly from the wall which was papered with yellow wallpaper. Lopatkin could only make out a hook made of thick wire in Busko's hand. The old man turned his back on his guest, fumbled furtively with the hook, and a little low door opened in front of them. Inside the door was a huge wooden bolt containing all kinds of screws and springs.

"Shnip-shnap-shnurr!" Lopatkin said in a fierce voice as he looked at this device.

"What's that?" For a moment the professor was startled. Then his alarmed face twitched and he smiled diffidently. "That's from Andersen, isn't it? To my address? Right up my street! All right, have your laugh! This is my faithful watchman, and there are things worth watching in here."

He put on a bright light and they entered a small room that felt cold and neglected, as though no one lived in it. The first thing Lopatkin saw was a large porcelain mortar on a table in the middle of the room, and beside it a saucepan containing a bluish grease. The cover of an open book printed in Latin type was thrown on top of the saucepan and was sticking to the grease. On the same table, beside an unwashed glass, lay sheets of manuscript spread out

186

fanwise and held down by heavy ceramic tiles and cubes, which were obviously the professor's own handiwork. On the floor and on the chairs books, some singly, some stacked in piles, were collecting dust; on the window sill were dirty test tubes and curiously curved flasks, plates, a teapot shining with a dim luster, and kiln-fired slabs and cubes stacked in little pyramids. Half the wall space was taken up by a large cast-iron stand, a "drawing combine," and beyond it, on a long chest, was the crumpled unmade bed of the room's occupant.

Lopatkin scrutinized every detail of this room as though he were in a museum, while the old man switched on an electric hot plate, lit a kerosene heater, and hung his overcoat on a nail. He was now clad in a short black jacket, shiny at back and at elbows. He stood facing his guest, rubbing his hands and revealing yellowish cuffs with old-fashioned cufflinks.

"Now it's warm, sit down. Bring out your tobacco, we'll smoke and go on with our conversation. Oh, yes, where was I?"

He put a heavy ceramic cube into Lopatkin's hand and began telling him the story of his second invention—a ceramic that did not require a special type of clay. There was still hope that this invention had not yet drifted away to foreign countries—at least, if it had, the professor had not heard. And how all these stories resembled one another!

". . . then I wrote a complaint about him to the higher authority and of course it was sent to Fomin and he organized a technical conference to crush me for good. Thirty persons, all of them subordinate to Fomin, took a decision in my absence, all of it dictated by Fomin. 'Busko is a hooligan, Busko must learn how to approach people in the correct manner!' But he is a public man, it is he who ought to have the correct approach! You may dislike the inventor, but the invention may be good for all that! But they—instead of *ad rem,* look, *ad hominem!* Not 'what has he invented?' but 'who is he?' And then the same members of the commission pinched my technology bit by bit."

187

"Yes," said Lopatkin, sighing vaguely for appearance' sake. He both believed and disbelieved the old man.

"I see that you don't know anything yet!" The professor snatched the cube from Lopatkin's hand and threw it angrily on the table. "You are in good health, you are gifted, cheerful. Are you any judge of men at all?"

"One must expose these dodgers more actively!" Dmitri said in a jocular tone, still looking about him in wonder.

"More actively! Scientists are not always adapted to fighting such battles. You can drag some of them to the fight by the ears and they are still incapable of it!"

"Evgeni Ustinovich, have you ever written anything? Not about technical journals, but about yourself?"

Instead of answering, the old man walked silently to a corner, dug into the heap of books there, and threw on to the table a packet of envelopes with black and colored rubber stamps on them.

"Here, have a look! There are eight letters here, I believe; I haven't counted them. They are merely rubber stamps, my dear fellow! Don't look at the rubber stamps, look here—at the signature. Who, for instance, is this Minayev? I don't know him. But from the answer it is obvious that he is a youth, and that all he can understand is that the matter concerns such and such a department, such and such a section, and so must be sent there. All letters revolve in an orbit of their own. The rivers all flow into the ocean but the ocean never overflows; nor does it revolt. The rivers return to the point where they rise and flow again. Besides, about whom am I to complain?"

He stopped. Something powerful—perhaps a great but sorrowful mind, perhaps madness, radiated from the dark eyes that seemed to float behind his spectacles.

"You don't believe? You need evidence? Here you are!"

He ran to the corner and from there began to throw on to the floor at Lopatkin's feet soiled blue-green sheets of paper with red seals on silk ribbons. Lopatkin gasped in spite of himself. They were all certificates of authorship. Lopatkin had only one such

188

certificate, but here were six—no, eight!—stiff blue-green sheets of paper falling at his feet! Lopatkin hurriedly picked them up.

"People are walking in the street," the old man shouted, becoming more and more excited, knocking at the window and still shouting. "And I cannot give them all this! Not even as a gift! I would give my life for good measure . . . and . . . I am not allowed to!"

He turned away, raised his sleeve stealthily to his face, wiped something away, and sniffed.

"I am like a savage now," he said, growing calmer. "My mind is still alive, I dream of airplanes, but—I have no means of making one! I am constantly being defeated. I have no laboratory, no assistants. With a single technical assistant I could get into production! Look, I even howl! And the time will come when you, too, will start crying! Go running to them!"

"Evgeni Ustinovich! Take me, for example, if I had not registered my invention, I would offer them coauthorship. Let them have nine tenths, or the whole of it, devil take them! That's not the point, after all!"

"And are mine not registered? I, too, have been fool enough to register them! Now they will look for a solution of their own; nothing else will do. 'No one would work for *you!*' is what they would say. Besides, what do you want?" The old man's voice hardened. "To fatten the Fomins? That the damned Poles should get my cradle? No, rather let it burn, and me with it, like Taras Bulba!" He squirmed like a madman. "They would take everything that I have lying in this chest, and sell it abroad. Catch me giving it to them! Now, I don't register my finds any more. Thank God! for the last five years, if I have gone there, it has only been in order to reconnoiter. That is enough. There is no point in having more enemies than one must. Now I pack everything away in the chest; at least spies cannot get at the stuff there!"

"Perhaps one might say that these inventions are already . . ." Lopatkin was about to remark.

The old man looked into his eyes and guessed his doubts. With

189

an unexpected and astonishing strength he pushed the heavy drawing stand aside with one hand and threw the bedding off the chest. He unlocked the massive lock, raised the lid, smiled with avid satisfaction as he gazed down into it, and silently invited Lopatkin to look at his treasures. Coming closer, Lopatkin was surprised: there was strict order inside the chest, which shone bright and burnished in spotless cleanliness. The professor's treasure consisted of a few dozen books and files, ranged in stacks on the bottom of the chest, which was lined with fresh newspapers. Test tubes glittered in cardboard boxes; red, yellow, and dark brown ceramic cubes were all placed separately, and along the sides of the chest glass jars containing white, yellow, and gray powders stood in rows.

"I am a 'miserly knight,' and this is my wealth. Millions! You think it is of no use to anyone?" the professor said, leaning with a proprietary air against the lid of the chest. "No good to anyone? Is that what you wanted to say?" He took out the smallest of the glass jars and shook the fine white dust off it. "They have stolen my powder which puts out any flame, and are selling my fire extinguisher in every foreign country. But now I have a new discovery in my hands, and no one knows of it. This powder is three times as effective as the one used in America for putting out fires in oilfields. I'll show you, if you like."

As he said this, he deftly took a broad paintbrush of the kind artists use out of the chest, and thickly strewed it with powder from the jar. "That's the appetizer," he said very softly, laying the brush on a chair and taking a large glass bottle full of a transparent fluid out of the chest. "And that is the drink to go with it." Lopatkin had not yet understood what sort of drink was meant, when the professor, with a frown of determination, shook the bottle and drenched the whole table with gasoline; Lopatkin smelled its sharp odor. The tablecloth quickly darkened. "Stand away!" the old man ordered, pushing Lopatkin aside. The whole table burst into brightly leaping, hissing flames—the professor had thrown a lighted match on to it.

"There you are. You see it, don't you? A fire!" said the old man impatiently, picking up the paintbrush with the powder on it.

He went up close to the fire, holding his bent arm in front of him, as though to shield his face, then slapped his wrist sharply with his other hand. The flame made a plopping sound, like the sound of a sheet flapping in the wind, and went out. The old man glanced at Lopatkin, silently, and hurriedly wrapped his paintbrush in a piece of newspaper, put it in the bottom of the chest, closed it, and threw his crumpled bedding on the top.

"Well?" he asked, pushing the drawing stand back in its place and coming back to the table. "What was it you said just now? 'Shnip-shnap-shnurr?' Don't bother about the table; it will all be dry in a minute. It's B70 aviation gasoline; it leaves no trace. Tell me, rather: is there any point in experimenting with the stuff? On a larger scale? Is there?"

"In my opinion it is urgent that you should at once. . . ."

"Oh, so it's urgent even! Fine! But now forget all you have seen here. Or else you, too, may begin thinking the kind of thoughts I do, day and night, and begin to lose your mind! Better, instead, tell me about yourself. If I were fool enough to take this and register it—what would happen? Expert opinion would be taken, I would be called a rogue, a blackmailer, a get-rich-quick on public money, and so on and so on and so on. I can't compete with them in that kind of billingsgate."

He opened the window to let out the fumes.

"Ah, it's freezing! Good!" he boomed, and pulled in a stocking hanging by a string from outside the window. He emptied twelve ceramic cubes out of the stocking, and made a note in a little notebook.

"I am testing these. I freeze them and thaw them by turns all winter. After that we'll test them for mechanical strength. . . . But I am listening to you. Tell me about yourself."

Lopatkin, somewhat abashed, keeping his eyes on this half-crazy sage, told his own story. It seemed very short and colorless. The old man stopped listening, while Lopatkin was still in the middle of it—

he sat motionless, lost in thought, staring at the table. Lopatkin soon ended his narration, and there was a silence, broken only by the old man's pensive sniffs.

"Aye," he said at last, shaking off his torpor. "And where do you live? Oh yes, you are no Muscovite. In a hotel? Two months in a hotel?" He pondered this for a while. "Look! come and live with me! The thousand roubles you still have left—why, it's quite a fortune! It would give us the opportunity to do some work until the summer, and then I'll teach you how to earn some money. Let us do that!" He jumped up and quickly began rearranging the furniture in the room. "Give me a hand. We must clear this corner out first of all. As quickly as possible. Everything should be done at once! Routine labor deprives us of time. And life is measured by time. Everything should be mechanized, so that people can still have the maximum of time left for thinking. . . ."

Between them they quickly cleared half of the little room of the cases full of clay and cement, of books and rubbish. Then the professor moved the drawing stand to the middle of the room, thus dividing it into two halves.

"This will be your half," he said. "And don't thank me, please. So far as I am concerned the more the merrier. And here is a drawing board. An excellent German contrivance. See, it's got counter-weights, everything is balanced. It can be moved very easily. I am giving it to you—I have no more need to work on it. Now let's see, is there anything else?"

There are still people who would not have understood either the professor or Lopatkin; the former because, having no money himself, he gave to an unknown person something he might have sold for three thousand roubles, and in addition did it as unobtrusively as he could; the latter because he did not thank the old man effusively for such a regal gift, but behaved in the same spirit: merely tapping the enormous drawing board with a finger and remarking: "A nice bit of work!"

Having finished all the work, they sat down and again lighted

192

cigarettes, placing their chairs in the no-man's land surrounding the table.

"At one time, fifteen years ago, I was a professor," the old man said. "I was a scientist, I lectured, and had a seat in all sorts of councils. Then I became a tiresome inventor. I began to dispute certain opinions and so was driven out of Paradise. The director of S.I. said to me: 'Perhaps you should move to another climate, Evgeni Ustinovich?' He gave me my salary for two months in advance, and I went away. I was still listed as an employee, but no longer went to work there. That's how it was," he said pensively. "But you have to live after all. You must go on living, you absolutely must. Otherwise you develop strange ways, as all those who concentrate exclusively on one thing do. I see that you think the same. I see everything. I am clear-sighted. All the same listen to what I say! Some of it may come in useful. Most of the time I have been a failure. You will have to find a different way. But above all, live! Do gymnastics. Go to the theater, to the art gallery! Read books! Find friends; a girl friend who looks at things with a childlike smile and believes every word you say! Such people will prevent you from becoming hard. With them, in their company, you will make discoveries: you will find out that there are such things as the sun, the cool of forest shade, gay birthdays, flowers. . . . Among such people you will rest, you will restore yourself."

There was a pause. "Cheerily, brothers, cheerily, cheerily, brothers, live!" the old man suddenly burst into song. "For with such a chief we don't need to grieve!"

4

SPRING had come. The changes spring brings to Nature are especially perceptible from a small room enveloped in the soundless dusk of semi-darkness. From early morning an invisible happiness enters the room. If you approach the window, the radiant sky calls to you. In the morning the sky is not blue, but infinitely pale. You look up at it, and imagine that something is waiting for you somewhere. But there is no one waiting, and it is better not to think of it.

An hour later, behind you, beyond a dozen stone walls, the sun rises. It is the sun for which you had been waiting, that cleaves the sky. If you open the ventilator, you sense the icy-cold scent of the snowdrop, the first, the sweetest flower of spring, which can no longer be seen when summer comes. You breathe it in trustingly, forgetting all else, like a boy who accidentally lifts to his face a woman's little glove. What are you to do? Where are you to go today? Nowhere! The flower is not for you! Better to sit and mend your coat, racking your brains as to where you can find two pieces big enough to cut out for patching the elbows. And for the trousers also. Couldn't you manage without the turn-ups? And the overcoat? It is still quite decent on the outside, but the lining is in rags, revealing all the secrets of the tailor's craft.

Dmitri had been living in Professor Busko's little room for two months. They got up early, punctually, in accordance with a timetable that Dmitri had pinned up on the door. His day began with a limbering up. When he had performed the deep knee-bend the prescribed number of times and swung a heavy pressing iron in every direction to unknot his muscles, he sat down at the table where the professor was already waiting. The two friends drank tea and ate black bread, smoked, and then each betook himself to his own working spot. The old man, humming "Cheerily, brothers, cheerily," would rub something to a powder in his immense mortar, or heat something else in his small homemade electric furnace. Dmitri sat for hours at the drawing board on which a sheet of paper was fastened, showing the faint outline of his machine.

Sometimes, usually in the morning, there was a soft knock at the door, and Zavish, a black-eyed rouged woman in a dressing gown the color of mother-of-pearl, brought Lopatkin a large envelope on which was the rubber stamp of some committee. Professor Busko neither wrote nor received letters. Zavish lingered, devoured by curiosity, her small swarthy hand relinquishing the envelope with reluctance. Sometimes the envelope was brought by Tymiansky, Zavish's husband, or by Bakradze, a tall, somewhat dandified engineer and black marketeer in fruit. Occasionally the envelope was brought in by Petukhov, an inspector of State Insurance, his wife, Zavish, and Tymiansky. That meant that the envelope bore the stamp of the Ministry. They waited to see what would come out of it. But one of the inventors would tear the envelope open, glance over the contents, throw it irreverently to the other, who would look at the letter and push it carelessly into a drawer.

The door would close with a disappointing squeak, and inside the room various dialogues and monologues would then take place.

"What a bunch!" the old man said. "And yet they have some sort of understanding. See how they push in to get a peep at the sacred flame. Like a shoal of sprats. They believe, I suppose, that the Minister himself is writing to us!"

"Yes, happily our fever passed them by. Though it is quite infectious, by the way!"

"Don't be afraid! In that respect they have iron health. Why should they worry, why try to push something through, why wait anxiously for anything? Innumerable discoveries have already been made and are at their disposal! Pay three hundred roubles and you can have a gramophone. In a luxury cabinet, too! Five roubles— and there's a record for you—Utesov! Double-sided! New discoveries?

What for? The world is already too full of amenities, and you need not be afraid that the mass will exchange them for letters from the Minister. God forbid!"

The professor burst out into his deep-voiced laugh, and Dmitri lowered his eyes. He saw that the neighbors were drawn, nevertheless, toward the little flame. . . .

"No, my dear fellow, there is a reliable immunizing process at work there!" the professor boomed. "They may make friends and love, but they take good care that such love should not upset their material balance. A woman of their kind would never marry a penniless genius. No, let Dmitri Alexeyevich show them his stocks and shares first!"

"So that's how it is!" Dmitri thought, and laughed. "She will never marry me. Yet it wouldn't be bad to appear before her as a victor, with every sign of success—a good quality coat and theater tickets."

But he at once admitted to himself that in Jeanne, too, there was a different, a new human being who occasionally looked at the world with clear eyes; that was the real secret of their relationship. That was how it had all begun.

"Yes, all right," he thought. "The professor understands that deeper side of life perfectly well. Then why these whimsies? Why does he behave like an old actor who has lost his voice? His voice isn't lost! After all, the powder exists!"

One day he said to him: "Evgeni Ustinovich, you are the luckiest of mortals. Your powder, of course, is something great. . . ."

"Is it?" The old man listened benevolently to this part of his remark. "Well, go on."

"But why don't you try and *do* something about it? Why don't you write or go anywhere? I think that in this itself there is a certain . . ." Wanting, with a joke, to mitigate the embarrassment he already felt, he added: "I find a certain kind of satisfaction in all this."

"What sort of satisfaction?"

"A certain element of play. Hope. . . ."

"Ah yes, hope. Do you know what Diesel said about it? He said: the older one gets, the less disappointment one suffers. Because one loses the habit of hoping. Hopes are cherished only by youngsters. You are right in saying that I am the luckiest of mortals. I could be that. Because an idea like this"—he laid his hand on his breast—"is a mountain, a great happiness, a treasure. It is only that Nature does not like injustice. For one happiness she gives you, she always forces a compulsory assortment of other things on you as well, counterbalancing happiness with cares. And she produces as many of these as are needed to balance the scales. But I am tired, Dmitri Alexeyevich. I am forced to renounce both."

"But why renounce the first, when you already have it there!"

"No, my boy. When one knows in advance that this thing will never see the light, when between you and others there lies a long road which one can no longer travel to the end, then it is as though the happiness had never existed. Only embers, as in the fairy tale. You know well enough how long the road is to the completed machine. Or rather, you don't know, because you have not yet traveled even half of it!"

"But your powder is ready. Why not show it to them?"

"Do you think I haven't shown it? Oh, they look at it with pleasure. An interesting toy, and ask very sensible questions. But as for making an official test, with minutes, and a copy of them to the inventor—ah, that's a different story!"

"But why? The thing is so convincing. . . ."

"The fakers, like Fomin, can also give a demonstration of that kind of thing. And in order to distinguish the genuine thing from a circus turn, one has to possess a certain knowledge. It is not enough to be an economist. And that is where the power of a gang of 'learned men' started."

It was after the first of such discussions with the professor that Dmitri, silenced but still obstinate, had pinned up the timetable on the door, to which he now subordinated his whole life. He watched the old man carefully, taking into account his experience—experience of which the old man himself was quite unaware. Dmitri realized that what must be fought first of all was weariness, the betrayal of one's self.

According to his own strict timetable, Dmitri always went for a walk at twelve o'clock. He turned up his collar, plunged his hands into his pockets, crossed several squares with long strides, turned into Gorki Street and walked along it to the Bielorussian Station, then turned and walked back the same way. These walks became a habit—a part of him.

From his first few paces after leaving the house, Dmitri forgot everything; his soul left his body and flew to a world of machines, while his legs worked automatically, like clockwork wound up for the day. Along the gutters workmen were laying drainpipes. Dmitri's feet went in the right direction of their own accord, while his thoughts were busy in a workshop, with a machine that was turning out of its entrails just such pipes as these, though they were not yet cooled, but still glowing cherry red. When he had produced a dozen such pipes, corrected certain defects in his machine, and written down a good idea in his notebook, Lopatkin's mind would leave the imaginary workshop and his legs resume their walk. They took him along the pavement, always farther, while he still remained unaware of the reality surrounding him. Now he was face to face with a narrow-eyed Drozdov, arguing with him: "But Leonid Ivanovich! What sort of genius am I? I am just a plain fellow, like that peasant in Dostoevski's *Adolescent* who got the better of the foreigners. The one who said: 'That's just the point, that it *is* simple, and that you, you ass, didn't know it!' That is the sort of fellow I am; what has genius got to do with it?" Then, suddenly, a new thought attacked him: "What have I lived to see! A Russian sitting opposite you and threatening you with a terrible danger: that you might become a genius in your own country! But you must on no account be a river, you must be nothing more than a mere drop. And he who thinks like this is the citizen of a country which can count its great talents by the dozen, in vast shoals! To hell with him—and with me; my machine is a mere trifle, and yet it might just as well have been another Lomonosov who came to Drozdov!" Lopatkin's legs by now had carried him to the cast-iron standard of a bus stop. "Ah! It's hollow! A pipe!" he said to himself, tapping the standard with his fist; then his face clouded. "Yes, you might try to make a pipe like this, too, but the tapering . . . how to manage the tapering?" he thought, already forgetting Drozdov.

After finishing his five-mile walk, Lopatkin got back to his room at three o'clock sharp, and by that time a saucepan with hot potatoes was always standing on the table, sometimes with a pickled cucumber on a plate. The two friends sat down to eat.

"Dmitri Alexeyevich," the old man asked thoughtfully one day, "how much money have we left?"

"Two hundred and twelve roubles," Lopatkin replied.

"Good. Soon my lads will come. There will be a nice little job for us."

In May, one Sunday, two working men, in unbuttoned sweaters, came to see them, one elderly and one young.

"Well, Granddad, ready for the job?" asked the older one, sitting down and licking a cigarette paper.

"Anything going?"

"Barulin seems to have something in view."

"Anything good?"

"Looks all right. On Metrostroy Street, the second house from the corner, the one that has the shop in it. New iron roof. Strip and re-cover. Large roof, U-shaped."

"Isn't Molokanov the superintendent there?"

"That's the man. Got a grudge against me, the swine! Can't forget last year."

"We'll put it right. Take it on. We can get it done quickly. Here's one more—he'll do the folding over."

"We won't fall down on the job, Evgeni Ustinovich. Just you go and see Molokanov today and have a look at the roof."

Toward evening Lopatkin, who, during the three months he had spent with Professor Brusko, had reached the point of being surprised by nothing, went with the professor to Metrostroy Street.

That year May was cool, and the two friends wore their overcoats over their shoulders. The old man walked faster and faster, pressing forward as he told Lopatkin all about the prospective job.

"Our cooperative gets together like this every summer. And we make good money. We do all the work on the principle of continuous flow, and on a single holiday we get more done than the average roofer of the fourth grade finishes in a whole week!"

But Lopatkin's thoughts were elsewhere. "What if it turns out to be the very five-story house? And he, the hero, all soiled with rust is banging away at the iron in the yard when she goes by with her little officer? The captain would smile, but there would be tears in her eyes, because she would have told the captain everything, and now she would not know what to do—whether to say hello to the roofer, or pretend not to see him. But the roofer's stern silence would mean: in spite of everything, victory will be mine. And then she might run to him, thrilled by his persistence, energy, and staying power. And the rust would seem brighter to them than all the military buttons in the world. Perhaps—as they wrote in the old novels—she would want nothing more than "to kiss those patient hands" that had held the hammer, and the schoolmaster's chalk, and the designer's slide rule, and now had taken the hammer up once more." At this Lopatkin laughed bitterly, and the professor, who had never stopped talking as he walked beside Lopatkin, was offended.

"You don't believe me? I give you my word! Last year we recovered the cupola of a church. It's on the Taganka, you can go and have a look at it. See for yourself!"

The house where the job was waiting for them proved to be almost opposite the five-story house that Lopatkin knew so well. The professor went off to find the superintendent, then came back with an aproned concierge, who walked silently before them up the stairs to the top landing, then to the attic, and finally to the roof, where a cold May breeze was blowing.

The professor pulled his cap down over his ears and turned up his collar.

"Whew! Enough space here!" he said, taking in the expanse of a rusty, much-repaired gabled roof bristling with dusty brick chimneys.

Some invisible being seemed to be sighing loudly and fitfully on the roof, now here, now there. The two friends climbed on to the ridge, and holding down the skirts of their coats, which billowed in the wind, walked along the ridge to the end. From there Dmitri looked down into the deep chasm of the street, criss-crossed by many wires, on to a multitude of gray-brown roofs, and, in the foreground, on to the sunlit house where Jeanne lived. Four or five of its windows were wide open. At one of them, in deep shadow, someone was sitting on the sill—perhaps it was she.

The professor climbed to the highest, most convenient spot, and, his spectacles gleaming, gazed down with narrowed eyes upon Moscow, on its roofs, and on some bright objects that were scarcely identifiable in the misty, darkening distance.

"It's beautiful! Dmitri Alexeyevich, come here!" he called. "Look how clearly one can see it all. This is how the discoverer of something new sees his case. He has climbed, one might say, to the second floor of a building, and can see from there the inconvenient paths along which men are proceeding toward a better life; he can also see the pitfalls where they will stumble and break their noses. He says: 'Look! Here! This is how you ought to go!' He cannot create *first-floor* values, because they are already behind him. It would be like making copies instead of creating great originals. With no thought for himself, the second-floor man hastens to grasp and to pass on to others everything he sees. He creates vast new values, and says to his first-floor disciples: 'Propagate them, popularize them!' But they don't understand. They are down there, among familiar, accustomed surroundings, dishing up the old stale stuff for new. For instance, they are working out a process that has already been discovered by Siemens! They develop it beautifully, complete with quotations and everything else. But genuine inventors they declare to be cranks or madmen. So what is one to do? You saw how I put out that fire. I am getting on toward seventy—

201

and here I am on this roof! Tomorrow I shall begin to produce a strictly first-floor value. Why are you turning your back to me? You are engaged in a conversation, and you turn your back on the object of it, so to speak!"

"I must make a confession to you, Evgeni Ustinovich. A friend of mine lives in that house."

"I see. Let's go and visit her."

"The trouble is, she is strictly a first-floor person!" Lopatkin was speaking softly, as though afraid that Jeanne might hear. "She is no dreamer, no romantic. If we were to gate-crash . . ." He laughed. "I must not present myself without some serious achievement to my credit, and it must be on the first-floor level at that. I mean that it must be acknowledged as such, and published in the newspapers. If a man has no gong to beat, he is not a hero—that is their psychology. In her eyes and in her parents' eyes I am a lunatic."

"Already! Unlucky man! How old are you?"

"Thirty-two, Evgeni Ustinovich, thirty-two. At present it seems to me that she is not yet quite convinced that I am crazy. I promised her too much. But if I were to put in an appearance looking like this, all her illusions would collapse."

"Then why do you still stick to her? To a mere skirt?"

"Somehow I can't help it, Evgeni Ustinovich. It used often to seem—and it still sometimes seems to me, that something stirs in her that cannot be completely awakened. Perhaps it is only my fancy. Well, that's all. But I would like her eyes to be opened."

"Such an operation would cost you dearly. She would have to see your sufferings and to realize her own guilt. She might see the first; she might see it even now, if she looked at you. But the second—her own guilt!—no, that they can never see! No! No!"

The old man glanced at the house with the open windows.

"In that case it is for us to go downstairs. We have had a look at the roof, and this one roof will keep us busy till the winter. All right, let's go."

He put his arm round Dmitri and gave him a gentle push. Without looking back, they walked along the ridge to the spot where the taciturn concierge was waiting for them by the attic door.

"This first-floor psychology is a great evil," the professor said meditatively, as they walked down the stairs. "It has seized many fortified positions. By the way"—here the old man lowered his voice and stopped, waiting for the concierge to go on—"by the way," he whispered, "foreign intelligence is taking advantage of all this. Spies are among them, making themselves pleasant, shaking hands, addressing them by name, and patronymic, and all that . . . and stealing our best ideas, because the first-floor crowd doesn't guard valuable ideas, it guards only its own handsome popularizing booklets."

Whenever Professor Busko mentioned spies, his yellowish whiskers quivered slightly; he sniffed as though a gnat had got into his nose, and his large, dark eyes gazed through his spectacles at Dmitri with a tormented expression. He held forth without noticing his companion's fixed gaze. Dmitri no longer answered him or tried to argue with him.

Two days later, when Dmitri returned home after his walk, and sat down at the table opposite the little iron stove on which potatoes were cooking, he noticed that the professor's wrinkled red hands were shaking as he lifted the saucepan off the stove.

Lopatkin helped himself to a potato and slowly put salt on it. At that moment the professor asked in a firm, ominous tone:

"How much money have we left?"

"Sixty roubles." Having said this, Lopatkin bit off half a potato with gusto.

"These are our last potatoes," the old man said. "We shall have to change over to the inventors' diet."

"Fine. And what is that diet, may I ask?"

"First of all, I must tell you that Barulin has let us down. We have nothing more to do with roofs, until we get a nibble from some other Barulin."

"Fine. Do eat, Evgeni Ustinovich, please!"

The two friends each ate a potato in silence.

"And what is this diet?"

"There are some bottles standing behind the chest, worth about fifteen roubles—a memory of better days." The professor sighed. "That will be enough for a month. We will buy black bread and fish oil. It is cheap and rich in calories. Though the discovery is not mine."

"As a last resort we still have another expedient," Lopatkin said, calmly sprinkling salt on a potato. "I am a seventh-grade engineer, you know. It's true that for the time being I am not very anxious to turn my hand to it, because I have a hunch about a certain matter, which concerns the casting of water pipes. And I think my machine could be a universal machine. So I ought to read all the literature, and get the hang of the thing. But if I go to work in a factory . . ."

"Why should you? Whom do you have to keep? Me? Rest assured that I can collect enough bottles to buy bread for us both. Besides, I've got another Barulin in a timber yard. If we load timber on to freight cars for two days, we shall have enough to live on for a month. We can easily make a living."

"Well, if we can, let's do it!"

However, they did not keep to this longer than a fortnight. The weather turned warm, which was just the thing for inventors. During this time the city was their workshop. The earth is a good drawing board. You can sit on a bench and think deeply. You can sleep at night with the windows open. One man wants love and the sound of leaves rustling, but another, a man of affairs, wants to save time. And with the window open you can get enough sleep in four hours without needing six. This is as well authenticated as the value of the fish oil. Another possibility is not to sleep at all and so earn a hundred roubles in a single night—enough for a whole month. You can go to the freight yards and unload freight cars, throwing off stones, or timber. And if there is early cabbage in the cars, you can take a bag along; they give you as much as you can carry away, if you only work with a will.

Lopatkin and his gray-haired but undaunted companion had

plenty of work during the summer. They bought themselves a cowboy shirt each, and Lopatkin, in addition, acquired a pair of gray half-woollen pin-stripe trousers. He even ventured to give the old man a present. Having guessed at a certain weakness of the professor's, he one day brought home and placed on the table before him a bottle of vodka. How many speeches were made over that bottle!

But the important thing was something else. Lopatkin had fixed a large sheet of paper on the drawing board, and on it could be seen the outline of a new universal machine for the casting of iron pipes of any shape up to a length of eighteen feet.

In August, when a train with watermelons arrived at the goods yard, and a watermelon diet had begun for our two friends, Dmitri started work on a sketch of his project.

The month passed in work on the drawings and nightly drudgery at the freight yards. It passed uneventfully, if one disregards a certain incident which remained unexplained for about six months and which ruffled the professor's peace of mind. One day, when Dmitri returned from his stroll, the old man, putting on a mask of indifference, examined him in detail as to whether anyone in the city, except the dispatching clerks in the Ministry, knew his address. Did he have meetings in Moscow with any women? Had he not seen any suspect individuals in the street shadowing him on the quiet? But to all his questions the old man got the same answer: "No! Didn't! Haven't noticed." And then, with a dark frown, the professor informed him that an unknown woman had called at the house in his, Dmitri's, absence and asked whether Comrade Lopatkin was living there. She had refused to wait, although the professor had tried amiably to detain her. She had gone away without giving her name or explaining why she had come. The woman seemed to be somewhat excited, she had fumbled with her handbag, and stared about her at the walls. She was intelligent enough—at first she had agreed to wait, and with that pretext had come into the room, had sat there for a little while on a chair, fidgeting, and had then gone away. She was young, she might have been a student. Her clothes were simple, severe, but of very good quality and well made. She wore a dark suit.

Dmitri frowned.

"Was her forehead high?" he suddenly asked. "And pink? With little curls combed down on it? Did you notice if she blushed all the time? That the blood came and went in her face?"

He thought that perhaps Valentina Pavlovna, on her way to a holiday resort, might have stopped over in Moscow. But the professor, looking past him into the distance with a sharp, uneasy glance, answered that no, her forehead had been low rather than high, although it was certainly covered with hair, and the hair did seem to curl. But she had not blushed; on the contrary, she had been pale.

This incident remained unexplained; the guest did not come again, and the two friends forgot all about her, Dmitri immediately, and the professor a little later. He was afraid of ambiguous situations and so, just in case, hid some of his notebooks and the little bottle with the white powder under the floor boards.

But the remainder of August passed very well. Dmitri made drawings of several features of his new machines and drew details of each feature on separate sheets of paper. The professor, too, had done well. He had at last found various different ways of making pottery, not out of kaolin, but out of ordinary earth dug up in the hills around the Leninsk Hills. In addition Lopatkin had exchanged letters all summer with various ministries, committees, and newspaper offices, and now had a fat file in which all these papers were neatly put away.

5

AUTUMN came; a damp fog descended on the street, and drops of moisture pattered rhythmically outside the window. A fire was made in the stove for the first time, and the crackling of wood told their hearts what words cannot express: that everything was provided for, that everything was ready for the winter. There was firewood in the woodshed. In the savings book there were funds enough to carry them through till spring. There was drawing paper in the chest, as well as several reams of other kinds of paper. One could fight on.

Life in the inventors' little room went according to a timetable, moving swiftly and silently, and it was due to this speed and accuracy that our friends were one day put to an unexpected and catastrophic expense.

On one of the cloudiest days Lopatkin noticed that the professor was silently and vigorously pounding something in his mortar. The old man had not delivered a single monologue that day, but had several times started humming to himself in his cheery, vibrant bass. Next day he was even quieter, but his movements even quicker. He would suddenly leap to his feet, rush to the kitchen for water, and sometimes leave the door open when he came back— a thing Lopatkin had never known him to do before.

And then a real commotion started. The professor urgently needed a press in order to make extra-solid ceramic cubes. The old man began to absent himself for whole days on end. His face grew haggard and an expression of urgency appeared on it. During the night he moaned in his sleep and in the morning again disappeared —he could not lay his hands on such a press.

Lopatkin recognized himself in the old man—his own silences and his own unrest, at the time when the first model of his pipe-casting machine had been in process of birth. And because he understood it all, he did his best not to hinder and kept as quiet as a mouse.

Finally the press was found, bought, and converted according to the professor's drawings. This swallowed up their entire fund. In their ardor, incidentally, they had never given a thought to the fund—they were watching only for results. Then the professor brought from the boiler room of the house next door a few raspberry-colored cubes, which had been "fired," and once more they had more important things to think of than the fund. The professor put a piece of an ordinary Metlach tile on a steel plate, grunted, and hit the tile with a hammer. The tile reluctantly broke into two. Then the old man solemnly placed a raspberry-colored cube on the plate. He handed the hammer to Lopatkin, for the blow had to be a true one, and the old man's very teeth were chattering with excitement. But even Lopatkin missed twice, for he was as excited as the professor.

Finally he hit the cube with the hammer. Splinters of stone flew in every direction; only a lump of pink crumbs pressed together by the blow remained sticking to the plate.

"Bother!" The old man lost his temper, but took himself in hand at once; he looked the other way and let the first minute pass in silence. "You certainly went to town, eh? Gave it a bang! Give me that hammer. This is how it must be done; simply by the weight of the hammer; it weighs two pounds, you know!"

And, putting a fresh cube on the plate, he hit it, with the weight of the hammer alone. He hit it diffidently, for he knew well enough what would happen. And of course the cube was smashed into tiny pink fragments.

That day all Busko did was to smash one cube after another with the hammer. Then he began whispering something to himself and went off to the boiler house, or sat for hours on a chair making it creak, rubbing his forehead, suddenly bursting out with "the devil!" and again taking up the hammer. Finally he admitted himself beaten—he took a broom without a word, and began to sweep up the stone crumbs.

"It is the right way," Lopatkin heard him say from behind the drawing board. "This is not the end, it is the right way." The old man had already calmed down and wanted to argue. "But the color was attractive," he said a little later. "Such a lively red! See, something of a man has even gone into that. And perhaps it isn't all lost, if I do succeed. . . . After all, I didn't put out the fire either at the first attempt."

But another day went by, his emotion subsided, and the severe summons of the timetable again called the two friends to work. The professor, after counting out the money that was required to pay the rent, the gas and electricity bill, again said that it was time to change to the inventors' diet. But now the dripping at the window was the promise neither of a pleasant autumn nor of good earnings. The two friends ate the last of the potatoes for dinner. Then the old man wiped his mustache, blew out his cheeks, and did not miss the opportunity of saying:

"Yes. The last belch! As you see, some people are willing to accept ups and downs of this sort. Such amplitude! And a man can still be happy. He experiences a new kind of happiness."

The old man felt that he was to blame for this "amplitude," and did his best to talk as much as possible in order to raise his companion's spirits.

"A simple diet now and then can do us nothing but good," he said, and went out to the kitchen to wash up. When he came back with the plates which he put away in a cupboard made out of a stool boarded all round with plywood, he continued in a cheerful tone:

"When I was working at this thing"—he put his foot over the spot on the floor under which his notebooks lay—"when I was getting close to my discovery, I didn't eat for two days and I never noticed it. By the way, do you know what hunger tastes like? I have observed it: it tastes like a copper spoon that hasn't been washed.

As I was saying, I didn't eat, although I could have postponed the work and taken a job, to earn a thousand roubles, if not more. Or I might have gone and exchanged bottles for bread. But I was following a red-hot trail. It was like a chase and I could not turn aside until it—this thing here—was in my hands—until it surrendered to me!"

"It seems as if you are trying to convince me," Dmitri said with a smile. "Let's have a smoke; I don't need any convincing! I, too, have sucked the copper spoon in my time, and didn't find it so very dreadful. Worse things happened in the war."

That day the professor bought a bottle of cod-liver oil at the chemist's, a good big bottle, and the two friends gaily celebrated their adoption of the inventors' diet.

Now their life proceeded evenly again, the quiet broken only by the resolute hiss of a pencil drawing a thick line on the drawing paper, by the crunch of sand in the mortar, or by some sudden comment of the professor's.

On a gloomy October day the old man explored the battered gas-mask case hanging on a nail in the passage, and found about a dozen potatoes in it. In his absent-mindedness he must have forgotten them. Sometimes, it seemed as if being forgetful might even have its advantages. The find was divided into two parts. One half the old man put in the pot and with assumed indifference carried it to the kitchen to cook, even humming a song as he did so. The other half he kept for next day. But the next day provided them with some food for thought.

When the professor was about to cook the potatoes he had left in the gas-mask case, he found not six, but about twenty, large potatoes. The case was filled right up to the top! The old man showed Dmitri this find.

"Cook some!" Dmitri said. "We can discuss it afterward!"

"I agree with you," the professor said, looking at the potatoes with distrust. "But what shall we do with the case? The unknown good Samaritan may think that we like his idea and have hung up

210

the trap again in the hope that something will be caught in it. What do you think?"

"Let's divide the potatoes to last us three days, and not hang the case up any more," Dmitri said.

When the pot with the hot potatoes appeared on the table and the two friends sat down to eat, they looked at one another silently for a while.

"Yes," Lopatkin said. For who knows how many times he had the feeling of a debt unpaid—a debt owed to an unknown, ordinary human being, who had suddenly laid bare to Dmitri his simple, generous soul and at once receded again into the elusive shadows.

"I can't keep silent!" said the old man, shaking his head. "And it is impossible to speak of such things in simple words. It is a miracle how a common potato can turn into a choice dish, an ornament to the table, because it has been in contact with a sterling human being!"

This occurrence caused Dmitri, and even the professor, to regard their fellow lodgers with fresh eyes. Now, as formerly, little painted Mrs. Zavish came in in her mother-of-pearl colored dressing gown and lingered as long as she could while the inventors tore open the envelope. But now Lopatkin saw in her eyes more than mere curiosity; he saw revealed in them the sadness of a lonely young woman, lonely though she had a husband, a husband with a weary look in his eyes and with modest little sideburns. Tymiansky came also, and Lopatkin thought: was it possible that it could have been he who had done this? Why shouldn't he have, after all? One can shave one's eyebrows out of simplicity, because others do, and yet remain a kind soul, and even be unhappy—and they had no children either!

Thus they regarded each fellow lodger with fresh eyes, not knowing which of them to thank, if only with a look. And there were many fellow lodgers in the flat, each of them an enigma, and each with a separate bell on his door.

They no longer hung the gas-mask case up in the passage. Twice a day—like monks—they sat down to a meal of bread, and while they

211

broke and chewed the bread, they discussed calmly the nature of men and of things. Now the professor talked mostly about their unknown friend, for whom he was making all his efforts.

"He is no savant, but he will understand everything!" the old man declared. "Show him my fire extinguisher, and he, after soberly weighing everything, will say: 'It must be tested. Perhaps it is useful!' The trouble is that between us and that man there is a middleman of imposing presence who regards himself as a devotee of science, as a servant of the state. He lectures conscientiously, year after year, always with the same text, gives expert opinions, writes reviews. Or else he is a gloomy departmental head, content to diestamp the same aluminum spoon for a thousand years; naturally fulfilling the plan to the extent of one hundred and two per cent! These people stand between us and the genuine common man, who, by the way, would be glad to have your pipes and my fire extinguisher."

"These are merely unsupported statements," Lopatkin baited him one day, gaily. "Simply music in aid of the digestion! To go with our inventors' diet! Tell me instead how to fight them."

"I have messed up my own fight. I used the wrong tactics. For the first ten years I tried to clear a sort of beam out of my way. My enemy, that Fomin of whom you have heard. I wrote complaints the whole time. But he is still doing well. Your Arakhovski was right, when he said that one should not give oneself away to the enemy. I gave myself away."

"But surely, if we hide our faces from our enemies, we also hide them from our friends. No. One must go into battle openly, always openly. And with our flag unfurled, clearly displaying our device. Written in large letters."

"And what is that device, pray? I don't seem to have heard of it."

"But you have read it. That is how we two came together."

"We came together because I liked you. That was all. I like visionaries, who live not by bread alone."

"That's right! You've almost hit it." Lopatkin bit off a sizable mouthful of his slice of bread and, chewing it vigorously, looked out of the window. "When I got all wrought up about that"—he nodded toward the drawing board—"at the same time I also had some general ideas. Do you believe in the building of Communism?"

The old man reddened.

"Somehow I haven't thought much about it."

"I never did believe in vulgar Communism," Lopatkin went on. "Those who think that under Communism everyone will strut around in cloth-of-gold are mistaken. The petty bourgeois whose heart is in the good things of life expects from Communism merely the filling of his belly. But in true Communism, many objects of crazy luxury, born out of the idleness of the rich, will be abolished."

"Excuse me, don't smother me in words. What has all this to do with the device? How does it tie up with your machine?"

"Quite simply. When I realized the significance of this machine and understood that it was needed, and that for its sake I should have to draw in my belt, I did not hesitate for an instant, but jumped gladly into this cold water." Here Lopatkin drew his belt in very tight. "To the last hole! See? Then I suddenly understood that Communism is not a construction thought out by the philosophers, but a force which has existed for a long time and which is covertly training cadres for a future society. This force has already entered me. How did I come to feel it? Like this! Never in my life have I worked as I am working now. I am working to capacity. Without ever looking back. I save time for no other purpose but for my work. Now about my needs. I could go and work in a factory now. I could earn two thousand, and buy a mountain of bacon as thick as my hand is broad. Or put my name down for a motorcar. Or money in a savings account. The account would grow and I would earn more and more. But I am not that sort; I have other needs; I want none of those things. I don't want that sort of happiness, the kind one sees in the movies: good food and plenty of it, a nice flat, a bedroom suite, lace petticoats . . . That is, of course, I would not refuse them. But if I had only those things I should not be happy. But if I get this job through to its conclusion, I shall be happy, even if I have no bedroom suite!"

"Rainbow chaser! What sort of Communism is it if you have to give up something that is dear to your heart in order to earn a living?"

"I don't say that we have got Communism yet. But I would like to have it now, not in order to get things for myself, but in order that I might give without being prevented."

"Now we have arrived at my proposition. Remember, I said that we were born too soon? So, come, hide your stuff under the floor boards, as I do."

"No! No hiding or camouflage for me! We must be frank with ourselves, it's the only way for us to discover one another. Why did you and I get together? Because we saw each to be what he is!"

"And what good was that?" the old man suddenly shouted. "We got together, so what? What if twenty fools like ourselves, all looking amiable, got together in this room? We would only sit, like slugs, under a wet rag. How do you help me? How do I help you? Flag indeed! Device!"

Lopatkin checked himself suddenly and did not answer. Biting his lip, he looked Busko up and down several times, as though he were an apparition standing there in front of him.

"Look at me as much as you like!" Busko said. "Make what faces you choose! What you see is your own future. And I look at you and I also make a face! Because in you I see my own damn-silly past!"

Lopatkin wanted to reply with a philosophical tirade, but realized that he really was facing an apparition who was incapable of hearing him. He walked to his drawing board and set to work. "I am thirty-three," he thought, "and you, Uncle Evgeni, are twice that age. It is very good that I found you: I can turn the rudder away in time—away from your old chest, closer to my fellow men, even if they are only these ones here, with their bell buttons on the door. I will look for kindness and fidelity in them to the end; they are here, and one cannot live without them. I have faith in them. Thirty years! How many more meetings there may still be for me!"

He worked in silence for a long time and the professor sat at the table and watched him. When he saw him pause for a long time, the old man called to him:

"Dmitri Alexeyevich! What's that you are counting on your fingers? If you are calculating terms, counting what you must have ready by such and such a time, kindly multiply by 'pi'!" A short, good-natured chuckle almost shook him off his chair. "Don't forget to multiply! By three point fourteen!"

"I have already seen!" Lopatkin said grimly. "And you, too, will see. More actors are due to appear on our stage, who will—"

"Who will be the same as Fomin."

"Who will help us as though they were helping themselves."

The old man shook his head skeptically: after all, he was sixty-nine. He had seen enough of this world.

But life is such that it can astonish a man—even in his seventieth year.

On the eighteenth of October, at twelve o'clock, soon after Lopatkin had left the house for his morning walk, there was a vigorous knock at the door, and a short woman who looked like a messenger, with a knitted shawl on her head, carrying a shopping bag made of many triangular pieces of leather, came quickly into the room. Out of the shopping bag she took a small, thick, oddly shaped package and put it on the table. It was wrapped in strong paper and pasted up; it bore the inscription: *Comrade Lopatkin. Personal.*

"Are you sharing with Comrade Lopatkin?" the messenger inquired. "Give this packet into his own hands."

"Who is it from?" The professor emerged from his half of the room, where he had been drying some reddish earth on the stove.

But the messenger seemed to be in a hurry. She was gone, loudly slamming the door. The professor looked at the packet, pushed it into the middle of the table, and wrote on its side: *18th October, 11h. 20 min.* He was not to be caught napping!

At two o'clock he cut a pound of bread into two halves and put the half which looked to him the larger in Lopatkin's place. Then he began to hum "Cheerily, brothers, cheerily," and went on stirring the red earth in the pan.

215

At that moment Lopatkin returned from his walk, wet, with reddened but hollow cheeks. Panting after his fast walk in the rain, he took off his overcoat, glanced at the package, hung his cap on its nail, wiped his wet hands, turned the package over and tore it open.

"Whew! My hat!" he exclaimed, and quickly took it apart. "Evgeni Ustinovich!" he called.

"I see, I see!" the old man said glumly from behind Lopatkin's back.

The package contained a solid wad of bank notes. Lopatkin weighed it silently in his hand, glanced at the old man, then sat down at the table and began counting the hundred-rouble notes. While he was counting, he cast friendly glances at his ration of bread. Then he broke off a piece of it, spread it with cod-liver oil, put salt on it, and as he chewed, went on counting the money as efficiently and indifferently as a cashier in a bank.

He had counted three thousand, and only then did he see a sheet of paper in the torn packet on which a short message was written in ink. He drew the note out and read:

Comrade Lopatkin, this money is yours. You are entitled to make what use you wish of it.

"This note must be preserved," he said, showing it to the professor.

"And the money?" the old man asked in alarm.

"Now we needn't bother any more about money. We've got it."

"I am amazed at you! You are just like a baby! Give me that money! I'll take it to the proper place at once, and the note, too. Can't you see that it comes from *there?*"

"I can see above all that the money is genuine," Lopatkin said. "I should say there is six thousand here. Yes, there is, this is the sixth thousand. And if it's from *there,* we must spend it all the quicker. After all, we haven't given the devil a receipt written in blood."

"In blood!" The old man's eyes widened alarmingly. He dashed to the door, opened it a crack, closed it again, and shaking his fingers in Lopatkin's face, began to beg him in a passionate whisper to have nothing at all to do with this money. He spoke convincingly. He said that he himself had often been lured into a similar trap, he had carefully studied the methods of foreign spies, knew for certain that the fact of this money having been handed to Lopatkin was already registered. *They* had elaborate means of effecting this. There was only one way of salvation, and that was to take the money at once to the proper place, and even that had to be done with caution, in order to deceive the enemy.

"You have convinced me," said Lopatkin.

"It's best to do it between five and six o'clock, when people are going home from work," the old man went on, shaking his head with an air of mystery.

"Let me have my say!" Lopatkin split the packet in two and calmly shoved the money into the pockets of his overcoat. "You have convinced me that I must buy myself a new suit and overcoat immediately, and replenish your wardrobe also. And it won't be a bad idea either to put something into a savings account, enough to last us six months. When we have done all this, at supper this evening we will go seriously into the question of who could have given us the money. But now let's go to the department store."

The professor looked at him, turned his back, and went over to his electric furnace. Dmitri said nothing, but began putting on his outdoor clothes. When he had buttoned up his overcoat, he put his hand on the doorknob and asked cheerfully:

"Well, are we going?"

The old man went on stirring the earth in the pan as though he had not heard.

"Evgeni Ustinovich!"

"Kindly leave me out of your unsavory affairs!" the old man said, very distinctly, looking out of the window as he spoke.

Dmitri went on his shopping expedition alone.

Who? he asked himself as soon as he had left the house. Who

could have sent him the money? The Sianovs? Where could they have got such a sum? Besides, it had not been sent by post. That's right, he must send Mrs. Sianov a thousand roubles. But who was the money from? Perhaps from Valentina Pavlovna, on her way through Moscow? Or Arakhovski? The latter was the more likely. "Well, whoever sent it, it was most timely!" he thought to himself with a sensation of youthful buoyancy in his feet. "It was very, very timely!"

That evening, when Dmitri got home again, he made an impression even on the absent-minded professor. He was wearing a black overcoat and a black hat. And when he took off the overcoat, there was a new suit underneath.

"Oh!" The professor could hardly suppress his disapproval. "How could you buy such a thing? The suit is much too tight. One can see at a glance that it belongs to an inventor! You look like an earthworm in it! You ought to buy a suit made for a stout man, so that the folds would fall loosely. You must exchange it at once!"

"It doesn't matter. Anyway, I've messed it up already!"

"I feel sure now that one day you will be a member of the Academy of Science!"

He examined the overcoat, praising it with reservations. Dmitri took a black hat out of a round box, and unexpectedly put it on the professor's gray head.

"I had an idea that you might not want to live alone in the trap after all, and so I bought you a hat!"

"Funny fellow!" said the professor. "I have merely thought the whole thing over and realized that we could set a trap for them, too, if we went about it in the right way."

And he went over to where a fragment of mirror was hanging on the wall.

"Ah! it's just as Ludmila behaved in Chernomor's house!" Dmitri laughed. "She thought it over, and began to eat!"

"To be properly dressed is useful," the old man remarked in an offhand manner. "I knew a man once—he had none of your gifts, nor your medieval chivalry—nothing but looks. Tall, an 'intelligent' voice, and well-dressed—a good overcoat, a shawl collar and all the rest of it. And, do you know, he got away with it!"

"Very well, I'll try. Perhaps I can get away with it, too!" Dmitri said.

6

Now that domestic needs were provided for, an inner voice again reminded Lopatkin that a man must *live*. But this time the reminder was more emphatic.

Yes, it was necessary to relax, that was obvious now. A man sometimes had to come out of his seclusion and mix with people. To live the life of ordinary people, who had everything except the habit of thinking concentratedly about ferrostatic pressure!

But here Lopatkin laughed, realizing at once that his position was like that of a man with stomach trouble, who has been advised to chew thoroughly everything he eats. One may chew and chew, thoughtfully and painstakingly, but it will never be anything like real life! If one prescribes to oneself: live!—things are doomed from the start. One must live without a recipe, for we all live as we can.

To laugh was all very well, but Lopatkin suddenly remembered how frightened the professor had been at the sight of the money sent by an unknown patron. "There's still a long way to go before I'm seventy. Until then one can pick up a bit more than that!" And he decided to try to plunge into the sort of life which until then had been, as it were, flowing past outside his window.

He began going to the theater with the professor, three times a month. In the Bolshi theater they saw two operas, in which two of the greatest geniuses had come together—Pushkin and Tchaikovsky. But the old man hampered him in playing his new role of young man of thirty. He scrutinized the public in the stalls and boxes, and, like Mephistopheles with Doctor Faustus, was constantly whispering in Lopatkin's ear, reminding him that he had sold his soul. In the theater the professor looked at nothing but the public. He studied those who sat in the stalls, and those who crowded the balconies. He imagined he saw enemies everywhere. But sometimes, pulling at Lopatkin's sleeve, he would point to someone in the gallery: "Look! that is certainly an inventor!" In short, the only things he took seriously were those connected with science and invention.

Soon it was evident that the professor detested symphonies also; he had no ear for music, and this fact provided Lopatkin with many happy moments. He began buying cheap tickets for the Conservatory concerts, and there, close under the roof, he sat in complete solitude, and the emotions of great fighters and long-dead martyrs came to life in him once more—emotions that had happily been recorded and which therefore lived on forever. He heard their sincere and ardent voices as if they were addressed directly to him. One day he went to a Sunday matinee concert for schools. The first thing to be played was the Second Piano Concerto with Orchestra, of Chopin, a plaster cast of whose small and childlike hand he had just seen in a glass showcase outside in the lobby. Lopatkin did not know the conductor, a little snub-nosed man with a composer's curly mane, nor the pianist, heavy, bald, and wearing a black frock coat. Schoolboys and schoolgirls with red Pioneer scarves round their necks were sitting all round him. The younger boys pelted each other with tightly screwed-up, well-chewed pieces of the program. The older girls, who already showed the promise of future beauty, glanced sideways at Lopatkin and giggled as they hugged one another. And perhaps simply because the audience was immature and was as yet ignorant of the soul's dull anguish—though Chopin, when he wrote his concerto, had been in need of sympathy and tenderness—perhaps it was just for this reason that the composer seemed to be picking one listener out from among all those in the hall—a pale, lean man with gray, softly glowing eyes and large, strong, thin wrists. At first he appealed to Lopatkin very softly, and he gave a start, feeling that he was being addressed. They understood one another instantly, and then the story, which was also Lopatkin's story, pealed out in full tones. He saw the hero, burning like a comet in the dark sky, a small man with the hands of a ten-year-old boy, and a gigantic

221

power of the spirit, who, at the cost of his own person, at the cost of his life, wished to blaze a path for multitudes of men. In the murmur of the violins against this fearful multifold background he glimpsed a desperate, single-handed struggle against the deep booming of the basses.

As Lopatkin went out into the street after the concert, his fists were clenched in his pockets. When he reached the corner of the street he thought to himself with a wry laugh: "Well, I've been to the theater! That was a fine relaxation!" It was useless trying to creep out of one's self.

Yet a few days later he again bought a ticket for a Conservatory recital. And this time it was Rachmaninov, with his Second Concerto, who expressed the same things to him. He expressed them from the opening, from the very first chords: men are not born to accept humiliation, to lie, and to betray, for the sake of rich food and a good time. The happiness of worms who are warmed by the sun is not man's destiny. For the sake of that sort of happiness it is not worth while being born a man—far better to be a worm. But man must be a comet shining brightly and joyously, not afraid to burn up his precious material energies.

Lopatkin went out to the lobby during the interval, feeling as though he had parted from a great companion to whom he had just said farewell, and as though that other, leaning back in a deep armchair, stricken in years, were still following him with his gaze.

"It must be my own thoughts that are so tensed; that is why I find special echoes everywhere of exactly what I am thinking about all the time!" But he remembered at once that there was another kind of music also, in which he felt nothing, in which there were no echoes at all. "So these echoes depend not on me, but on the composers!" he discovered suddenly. "These are their thoughts, after all! They have remained alive!"

Here his thoughts were interrupted by a young and very lively woman, who had recognized someone standing next to him and had broken away from the slowly-moving stream of people. "Sergei Petrovich! Fedia!" she cried, and pushing Lopatkin aside, seized her two friends by the hand—one was a large, tired-looking fat man with hair graying at the temples, the other a small, yellow-faced, wrinkled one. She shook their two hands simultaneously—the heavy and the light one, and began chattering very fast: "You know, I was late. As you are the organizer of today's outing, I must explain. . . ."

"All right, think up some excuse!" the big man said good-humoredly. "Or I won't let you go! I'll give you a good dressing down!"

"No, but this is serious! I have been trying to get a copy of Kuznetsov's *Physics of Solids* for Ivan. There wasn't a copy in our library. Has Ivan come?"

"Did you get the Kuznetsov book?"

"Yes, I did. I must go and tell him."

"All right. Go! Go! Put his mind at rest!"

"Listen, Sergei," the giant said slowly, following her with his eyes. "You might do something for our librarian. Something, perhaps, on the pay roll. And perhaps a bonus as well. Go slow on that, though . . . perhaps five hundred or so."

"It had already occurred to me." The little man scratched his ear.

"Well, let it occur again! She is a wonderful girl! And she has kids as well."

There was a pause.

"Ivan is worried," Fedia began again. "I heard that Bukhantsev was meaning to come; I'm scared. He does hit out so at times: guarding his Parnassus. How he went for Alexander Fiodorovich the other day!"

"Well, if he takes it lying down!" the little one said sharply, his eyes flashing in anger. "We, too, have our 'quick-witted Newtons'! We shan't let Ivan down!"

"No, we can't let Ivan down," Fedia agreed, and both were silent again.

Presently Fedia stirred. "Let's go and find the boys!" He turned the little man round by the elbow, and they threaded their way quickly and deftly through the crowd, as though both of them were suddenly driven by the same emotion.

This sudden move seemed to carry Lopatkin away as well, for he, too, although he did not yet understand what it was that moved him, began pushing his way through the crowd in the wake of the tall Fedia, striving not to lose sight of him.

But he did lose sight of him all the same, running round the lobby in an almost complete circle, and then just as suddenly finding him again. He caught sight first of a long divan, of the enormous Fedia, sitting in a corner, taking up hardly any space on the edge, his spectacles gleaming mildly. "Pierre Bezhukhov," Lopatkin said to himself. Sergei Petrovich sat on another divan, the librarian on a third. They had been obliged to sit down wherever there were unoccupied seats and were now conversing simply with a brief word now and again, or a gesture or a movement of the eyes, in order not to inconvenience the other people sitting near them, in all the brilliance of the evening dress they had put on especially for the concert. Along the wall were more divans, and armchairs in white dust covers, some of which were occupied by friends of these three; for here and there a head was raised in greeting; they were all talking about Ivan, who was sitting there among them and seemed about to undergo some serious ordeal. Their talk was like the chattering of a flock of birds that had just alighted in a garden.

Dmitri was seized by a sudden desire to join them, to perch on the same tree. He moved closer, and, by good fortune, the woman sitting next to Fedia got up and went away. Dmitri quickly sat down in her place; he did it so hurriedly that even the imperturbable Fedia was distracted from his conversaton. But it was a completely different man now who was looking at Dmitri coldly through his spectacles. The large, tired, gray-haired Fedia was guarding the boundaries within which he lived so comfortably with these young and not-so-young "boys."

Dmitri lowered envious eyes. He realized that these must all be workers from the same institution, most likely from a scientific research institute. They had probably studied together, perhaps or-

224

ganized their institute together, and fought for it together. At all events they were united by some very strong tie. They were here, beside him. Dmitri was even in close physical proximity to one of them, and yet saw no way of crossing the boundary and joining them. Yet he would have been the most obedient and diligent of workers. But to get *there*—not into the institute, but through to *them*—was possible only by undergoing a test and receiving a silent "yes" from each of them.

"Perhaps I am only imagining all this," he thought. "Am I simply tired of being unjustly branded as an individualist, and do I merely want to attach myself to living people?"

A bell rang in the distance, the light in the lobby was dimmed, and the "boys" all stood up; there were eight of them. Lagging behind the rest of the public, they moved toward the concert hall in a straggling line. Dmitri followed them with his eyes and then hurried to the stairs leading to his gallery.

"Yes, I am alone!" he thought. "I am alone even when I am sitting in the room with the professor, for he and I lack something, we lack whatever it is these people have. I need to talk about a lot of things, to check up on myself, but the old man! Something fundamental has been broken in his soul. We cannot open our hearts completely, because we are incomprehensible to one another. Ah, Sianov, Sianov! Valentina Pavlovna! It is they whom I lack."

But there was also the girl—the one who looked at everything with the smile of a child. He remembered her constantly. The thought of her pulsed in him, strong yet imperceptible, like a second heart. And now that he had a new overcoat and hat, he could go to see her. Nothing any longer stood in the way.

And one day he diffidently waylaid Jeanne as she was hurrying home, with a little brief case in her hand. She was wearing her black coat and a small light-green fluffy cap with ear flaps; a leather belt was drawn tightly round her waist, and she kept one hand in her pocket.

When a tall man in a black coat and hat suddenly blocked her way, she frowned and without raising her eyes any higher than

Lopatkin's chest stepped to one side, into the road, then raising her angry eyes by accident, and swinging the hand which was holding the brief case, with which to hit this impertinent fellow, she suddenly gave a start and began to run away, but Lopatkin laughed and seized her.

"Is it really you?" she asked doubtfully.

"Is it really I!" said Lopatkin, still holding her hands, and kissing her several times, as they stood in the road.

This seemed to convince her; she blushed and laughed doubtfully but happily.

"Let's go somewhere else quickly; there are people here!" she said, and they ran hand in hand, and turned up a side street. Here Jeanne stopped and kissed Lopatkin several times.

"So it *is* you? Listen, was it you that other time?"

"When?"

"Over there—by the shopwindow."

"What shopwindow?"

Lopatkin was able to give a loud and natural laugh.

Jeanne looked into his ashen face, and her brows twitched as if she were in pain. Something good, understanding, and kind seemed to break through, something that came from the bright sunlight, the forest coolness, the holiday in her soul.

"What shopwindow?" Lopatkin asked again.

"Oh, it's nonsense! I am always dreaming of you! Waking dreams!"

"That is nonsense, of course!" Lopatkin said. "Dreaming is not worth while—especially dreaming about me!"

"Well, and so you have come to Moscow! How are your affairs going?"

"What shall I say?" thought Lopatkin. "Which of her selves is it today?"

"Are you still Martin Eden?" she asked, smiling without much hope. "When you shave, do you still hang up something in front of you, to read at the same time?"

"No!" said Lopatkin, looking into her eyes still without discarding his inward mask. "I simply don't shave: that's an even greater saving of time!"

"Are you still inventing?" she asked softly.

"Yes," he said curtly, raising the mask for an instant.

"Where have you just come from now?" she asked, stepping back a little and looking him over. "You've bought a good coat."

"Where from? A concert," he said.

"No. Really? So you have had some success?"

"That's right. You can see: a new coat. And a Conservatory ticket in my pocket!"

She looked incredulously once more at his colorless face and the stricken eyes ringed with brown.

"I can't understand it! You were such a good teacher! An excellent one! Everyone liked you, both the boys and the girls."

Lopatkin shrugged his shoulders; he had forgotten to take the smile off his face, and this forgotten smile seemed to be waiting for someone to find it, in this inconvenient, exposed place.

"Listen, Dim. Let's go off somewhere together and take jobs as teachers." She gave him a quick, piteous look and turned away.

"Little Jeanne," Lopatkin said, "I have a very big job on my hands and I can't give it up. It is a certainty! I have already almost swum the Channel and I can see land!"

"Is that all?" she asked bitterly.

But it was not mere frivolity that prompted her. Lopatkin understood how much he had exhausted and aged her. For years past he had been describing his machine to her with an eloquent pride and each time the term ended she had still before her only an emaciated face, shining eyes, and a shabby coat.

"I am constantly coming across very fine people," he said quickly. "They are continually coming to my assistance and soon we shall really break through with our machine. Jeanne! Are you listening? You still have two more terms to finish, haven't you? My dear, in that time I shall move mountains!"

"But I can see no solid ground," she said, "neither for myself nor

227

for you. I have seen a great deal of all sorts of things. And I try not to think. I find it is better, you see."

There was a silence. Jeanne jerked at her brief case and turned to go, looking sadly at Lopatkin. He could not restrain himself. He put his arms round her, drew her close to him, and kissed her cool cheek. Tears seeped from under her closed eyelids, as though the kiss had pressed them out. Seeing them, Lopatkin drew her yielding head closer and he, too, half-closed his eyes.

"Dimka, you are betraying me!" she said, now sobbing openly. "Why did you go-o-o . . . ?" She moaned softly and bitterly, pressing her head against his chest. "Why? Didn't you know I loved you? What more did you want? If you like, I will give up everything! At least let me kiss you once more! Don't go away!"

They were silent, shielded from the street by Lopatkin's broad back. They stood without speaking, swaying a little, and feeling a strange relief and emptiness after their tears. Jeanne took out her handkerchief and blew her nose, smiling piteously at Lopatkin.

"Are you staying in Moscow long?" she asked him.

"I am leaving tomorrow," Lopatkin lied. "I haven't much more to do here. Soon we shall start making the machine. I am leaving for the Kuzbass tomorrow morning to discuss it with a factory."

"Is that really true?" Jeanne asked, brightening.

"Word of honor!" Lopatkin said stolidly, taking yet one more sin upon his soul.

"Then write to me. Are you coming back soon?"

"No. I don't want to correspond. All sorts of unforeseen things can happen. And you write very unpleasant letters. At difficult moments letters like that don't make things any easier!"

"That's because you don't do things as other people do!" Again her tone was unpleasant. "Most of my friends go in a certain direction, and they are all happy. And I can understand it. But no one can understand you: you see? You fly into a rage as soon as I begin to say this."

They walked along in silence for a time, waiting for the coldness which had come between them, from where, neither knew, to dispel

228

itself. Finally they parted, and Dimitri walked home with his long, even stride.

So there it was. He had had his relaxation in the company of the girl "with the smile of a child"! he had had his taste of forest coolness, of the sun, of merry birthday parties!

Suspicious and sharp-eared, the professor listened for a few days to Dimitri's furtive sighs, and realizing that something was wrong, asked him what it was. After having heard his confession out, the old man flared up, glared angrily, and was about to hold forth against "these low-minded clods," and to annihilate "that creature, what's her name," but instead suddenly shut up, pondered for a while, and said after a pause:

"Many genuine discoverers I know . . . indeed all of them . . . none of them have families. The reason . . . well . . . better not to think about that! Just set to work, and in another week you'll have forgotten all about it!"

He was right. By January Dimitri no longer thought about Jeanne. Only, as he sat at his drawing board, he would hum to himself the things that Chopin had told him, and that Rachmaninov had confirmed in his Concerto. His task was rapidly nearing its conclusion and Dimitri became more cheerful, and began once again to go to the Conservatory concerts.

One day, after hearing Liszt's Preludes for the first time—they were still vibrating in him and making him feel strangely restless— he descended from the gallery to the lobby to stand by the same pillar as before. With other silent young men, he leaned against the column, so as not to stand out conspicuously from those around him while he furtively scrutinized the faces of women who, against his will, still attracted him. Almost all the prettier ones had solid-looking escorts who were constantly making witty remarks. "Laugh louder!" Lopatkin thought. "There is no need for alarm! Shutikov and Avdiyev themselves have assured you of that! All roads are wide open to our innovators!"

"You always make such a face that one could find it by the description, even if one didn't know you!" he heard a voice say, as if through a fog.

"Yes, they are all too unconcerned," Lopatkin was thinking. "They get their ideas of what is going on in our corner only through reading articles by such *undoubted partisans of progress* as Shutikov!"

"What are you staring at, Dmitri Alexeyevich?" someone said close to him.

His thoughts were in a state of confusion. He resisted this enforced awakening for a second or two, then suddenly became aware of a plump, pretty young girl with a velvet birthmark on her cheek standing in front of him. He looked again, and a miracle happened —the young girl turned into Nadezhda Sergeyevna Drozdov dressed in a severe tailor-made suit of dark gray shot with mauve.

Dmitri gave her a calm, straightforward look, as he had done two years before in Muzga. Their glances clashed for an instant. Dmitri felt a slight and pleasant catch of the breath, and she blushed. Perhaps it was because the pure, true music of the Preludes was still echoing in Lopatkin's memory. He looked at Nadia once more and even gave a hint of a cough to break the silence. She held out a soft, warm hand. He took it and said something in reply. Nadia turned away for a moment and he caught sight of her neck— proud and white as unskimmed milk.

"Do you know . . ." he began. "Something has happened to you. You have blossomed, one might say. . . . Excuse me, but I simply did not recognize you! Or, rather, I did recognize you, but felt: this is not the same Nadezhda Sergeyevna!"

"Yes," she said thoughtfully, gently disengaging her fingers from his clasp. "Yes, I am not the same. And you? You have not yet lost your head?"

"Not really. I knew in advance . . . that it wouldn't be all fun. I foresaw it all and so I felt no painful shock."

"Come, let's go and join the general merry-go-round." She slipped her arm through his. "Tell me, how are things with you? In detail, about everything. I see a new suit."

"Not only a suit! There is also an overcoat and a hat!"

"Well! So you are rich now!"

"And that certainly is a story!" Lopatkin began to tell her about the six thousand roubles. But the dangerous encounter of their eyes at once ceased and the echo of the Preludes died away. Now Lopatkin was merely relating to a Comrade certain interesting and amusing matters. And the *Comrade* was hanging greedily on his every word.

" 'Foreign espionage!' " Lopatkin said. " 'A trap!' The old man dug his toes in and refused on any account to take the money. But I put it in my pocket: and while they are carrying out their schemes, we shall have eaten it all up!"

"Quite right!" Nadia laughed, looking at him with a sidelong glance.

"The little parcel came in the nick of time! We were just wondering, the old man and I, whether I ought not to take a job in a factory. And if I had, the business with my machine would have had to be put off."

"But it seems that that has happened anyway! Drozdov told me that you had reduced your offensive. I don't like that! I worry about you, you know."

"Oh, I am going into battle soon. I have worked out a new . . ."

Here Lopatkin checked himself with a cough; he had suddenly remembered to whom he was speaking.

"What is it? Why didn't you finish what you were saying?" Nadia asked softly; then a numbing thought seemed to strike her. "You . . . You think that I . . . !" She shook her head and her gray eyes grew big with tears.

"I don't think that!" He too, blushed. "Yes. . . . Yes, I am afraid . . . No, I'm not afraid, but it is not in my interests. . . . You see, Nadezhda Sergeyevna, if we are to talk frankly," he said firmly, and puckered his lips wryly, "you are the wife of my adversary. For you this is simply a spectacle. At best a duel of gladiators. But I am afraid to the last degree that—"

"I have nothing to do with him! I never want to see him again!

Be quiet!" she hissed, and several people in front of them turned round at the sound.

They walked halfway round the lobby in silence.

"Is that true?" Lopatkin asked at last. "Since when?"

"Almost two years. Incompatibility of temperament."

They walked a few paces again in silence. Then Nadia raised conscience-stricken eyes to his face.

"Dmitri Alexeyevich, I will never betray you! I give you my word of honor. I swear by my son!"

Without moving his elbow, he pressed her hand, then let it go.

"Nadezhda Sergeyevna, I have designed a new machine. A universal machine for the casting of every kind of pipe. Now I realize it myself . . . it seems to me that I have made a serious discovery."

"They, too, are making a machine."

"Who?"

"They are already finishing it." Nadia was frightened by her own words, and went on hurriedly. "I'll tell you who. Those two who were with you: Maxiutenko and Uriupin. Drozdov 'superintends,' and Fundator, Avdiyev, and a few others give advice. . . . Which others, I can't remember."

From the expression on Lopatkin's face and the way he drew the air sharply into his lungs and stiffened with the shock of battle Nadia suddenly understood everything.

"Dmitri Alexeyevich," she cried softly, stroking his sleeve. "Dmitri Alexeyevich! I'll find out everything. Everything."

A bell rang. It was the third signal, and the lights in the lobby were lowered.

"Come to me a week from today! On the nineteenth. In the daytime. Everything will be there! Come at noon."

"Where to?"

"Anywhere. To the music shop on the Neglinka, say. Don't worry! Wait before you begin worrying!" She pressed his hand. "I will help you without fail! Good-by."

Perhaps she was expecting him to suggest that they should meet after the concert. But Lopatkin pressed her hand, turned without a word, and disappeared into the crowd. He did not even stay for the second half of the concert, but went home at once.

On the nineteenth of January at noon Lopatkin walked along the Neglinka. The collar of his overcoat was turned up and his hat was pulled well over his ears, for a wet snow was falling. He stopped in front of the music shop, looked to right and left, and was just about to push down the bronze door handle when a woman came up to him, dressed in a full black cloak and wearing a large beret of smoky-blue felt pulled forward on her forehead. . . . It was Nadia. She had been waiting for him.

"Good morning," she said in a voice that was almost inaudible, giving him a hand in a thin black leather glove.

"Nadezhda Sergeyevna!" Lopatkin cried joyfully, but stopped when he saw the look on her lovely, unhappy face that was quickly hidden again by the slanting blue shadow of the hat as she bowed her head. "Nadezhda Sergeyevna!" he said quietly. "Something has gone wrong?"

"Simply that I couldn't get any news for you."

"Never mind. To hell with them! There's less worry this way!"

"Dmitri Alexeyevich, we must go somewhere to talk, I have a lot of things to tell you. It is this: they have robbed you, I realize that now. I wanted to make a drawing of their machine for you, but nothing came of it. I only had a glimpse from a distance once of a thing like this in their drawing. I quickly made a sketch of it."

She took a sheet of paper folded in two out of her handbag. Lopatkin unfolded it, and again, for the third time, he saw the same familiar circle with six smaller circles inside it aimed at him like the barrel of a revolver. It was Maxiutenko's and Uriupin's machine.

"They are making this machine in our factory, under Ganichev."

"All this is very important," Lopatkin said thoughtfully, as though talking to himself. "Very important." He shook his head. "Look how this business has been developing, while we were unloading cabbage here. . . . Ye-es. All right." Suddenly he came down to earth again. "Let's go. Tell me what you know—whatever you can say to please me. Don't worry, you really are pleasing me! You are arming me, giving me a shield and a sword. Only, if it isn't a secret, I should like to know why you are doing this?"

He looked straight into her eyes and she lowered them. She stood a long time like this, motionless, her hands and her eyes lowered, smiling and blushing by turns and saying nothing.

"Well . . ." she said, not answering Lopatkin. "Of course you remember that Avdiyev's machine was made first. . . ." And she began telling Lopatkin about centrifugal machines and pipe-casting—things he himself knew perfectly well.

7

AFTER their move to Moscow, relations between Nadia and her husband had still remained just as indefinite. But by now she was well aware that she had made a mistake in marrying her Siberian hero. If in the first days of her married life she had been proud of his power over men, and had listened in delight when she heard him cracking jokes as he talked on the telephone at night, that terrifying place Moscow; if Nadia had later pitied him, as a man tormented by the harrowing cares of the *kombinat's* affairs, and because of this, had forgiven him his lack of literacy or of the slightest trace of musical understanding, now she could scarcely restrain herself from telling him, with offensive calm, how much she hated him. She hated his way of closing his eyes, because in it she saw clearly the affectation of the high official wishing to show how much he was wearied by the cares of state. When he ate with uncouth noises at the table, she reddened and lowered her head. But she was even more irritated by Drozdov's philosophical discourses; he knew so well when to insert glibly catchwords such as "basis," "state duty," "collective," and so on, using them to hide his own personal interests or weaknesses. It irritated her even more that Drozdov, when he began to talk in these phrases, somehow, in an odd way, disarmed her, depriving her, as it were, of the power of speech. And although she realized that her husband had once again been party to an injustice, she found no words to oppose him. This infuriated her, yet when she stood facing him, from old habit—a stupid, servile habit—she still nevertheless deferred to him.

Drozdov himself was not changed by becoming a Muscovite. As in Muzga, he still surveyed his surroundings with the glance of an eagle sitting on a telegraph pole in the steppe; and there was a metallic glitter in his eyes. In Moscow he found himself in immediate contact with many men of superior rank to his own. At his house the telephone often rang in the middle of the night. Speaking in an earnest "business" voice into the receiver, saying, "Yes. Yes. It will be done," Drozdov remained exactly the same as before—he would close his eyes, sniff, and wink at his wife, as if to say, "All right. That's what *he* thinks, but we shall see about it!" Only on rare occasions was he roused to a quiet fury—when he was required to commit some stupid blunder. But even at those times his superior heard only the weighty arguments he would bring against such action, and as a rule Drozdov had his own way. But if his superior insisted, Drozdov would say: "Very good. It shall be done!" For the benefit of his wife, however, after he had hung up the receiver he would quote Suvorov's words: "Before you can command, you must learn to obey."

Already, during the first year in Moscow, Nadia had begun withdrawing to her own room. There she would play with her little son, and was delighted when he said quite clearly: "Give-give-give!"—words that, as Drozdov said, already insured him a firm position in the world. In order to conceal her physical repugnance for her husband, she sometimes complained of pains in her back, and began swathing herself in a woollen shawl. Drozdov sent her to a clinic. She explained at length to the puzzled doctor what it was that was upsetting her, told him about her unfortunate pregnancy, and the result, as she had hoped it would be, was that the patient was prescribed warmth and rest. Soon after, Nadia finally overcame her husband's distrust by cluttering up the window sills in her room with little boxes full of "pulses"—as Drozdov called her homeopathic remedies.

Nadia felt now that there was no turning back, that a great change in her life was approaching, and she prepared for it earnestly. Lying on the sofa in her own room, with a book in her hand, she sometimes thought of Muzga and sighed, as though she had left her youth behind her there. Frowning, she stared at the mauve wallpaper; but what she really saw was dusty, narrow East Street along which she had walked once—no, twice—to the very top. "Dmitri Alexeyevich," she whispered, hardly moving her lips. Yes, that had been her youth. *Had* been, and now it had passed, leaving only a warm breath behind. What happiness it might have contained! *He* was probably still walking there, along East Street, preparing to fight alone, not believing that he would get help from anyone. Although perhaps Valentina Pavlovna . . . "What fine people! What have I done!"

Old Mrs. Drozdov had brought Shura from Muzga as a nursemaid for her grandson, and Nadia, disregarding the family's objections, at once took a job teaching geography in a school. Everything went on in its usual placid way, but one day Drozdov, on his return from work, rudely disturbed the even tenor of this life.

"Nadyush! That chap of ours! Our fellow countryman! What a row he made in the technical council!"

"Whom are you talking about?"

"About Lopatkin, of course. Our inventor!"

"Is he in Moscow?" Nadia asked with apparent indifference, but the room around her seemed suddenly to fill with light, so that she had to lower her eyes.

"I'm telling you! He has recently defended his project in the C.S.I.F.R.!"

"You haven't seen what a nice little suit I have got for Nikolashka," Nadia said, laying aside the geographical atlas which she used for preparing her lessons and propping herself up on the divan.

"The suit can wait! I tell you, Lopatkin has moved to Moscow!"

"In the end he will have his invention accepted. You know what kind of man he is!"

"Our bigwigs are on the alert." Drozdov took up his favorite facetiously majestic pose. "Science is jealously guarding its frontiers against every kind of . . . er . . . incursion!"

"What! Have they rejected it?"

"He went away barely alive! Reeling, as the saying goes. They hit hard, you know—though without leaving bruises!" Drozdov smiled, puckering his yellow face up into innumerable wrinkles of amusement.

"And he? How does he look?"

"He came to see me today. In his . . . uniform. Did I tell you? He would not accept a suit from me. I offered him one back in Muzga."

"Do you want to have dinner?" Nadia asked, getting up from the divan. She was wearing a long house coat of dark violet silk patterned with small, widely-scattered red and gold twigs and half open over her breast.

"Dinner?" Drozdov asked, embracing her and drawing her close to him. As he did so, he felt for the woollen shawl—was it still there? The shawl was in its usual place. "M . . . ye-es," he replied, somewhat disappointed. "Yes, I suppose so. . . ."

They went into the next room, where the old woman had already laid the table. Drozdov sat down in his place and picked up the decanter at his right hand. He drank a glass of vodka, and with his fork fished some sauerkraut out of the dish and laughed as he crunched it in his teeth; he had remembered something funny, but the sauerkraut prevented him from speaking.

"Maxiutenko!" he said, unable to refrain from a burst of laughter. "Oh, what a headpiece! Do you hear? Our Don Juan of Muzga! I wanted to put him up to something, knowing the sort of chap he is, but he was in it already—off his own bat! He had submitted a machine design of his own! Every zero wants to seem a hero! He pinched the idea from Lopatkin, added something from foreign designers, and it seems as if the swine has chosen just the right moment!"

Drozdov poured himself another glass, tossed the vodka back into his mouth with a quick movement, and began noisily eating his soup.

"Mother, we're just ourselves here, give me an old wooden spoon!" he said, and Nadia suddenly remembered how delighted she had been long ago, when he had said the same thing on the day of her marriage.

"You say he has chosen the right moment? How?"

"Oh, I haven't told you! It's quite a story! Shutikov—our deputy chief—it's not for nothing that he occupies himself with pipes! We have no plan for them, at least we have a plan for drainpipes, of course, but only for inside use. For our own building. But our deputy reads the papers, and he was present at a conference held by an august body when the construction of a centrifugal machine was discussed. He was also present a year later when a few ministers were hauled over the coals for not being able to produce such a machine. The ministers are reprimanded once, then twice, but our darling still just sits there—and not a squeak out of him! Oh, Shutikov is a man with perspective! He gets busy. The others all make promises and then ask for money, but he simply decides to make this machine on the quiet, and then modestly to report it. But if it was to be done modestly and quickly, it wouldn't do to quarrel with the institutes! A common language had to be found. Well, it *was* found: they made the Avdiyev machine! That a lot of money was lost didn't matter!"

"But why didn't he back Lopatkin?" Nadia exclaimed, growing pale, but Drozdov did not notice.

"Wait a minute!" Drozdov liked to tell his stories in his own way. "Wait, Comrade . . . er'm . . . Drozdov! Perhaps he *might* have backed Lopatkin; Shutikov didn't care who it was—what *he* was after was to make a machine, and then to produce a pipe, all complete on the table. But Lopatkin is a dark horse. Set up a separate design office for him? Too much trouble. Hand the design work over to the Institute? Impossible. He wouldn't get on with Avdiyev. It would only be a waste of money. The man wanted here is one who will make concessions. The scientists have their own interests to consider. What they need is for all machines to be based on their own long, creative, profound, fertile research work. And Shutikov knows perfectly well that 'with the elements of the Lord' . . . how does it go on, that thing you read to me?"

239

" '. . . even tsars cannot cope,' " Nadia prompted.

"That's it. 'With the elements of the Lord, even tsars cannot cope.' If Lopatkin, from the start, had managed to find a language in common with the institutes he would have been all right. True, Avdiyev is difficult, he's made of flint. One must simply defer to him and throw oneself on his mercy. But Avdiyev has some sense—he would have thrown him some sop from his own table. In other words, Lopatkin's strategy was miscalculated. And now that the thing is patented, the institutes won't touch Lopatkin with a barge pole!"

"A pity!" Nadia said with a sidelong glance at her husband, waiting for what would come next. "Try the veal, it's very tasty today."

"Veal? Ho-ho!" Drozdov said, truculently helping himself to a piece that weighed about a pound. "Well, to go on . . ." he said, chewing vigorously, so that his whole face was in motion. "Maxiutenko . . . Mother, you've done this veal very well today! . . . As I was saying, here's Maxiutenko. He's a fool, but he turned up at just the right time! So now he is being kissed and petted. And quite right, too. They were deeply involved with the Avdiyev machine and all their theses about it. Now they were forced to write off, not merely a little surprise, but big losses. And now they *can* write them off, they will say that the money went for research, for development, for promoting the new machine. Well done!" He chuckled, and began noisily cutting up the meat on his plate. Having done so, he put a large piece in his mouth, and a hard bulge appeared in his cheek, as though he had stuck his tongue in it. Nadia, her nostrils twitching nervously, looked fixedly at this bulge, and then turned away.

"Still, it is a dirty trick!" she said. "The man has worked for years and years . . ."

"Yes, of course. But if you look at it dispassionately"—Drozdov raised his eyebrows, skewered a fresh piece of meat on his fork and pushed it all round the plate, smearing it with mustard—"to invent, to discover, is only a tenth part of the business. How many good

240

intentions have been swallowed up in history without leaving a trace! All because they didn't go about it in the right way, because they didn't find the right *organizer*. And that a man like our Lopatkin is preyed upon by men like Maxiutenko, Avdiyev, and Shutikov, is only natural! An idea, if it is a correct one, begins to have an independent life of its own and seeks out for itself a strong man —a man who will make sure that it will prosper. Ideas prefer marriages of convenience to love matches!" Having said this, Drozdov gave his wife a look of triumph. "Ideas gladly break faith with their first lovers in favor of influential and energetic patrons!"

"But the real creative part can never be played by a fixer!" Nadia said almost inaudibly. She said it so softly that Drozdov was quite justified in not answering. He pretended not to have heard. And Nadia understood everything.

The dinner dragged on for a long time. It was not Drozdov's fault—he dealt rapidly with the food, demolishing it at a furious rate. It was Nadia who lingered over her dinner, merely prodding at the plate with her spoon, and eating almost nothing. "This is it! It has come!" she said to herself, frightened and at the same time glad. And Drozdov, seeing her make no move to get up from the table, helped himself to more food in order to pass the time. Having eaten too much, snorting with overindulgence, he finally went off to his bedroom for a nap.

Nadia decided to look for Lopatkin. Next day, on her way back from school, she stopped at an information booth, and after buying an information bureau form, she filled it with the name "Lopatkin, Dmitri Alexeyevich." An hour later she got the answer that he had no address for "such a one." "Yes, of course, it would be like this! Where could he live in this town?" she wondered sadly, walking slowly along the street; she tore up the slip and let the wind blow the tiny scraps of paper out of the palm of her hand.

That evening she asked her husband, *en passant,* and with an air of absent-mindedness, where he could possibly be lodging—that inventor. After all, it was winter! "The devil knows where! These fellows have hides like wolves, they're not afraid of the cold,"

Drozdov replied. She did not venture to repeat the question, and life once more went on evenly: lunch at one, dinner at seven, supper at eleven. Drozdov did not mention Lopatkin again. If he told her stories, they were anecdotes about the Ministry. For instance, that Shutikov had an assistant in his department whose name was Nevraev but whom everyone called "the ministerial barometer."

"The youngster is fond of the bottle, it's true, but his intuition . . . I've never seen anything like it!" Drozdov said with an approving smile. "He is the terror of all the smaller fry in the Ministry. If he makes himself agreeable to you, you can rest assured that all is well. If he comes up and greets you, you know that you will soon go on a mission abroad or be made head of a department. But if you go to see him and he is busy, doesn't notice you, must go off somewhere else in a hurry, then you know your number is up. Your name will be in the Ministry's order of the day, either next day, or the one after. It's a certainty. At times he does better even than our Oleg the wise: 'Your death, it will come through your favorite steed.' "

At the end of February at dinner one day Drozdov said to Nadia:

"Shutikov has an article in tomorrow's paper—a feature about innovations and innovators. Of course it wasn't he who wrote it, it was Nevraev. That is, Nevraev and the newspaper chaps between them. Shutikov only got the proofs. He signed them—listen to this! —read them after signing, and said: 'I've made it a bit rough here. Put it right! *I've* made it!' "

But somewhere at the back of his shrewd and knowing smile there was a momentary flash of resentment that vanished again instantly.

"I suppose you wouldn't mind having an article in the paper either?" Nadia said with an air of innocence.

"Nadezhda!" Drozdov's voice held a warning note, though it was as cheerful as ever. "I understand you, Comrade . . . h'm . . . Drozdov. If ever *I* have an article in the paper, the ideas in it will be my own! It happens sometimes that illiterate muzhiks can dictate to those who can write. And then again there are *literate*"—he stressed the word—"highbrows, who can only write down other people's ideas. And one can't reverse the business. The muzhik can't write and the clerk—ha!—can't dictate! If I publish anything, the collaboration will be between a muzhik with brains and a pen pusher!"

Having said this he sat lost in thought, chewing his food absentmindedly, and Nadia sensed even more clearly than before the secret resentment which was even affecting his appetite.

The spring brought no changes that year. The month of May passed in school affairs and in examinations. In June, Nadia, the child, and Shura, took the car and drove to a place on the Volga. The summer was sunny, without wind or rain, but it was a restless one for Nadia. She walked long distances alone over the sands, and there, on some sandbank amid shallow inlets and backwaters, she tanned herself, began to read *Lost Illusions,* dropped it again; she could not understand what was the matter with her. She bathed; sometimes swam, yielding herself up to the cool current of the river, sometimes wallowed in the warm ooze of the inlets, and it was all pleasant; but the quiet unhappiness and the strange outbursts of anger still persisted. In the silent heat of July the crops in the fields beyond the village began to get scorched. Nadia saw the members of the kolkhoz on the porch of the kolkhoz office; they were sunburned, with white patches of salt on the backs and shoulders of their faded blouses. They smoked in silence, spat on the ground, and watched the "woman from Moscow" out of blue eyes that seemed to have been bleached by the sun. Nadia realized that disaster was approaching them, and there was nothing she could do to help them. Now she could no longer walk on the sands to get away from it all; the sands were too hot and drove away the suntanned, bored, lonely little lady wearing a *sarafan*. Nadia hid herself in the cool cottage, where no one would be able to see her gay sunshade and her books. At the beginning of August she could bear it no longer and sent her husband a telegram. The car arrived and the summer guests fled back to Moscow during the night.

Drozdov met her with his usual shrewd smile. He wanted to pat his wife on the shoulder, but somehow it didn't come off. "My affairs are not too bad," he answered her indifferent question with an air of mystery. But that evening visitors came. Nadia recognized Maxiutenko at once. He had put on flesh and was wearing a dark-blue suit with drooping shoulders. As soon as he saw Nadia, he went quickly up to her and put a little box containing a bottle of scent into her hand—the scent was "Lilac," made in Leningrad, about which there had been a lot of talk at the time. The other guest was a thin graying man with a metallic note in his voice. He squeezed Nadia's hand slightly, but nonetheless painfully, and introduced himself by the name of Uriupin.

Nadia had expected them to drink and sing, but the guests and Drozdov shut themselves up in the middle room, the one they called the dining room or the reception room, and unrolled drawings on the table. Their conference lasted for three hours. During all this time, from her own room, Nadia only once heard their voices—in a general burst of laughter: her husband's moaning sigh, Uriupin's martial guffaw, and Maxiutenko's horsy neigh.

Then tea was served, and Nadia was asked to come to the table. A more manly "tea" was also poured out for them, but this Nadia refused.

"Look!" Maxiutenko turned to Nadia after the first toast, and with his empty glass pointed to Drozdov. "He won't help us!"

"Don't exaggerate, Maxiutenko!" Drozdov said severely, closing his eyes. "I am not refusing to help, but I don't want to be a co-originator. But as for helping, of course I'll help! On the contrary, if you'd like to know, if you haven't forgotten, it was I who put forward your candidatures!"

"That's why we want you to be with us, Leonid Ivanovich!" Uriupin said. His bony face broke into a smile and his thick gray hair suddenly, as though of its own accord, moved forward on his wrinkled forehead.

"Go on, go on!" Drozdov laughed loudly. "Go on! Do it again!"

Uriupin gave Nadia a quick glance and frowned. He did not

like this disability of his to be laughed at, and for this very reason his hair moved even more rapidly than usual, down to his brows and back again.

"You are nervous!" Drozdov said. "Your hair gives you away!"

"Well, what are we deciding?" Uriupin asked, getting red.

"I can't be a member of your group in outward appearance, for the sake of a future medal. Nor will I take part in the projecting. I have other work to do. I am going the rounds of the factories. You must rope in those I mentioned: Volovik, Fundator, and Tepikin. Only, mind you, they won't come to you of their own accord. They are beautiful maidens; they would like to, but their position compels them to be coy. I have already prepared the way. Now it's up to you! Of course it would have been good to get Shutikov in as well, but you yourselves, silly asses, messed that up! And you put me on a spot, too! I don't know what his considerations are, but in general, friends, there are certain orifices which one should always keep closed. Now he doesn't speak to me at all. Two words: good morning and good evening, that's all! So you see what you have done!"

While Drozdov was speaking, Maxiutenko, reddening guiltily, was exclaiming over and over again, "Leonid Ivanovich! Leonid Ivanovich!" When Drozdov angrily ended his tirade, Maxiutenko said once more: "Leonid Ivanovich! . . ." Drozdov looked at him with an ominous smile. "At ease, Maxiutenko! Just do as I say!"

The guests soon left. Drozdov saw them to the door, stretching and cracking his joints in the hall.

"Out of sheer stupidity they have got me into a nice mess! They went to see Shutikov and suggested that he should be the head of the group and told him straight that Drozdov had advised them to include him! He only smiled, of course, but later, when we were alone, he said to me: 'Why are you trying to involve me with this . . . er . . . this group?' To that I said: 'But it was through your own initiative, Pavel Ivanovich!' At which he fairly hissed at me: 'What initiative of mine? Don't talk so much nonsense!' And to this day he gives me black looks. He's an old wolf, so he imagines he smells hounds everywhere! Ah, Nadyusha, life is no simple matter!"

Nadia did not hear him out to the end, but went silently to her room. Drozdov followed her to the door.

"May I come in?"

"On no account!" Nadia said. "Never!"

"Why so stern? But I am coming in all the same! By force of the marriage certificate!" He laughed and entered.

"All right, come in. And I shall go out!"

"What is this?"

"I don't love you."

"That's all wrong," he said. "You *must* love me."

"Look, don't make me angry! You have turned out to be such a petty . . . You ruin a man for nothing at all. He has never so much as crossed your path. It was you, you who barred his way. He never suspected you and yet you put a noose round his neck to throttle him. Look at him, how determined he is, how he refuses to give up, while you just go on throttling and throttling . . ."

"Oh, come, one can't throttle a fellow like that!" Drozdov tried to turn the matter into a joke. "Now just listen to me . . ."

Nikolashka, a fair-haired little boy, was standing by his cot, banging at it with the bottle of Lilac scent from Leningrad and laughing as he looked at his parents. Nadia picked him up, held him tightly, and turned her back on her husband.

"Now listen!" Drozdov said, frowning. "Lopatkin would have ruined his idea in any case. We had to step in, in the common interest, if you like; we were obliged to interfere. What we need is pipes and not your Dmitri What's-his-name. . . ."

"I don't want to listen." Staring into the distance, she pressed her lips to the child's warm little head. "You always say something that justifies you for the moment. You are always right. Throttle him then! But I am no longer your wife!"

After this conversation everything seemed to go on as usual. They sat down to their meals together, and even exchanged a few words—about the weather, the boy's health, or about the fact that

246

there were a lot of moths about. But Drozdov told no more anecdotes, and Nadia never smiled when he was there.

Toward the end of August she asked her husband for the car, and drove with Shura to the center of Moscow, to buy winter clothes for the child. As the car was passing the Belorussian Station, and was waiting at the traffic lights, Shura suddenly pulled Nadia by the sleeve.

"Look! There he goes! The schoolmaster from Muzga! Look at the long steps he takes!"

Nadia started. The blood rushed painfully to her head.

"Oh, how you startled me!" she said. "Who was it you saw?"

Looking out of the slanting window of the car, she immediately caught sight of Lopatkin, who was walking along the pavement toward the city center. His face was stern and set; he was just as he had been in Muzga, seeing and hearing nothing of what was going on around him, so deeply occupied was he with his own thoughts.

The policeman at the crossing waved his little stick and made a half-turn; above him the traffic lights changed to green, and the car moved on along Gorky Street, leaving Lopatkin far behind.

"Stop here!" Nadia said to the driver. "I will shop on foot."

The car slowed down and came to a stop at the curb. Nadia got out and with difficulty, controlling the tremor in her voice, began slowly going over with Shura everything that she had to buy for dinner. "The best thing is to get sturgeon, if there are any big ones to be had," she said. "If there is smoked eel, buy some, Leonid Ivanovich is very fond of it. And of course make sure that you get a chicken. . . ." She slammed the car door, then waited a little, until the car was swallowed up in the distance by the general stream of traffic. Then she turned round and ran back, muttering to herself, her face radiant. As she ran, she racked her brains for some lie to justify her sudden appearance to Lopatkin. But she could think of nothing.

Then she stopped: it occurred to her that it would not do to jeopardize such a lucky chance in this way, for a second meeting might never come about at all. And Dmitri Alexeyevich might be in a bad humor. He might not want to talk to anyone just now, and especially not to Drozdov's wife. He would only say "Good morning," and go on. No, this was not the right way.

Nadia turned quickly to a newsstand. She was just in time: hardly had she opened her handbag and looked at herself in the mirror when the greenish blouse appeared among the crowd. Nadia raised her handbag higher, but the precaution was unnecessary. Lopatkin, with his rapid, elastic step, seemed to spring out from among the stream of pedestrians and to disappear no less rapidly. Nadia snapped her bag shut and hurried after him. Soon she overtook him; he was still walking as evenly, neither increasing nor decreasing his pace.

Nadia walked in this way along the whole length of Gorky Street, Mokhovaya Street, and Volkhonka Street, some fifty paces behind Lopatkin. A fine task he was giving her! At times she imagined he had seen her and was wandering about on purpose to make fun of her. At this thought she blushed and slowed down, lagging behind, so that he should not notice her even if he did turn around, and even if he suspected that something was wrong.

But Lopatkin never once looked around. He calmly finished his five-mile walk, turned into his own Liakhov Lane, crossed the yard, passed the sheds and dovecotes, and mounted the steps to the entrance of the old house with the dilapidated colonnade. Nadia scrutinized these columns from a distance. The lower parts were covered with inscriptions unmistakably characteristic of the middle of the twentieth century. She scrutinized the courtyard, memorized the number of the house, then returned to the boulevard and took a taxi home.

A few days later, after long hesitation, she decided to pay Lopatkin a visit. On the morning when she took this decision Nadia began singing to herself for the first time since she had lived in the Moscow flat. At nine o'clock she washed her hair, and then took a long time drying and combing it. Her not very long, thick chestnut hair seemed to have gone mad after the washing—it stood on end and crackled loudly under the comb. When she had combed it out, she plaited it in two thick plaits, which she twisted into a tight bun at the back of her neck. At the back of her neck everything was tidy, but in front and all round her head sprang a lot of reddish threads, as fine as spiders' webs—the sweet down of youth, which vanishes with the years. But Nadia did not like them; she undid the plaits, and began angrily combing her hair again. "What am I doing?" she asked herself suddenly. And all of a sudden she understood the reason for her annoyance, and although she was frightened of the simple answer which had already come to her, she began to laugh and sing with an incomprehensible joy.

So it was with her hair carefully done, but still with the spiders' webs, that she appeared before the professor, who at once began artfully to question her. But all his art was foiled by Nadia's absent-mindedness. She answered "yes" to nearly everything the old man asked her, thereby arousing his serious suspicions. Her absent-mindedness was of a peculiar nature. First of all she noticed the whole flock of bell pushes on the door and wondered. Then, learning that Lopatkin was not in, she remembered the bell pushes and thought that every one of them represented a neighbor, and, it seemed to her, an unsociable, ill-intentioned one. The little old man asked her in and offered her a seat; she entered a room redolent of tobacco smoke, and sat down on a rickety chair. It was here that the professor heard all those "yesses" from her, which put him on his guard. On the dirty little table Nadia saw two slices of black bread of exactly equal size, placed accurately opposite each other, with half a pickled cucumber lying on each slice.

"Do you live here together?" she asked.

"Yes, yes," the little old man replied, then he, too, asked a question to which she answered, "Yes."

She caught sight of a drawing board and on it was a sheet of drawing paper with a drawing. She wanted to go and look at it, but the old man said, "I beg your pardon!" and intercepted her, nimbly covering up the drawing with a newspaper.

"Yes, yes," she said to him, glancing again at the slices of bread and fumbling with her handbag which contained two hundred roubles. Then she went out into the passage, and, without answering the old man, walked quietly to the exit.

She made up her mind at all costs to help these two, one of whom had that day risen even higher than before in her eyes. "But how is it to be done?" she asked herself. "Two hundred, five hundred roubles—that is far too little!" Yet she could not get hold of any more, since housekeeping expenditures in the Drozdov family were in the hands of Drozdov's mother.

Six weeks went by. The rainy season had come, and Nadia was still in search of money, and could think of nothing. Then one day Mrs. Ganichev telephoned, and came to see Nadia during the course of the day. She was on a visit to Moscow for several days. Bandy-legged, rouged, reeking of the same violent scent, she hugged Nadia and kissed her, peering at and noticing everything round her as she did so. She immediately spotted the little bags of naphthaline on the table and the open wardrobe.

"I have just been having a look at my fur coat, to see whether there were any moths in it," Nadia said. She glanced at Mrs. Ganichev, and shivered suddenly.

"Wait a minute! Let me try it on!" Mrs. Ganichev seemed to have read Nadia's thoughts. She put on the fur coat, scattering mothballs all over the carpet, and went to the mirror.

"A bit too long," Nadia remarked.

"That's nothing." Mrs. Ganichev turned first one way, then the other, in front of the mirror. "Listen! Will you sell it to me? Oh, do!"

Nadia said nothing.

"My goodness!" said Mrs. Ganichev. "How much did you give for it?"

"Twenty-two thousand."

"I haven't got as much as that. And with the currency reform . . . But I'll give you nine for it."

Nadia was silent. She grew pale, and stared into space. It was impossible—to sell something that Drozdov had bought her. Precisely because it was Drozdov who had bought it, who had himself paid for it, had himself counted out the money. If she, Nadia, left him, she would have to leave the coat behind with him. But nine thousand roubles!

"Well, what about it?" Mrs. Ganichev said. "Look, I'll give you ten. And that's my last word."

"Zinaida Fominichna," Nadia hurriedly began, "I need money badly!"

"And what am I offering you? Isn't that money?"

"But my husband must not know on any account. Until the winter."

"What's the matter?" Mrs. Ganichev lowered her voice. "Oh, all right. Don't tell me. It's no business of mine. So, what have we decided?"

And Nadia decided. Next morning Mrs. Ganichev brought her six thousand roubles, and promised to send the rest to her from Muzga. The coat was already wrapped in newspaper and tied with string. Mrs. Ganichev deftly carried it out to the staircase, indicated by a gesture to Nadia that "mum was the word," and took herself off.

Two hours later, when everything had quieted in her soul and the nerve-racking smell of naphthaline had vanished, Nadia packed the money in coarse gray paper, stuck down the corners of the packet, and taking Shura with her, went to the town center to do some shopping. They got out of the car in Liakhov Lane. Shura at once understood the part she was supposed to play, threw Nadia a sprightly, encouraging glance, and ran off through the archway.

It was in this way that Lopatkin came to be the owner of a new suit, and overcoat, and a hat. When she caught sight of him at the conservatory, Nadia, before speaking to him, first examined him from every angle and decided that the suit was a good one and had been chosen with taste. In contrast to the professor, she saw in the suit only its positive qualities. And as she looked at Lopatkin she at last overcame her feeling of guilt toward her husband.

A long-forgotten sense of freedom seemed to sustain her, and she flew as one flies in dreams. All her movements now were hasty but collected. She moved quickly even in her own room, for she was short of time. First she had to hurry to school, then she had to get back to her little boy, Nikolashka, before it got too late. She could make no excuses to him, especially when, bored with waiting for her, he ran to meet her and fell, not being as yet completely sure on his feet. Though it was he who fell, it was she who felt the pain. But Nikolashka, sitting on his mother's lap, slipped to the floor to pick up a button and put it in his mouth. He was perfectly serene, nothing had changed in *his* life. All the unrest, it seemed, burned in her alone.

"Where do you disappear to in the evening?" Drozdov asked her in a jocular tone, catching her one day in the passage as she ran out of the bathroom. "I believe you have got a temperature, Comrade . . . Drozdov!" he said.

"Oh Lord!" She shooed him away angrily. "Please leave me alone!"

It was getting toward evening, and she was in a hurry. She was not going either to the pictures or to the theater. She must dress as *simply* as possible, and it was not so easy. She had only an hour and a half left altogether—that was all! And she still had to lock herself into her room, to do her hair, arrange her plaits, powder the hot, dry bloom on her cheeks, and make an attempt to understand the strange and crazy woman who had appeared in her mirror in recent days and who frightened her.

8

BY this time Nadia was quite at home in Liakhov Lane. Things had just all happened. But how? Only the woman in the mirror could have explained. She revealed herself only to Nadia, and only when Nadia was alone, but when Nadia left her own room, she at once became quiet and modest and hid herself away and had disappeared completely by the time Nadia reached Lopatkin's and Professor Busko's room.

That room was by now much changed. There was oilcloth on the table, the water was boiled in a new kettle, the tea was brewed in a small round pot with a sharp spout and poured into unbreakable white German mugs with sides as thick as a man's finger. All these things had been brought by Nadia, after Lopatkin himself had escorted her to the room and formally presented her to the professor.

Nowadays she simply entered boldly, but quietly, so as not to disturb the inventors. She always brought something fresh to put on the table, some trifle, such, for instance, as a good, solid sugar bowl. Lopatkin would have liked to object to her making such purchases, but he could not, since Nadia did everything sensibly, and everything was inexpensive—and necessary. While she was buying these things she always kept in mind the character of their future owners. In the shops she was guided by that other woman, the artful one whom she saw in her mirror.

It was *her* voice that one day prompted Nadia to buy Lopatkin a shirt and necktie. When he unwrapped the parcel she had carelessly thrown on the table, he blushed, and so did she. Then he carefully examined the things. The shirt was made of extra-strong corded silk. He thought: "It will outlive us all!" During his hard times he had developed an overwhelming passion for good quality, for things that were durable. And even if his spirit on those occasions still protested, his hand willingly accepted the gifts, so that he could not resent them. And that other—the crazy, artful one, peeped triumphantly for an instant out of Nadia's eyes, taking the offensive—and Lopatkin was defeated.

Nadia's typewriter also stood on the table now or in its case on the floor. At last a worth-while permanent job had been found for it. Nadia took it upon herself to deal with Lopatkin's correspondence.

A peculiar relationship developed between her and the professor. When she had first entered the room, followed by Lopatkin, the old man had jumped up, aghast. Lopatkin had introduced Nadia. "We have already met," she said, and the professor answered, yes, he had already had the pleasure. He had guessed something, did his best to efface himself, and if, by chance, his eye alighted upon her from behind the drawing board, it was with a cheerful, knowing expression, and Nadia felt a pleasant confusion, and blushed a little.

During the first days of February, Lopatkin gave Nadia some sheets of paper covered with writing in a large, vigorous hand.

"Type this, please! With three copies." He spoke as one speaks to a secretary, trying not to look at her.

In five days the whole text was typed; there were twelve pages of it. It was a letter addressed to several top-ranking bodies and ended with the words: *Look at the number on this complaint, consider what it means, and summon me for an interview, even if only for five minutes.*

"Do you approve of the text?" Lopatkin asked.

"Yes," she whispered.

In the letter Lopatkin had briefly outlined all his hopes and disappointments, beginning with the first day he had submitted a small drawing to the inventions department of the Muzga *kombinat*.

"There is no better way of associating you with our struggle,"

Lopatkin said. "You must take these letters yourself and hand them in at the proper windows. But the answer will come from one of Shutikov's assistants, or from a scientific officer in C.S.I.F.R. Pay attention!" he laughed, and Nadia gave a start. "Please make a note of the day—it is the seventh of February. Nadezhda Sergeyevna, I am entrusting this business to you. Please be good enough to enter it in our register. This will be complaint number? . . ."

"Forty-six, forty-seven, and forty-eight," Nadia said.

"Now I realize that one must send letters to several addresses at the same time," Lopatkin said under his breath to the old man. "One must aim, not at a single target, but at whole surfaces, with grapeshot. . . . One gets the feeling of the situation sooner in that way. . . ."

Nadia was amazed that he uttered these improbable words quite calmly, not as though it were a joke, but an ordinary, businesslike remark.

A few days later an answer came in a special handsome envelope.

"Please open it yourself," Lopatkin said, going on with the work he was doing.

Nadia cut open the envelope. It contained a form: *Your complaint has been forwarded to . . .* (here the letters *C.S.I.F.R.* were written in in ink) *to be dealt with in order of importance.* Nadia received two more forms the same day: the complaints had been forwarded, one to the Minister, the other to—C.S.I.F.R.

"Why, they didn't even read it through!" Nadia was amazed. "What does it mean?"

"Indifference!" the old man answered from his working bench. "A survival from capitalist times."

Nadia laughed loudly, and the old man, surprised, stuck his head out from behind the drawing board.

"My husband often says such things!" Still laughing, she shook her head and began filing the forms in the incoming folder.

"Nadezhda Sergeyevna!" the old man said in a tone of protest, choosing his words carefully. "You look on this affair somewhat

255

superficially, and I would even say academically. But books are one thing and life is quite another. Books, as you know, reflect life, but not always the right way—sometimes in reverse. Survivals do exist. True, sometimes they are not at all like what we read in the books. But life has many secret, unexplored aspects, in contrast to the more obvious ones. Let's take, say . . . Whom shall we take? Well, take the roofer who works for our house management. He gets four hundred roubles a month, he has a wife and child, but doesn't go off to a job in a factory because here he has a lot of free time. In the morning he makes mattresses in the yard, and on Sundays he organizes a private enterprise with other roofers like himself, and earns a bit on the side, building and painting garages for the owners of Pobeda cars. Recently he has bought a television set. There you have two aspects of the same man. Now take our neighbor, Bakradze, an engineer. He earns a great deal more than the roofer and has no family. And yet he deals in fruit and bay leaves that he gets from Abkhasia and sells in the market. There is his second face for you. Now let's go still further. Take the head of that office who passed our complaint on without reading it. He isn't a black marketeer. Oh, dear no! He sometimes even makes speeches! About democracy, and consideration for the people! But if he had any consideration, if he enjoyed defending the righteous and punishing the guilty, he would have to work, to bestir himself like a squirrel in its revolving cage! Because our complaint alone would provide him with enough hard work for a month. And our complaint is not the only one. He would have to forego his night's sleep to work out a method of dealing with complaints which would take everything into account. So that complaints about Avdiyev are not sent to Avdiyev! Good-by to his country cottage, good-by to his fishing excursions and football matches! Or he would neglect the routine of his department and be sacked. Whereas now if you were to look into his business you would find it completely up to date. With everything nicely arranged in little boxes and card indexes, like the keyboard of a piano accordion. And he can enjoy his private life splendidly, without any trouble, without any suffering, without any pain. And make speeches about 'consideration,' too! Here again are two aspects: the hidden one and the visible one."

"Yes," Nadia said thoughtfully. She was thinking of Drozdov. Here was the answer to all his endless speeches.

"So there you are, Nadezhda Sergeyevna, that is what the residue of capitalism looks like in its natural conditions. One can shut oneself away from it between four walls, stick posters all over the walls, stop fighting it, sit contentedly, priding one's self on one's righteousness, and it is already there inside one! It has broken in!"

Discourses like this took place quite frequently in this room, and the professor always liked to give them a twist at the end that revealed to Nadia one more of Lopatkin's merits standing out brightly against a rich background. On these occasions Lopatkin silently gave the old man one of his dark, threatening glances. Nadia listened modestly, like a good pupil. But the other creature inside her leaped and struggled to get out, and it was to her that the professor was addressing his somewhat old-fashioned wiles.

The same being, self-willed and spiteful, prompted Nadia to put on something new, and *as simple as possible,* each time she got ready to pay a visit to her friends in Liakhov Lane. If, on the previous day she had worn a rather old dark-blue jacket, against which the color of her neck stood out delicately, then on the following day the jacket would be given a rest, and she would put on a narrow black skirt and a thin white blouse, which Nadia had not liked until now because it molded the breasts too tightly. Then on another day, instead of the blouse there would be a mauve elastic jumper which evened out all the curves chastely, in which her neck seemed thin and her waist almost the same thickness as her neck, but in which, to make up for this, there seemed to be twice as much hair!

Lopatkin did not realize that these transformations of Nadia's had anything to do with the *simplicity* of her clothes—that it was merely an optical illusion. It seemed to him that another magnetic storm raged in his heart and that his compass had lost its north and its south. He remained grimly silent as he sat at his drawing board.

But Nadia's every appearance was unexpected, and confused his thoughts; he chewed at his pencil, struggled to concentrate, and blamed himself alone. But Nadia calmly put the typewriter on the table, and, with her mouth tightly pursed, began searching for the right keys on the keyboard, and the diffident tapping to which he was already accustomed sounded in the room.

No more replies came in answer to his complaints, and even the professor, who foresaw everything, began to wonder, because the full cycle was not yet completed. The wheel was to come full circle with a circumstantial answer under several headings, which proved that Lopatkin's machine was expensive, uneconomical, unproductive, dangerous in use, and as to its underlying idea, not even new. And, needless to say, "intricate and clumsy."

Toward the end of February, when Nadia came at dusk one day, Lopatkin, with a bitter laugh, handed her a new document, holding it, with weary carelessness, between the index and middle fingers.

"Register this . . . er . . . under incoming, please."

To Citizen Lopatkin, D.A., was typewritten on white art paper. *On receipt of this you are required to appear on February 21 at the district prosecutor's office, room No. 9, to Deputy Prosecutor Comrade Titov, for explanations regarding a question concerning yourself.*

Nadia read, cast her eyes down, and silently opened her ledger.

Lopatkin had been prepared for such a contingency. He knew that he could answer any question, and the sadness and weariness in his eyes were not due to his fear of any possible trouble. It was simply that that morning he had caught a glimpse of the long and endless road that lay before him, with its uniform milestones: 33, 34, 35 . . . familiar figures, because soon he would be thirty-three. Somewhere at the end of that road stood his completed machine. But which figure would be carved into that milestone?

Sorrow suddenly pierced him like a needle, soundlessly, and when he glanced at Nadia, it pierced her, too. But he was a stern and hardy traveler. He frowned, his face clouded darkly, he lifted the bundle higher on his shoulder, and tramped on, not back, but forward. But Nadia was stunned. She said nothing to him then; it was only two hours later, when Lopatkin was escorting her in the darkness along Liakhov Lane, that she suddenly took him by the arm and stopped.

"Dmitri Alexeyevich! Why have they sent for you?"

"Which 'they'?" he laughed. "I assume that Avdiyev wants to clarify our relationship."

"Why make fun of it like this?" She was offended; tears glistened in her eyes in the darkness. "I asked you seriously."

"Nadezhda Sergeyevna." Without thinking, he put his hand on her shoulder, but quickly took it away again. "It is a pity that you can't see how serious my answer was. It is a very serious business altogether!"

On the twenty-first of February Lopatkin, freshly shaved and wearing his new tie, knocked on the door, and entered Deputy Prosecutor Titov's office, which was brightly lighted by the winter sun. The prosecutor was a severe-looking woman with closely cropped hair, a brown coat with green facings, and narrow white shoulder straps. On the table in front of her lay documents in folders, and on top of the folders a packet of White Sea Canal cigarettes, and a box of matches. When Lopatkin came in, she was telling someone off on the telephone in a toneless voice, smoking all the time, and, without looking, flicking the ash all over the documents.

"Stop giving me that, Comrade expert! . . . Just stop! Look here, Uncle Kolya, this expert opinion of yours would take at most four hours."

Having come to the end of the conversation, she hung up the receiver, gave Lopatkin a quick, unpleasant glance, said: "Sit down," and lit herself a fresh cigarette.

"What is this, Comrade . . . er . . . Lopatkin, isn't it? Yes, Lopatkin." She shifted the documents on the table, drummed nervously on the table with her fingers, stood up, and walked to the window. "What *is* all this, Comrade Lopatkin?" she asked, looking out of the window. "Some people advance Soviet science and industry, doing creative work, and others fling dirt at them. How does that strike you?"

Lopatkin said nothing, merely scrutinizing her with curiosity.

"Is that how it is?" She sat down once more at the table and again fumbled with the papers on it.

"I fling no dirt at anyone," Lopatkin said quietly. "You have been misinformed."

"Then what is this? And this?" She opened the folder and handed Lopatkin typewritten copies of seven or eight of his letters, applications and complaints, written at different periods. A copy of the letter he had written to the editor of the newspaper in connection with Shutikov's article was there also. The letter had been sent to the institute, and the "experts" had sent it on here.

"These are complaints," Lopatkin said in a soft, even voice. "Criticisms."

"There is such a thing as criticism, and there is also libel directed at honorable men."

"Perfectly true," Lopatkin answered. He could not refrain from smiling at her stern look. "Who is to decide for us what is libel and what isn't?"

"A group of scientists has complained to the public prosecutor's office."

"Oh, I see! May I have a look?"

"Here you are." She handed him the complaint, typed on eight pages; half of the last page was taken up by the signatures.

Lopatkin read it through attentively without hurrying, raising his eyebrows when he came across particularly strong expressions, such as "unprecedented attack," "with incomprehensible fury," "compelled to seek protection in Soviet law."

"Well, how do you like it?" Titov asked.

"Not badly worded," Lopatkin said, somewhat taken aback at seeing himself described all of a sudden as a "dangerous calumniator," "sham innovator," or "blackmailer." He said nothing, then nodded to Titov. "Not bad. It fits the case."

"Perhaps. But *we* don't like it, Comrade Lopatkin." Titov now raised her eyes to Lopatkin's face for the first time. "We don't like it at all."

"That is your own fault, Comrade."

"What do you mean?"

"Excuse me, how long have you been working as prosecutor?"

"I don't understand. Well, say, eight years."

"And how many people have you prosecuted for suppressing technical innovations? None? Well, that is why *we* are complaining."

A light suddenly appeared in Titov's lusterless eyes. For an instant she smiled, put her cigarette to her mouth, and disappeared behind a cloud of white smoke.

"The point is that you believed them." Lopatkin's voice grew firmer. He leaned toward Titov and stretched out his strong, bony hand. "And yet all these scientists, Avdiyev, Fundator, Volovik, Tepikin, are still riding along on the technical methods of the day before yesterday. Like the silkworm, they spin cocoons for themselves out of their own spittle. Perhaps at some time you may have seen this: a foreign motorcar with a little flag on it standing in the street. Like a living bird. All shiny. And around it a crowd of our people. Have you ever seen that? Well, when I see such a thing, I feel at once as though something was burning me here in my left side! I feel that if I stay there another minute looking at the scene I shall fall and never get up again. And it is these people, Comrade Titov, who force such disgrace on us. It's a monopoly. They do not allow any leaps forward, only a gradual, scarcely perceptible ascent. And they strike at everyone who thinks differently. But it is impossible to destroy those who think differently—they are needed, just as a conscience is needed."

"In other words, you think we ought to spare our enemies, too?"

"There you are! They regard all those who differ from them as enemies! And that even in technical matters! What sort of enemy am I? Yet here they are trying to give me a bad name and hang me! One man doesn't like my machine, so at once they try to label me

261

some sort of Weismannist-Morganist. To stick it on my back, and there I am with a black mark against me. But the matter is not so simple. Everything depends on the purpose. If you are pursuing the same high purpose by different means, it is possible to argue. And such arguments can only be of advantage. A probing of the matter would result in doing away with parasites, both greater and lesser ones. Remember that I am convinced Avdiyev is wrong. He appears to be right merely because of his position."

Lopatkin's gray eyes lit up with a soft and velvety warmth. He placed each of his words firmly in front of Titov and underscored them with a strong bony finger. He was not giving an account of himself to a public prosecutor—he was a schoolmaster in his class, teaching and persuading. Titov no longer concealed her smile; she smoked thoughtfully, scrutinizing this strange propagandist with the limp, lusterless hair.

"It is quite true that they and I are enemies. We not only hold different opinions, we are pursuing different objectives!" Lopatkin explained patiently, his voice softening. "Our aims—it's the aims that are different! I am saying this in full possession of my mental faculties. They are already looking back, not forward. Their aim is to stay put in their easy chairs and to go on getting richer. But a discoverer of new things is serving the people. A discoverer always thinks differently in any sphere of knowledge. Because he has found a new and shorter way, he rejects the old habitual one."

"All right," Titov said, after a pause. Her cigarette had gone out; she took a fresh one. "All this is true. But let's come to the point. What have you to say about the case in hand?"

"I dispute the allegations, of course. Both the accusations and the accusers. There should be a single answer to my complaints: to make the machine and see which of the disputants was right. But they are afraid of arguments and experiments, for they would be the death of them. They prefer the public prosecutor. Please keep in mind, Comrade Titov, that there is another group of scientists, who supports me. But alas, it is a minority!"

"Very good. We'll check up." Titov sighed and stood up. "There is a table over there. Sit down and write an explanation. Only, please," she smiled, "keep to the facts of the case!"

An hour later the explanation was ready. Lopatkin handed it to Titov, shook her hard, dry hand, and went out of the bright sunlight of the office into the dusk of the passage. Here someone brushed gently against his chest. As his eyes grew used to the half-light, he saw right in front of him Nadia's large gray-blue beret.

"Excuse me, Dmitri Alexeyevich," she said softly, raising her eyes and then casting them down again. "I suppose I am being very bad!"

Lopatkin looked first to one side, then to the other; this helped him to hold back the tears which had unexpectedly welled up in them. "Hell! There is something wrong with my nerves!" he thought. He quickly held the beret against his breast, they looked at each other, and began laughing happily. Still laughing, Nadia firmly gripped Lopatkin's arm, shook him, and they set out quickly, walking in step, without saying anything, from the passage to the stairs, down the stairs into the street, and along the streets and alleys. And both of them felt, with alarm, that some change had come over their relationship.

That same evening Nadia wrote a letter to Valentina Pavlovna in Muzga. The letter began with the words:

Dearest Valentina Pavlovna,
I have met and it seems fallen in love with your . . . you know whom. I had never known love, now I know it, and understand you! And I know you will forgive it me—for, after all, I could not help it! Besides, I share your fate—he will only allow friendship.

Here Nadia laid down the pen and blushed with a joyous hope, as she remembered what had happened three hours ago—that short blissful walk with him after the visit to the prosecutor.

9

SHE decided to invite them to her house. "Them," because she knew Lopatkin would not come alone without his friend. She wanted to arrange it as a simple friendly occasion. To make them sit on the divan, brew them strong tea, and chat with them (with him!) when there was no drawing board around; perhaps even play them something on the cottage piano.

The idea gave her no peace for several days. She worked out a detailed plan, but it almost came to nothing. For Lopatkin, too, had a plan in which an evening party at Nadia's house had no part. It was the professor who saved the situation. He remembered a long-past conversation about the necessity of *living,* and about the dangers of excessive concentration on one thing; Lopatkin unwillingly agreed. He was apprehensive about something, and frowned as he accepted the invitation.

On the appointed evening they rang the bell. They were freshly shaved and did not speak to each other. They entered the hall and stopped, keeping close to one another; they were not used to going out on visits. Nadia, prettily dressed, gaily took their hats and hung up their coats. At that moment the professor trod on Lopatkin's foot, and glanced meaningly at the hat stand. A shopping bag was hanging there, made up of many triangular pieces of leather. It was a striking-looking object. Lopatkin glanced at Nadia and said, "Hm. . . . Yes. . . ."

In truth, he had already guessed one or two things when Nadia had begun bringing them her carefully thought-out inexpensive presents. But at that time they had merely been unconfirmed guesses. The shopping bag was a different story; even the professor gaped at it open-eyed, and he most certainly knew the value of evidence.

"Once you've hit his trail, go on and catch your spy, quick!" Lopatkin growled under his breath, and looked to see whether Nadia could have heard him. But she was no longer in the hall. She had run to the kitchen and was talking softly there with an angry, deep-voiced old woman.

Then she came back. She showed the guests to her room, and they all sat down in a row on the divan. Nikolashka stared at them round-eyed from behind a chair. Lopatkin shook his finger at him, the little boy looked at his mother, his eyebrows rising piteously, and began to cry.

"Don't be frightened, darling!" Nadia took him in her arms and hushed him. "This is a nice uncle."

"A very nice uncle indeed!" the professor confirmed.

Nadia put her son into his bed, but he howled so loudly that he had to be taken out again, and put on the floor. He at once hid behind a chair, stuck his thumb in his mouth, and watched the "uncle" closely.

"Nadezhda Sergeyevna," the professor began. "We have often talked about you, about it all, as it were . . . and about certain mysterious actions on your part which we have learned about, so— who are you?"

Nadia stood at the table, moving the delicate cups. She turned quickly and looked at the old man without speaking. Then she answered simply:

"I am one of Dmitri Alexeyevich's defaulting debtors!"

Meanwhile Nikolashka, picking up courage, emerged from behind the chair and even took a step or two toward the "uncle." Lopatkin showed him a "horned goat" with his hands, and the child dashed back behind the chair, but his eyes shone.

Nadia poured out the tea. The first cup was naturally for the professor, and he expressed his thanks with a slight inclination of the head.

"I like you better and better, Nadezhda Sergeyevna!" he said.

"Put some jam in it, it's nice like that," and Nadia pushed the jam jar toward him.

"Hi, you rascal!" Lopatkin said, glaring playfully at Nikolashka. Nikolashka skipped and stamped his feet with a mixture of terror and delight, hid behind the chair, and then peeped out again.

"Shameless creature!" the old woman said outside in the passage, speaking in a deep, mannish voice that seemed to come straight through the keyhole. Then she departed, shuffling the soles of her bedroom slippers. But inside the room no one started in alarm, no one stopped talking or winked an eyelid—probably because they had already had enough trials in their lives.

"I like this kind of tea," the old man said. "And you make it very well. But I want to tell you a secret! Strong tea is dangerous, it truly is; and you have a lovely complexion!"

"If you knew what a lot of trouble I take over it!"

"You don't need to. Where nature has provided so generously there is no need for feeble human efforts!" the old man said with a courtly little bow, moving his empty cup toward the teapot. Lopatkin raised his eyebrows quizzically and Nadia thanked her cavalier with an appropriate acknowledgment and poured him out another cup of strong tea.

"Thank you." The professor took the cup from her hand, and, not forgetting the jam, went on: "I have often pondered on the natural, physical beauty of men and women!"

"There is no such beauty!" Lopatkin suddenly said.

"Miron, Phidias, and Praxiteles have given us splendid examples, which . . ."

"Don't trot out any authorities, please!" Lopatkin retorted, laughing. "Most people like what is *attractive,* not what is beautiful. The very word was born to stress the difference between a mere regularity of feature and an inner spiritual beauty."

"But why is it that we can be so mistaken?" Nadia asked in a soft, despondent voice. "We may meet someone with an unhandsome exterior, and be attracted by an inner beauty, which later proves to be non-existent."

266

Lopatkin at once understood of whom Nadia was speaking, and pondered the matter. He had to answer in such a manner that would not show Nadia that she had unintentionally given herself away, and that would not embarrass her.

"There are always some deviations from the rule," he answered, then paused. "There is a long gamut of deviations."

"But what about my example?" Nadia asked. She understood Lopatkin's caution, and with a look gave him permission to speak without any reserve.

"Lovers take on special mating apparel, and a festive display of every color in the rainbow," the professor said, looking approvingly at Nadia.

"In those cases it is useful to see how a man like that behaves when *she* is not by!" Lopatkin added. "What he is like with other people. A lot is revealed in that way. . . ."

"Yes," Nadia said absent-mindedly. "It's quite true. A lot is revealed!"

She raised her eyes and gazed for a long time at Lopatkin, as though she were testing her relationship to him. Lopatkin recognized the look, and turned his eyes away; Valentina Pavlovna's tenderness and devotion now seemed to have been transferred to Nadia. He glanced at her once more, and again turned away his eyes—she was still looking at him with the same gentle devotion.

"The question sometimes remains insoluble even for very sensitive people," the professor said, as though awakening, "or insoluble until very late. A young man, very gifted spiritually, I think, was one day traveling in a railway train . . . No, we won't begin like that! I knew a woman once who dreamed of getting married. And somehow, on a train journey, a young man fell in love with her. He fell in love so completely that he proposed that she should leave the train with him and marry him. But she said: 'How can I? Suddenly, like this?' She was a vulgar-minded woman, and a Muscovite at that, and this was somewhere in Belgorod, a world away. She thought there would probably not even be bread to be had there, and so she said no, although she was very much attracted to the young man. So they parted and she regretted it afterward for a very long time. I think even now she regrets it. She never did marry, by the way. And of course he, too, was sorry. But if I were to meet him, I would say to him: it was your great good fortune that you did not succeed in persuading her. Your wife should be a woman who would be glad to jump boldly off her train with you! I want to tell you this, Dmitri Alexeyevich, so that you will not be so hard on the poor devils of vulgarians! Let them live, thinking only about the rags on their backs and about their captains! Don't disturb them! Oh, by the way . . ." The professor suddenly slid along the divan to a little bookshelf that was crammed with books. "So you've got Balzac! Ah!" He took out one of the books, then, recollecting himself, searched for his cup with his shortsighted eyes, drew Nadia's cup to him, and took a sip. "Aha! *Lost Illusions.* How I love it! There are some wonderful passages in it! This is genuinely great literature!"

He began with trembling fingers to turn the pages of the book, and Nadia and Lopatkin were suddenly left to themselves.

"Shall I play you something?" Nadia asked softly.

"Yes, do, please," Lopatkin agreed, bending, as it were, under the weight of her glance.

"What shall I play?" She went over to the cottage piano, opened it, and began to play. "You know what this is?"

Lopatkin recognized it. It was the second movement of the Second Concerto, the passage where the hero's melancholy musing begins and where Chopin, believing there is one human being in the world who is receptive to the message, speaks to him about how hard life sometimes is and how precious is the sympathy of a friend.

If Lopatkin had raised his eyes at this moment, he would have seen a strange being at the piano, a being very like Nadia, looking straight at him, sorrowfully radiant. But he did not raise his eyes. He wrinkled his forehead sharply and hung his head, as if he were looking under the table.

"Please, play that passage again," he begged.

And Nadia repeated the passage, again and again, because she herself also liked it. She was thinking of Lopatkin, and as she softly pressed the keys, she gazed at him, as though telling him in sound what she could not tell him in words. And he listened and understood the sounds in almost the same way as she did. But there was a point where his feelings and Nadia's diverged. To him it seemed as though it were his mother, who had died in loneliness, but who, forgetting her grief, was now looking lovingly at him, shedding tears of joy, as she gazed at her large and splendid son.

"Here it is!" the professor broke in, and Nadia stopped playing. "A masterly passage!" He began to read, unaware of Lopatkin's and Nadia's smiles. " 'Not all inventors possess the grip of a bulldog, which will die before it lets go what it has once got its teeth into.' How marvelously put! What force!" Here he glanced at Lopatkin and Nadia, and noticed their smiles. Exclaiming "Oh!" he waved the book, and again settled down on the divan to read it. Even in literature, he understood only what was related to inventors.

Nadia let her hands fall softly on the keys.

"I know what you like," she said. "You like this!"

With her lips compressed she touched the keys—it was the passage where, after momentary weakness, the hero rises again and pushes forward. After a few seconds Lopatkin, too, began to hum the orchestral part very softly, to aid the hero.

The battle was over. Nadia let her hands drop, and this time Lopatkin did not ask her to play the passage again, for such things cannot be repeated. There was a silence.

"Oh, you wascal!" The words were suddenly spoken quite clearly near the divan. It was Nikolashka who had at last made up his mind to approach the "uncle." He had already touched his knee several times, and was now prodding him, inviting him to a romp.

"A-a-ah!" Lopatkin roared, seizing the little boy and tossing him up in the air, then he seated him on his knee, and opened his mouth, pretending to swallow him. Nikolashka puckered up his face, but laughed at the same time, showing his wide-spaced little teeth. Then he settled himself firmly on Lopatkin's knee and began seriously to examine this big "uncle," and play with his buttons.

"Now he will give you no more peace!" Nadia said, and began to play, quite softly, something unfamiliar, losing herself in thought.

"Here!" the professor shouted triumphantly. "Just listen to this, Dmitri Alexeyevich! Your very words! 'The Cointets will make money out of my inventions; but, after all, what am I compared with the country? A man like any other. If my invention is of benefit to the country, why, I shall be happy.'"

Taking another sip from Nadia's cup, the old man again seemed, as it were, to disappear from the room, and it was then, to the soft sound of the piano, as he tickled Nikolashka's neck with his nose, that Lopatkin suddenly asked himself: "What am I doing? And why?" And he saw Jeanne, her tears and her confusion. He had loved her once, he loved her still, he could not simply give her up, desert a young girl who was unable to find a proper place for herself in the world. . . . She would perish! And there was that captain . . . He might marry her, buy her a blue fox fur, and make her embroider table napkins all day. . . . "But then why am I so drawn to this one, sitting there? She invited me to come here and I was glad!" Frowning, he glanced at Nadia. She read his thoughts, cast her eyes down modestly, and went on playing.

"Aren't we staying too long?" he asked in dumb show, and coughed. "Aren't we disturbing the great man's rest?"

"The great man is not in!" Nadia answered with a shake of her head. And without pausing in her playing, she added in a whisper:

"He has gone to Muzga. They are making the machine there."

"And he?" Lopatkin inquired, also in dumb show.

"Unofficially. But he has already taken the lead," Nadia said, speaking very clearly.

"I must go!" Lopatkin thought, and he stood up with a suddenness that surprised even himself, almost dropping Nikolashka. He was in a hurry to get back to his drawing board, and no one could have detained him.

By the middle of March Lopatkin had completed his new design. It happened one evening. He stood up, grasped the upright of the drawing stand, stretched himself so vigorously that the stand shifted from its usual position, and for the first time in several months he gave Nadia a brilliant smile.

"Done!" he said, coming out into the middle of the room; he picked up the flatiron and began doing his exercises with it. "Now we'll start our run-around again! Right from the beginning. We'll start a brand-new, splendid, everlasting run-around!" he sang gaily, spinning round and round, swinging the flatiron. "Tomorrow I shall be thirty-three. Uncle Evgeni!" he cried, "now I am no longer an infant either—I am an inventor of six years' standing!"

"March on!" the professor responded. "Diesel used to say . . ."

"I know what he used to say." Lopatkin changed the flatiron over to his other hand. "There is a terrible irony in those words! Really terrible. But there is no sense in them. In real life the opposite is true: the older one is, the more hopes one has. The chances improve and the hopes grow. It is the hopes that draw us on, that draw us further and further into this business!"

"But have you ever been an old man?" the professor asked in an innocent tone. "You haven't? Ah, that's just the point!"

"You, too, harbor hopes, Evgeni Ustinovich," Nadia said. "You like a drink, I know. And yet you seldom do drink. That is proof number one."

"Nadezhda Sergeyevna, one mustn't drink if one holds a treasure in one's hands which one has to hand over to . . . to the people, so to speak."

"Ah! So you *do* hope to hand it over someday!"

"No, I am convinced that I never shall. But while I am alive, I must keep it safe. That is the important part of me. A human being is made up of two parts: the physical shell, which inevitably dies, no need to regret it—and of a cause. The cause may go on forever. If at any time it does get into people's hands . . ."

"Evgeni Ustinovich," Lopatkin said solemnly, "if ever I hand over my own, my second job shall be yours, without fail!"

"Don't make promises! You promise and already enjoy, free, the pleasure of having helped a fellow human. And you receive thanks in advance!" The old man stood up and made Lopatkin a bow. "So

271

that perhaps you won't even want to receive the same thanks all over again. Especially as you would have to pay for a second pleasure—you would have to keep your promise."

"Very well. I take back my word."

"Don't make promises," the professor said once again, taking a little clay cube out of the press. "Particularly not in front of other people. A public promise gives greater pleasure, but, on the other hand, later you begin thinking, not of the debt, but of the interest, of people remembering that you had promised. Vows, even of love . . ."

"Yes, you can't make promises about love. That is true," Nadia said. "One should just love. But it is so pleasant to listen to vows of love."

"Yes, it may be true, that those who love or those who hate do not require formal vows," Lopatkin agreed.

"I see that we all agree about this," the professor went on. "And in fact it is so! No one, for instance, exerted any pressure on Dmitri Alexeyevich, to make him remain faithful to his idea. Nadezhda Sergeyevna types your complaints, Dmitri Alexeyevich, although no one made her swear any oaths to do so! What is more, she even infringed certain obligations she had formally taken on herself, because the name of Drozdov is mentioned in these complaints, and soon people will begin saying that she has acted contrary to man-made laws."

"They are already beginning to talk," Nadia murmured thoughtfully, stroking the keys of the typewriter with her fingers. The old man stared at her in alarm.

"Nadezhda Sergeyevna! Do you mean me? If it was I who said it first, forgive me, please! It was because I understand you and speak to you as if I were talking to myself!"

"No, Evgeni Ustinovich," Nadia said, coming out of her abstraction, "I was thinking of something quite different." She sighed. "Dear Evgeni Ustinovich, it was something quite, quite different."

"Well, comrades in arms, don't make vows. But if you do want to make some great resolution, do it only once in a lifetime, and do it in silence; don't make an exhibition of yourselves. Climb up somewhere to a great height, from which you can see the whole earth, and make your resolution in silence. In such circumstances you will at least be troubled by your conscience, by the fear of being a coward, a small-minded creature."

There was a silence. Lopatkin bent his head, went to his part of the room, and without a word began to pack up his drawings: a drawing, then a sheet of newspaper, another drawing, another sheet of newspaper, and so on, until all fourteen drawings were assembled. Then he rolled them up into a tube and tied them with a bit of string, singing with great concentration the whole time. Nadia watched his punctilious procedure, looked at him from under her knitted brows with such an expression of restrained love, that the professor paused in his work, directed his misty spectacles in her direction, drew his head in between his shoulders, and said nothing more.

It looked as if Nadia were making her great resolution silently there and then—she had no need to climb to some high place in order to see the whole earth from there; she made her vow, not to the earth, but to one man.

Next day, toward evening, when they had just switched on the light, Nadia came again. In her hand she carried a huge roll tied lengthwise and crosswise with string. Lopatkin glanced at it and frowned slightly—Nadia had again brought a gift. He felt that a decisive moment was coming when explanations would have to be given—explanations that would be unpleasant for him, and particularly so for her. It is not good to overdo things.

Nadia took off her beret and her black coat wet with the March snow, and revealed a blouse of some delicate fluffy bright green material. These blouses—with very short sleeves—had just begun to be the fashion among young girls for dancing. But this fashion had not spread in the usual way; having come from abroad, it had first taken root on the outskirts, broken out like an epidemic in Muzga, and only later found its way to Moscow.

Arms bare almost to the shoulder and as delicate as a baby's and against them the thick warm fluff—January and July side by side—great daring was needed to demonstrate such a combination in winter, even at some club or other. That Nadia was wearing such a blouse was, of course, due to that other self, the crazy one, who had lately grown dangerously bold. Because of this, Nadia, when she had taken off her coat and felt Lopatkin's stern gaze upon her, blushed furiously, close to tears, then plucking up all her courage, and feeling as though she were naked in the presence of the two men, she dragged her enormous roll on to the table and began peevishly slashing at its string with a knife.

"What is this? Another present?" Lopatkin asked, laying his hand on the roll.

"Please, don't say anything." Nadia glanced at him and at once dropped her eyes.

"Very well, I won't," Lopatkin's eyes replied inflexibly. In the silence that followed, Nadia again began cutting and tearing at the strong string that tied the parcel. Then she paused, and, facing the two men, said:

"Don't look at me, please! I did a dreadfully silly thing—I put this on for the festive occasion. It was the girls in Muzga who invented the fashion!"

"I must say our Muzga girls are very intelligent creatures," the professor intoned nasally, under his breath.

But at that moment Nadia peeled off the last layers of wrapping paper like the leaves of a cabbage, and pulled out a large, dark-brown brief case made of the thick leather from which cavalry saddles are made. It had a very convenient handle, and was stiffened by a brass frame.

Lopatkin averted his eyes from the brief case and said:

"Nadezhda Sergeyevna, I am not able for the moment to return the money you sent us, but I am keeping the debt in mind. But we shall not accept anything more from you. Let me help you wrap it up again."

"Don't be in such a hurry," Nadia retorted, sticking out her chin obstinately. "Stand up straight. Evgeni Ustinovich, come closer.

Just let me see him try . . ." She ceremoniously stepped forward, holding out the brief case, and said to Lopatkin: "My congratulations, comrade inventor, on your birthday! May the projects you will carry about in this brief case all be approved!"

"And may they serve the people reliably!" the professor added.

In the end Lopatkin was forced to accept one more gift from Nadia. He opened the brief case, clicked its massive locks, and smiled like a child, because grown men also like toys. Meanwhile, Nadia was undoing a mass of wrappings, little twists of grease-proof paper, small parcels and packages, some rolls, and finally she placed on the table one by one no less than four bottles of wine.

"I don't know who drinks what," she said. "This is a Cáhors, it is what I like. This is port. And this is port, too, but a different kind. And this one I have heard called wine by those who drink and vodka by those who don't. I don't think there's any harm in celebrating the birthday of one of us, especially as he finished an important piece of work yesterday."

"Quite so," said the professor, and began carefully clearing the table. He wiped the oilcloth, which was already clean, cleared the cigarette stubs from the chairs, and carried the whole bundle of wrapping paper to the kitchen at a run. Then he came back and began to uncork the bottles.

At last the preparations were complete, and the three friends sat down to the table on which were plates of salmon, caviar, cheese, ham, butter, and a huge pile of sliced bread.

"Well, shall we drink?" Nadia asked. "You, Evgeni Ustinovich, will want *this*, I suppose?"

"White wine, please," the professor replied, holding out his cup.

"And you? White wine or vodka?" Nadia asked Lopatkin, and laughed. "Oh, do you know, I seem to be drunk already!"

"Very little for me," Lopatkin said, pushing his cup toward her. "That's enough."

But Nadia managed to pour a little more into the cup and again laughed. For herself she poured out half a cup of Cahors.

"Let's drink to each of us in turn," she proposed. "First to the one with the birthday."

"Your health, Dmitri Alexeyevich!" said the professor, and made Lopatkin a bow.

"Your health, Dmitri Alexeyevich." Nadia laughed, copying the professor's bow.

They drank, each of them in his own way, Lopatkin as though he were drinking water and even felt surprised at the weakness of Moscow vodka. The professor grew crimson in the face, wiped away tears, and quickly grabbed one of the sandwiches which had been prepared in advance. Nadia drank her Cahors in sips, and without any reason laughed into her cup.

"I don't know what's got into me."

"I'll explain," the professor said, chewing his sandwich. "It's all quite simple. You yourself are a wine. There was a time—hm—when I, too, felt the same, but now, as you see . . . in order to rise to the level of your temperament in my conversation I must, I am forced . . . This tones one up very well." He took the bottle and with a melancholy air poured himself out half a cup of vodka, exclaiming to Nadia: "To your wine!" gulped down the vodka, and again attacked the sandwich.

"Why are you eating so little?" Nadia asked, glancing quickly at Lopatkin and piling on to his plate some of the good things on the table.

"He doesn't eat on principle," the professor declared, chewing rapidly. "He has some sort of theory about it. This delicate morsel is too good for him. I had better have it." The professor took a piece of salmon off Nadia's fork with his fingers and put it into his mouth, smearing the oil all over his whiskers.

Nadia laughed aloud.

"Just look at the professor! And what theory is that, Dmitri Alexeyevich?"

"There is no theory. You can see I am eating. Everything will be eaten up. This old vulgarizer went on arguing with me during the night, and in the end he argued himself into saying that in all human beauty it is the exterior that is of decisive importance. Have you never seen some sable-eyebrowed beauty who not only left you entirely cold but who was horrible to look at? The next thing he'll say is that beauty consists in clothes! Or in having a private motor-car."

The professor looked at Lopatkin over his spectacles, like an old badger suddenly attacked by an inexperienced hound.

"Dmitri Alexeyevich has a theory that food and clothing are evils. This theory satisfied us completely until an unknown agent brought us, in a shopping bag made of little pieces of leather . . . Would you kindly pass that bottle? I'd like to taste it. I have never drunk Armenian port."

"No, you must explain your creed to Nadezhda Sergeyevna."

"My creed indeed! It's the creed of the overwhelming majority of people."

"No, it's the creed of the consumer. Or isn't it?"

Lopatkin had been too hasty when he expressed a lack of confidence in the "metropolitan" vodka. He drank without turning a hair and in this way admitted a dangerous enemy into his fortress. The enemy went into action—making him speak in a loud voice. Lopatkin grew pale, as all exhausted, enfeebled people do when they drink strong spirits. His movements had become rapid and precise, and his eyes had darkened.

"Don't you think," he said, as he tried to cut himself a slice of ham, "don't you think that the external beauty of human beings is created not by nature so much as by those human beings themselves—by their characters? Stupid, greedy, unrestrained, lazy, and weak-willed people are generally stout. Those who see the meaning of life in the acquisition of worldly goods have a peculiar 'earthy' look."

"Wait a minute!" The professor tried to object, but at that moment Nadia cried: "Let's drink to beauty!" and Evgeni Ustinovich submissively bowed his gray head and held out his cup.

Lopatkin drank his second glass of vodka as though he were drinking a cup of tea, and continued his attack:

"Isn't it true that a first glance at a human being often gives a correct conception of him, even if only subconsciously? You, for instance, understood me at first glance; you even said something about a face and a passport. Remember? So there you are! It is not fur coats and bright eyes that walk in our streets, but characters, each one of them!"

"My dear fellow, you are quite different from me, you know. You understand more than a little about music, or at all events you are able to sit through a concert to the end. You have a certain firmness. I, for my part, am armed with nothing but mathematics and chemistry, although I make bold to assert that I have never heard more divine music than the music of the theory of numbers! I must say that you are talking much more clearly and logically today, but unfortunately I can understand nothing after all these toasts."

"For the sake of those last few words I am prepared to forgive you everything," Lopatkin cried, laughing.

"Then I have something to say." The professor suddenly spoke in his usual serious tone. "Fill our cups, please, Nadezhda Sergeyevna."

Nadia filled them, and then put the empty vodka bottle under the table.

"Comrades, it turns out quite unexpectedly that I must leave you," the professor went on quietly. "I told Dmitri Alexeyevich that I have to meet someone in connection with whom I have certain hopes. The meeting is today. I can't conceive how I could have forgotten it! What is the time, Nadezhda Sergeyevna?"

"A quarter to ten," Nadia said.

Lopatkin frowned.

"Oh! I am forty minutes late already!" The old man hurriedly put on his overcoat, stuck his hat on his head, then stopped and counted on his fingers: "The tram journey, then ten more minutes' walk—the whole will take about an hour and a half. I must rush! Excuse me, please!" He picked up his cup. "I drink to my not being too late! To the success of my enterprise, for whose sake I have to leave such a wonderful table and such good company!"

He drank the vodka, took a slice of bread from the table, laid a slice of ham on it, made Nadia a bow, and walked out chewing his sandwich. They heard the dull thud of his footsteps receding as he walked along the passage. A door slammed in the distance with a decisive, final sound that could be heard throughout the flat. Lopatkin and Nadia sobered instantly. As if by agreement, they both looked at their cups and pushed them away, although the professor had already proposed and drunk the toast.

"How suddenly he went off," Nadia said. "Just like that!"

"He said something about it to me three days ago."

"Is that really true? Did he?" Nadia cheered up. A sudden unsavory suspicion had almost spoiled the whole evening for her. "Where does this person live?"

"In Malakhovka."

"Oh, as far as that?"

Nadia was quite reassured. And then she felt her breast pleasantly constricted by a familiar, forbidden feeling, a sinful emotion that boldly overcame her soul, because it was already known to her. Nadia blushed and hung her head. She felt herself beginning to change into that other woman—the one who lived in the mirror. She herself scarcely knew her, and she was afraid that Lopatkin would be displeased by the change, but it was impossible by this time to control the other. The silence thickened around them and tingled in their ears.

"What is the time?" Lopatkin asked hoarsely.

"Three minutes to ten." Nadia rose and began walking up and down the room. "Oh, you have a wireless set! May I switch it on?"

The battered old loud-speaker vibrated with a stage baritone, sweet and passionate, like Mrs. Ganichev's scent.

Lopatkin and Nadia laughed aloud: the singer had in an instant driven all suspense from the room. He sang on, inserting little coquettish sighs before almost every word:

> "Oh, the first letter, oh, the first letter
> Oh, in it you'll find a tear between the lines . . ."

"What a lad!" Lopatkin said.

Nadia pulled the plug out of the socket and the baritone stopped singing.

"Why did you do that? Let him finish his song! Wait, and let's see what he'll be up to next." Lopatkin rose and turned to seize the plug, to set it going again. But it was Nadia's soft little hand. They both plugged the wireless in and took their hands away at the same instant. The baritone buzzed and vibrated wildly: "I was drunk with joy, with love and anxiety!" But neither Nadia nor Lopatkin heard him. A low-pitched ringing filled the room. Lopatkin lowered himself into his chair with unseeing eyes.

"Shall we finish the bottle?" he asked, clearing his throat. "There is still some left."

"What?" Nadia asked, and something prompted her to draw closer to him. "What was that you said?"

Lopatkin did not answer.

"You did say something, didn't you?" Nadia asked timidly. She came up close behind him and bent over. "Something about drinking?"

Then her fingers began creeping caressingly into his hair; they slipped through, tousling it.

"Dmitri Alexeyevich," she said in a strange new voice, pressing his large, yielding head to her breast. "Dmitri Alexeyevich!"

"For one moment of happiness with him I would give up everything"—those familiar words someone had once spoken flashed through her mind.

Lopatkin put his arms about her and swung her round, feeling stronger each minute. She seemed to envelop him from all sides. He wanted to press his face against hers, but Nadia took his head in her hands, held it at arm's length, and gazed at him, anxiously trying to meet his eyes; but he avoided her questing gaze, again feeling embarrassed for a moment. "My darling!" her look said. "Wait, let me look at you. You are mine at last! But what is a kiss? I am ready to give you the whole of myself, my life! Will you love me, Dmitri?"

And having said this, she herself pressed her face to his lips, to his eyes, to his hard cheekbones, laughing and whispering incoherent words.

At two in the morning Lopatkin, his arms flung wide, lay asleep on his bed that was made out of two packing cases, on the gray felt blanket crumpled into a bundle. Nadia had hung his jacket on the back of a chair and unbuttoned his shirt, revealing his bony chest with the strong, protruding ribs. He was breathing deeply and greedily and looked like a large, tormented fledgling. At this moment much could have been learned from his pale face with the harshly knitted brows, from the broad, weary chest which, in his student days, must more than once have broken the tape at the end of a race.

Nadia sat beside him, on the same blanket, and her mournful eyes never left his face. From time to time she suddenly clenched her hands, and the tears, running down her cheeks, dropped on to his shirt. "No, I shall not let you go!" she whispered, kissing his powerful chest and hearing his great heart beating underneath. But her tears soon dried and her face cleared; she sniffed, gently smoothing Lopatkin's hair, pushing it back from his broad forehead lined by a deep furrow that was not smoothed out even in sleep. "Heavens, and I was looking for a hero!" she thought, motionless in her happiness. "Can he really be mine? No, but now I shall ensnare you; you won't get away from me now; there will be no more Jeannes for you!"

She sat until morning, watching Lopatkin. At daybreak she went to the window and saw the deserted Liakhov Lane, gripped by a light frost; she saw the wide-open gate and deserted courtyard of the house on the other side of the street. Everything was quiet and dead; only from the housetops merry, glittering little streaks of water ran down, getting wider and wider, as the sun rose somewhere at Nadia's back.

She looked at Lopatkin and thought: "I, too, have jumped off the train!" It had been a leap that made her head whirl. She gazed with changed eyes at everything around her: this was the house to which an unexpected traveling companion had brought her. What awaited her here? She *had* dared to leap, after all! Although, now she came to think of it, she had not been pressed so very hard.

"I awoke at the misty dawn of who knows what sort of day?" she recalled Blok's verses. "She slept, smiling like a child—she was dreaming of me!"

But no, it was not she who slept, it was he, and there was no Nadia in his dreams. There was only something great and difficult to endure. And on that misty morning she, too, quietly awakened from her childish dreams. The forlorn smile faded slowly from her face. Nadia glanced at the huge drawing board that merged above her into the semi-darkness; she looked at the room where everything resembled a soldier's quarters during a campaign, and she recalled another line from the same poem: "The song of the nightingale cannot prevail over the roaring of the sea."

Then she turned her face again toward the lifeless street and started back, blushing. For there, on the pavement opposite, shuffling slowly along, his fists distending the pockets of his knitted overcoat, was the old professor. He halted, looked up at his house, at his own window, turned his collar higher, shook his head at the cold, and walked on, sidling, and stamping his feet, as the *dvorniks* do who are on duty all night. "To the success of my enterprise!"— Nadia remembered his chivalrous toast. "Oh, you deceiver, you sly fox, you horrid wretch!" she whispered, laughing and shaking her fist at his receding back.

Meanwhile the lane was getting lighter; a flesh-colored tint appeared in the greenish-gold sky, its tones grew warmer, and the live warmth increased. The joyful clarions of dawn seemed to sound beyond the brightly lighted housetops. Yes, a new day was beginning in Moscow, and for Nadia a new life as well. True, it was not beginning in a self-contained flat; it was a half-starved life, but it contained great joys and great sorrows, it was life in the raw. Happiness! It is never sweet and bears no resemblance at all to the insurance posters. It has an undertone of sorrow, as Nadia was very soon to learn.

At seven in the morning she cleaned and tided the room, kissed the sleeping Lopatkin once more, put on her clothes, and crept silently out. All was quiet, and she met no one in the passage. She closed the outer door behind her and sighed with relief. Then, quite suddenly, she had a vision of her deserted Nikolashka; his little face drawn and his wide-open eyes full of wonder. He was standing in his cot, not crying, but only looking at his mother's empty bed and at the door, his small brows piteously wrinkled—unable to make it all out.

"My darling, my sweet, how can one exist without seeing Mummy for such a long time, not at night, nor even in the morning?" Nadia gasped, and, blaming herself, she hurried down the stairs, across the yard to the gate. Far off in the lane the small green light of a taxi was blinking. Nadia ran to it, jerked the door open, and sank on to the soft seat. Only when the houses and columns began flashing past to right and left did it occur to her that now she would have to give up certain habits, such things as taking taxis. "This is the last time," she resolved. "We will live more austerely, in a way that suits a geography teacher!"

She found everything well at home. Nikolashka was sitting at the table in his high chair. Shura was feeding him porridge; he was blowing out his cheeks and stretching his hands out toward the bowl.

"Oh my golden darling, you!" Nadia sang softly, scarcely able to resist the urge to hug and kiss her little boy. But first she took off her coat and, still repeating, "My golden, silver darling," she hurried to the kitchen to wash her hands. Nikolashka began to howl because his mother had gone away. But she was already back and she took him in her arms, made sure that nothing was wrong with him, kissing him again and again, and, flushed with happiness, began to feed him.

"I'll tell Leonid everything! Everything!" her mother-in-law growled from the doorway. "Just you wait until he gets back!"

"Better wait until he comes and then nag *him*, not me," Nadia answered over her shoulder. "Nag him for having deserted his first wife with her two children!"

"Oh, so that's it, is it? She went of her own accord! She was the same sort of dirty tramp . . ."

"Well, his third will leave him, too, one day! And don't talk to me, if you please! I will have nothing to do with you!"

Nadia was at the school all day, teaching classes, and toward evening, alternately holding her breath and sighing deeply, she stood again in front of the tall door with its multitude of bell pushes which sat there like flies in the sun.

It was the professor who opened the door.

"Good evening, Mephistopheles," Nadia said softly.

There was a silence as they gazed at each other.

"Good evening, Marguerite," the old man chanted in soft nasal tones, and Nadia blushed. But he immediately realized that, having been away in Malakhovka, he was not supposed to know anything. He looked diffidently at Nadia and said: "Excuse me, but how am I to understand such an unusual greeting?"

"Jokes are all very well, but I must tell you one thing—in strict confidence," Nadia whispered. "I saw a foreign secret service agent!"

"Impossible! Where?" The professor's eyes opened wide behind the lenses of his spectacles. He looked over his shoulder, then bent an ear toward Nadia out of which protruded gray hairs like broken strings.

"I am absolutely certain that it was he," Nadia said. "He was keeping watch under our window all through the night! One ought to catch and punish the spy."

The old man stood with bent head, thinking this over, then gave Nadia a severe look.

"It is a serious matter. Yes. Very serious. But is it worth while punishing him? The poor fellow certainly caught a cold on the job!"

Hiding a smile, Nadia was about to pass on into the passage, but the professor stopped her.

"Nadezhda Sergeyevna, please don't tell Faust anything. He is in a bad humor today. He would eat me alive for this."

284

"What is he doing?"

"Still lying down. Scowling. Thinking."

Lopatkin had not yet got up. His head was aching. He lay all day on his packing cases, fingering his forehead, staring at the wall and thinking—always about the same thing.

"Hypocrite!" he told himself over and over again. "You have deceived and betrayed Jeannie! Very well, go on with it, and don't whine!"

He groaned and turned over on to his other side. "No, it was not a betrayal," he answered himself. "Anyhow, we'll soon see . . .

"*What* shall we see? And what about the other?" A new thought suddenly crossed his mind. "She will say that there is no good in this world!"

Then a terrible question stabbed him: "And what about *this one?* Why didn't I discourage her from the beginning? Why did I allow her to hope? Was it out of weakness? Or do I perhaps love her? She loves me, that is obvious, that is why she was ready for everything. She may ask for an explanation. And if none is forthcoming, she may ask why I deceived her. I shall have to tell her something, even if the awakening is painful for her. But—have I really deceived her? I liked her, so surely I could not have done so?

"Oh!" he exclaimed, turning on his back and covering his eyes with his hand. "And what about the other one?" he wondered, and the thought was painful. "She is only a slip of a girl. She is hoping that I am in the Kuzbas, she has allowed herself once again to believe that I am not a mere crank, that there *are* heroes in this world! Can I, at such a moment, betray her like this? And Nadia! Am I just to say to her: 'Nice to have met you! Good-by'?

"You're a fine one, you are!" A new firm voice now broke in. "Is that what you are going to brood about now? And the machine? After all, it must be *handed over* some time. And what is the figure on your milestone today? Thirty-three? Then what ought you to be thinking about? Solving childish riddles, or the important part of you, your cause?"

This new voice decided him. Lopatkin frowned and swung his legs off the bed. At that moment Nadia came in.

"Good evening," she said in a bright voice, concealing her anxiety.

Lopatkin looked away guiltily. He was slowly summoning the courage to speak decisive words to Nadia. But she already understood.

"Don't say anything, I understand," she said, sitting down beside him. "Dmitri Alexeyevich, please wait one more day. Give me one day. Let us be together, go somewhere together . . ."

"And never come back!" Lopatkin thought, smiling grimly.

"No!" He drew a deep breath, passed his hand across his forehead, and went on: "Yes . . . What I want to say is . . . we can't carry on with this . . . this business . . ."

Neither of them said anything more. The professor came in, gave them a quick glance, and began wiping the clean oilcloth on the table.

"Fine day today!" he cried, to dispel their confusion. "Oh, you young people, you young people! Why don't you go out into the fresh air?"

Lopatkin said nothing. Nadia looked at his pale face, read his thoughts, and understood everything. Something was happening in her in answer to his silence. At this moment she turned, as it were, into this huge man's mother. And that other sweet, crazy being whom only yesterday she had not been able to control now melted away imperceptibly and disappeared with her quiet tears.

Nadia rose, quickly took off her coat, and hung it up. She was dressed in her dark gray, severe school dress. She turned toward Lopatkin, as though she were awaiting his instructions about the work to be done—as though to let everyone see that if necessary she could be a completely different person. It was her answer to the first sorrow that had come to cloud her happiness.

PART
3

I

THE opportunity of witnessing genuine heroism does not often present itself. Not because heroes are few, but for quite a different reason. The hero rises to the summit of his glorious life without as yet wearing any attractive golden badge on his breast. And that is just when he really *is* a hero. His rise may take years, perhaps decades, and may even remain unnoticed to the end. It sometimes happens that we rub shoulders with a hero and never recognize him. That is no doubt why some people say that heroes do not exist; that there are only prudent sowers, who sow in order to reap a tenfold return.

But consider Lopatkin; his harvest has been ripening for six years, and still there are no ears of corn to be seen. If he had worked as an engineer of the seventh grade, or as a mathematics teacher, he might, during the two preceding years, have acquired all the worldly possessions shown on the huge household-insurance poster pasted on the wall of his alley. But therein lies the sublime and incomprehensible oddness of these people, that they do not take such gigantic and no doubt useful and necessary posters seriously, do not admit their essentialness, and are not afraid either of fires that devour property, or of natural disasters. Neither small nor large sums of money remain in their hands or in their current accounts, nor are ever transformed into worth-while property which can be insured. Among themselves, such people crack jokes about things which to some of us may appear serious. On the other hand, things that some people lightheartedly scoff at are sacrosanct to them. When an "initiator" goes to see an academician for the first time, he is modest and subdued. But if one of these scientists (Academician

289

Florinsky, for example) tells him that he is right, and that his discovery is of great value, then such a man is undone and may even prove dangerous. He will not give up his notion for any consideration, will never be deflected, but will try to force his way in, hammering with his fists at every door to the very last, even if he knows that the end is often a bitter one.

Professor Busko, quoting Diesel, said that with increasing years one loses the habit of hoping; but that was merely idle talk on his part. Never before had he so clung to hope, never held to it so firmly, as since his close acquaintance with Lopatkin, who tried persistently to convince him that friends might serve a useful purpose. When he told Lopatkin to "make no vows," he accepted the vow nevertheless, knowing in his heart that should this new friend of his be successful, he would at once stretch out a hand to help him, Busko, to pass on to the nation his fire-extinguishing powder.

Nor did Lopatkin himself lose the habit of hoping as the years passed. True, he put on a show of indifference when, for example, he handed Nadia a complaint, a letter, or a protest to type, he even laughed at them, but Nadia had already learned to read his feelings. It had been easy for her to acquire this knowledge, which was inaccessible to so many others. She knew that Dmitri expected results from even the most insignificant piece of paper. He considered his every move carefully for days before making it.

One day in May Nadia approached him to ask him some question. Lopatkin was sitting with his head bent, and Nadia caught her breath: a third of his light-brown hair, which had been constantly growing more and more limp, and lacked luster, a third of that crop which was so dear to her, was gray! That was what hopes had done to him, for the hopes were never fulfilled.

Yet Dmitri never exhausted fresh and untried hopes. He submitted his new, improved project to several institutions and had already been frequenting their waiting rooms for about three months, meeting everywhere with the familiar show of politeness and the surreptitious sneers. It was as impossible for him to get used to these as it was impossible for him to lose the habit of hoping.

Who were these sneerers? One could not be angry with them; they were all honest workers in their own departments, who knew for certain, however, that everything that could possibly be invented had already been invented during the past century. They thought it funny that the pedagogue—the nickname they had given Lopatkin—was writing about his *case* to the highest authorities. The crazy one! To imagine that he knew better than such authorities as Professor Avdiyev, or Academician Saratovtsev!

Some of these officials received Lopatkin sternly, spoke to him sharply, frowning. They looked down at him, as they believed, from the heights of governmental policy. "How much superfluous trouble these inventors of pickled cabbage do cause!" their looks said. "What a lot of money is wasted on all this idiotic correspondence with idlers and wastrels of this sort!"

But Lopatkin understood and bore them no grudge; he merely tightened his lips more patiently than ever.

So it was that one day, having received the usual rejection and returned the familiar formal smile with a polite bow, he was walking along a long passage in the Ministry that was flanked by cupboards and old writing desks. It was almost July, and the weather was very warm, even sultry. Noises, unexpected in a ministry, surrounded Lopatkin. The clatter of typewriters met his ears, and through one of the open doors he saw the walls and ceiling of an office that was hung with a cream-colored material. Then came an area of silence—Lopatkin was passing the reception room belonging to the head of the department. Through the open door he saw draped silk curtains, the shining glass of the wide-open windows, a table with telephones on it, a female secretary, and visitors sitting on the chairs and settees. In the room next door a conference was going on. Beyond it was a large hall with about forty desks, an official sitting behind each one. And everywhere, in the passages, in the doorways, in the angles formed by the cupboards, people were loitering in twos and threes, with their hands behind their backs or leaning against the wall, and they were all discussing something. Like an enormous ship, the Ministry was running full speed before

291

the wind; all the seamen were conscientiously standing their watches; no one wanted to be bothered with a harebrained project of a machine for the casting of iron pipes—a project not included in any plan.

Crossing the full length of this ship, Lopatkin sighed, stood still for a while, passed his hand across his face, and descended the stairs. In the lobby he threaded his way adroitly through the labyrinth of plate-glass doors and emerged into the street, bright with summer sunshine. On the pavement he almost collided head on with Drozdov's secretary, the one he had once nicknamed "Russian Dawn." The Dawn was wearing a tight dress with very short kimono sleeves that reveal the arms so attractively, making the shoulders appear sloping. Her hair was cut short, surrounding her head with a flaxen aureole and leaving her childlike neck bare. She was walking along eating an ice-cream cone.

Dmitri gave her a scarcely perceptible nod and quickened his pace. But the girl stopped him.

"Heavens, how you are changed. You *are* Lopatkin, aren't you?" She shook her head. "Still on the run-around?"

Lopatkin said: "Yes, still!" preparing himself to answer some unpleasant questions. But the girl gave him a quick look; the wrinkle between her eyebrows deepened with an expression of concern. She turned away pondering, looking hard at her ice-cream cone. She was wearing the badge of the *komsomol* on her breast, and at this moment it must have burned her with a demand for decisive action. She looked at Lopatkin once more and suddenly made up her mind:

"I'll tell you what, Comrade Lopatkin! Give me your project— the drawing and description. And now: come with me and write a short note to Afanasy Terentievich."

"Are you not with Drozdov then?"

"No, with the Minister."

Lopatkin nodded his head. They returned to the labyrinth of plate glass, and the doorman was about to ask Lopatkin for his pass when the girl boldly cut him short:

"By the invitation of Afanasy Terentievich!"

They went along a passage that was unfamiliar to Lopatkin, then climbed a narrow staircase to the second floor. Here they were met by another watchman and the girl again said:

"This comrade has been asked to come."

Dmitri found himself in a long, wide hall with a soft red carpet running along its full length. The girl conducted him to a round glass-topped table.

"Here is pen and ink," she said in a low voice. "Address it like this: To the Minister, Comrade Diadiura, Afanasy Terentievich. Don't complain about any particular person. Just say that you have been unable to get the matter moving for several years. Write! I shall be back presently."

She walked to the extreme end of the hall, along the red runner with its green border, with the special walk of the private secretary, neither hastening nor slackening her pace, and disappeared behind a tall polished door. In a short while she returned. Lopatkin had written the letter and silently handed it to her, together with a photocopy of the project in a reduced size. The girl took the papers, accompanied him to the stairs, and there, looking at him as sensitive people look at a condemned man—pityingly but afraid to touch him—she said:

"Ring up in two days' time, in the morning. Ask for the reception desk, Comrade Mikheyev. We'll arrange something. *He* likes to discover inventors and any sort of talented people in general."

Two days later Dmitri telephoned to the reception room of the Minister and asked for Comrade Mikheyev.

"How can I help you?" the disciplined voice of the ministerial secretary replied. "Oh, it's you, Comrade Lopatkin!" and the voice at once grew warmer. "Is that you, Comrade Lopatkin? Afanasy Terentievich will see you on Friday. Please be here at four o'clock. I'll see that a pass is ready for you."

During the two days remaining until Friday Lopatkin neither wrote nor drew anything. The professor stopped working also. In the evenings they opened the window and sat silently facing each other, without switching on the light. Now and then an involuntary word dropped into the silence, and only by this could it be known that a conversation was in progress.

"On Friday," Dmitri said. "Perhaps that will be the end of it!"

"Come, come!" the professor answered after a short pause, and then silence fell once again.

On Friday Lopatkin shaved, pressed his suit, and cleaned his shoes. At half-past three, carrying the brief case given to him by Nadia, he walked up the main staircase of the Ministry, to the second floor. Here his pass was checked once more and he entered a long hall with a carpet runner from one tall door to the other. Passing through a second door, he found himself in the waiting room. This, too, was large and square, the walls shining with polished wood, lacquer, and fresh paint. Settees with white covers stood along the walls. Visitors, obviously at home here, were lounging on the settees, waiting to be called; old and young men, dressed in white smocks holding enormous portfolios. At one of the two tables a young man with delicately penciled black eyebrows was sitting and listening with an enigmatic smile and without raising his eyes to a gray-haired, stout, amiable old fellow, probably a factory manager, who was bending down and appeared to be pleading with him. At the second table a stern-looking Dawn was lifting telephone receivers, two at a time, and speaking in a low voice into both receivers simultaneously.

Dmitri gave her a scarcely perceptible bow. She looked at him without moving a muscle. Lopatkin understood and went up to the young man.

"Lopatkin?" the young man asked without looking up. "Please be seated." And in the same tone, still without raising his eyes, he answered the stout man, who was offering him a cigarette: "Thank you, I don't smoke."

Lopatkin sat down on one of the settees. There was that complete silence in the room that exists only in rooms with good sound insulation. But in a few minutes the silence was broken; Shutikov, the Deputy Minister, and Drozdov, head of the technical department, came in quickly, noisily talking. Lopatkin stood up to greet his old acquaintances, but they did not notice him.

"Is he in?" Shutikov asked.

"Oh yes," the young man answered, standing up and pulling his coat into place.

After a moment's delay Shutikov and Drozdov passed through a gray curtain into the short passage that led to the Minister's office. Again there was silence. Lopatkin knew that he was being talked of at that moment in the Minister's room. "Oh, how long they are taking!" he thought, and felt a sudden violent pang. The electric signal behind the young man's back had come on. The young man stood up at once and went unhurriedly through the curtain.

"For me!" Lopatkin said to himself. But the young man came back and sat down at his table again as though nothing had happened. Again long minutes dragged by. Then the signal went on a second time, the young man disappeared behind the curtain, came back, and almost stunned Lopatkin with the softly spoken words:

"Comrade Lopatkin."

After going along the dark little passage, Dmitri opened a tall door faced with Karelian birch and saw another large room with enormous windows in two of the walls. This was the Minister's room. Near the right-hand window, close to the far wall, stood a writing desk and in front of it two easy chairs.

At the writing desk sat the Minister with a general's white shoulder boards and in the easy chairs were Shutikov and Drozdov.

Lopatkin crossed the soft, bright expanse of carpet, and when he was close to the writing desk the Minister stood up and hurried to meet him, with outstretched hand and body bent forward. He was powerfully built and about fifty. He shook Lopatkin's hand vigorously and said: "Sit down." Drozdov at once jumped up from the easy chair in which he had been sitting, and sat down on a chair near the window. Lopatkin held Shutikov's soft hand in his own for a moment, then shook Drozdov's small, dry, powerful hand, and sat down in the easy chair Drozdov had warmed for him.

"Well, I have gone into the matter, Comrade Lopatkin!" the

Minister said. He had a large, bony forehead, brown bags under his eyes, and his hair fell untidily over his forehead; he looked like the portraits of Beethoven.

"I like the idea," he said. "But I don't understand everything here."

"May I explain?" Lopatkin asked.

"Yes, of course! Let's see what you've got here."

Dmitri unfolded a large drawing and laid it on the table.

"Some inventor!" the Minister said, laughing. "He's even had a photocopy made!"

He listened attentively to Lopatkin's explanation without interrupting him. Only once he asked cautiously:

"What is this—here? Your connecting rod does not seem to be of even strength."

"He is not an engineer, Afanasy Terentievich," Shutikov answered in Lopatkin's defence. "We'll put that right."

And he radiated amiability with the yellow gold of his teeth and his spectacle frames.

At that moment the farther door of the room was opened a crack.

"May I?" asked the young man with the arched eyebrows. Tiptoeing forward noiselessly, he approached and laid on the edge of the table fifteen small, heavy, marbled, many-colored oblongs, with a label on each—samples, obviously, of some material.

"Are they all here?" the Minister asked. He stretched out his hand, fumbled with the samples without looking at them, while the young man tiptoed out as noiselessly as he had come.

"Yes . . . well, I like the idea," the Minister said to Shutikov. Then, laying his hand on the drawing, he turned to Lopatkin. "We are already making such a machine. Maxiutenko and others. Leonid Ivanovich Drozdov is looking after them. Are you acquainted with their machine?"

"Of course! I have had the opportunity!" Dmitri said with a caustic smile. Drozdov also smiled unpleasantly. But the Minister noticed nothing of this.

"Well, Leonid Ivanovich! A rival for you! You must be a chivalrous opponent! You will have to compete with him!" The Minister laughed and Drozdov bent his head with a smile.

Then the Minister frowned.

"You write here that you were given the run-around for two years?" After saying this, he took a huge brief case of strong chocolate-colored hide from a drawer and began stowing the samples one by one into its satin interior.

"It was the C.S.I.F.R. bunch. At first they didn't get the hang of it!" Shutikov said.

"This is what happened," Drozdov interrupted him with a serious air. "Permit me, Afanasy Terentievich. Comrade Lopatkin had another project at first, which met with various substantial objections both from our scientists and from . . ."

"Yet it was from that objectionable project that you took the idea for your machine," Lopatkin said to Drozdov. "For the one you are making now."

The Minister laughed and shook his head, bending forward over the table.

"Well done! Good for you! One can see at a glance that he's an inventor! On my word, they are all cut after the same pattern!"

Only now did Lopatkin realize that the Minister was in a hurry to get away. The Minister laughed, his movements were casual and easy, but his hand gave him away. It trembled, with the desire to drum on the table. It could not be controlled, it stretched out toward the brief case and loudly clicked the lock.

"So what have you got to say, Leonid Ivanovich?" the Minister asked Drozdov.

Drozdov, who, with Shutikov and the Minister had laughed, cleared his throat and with a gleeful sidelong glance at Lopatkin went on:

"That project met with various essential objections and Comrade Lopatkin knows it! As for the delay in connection with this new model, that . . ."

"Why didn't you ring me, Comrade Lopatkin?" Shutikov wondered amiably. "Didn't I ask you, when we had that personal interview: ring me up, come and see me? Alone, you cannot get even the most ideal project through. It is our institutes, you know, one must break through, like a salmon. Have you ever seen a salmon jumping up a waterfall? No? Then one day you and I must somehow pay a visit to the Karelian isthmus!"

"Just a minute, fisherman!" the Minister said. "The fish can wait!"

Shutikov, penitent but radiant, looked down at his knees.

"What are we going to do with Comrade Lopatkin?" the Minister asked.

"Get an expert opinion?" Drozdov suggested cautiously.

"Who would you propose?"

"Vassily Zakharovich Avdiyev."

"But won't he bury the project? Vassily Zakharovich . . . ! Let's have Florinsky for a change, eh? Avdiyev will want to justify himself now. What do you think?"

"He'll give an objective opinion," Shutikov said with assurance. "The opinion, in my view, ought to be definite."

"All right. If the opinion is favorable, set up a group and let them make all the calculations. Put the initiator on the pay roll. Well, I think that's all." The Minister stood up and the others did the same. "That's what we'll do. And you, Comrade Lopatkin, if there is any trouble, don't hesitate to ring me up at once."

When they left the room, Drozdov gave Lopatkin an amused glance out of his black eyes. "How on earth did you manage to get through to the Minister?" asked those shrewd bright eyes.

"Look at him, Pavel Ivanovich, why, this is a salmon!"

"Quite true, a salmon," Shutikov agreed, putting his arm round Lopatkin's shoulders and beaming at him with his golden smile. "Well, shall we go to my room?"

Shutikov's office was on the same floor, the second. A spacious reception room with a color scheme of pink and cream, like the Minister's waiting room, shone with fresh paint. In Shutikov's own room all four walls were paneled in dark walnut, alternating with frames of dark-green cloth.

On entering his office, Shutikov sank on to a large divan, which appeared to be made out of a large number of small leather cushions. He pulled Dmitri jovially by the coat, so that he fell on to the divan beside him. The divan received both of them gently. Shutikov produced a cigarette case and they both lit cigarettes. The perpendicular wall of an enormous chasm, the Ministry courtyard, was visible through the open window. In its depths a motorcar engine roared suddenly and a horn was sounded threateningly.

"He's gone already," Shutikov said.

Lopatkin realized that Shutikov was talking of the Minister.

"We have been holding him up," said Shutikov. "Mm. Ye-es." He smiled at the ceiling. "Really, it's very interesting how fates are woven! One looks on and behold!—the most unexpected chain of circumstances! It's you I'm talking about, Comrade Lopatkin!" he said, giving a sudden sheepish smile. "You always play up like this! Every step you take draws the fire toward yourself! Even I, I tell you candidly, even I was forced at times to bar your way! Because you see nothing and know nothing except your machine, and so you sometimes stand in the way of doing an important piece of work."

Lopatkin smoked furiously and frowned with the effort to discover what this amiable person, bright as a summer day, dressed in an expensive grayish suit of thin cloth, was driving at.

"You don't understand?" Shutikov asked, and laughed. "You'll catch on in a minute! Here am I. My superiors saw fit to saddle me with the responsibility for the production of pipes and notably for the production of pipe-casting machinery. When I studied the matter, I found that beside me there was a whole group of other people whose life was bound up with the same business—with pipes. Indissolubly tied up. They built themselves a sort of Scythian fortress, surrounded by a wall, divided the duties up between themselves, and now live according to Malthus, limiting fresh births. The fortress may not be visible, but all the same it exists!"

"So you want me to give up?" Lopatkin asked hoarsely.

"You catch thoughts in flight, as a trout does a midge! It is not

I who want you to give up, but *they* who want it. You can see for yourself how they have closed the gates against you."

"All right. But why do *you?*"

"Why do I, too, sometimes stand in your way? This is why: What is important from our point of view is not who gives us a machine, but that a machine should be produced. That is a task of national importance. We have a greater interest in such a machine than you yourself. We need pipes, good, cheap pipes, and we want them to flow out of the machines as nails do. That is what we need. Not we personally, of course, but the State. Do you understand?"

"But here it is—the machine! Take it!"

"Who can assure us that this machine will work? That it is efficient? Why, we have to take a risk which might lose us several hundred thousand roubles. We would trust you, of course, if you were a top-rating specialist in this field, like Professor Avdiyev. But in that case you would be inside the fortress, as their witch doctor number one."

"But hasn't this witch doctor of yours built a dud machine?"

"That affair of Avdiyev's error"—Shutikov blew out soft clouds of aromatic smoke—"that affair—really it is time it was forgotten!—has had its positive aspect as well. It was thanks to it that I at last had a possibility of checking up and of making demands. Now, instead of giving promises, they, with Maxiutenko and Uriupin, will give us a tolerable machine, and that is what we need."

"Then what about mine?"

"We will try to test yours. But the fortress exists, Comrade Lopatkin, the fortress exists! That we managed to see the Minister was one up for you! But the scientists are scientists. They are an iceberg that has sunk many a *Titanic!* Start a feud with them? No, that's not the best way of solving an economic problem."

There was a silence. Shutikov smoked and stealthily studied the inventor's face. The inventor looked back at Shutikov from time to time with his tired gray eyes. He frowned very slightly but did not tighten his lips or allow the muscles of his jaw to bulge in a threatening way. His expression was impenetrable—a sign of great strength of will.

"Yes, Drozdov is right," said Shutikov, putting his arm round Lopatkin's shoulders and nudging him in the ribs. "You are a salmon! The trouble is only that the most stubborn salmon, you know, those splendid five-foot specimens, once they have discharged their roe, sometimes float away to the sea stone dead." Shutikov laughed and again nudged Lopatkin. "You have a chance of achieving your object," he said, this time speaking seriously. "But many things have to be taken into account. What about your health?"

"My health is normal. My nerves and my appetite are good," Lopatkin said.

"Then there's this: one must also consider what you get out of this. Your machine is made, say, and you are of course awarded a certain sum, but it will disappoint you. The remuneration will be far from adequate to the inventor's expenditure. No, one can't base any calculations on *that*. H'm. Then you would have to go back to teaching, with a gap in your career."

He looked questioningly at Dmitri, but he said nothing.

"There is one other possibility for you," Shutikov went on softly, looking at Lopatkin with half-closed, momentarily dulled eyes. "You are a mathematician and a pretty good practical engineer. I am not trying to flatter you—you are better than many of our designers. Your vocation is in mechanics. And I am certain that you would be capable"—here he raised his voice—"that you would be capable of heading a department in that same C.S.I.F.R. But"—here he drew in his head between his shoulders and flung his arms wide—"first you must get rid of, or if you like acquire, certain businesslike qualities. Come to know what life is. In our epoch men are imperfect. Take, for instance, our fortress dwellers. They are living men with positive and negative qualities. One must know this and take it into account if one wants to work in a way useful to the community."

"I'll try. Perhaps I shall acquire the necessary qualities," Lopatkin said quietly, smiling faintly. He was not in earnest, and Shutikov saw it at once.

"I am speaking seriously." He raised his voice and pierced Lopatkin's faint smile with his heavy glance. "It's time you were out of short pants! What bug has bitten you with this inventing business? You only waste your energy, knowledge, and time on a senseless run-around! People with brains are always needed. I should be glad to entrust you with responsible work as soon as I can be sure."

Having said this, Shutikov got up and walked toward the exit. At the door he shook Dmitri's hand, held it for a moment in his own, and suddenly put on his beaming golden smile, the smile of a man who loves children.

"I am very glad to have been able to improve our acquaintance. I hope we shall understand one another and become friends. Oh yes, about your project. Give it to Nevraev, you'll find him in the room just beyond the waiting room. Well, Dmitri Alexeyevich, all the best."

A fortnight later Lopatkin was standing in Nevraev's office, at the open window, looking out into the street, his elbows on the window sill. Beside him, prone on the window sill, lay Vadia Nevraev, engineer, referee, and journalist. His face was round and chubby, his sparse brush of hair the color of straw, and his whole person seemed to radiate a rose-colored light. Vadia's light-gray jacket was unbuttoned, showing a pale-blue silk shirt and a silk tie all askew. He emitted a slight odor which might have been of violets or of vodka. Leaning a little way out of the window, he looked benevolently down at the street. His eyes were a greenish-blue, like the broken surface of glass, and the green street was reflected and vibrated in them.

Between Lopatkin and this good-natured young man of twenty-five, or possibly even thirty-five, who was fond of drinking, laughing, and discussing the "woman question," something very like friendship had established itself from the first day of their acquaintance. They had already twice gone bathing together to Khimki. In Nevraev's clear eyes, which took on a deep blue tone when he was on the edge of blue water, no reflection of the seamy side of life was to be seen. He regarded everything around him benevolently and was always very slightly drunk, though never to the point where Shutikov, who also took one or two drinks after dinner, would notice it.

"Here comes our darling Teddy bear!" Vadia said, without changing his position, and Lopatkin saw the long black Z.I.S. car driving down the middle of the street. The car slowed down, the horn sounded abruptly, and turned in under the arch of the Ministry building.

"Dmitri, I'm dying for a smoke. May I?" Nevraev asked.

"Why ask?" said Lopatkin, surprised. "And so far as I know, you don't smoke."

"But you don't mind, do you?" Nevraev said, with a straight face.

Lopatkin took out a packet of "White Seas" and shook a couple of cigarettes out of it, one into Nevraev's hand, taking the other himself. Then he struck a match and held it for Nevraev, who refused it.

"Just light yours while I get something."

While Dmitri hurriedly and avidly lit his cigarette, Nevraev took a drawing pin from a drawer and pinned his own cigarette to the window frame.

"This is a signal intended for certain coy inventors," he said, admiring the cigarette, but without smiling. "It means that they should not be too shy to smoke in my office! And that they should be less shy of me generally!"

After this they looked down at the street for a long time. From time to time the corner of Lopatkin's mouth turned up in a smile, and Nevraev gazed placidly down at the pavement, appearing not to notice these smiles.

"So," he suddenly said. "There is another firm rule in my office as well. That you should always smile as you are smiling now. The occupier of these premises likes that smile."

There was another silence, while for ten minutes they lay quietly on the window sill.

"And there is one more rule," Nevraev said suddenly. "Not to give way to nerves and not to get excited."

Lopatkin was indeed excited. For in forty or fifty minutes a conference was to meet in the office of the chief of the technical department, a conference specially called to discuss Lopatkin's project.

"The last rule is difficult to observe," said Lopatkin.

"In this office all the rules must be observed," Nevraev remarked placidly. "Aha! here comes Academician Florinsky's old jalopy! So, you see, you have no reason to be in a bad humor, Comrade Lopatkin!"

Nevraev slipped nimbly across to the telephone, dialed a number, and said:

"Lida, Florinsky has arrived. See that he is looked after."

An ancient Packard rolled slowly up to the main entrance of the Ministry, stopped, waited for a few minutes while a white-haired old man backed out of it with the aid of a stick, straightened himself up, adjusted his spectacles, and moved forward uncertainly, leaning on his stick. But two slim young men came running from the entrance, and one on each side, gave their arms to the old man.

"Grandpa's eyesight is going," Nevraev said. "Saratovtsev is two years older, and how he can put away the vodka! No, Dmitri, you mustn't get nervous in my office. Let us instead decide whether we shouldn't go and have one at the bar."

"Yes, let us go, but only after the conference, and if the decision is in my favor."

"Stop! I like a clear understanding," said Nevraev, still looking out of the window. "Which is the decisive proposition: 'after the conference' or the 'decision in favor'?"

"The 'decision in my favor' of course!"

"Then we can go straight away."

"Why?"

"Because the decision is already laid down."

304

"Where?"

"Here!" Nevraev got off the window sill. He was not smiling now, quite the reverse. "It is all laid down here," he said in an indifferent tone, pulling out a drawer of his desk. "You may read it, Comrade Lopatkin. It concerns *to you*, as Mister Tepikin, doctor of science, would say! Paragraph two. I finished formulating it last night."

He handed Lopatkin a typewritten paper headed: "Resolution passed by the conference called by the head of the technical department." The second paragraph read: "Instruct C.S.I.F.R. to work out the project of Comrade Lopatkin's pipe-casting machine with the participation of the inventor and taking into account the improvements proposed by the participants of the conference."

"And you are sure that this resolution will not be modified?" Lopatkin asked with a smile. He liked Nevraev, he liked his benevolent air, his serious voice with its sudden fadings.

"Quite sure," Nevraev answered even more softly than before.

"Why?"

"I took a long time over this resolution. I am sorry that I can't nail your smile down with the same certainty. Please, Dmitri, smile more often; I like your smile! Aha, here's someone else arriving! Vassily Zakharovich Avdiyev. It's time to go."

A tall man in a capacious pale-gray suit, white shoes, and an unbuttoned Russian blouse colorfully embroidered down the front, was getting out of a shiny Pobeda car. His luxuriant gray-and-golden hair curled on his temples into a multitude of rings, like a cut onion. He halted and looked along the street, and Lopatkin for a moment caught a glimpse of his menacing face, of that sausage red that is often seen in red-haired men.

"Let's go. You'll have plenty of opportunity to enjoy the sight of your opponent later!" Nevraev said, taking a folder from the table. He straightened his tie, passed a comb through his thin brush of hair, and they entered the same long hall, in which, a fortnight before, Lopatkin had written his application to the Minister.

The conference was to be held on the fourth floor, in Drozdov's

305

office. At twelve o'clock those who were to take part in it were gathered in Drozdov's waiting room. There were eight people there whom Lopatkin did not know. Some of them wore white tunics with white shoulder boards; these were engineers, others thin light-colored summer suits; these were the scientists. Nevraev changed into another man as soon as he entered the waiting room. His jacket was now buttoned up and seemed to have become stiffer, not only hindering his movements but even making it difficult for him to turn his head. Flushed with the effort, he went up to each of those present, with a waddling gait and a severe expression, shook hands with everyone, and then entered Drozdov's office without so much as a glance at Lopatkin.

He soon came out again and said:

"Come in, comrades."

They all gathered at the door, entered the office, sat down on chairs placed along the wall on which copies of Lopatkin's project were already pinned up. Drozdov was sitting at his desk, wearing a tunic of pale gold shantung silk. Next to him sat Academician Florinsky, his back humped, his hands on his stick, nodding every now and then, though no one had spoken to him. On the other side of the desk Professor Avdiyev was lounging in an armchair, shaking his yellow-gray curls. He was smoking, blowing the smoke toward the ceiling and knocking the ash off his cigarette into Drozdov's cast-iron ash tray. Avdiyev was a huge man with a broad pink face and powerful pink neck covered with yellow freckles. His eyes surprised Lopatkin; they were like round, pale-blue, lack-luster pebbles which yet seemed to contain a wild gaiety. Avdiyev's voice, too, was strange; it resembled that of a woman with a violent cold in the head.

"Comrade Lopatkin, make your report to the conference," Drozdov said.

"Why a report? Everyone has already seen the project," Avdiyev asked in a toneless voice, turning round and making his chair creak loudly. "Hasn't everyone seen it?"

"We have seen it. We know," several voices replied.

306

"What is your opinion of it?" Drozdov asked.

"The Institute maintains its former opinion regarding the necessity of a scientific development of the main questions connected with the essential peculiarities of this scheme," Avdiyev said all in one breath, still sitting in his chair. He spoke only to Drozdov and the stenographer. "However, taking into account our daily troubles, so to speak, and the already pressing need for such a machine, we consider possible the construction . . . mm . . . of an experimental prototype of the variant now proposed by the comrade inventor. The machine merits attention and testing on a level with the one now being made in Muzga, although the device now being made by order of the Ministry—I have in mind Uriupin's and Maxiutenko's device—is promising us a successful solution of the problem."

"Peter Innokentievich, I believe you wanted to . . ." Drozdov said to Academician Florinsky, then checked himself suddenly. "I beg your pardon, Vassily Zakharovich, have you finished?" he asked Avdiyev.

"There's not much more to say," Avdiyev said hoarsely, wriggling his powerful back and taking a fresh cigarette out of his case. "With one thing and another we shall obtain our pipes now." He turned and looked at Lopatkin, holding the cigarette between his strong teeth.

Before he began to speak Academician Florinsky nodded repeatedly and tightened his hold on the stick on which he was leaning.

"I am glad to hear Professor Avdiyev's positive opinion here. In amplification of what has been said"—here he raised his voice and spoke clearly and precisely—"in amplification—I beg to place on record this my fundamental thought." Here he took a deep breath and began dictating to the stenographer sitting behind him: "Comrade Lopatkin's project was born, as it were, at the behest of our new era. It incorporates . . . in the most profitable manner . . . the idea of continuous flow . . . and it provides at least a fourfold increase . . . the productivity of labor. But in order to realize . . .

307

the true value of this machine . . . one should multiply by two . . . the results obtained . . . because this machine . . . will occupy only half the space . . . required by any existing design. This is my opinion." He rapped the floor with his stick and nodded several times.

"Does anyone else wish to speak?" Drozdov asked. "No? Then permit me." He stood up. "The technical department cannot fail to stress the tremendous work done by Comrade Lopatkin in developing his machine."

He went on to make a speech of moderate length, praising the machine in a moderate fashion, pointing out a few constructional defects in it, and saying that support for progressive technical thinking was the first duty . . . et cetera.

While Drozdov was speaking, Avdiyev stopped smoking and gazed at him with his strange, pale eyes as though he had suddenly caught sight of a genius.

The next one to speak was Comrade Nevraev. Flushed with zeal, he came forward, breathed deeply, cleared his throat, and then read out the decision which was already known to Lopatkin—the one he had "formulated" so firmly a few days before. The resolution was approved by all present. Drozdov declared the meeting closed and everyone hurried to the exit.

Outside in the passage Lopatkin was overtaken by Nevraev. He was once more as amiable and uninhibited as before and his jacket was unbuttoned again.

"What's your hurry, Comrade Lopatkin?" he asked in a quietly menacing tone. "Explain yourself!"

Lopatkin understood. But he had no great desire to drink vodka. It would be much better, he was thinking, to be offering Professor Busko a glass. But Nevraev was inexorable.

"What's this? Breaking your word? I won't let you go, Dmitri!"

Suppressing a sigh, Lopatkin answered in the same earnest tone: "I am prepared to do as I said."

They went down the stairs in silence.

"Dmitri," Nevraev said softly and modestly when they reached the lobby, "I am prepared to treat you, on the basis of lend lease ... I know that you will soon be able to make return."

They went out into the street, crossed it, and entered the beer hall on the corner. The bar was crowded.

"Who is the edgemost?" Nevraev asked mildly.

"I am the *last*," an intellectual sot wearing pince-nez on his nose answered provocatively. " 'Edgemost' is not Russian."

"But Comrade Tepikin always says 'edgemost'," Nevraev objected in the same soft, even voice.

"Who is this Tepikin anyway?"

"If you don't know Comrade Tepikin, you don't know the new rules of Russian grammar!" Nevraev said. The man with the pince-nez stared. "Yes, I can see you don't know him. A great pity!" Nevraev swallowed hard and became calmer. "However, Dmitri, we had better consider what to rinse you down with."

2

ALTHOUGH Lopatkin's affairs were now going forward with astonishing rapidity, and progressing favorably, he still harbored suspicions, and was more nervous than he had ever been during his worst moments of hunger and stagnation. In the middle of work or of a conversation he would stop abruptly, overcome by some question that had suddenly struck him. Many questions arose in his mind, and there was no answer to any of them.

Why had Shutikov spoken so candidly? And had he really been candid? What was the meaning of his proposals? Had they not contained a threat or a warning? If so, of what? What ought one to expect? And then again: why had Avdiyev suddenly spoken *for* it? What had prompted Drozdov to make such a solemn speech and why had he changed his opinion so suddenly?

Lopatkin was sufficiently experienced by now to know that all this praise and these smiles were not owing to any sympathy toward himself, nor to any satisfaction felt at the successful solution of the problem of pipe casting. But he was unable to unearth the true reason of it all. Everything seemed strange; it was all running so smoothly with such menacing rapidity. The director of C.S.I.F.R. appointed his two best designers for the work: Antonovich and Krekhov. The latter was an engineer who greatly admired Avdiyev for having come into science little more than a peasant in bark sandals, "pushed hard, and carried everything before him." A group was organized in a single day, a special room was assigned to it, and the whole group at once set to work. The director himself paid a daily visit to the group, like a doctor in a hospital, to inquire how things were going.

The old professor was also rather worried.

"The forest is on fire, Dmitri Alexeyevich!" He opened his eyes in a wide stare. "The forest is on fire. But I just can't figure out where the fire is!"

This anxiety spread to Nadia also and one day, when she came to them after her schoolwork, she said:

"During classes today I remembered something Drozdov once said." She now referred to her ex-husband only by his surname. "I remember," she said, "that it was suggested Shutikov should participate in the development of the other machine, Uriupin's. And Shutikov refused, took fright, and even became suspicious of Drozdov; he thought that Drozdov was somehow trying to frame him, and he looked askance at him for months."

"That tells us first of all," the old man said thoughtfully, "that there is something wrong with their machine and that the whole business may blow up. Or why should he have refused? Your Shutikov seems to be prudent enough."

"Just a minute! Why should he have anything to do with pipes in the first place?" Lopatkin suddenly asked.

"That's simple," Nadia said eagerly. She had just recollected something, which seemed to her like a discovery. "Drozdov said that Shutikov had certain special interests."

"Yes, he would, of course!" the professor remarked, half to himself.

"No, wait! Shutikov often sits in at conferences in the Big House, so Drozdov said. And centrifugal casting was often mentioned there. But the ministers in charge of the competent departments were never able to master this type of casting. So Shutikov decided to make a machine on the sly, and then face them all with the accomplished fact."

"We urgently need a machine of that kind. Not we, of course, but the State." Lopatkin recalled Shutikov's words.

"Yes, of course, it's all the same to him who brings the pearl up from the bottom of the sea," the professor remarked thoughtfully, digging his finger into his ear. "What is important for him is to get the pearl and to sell it profitably. The buyer sees only the goods and the smiling salesman."

"As to that, he can certainly smile," Lopatkin observed.

"He would, of course! But why did he suddenly become interested in the other machine?"

"Dmitri Alexeyevich is a dark horse one can't bet on," Nadia said, looking into Lopatkin's face with an almost imperceptible tender melancholy.

"I don't quite get it. Is this a personal expression of regret or a quotation?" the professor asked suspiciously.

"A quotation. Of course Drozdov especially explained to me why they had picked Uriupin. It was because Uriupin would be amenable to any proposition that was put to him."

"But if you look at it more closely, you'll see that your Uriupin, too, is merely selling something over again. He didn't dive for the pearl either."

"One thing surprises me," Lopatkin said, frowning. "What are all these people, these designers, lecturers, engineers—the whole lot of them, who fill these buildings—what are they all doing? Or is there not a single honorable man among them?"

"My dear Dmitri Alexeyevich! Being honorable is only a fifth of what one has to be if one is to raise one's voice against the monopolies."

Lopatkin and Nadia realized that a sermon by a philosopher of antiquity was about to begin.

"The first thing, of course, is that one must be honorable," said the old man. "Most of them are, but not all. That is only the first phase of the screening. Then courage is necessary also, and that is not given to everyone. Furthermore, brains are needed. We have seen plenty who had courage but who brought the very idea of criticism into discredit by their foolish clamor. Finally, even those who are honorable, courageous, and shrewd may be prisoners of established formulas. That is another big hitch for you. The same Avdiyev—professor, doctor, a traditional authority—may tell a man of that sort that Lopatkin's idea is no good and that Lopatkin him-

312

self is an impostor, whereupon this honest man will honestly and with a consciousness of doing his duty beat Dmitri with a wagon-tongue until he turns up his toes."

"Then what is to be done?" Nadia asked in distress.

"What is to be done? One must think hard. I have the impression . . . I feel . . . I have the impression that they have spread a net for Dmitri Alexeyevich. I wouldn't let them get away with it."

"That goes without saying!" Nadia said hotly. "But if you love your country . . ." Here she suddenly stopped, blushing. Then she threw her head back. "Why are we ashamed of talking about such things? In the war we talked about them. . . . Because then there was danger. But I think now, too, there is danger. . . . Because the root of what we are fighting still lives, resists, and is growing. You must carry on with the work the country needs, even if it rejects your achievements. Even when it condemns you out of the mouth of those of its servants and judges who pronounce unjust sentences in its name. Your service will carry weight only if you can achieve what now appears impossible."

"But what is this, Evgeni Ustinovich?" said Lopatkin, who at this moment was not interested in philosophical discussions. "You are a wise man. Why are they in such a hurry over my project? If they go on like this, we shall have finished the whole thing by September."

"However unpleasant it is, we must let the enemy deploy his forces. In the end everything will become clear."

But the last days of June went by, and now it was July. Lopatkin had already received seven hundred roubles, representing half a month's salary as a project engineer, and the situation was still as unclear as ever.

"They are paying out money, speeding things up, they are working, and working honestly," Lopatkin thought as he contemplated the serious middle-aged men who were racking their brains over his project. Every now and then one or another of them came up to his table, bringing him honest ideas that had been thoroughly matured in the peace and quiet of the designing room.

"Are they in the know?" he asked himself, carefully studying the backs of their heads, the little bald patches on top. They all looked intelligent. No, all these men appreciated his machine, they accepted it and its inventor. Krekhov, an old designer, a very thin man with thick black eyebrows and a gold ring on his finger, who sat with his back to Lopatkin, said one day: "You are a lucky man, Dmitri Alexeyevich. I understand you."

He said this as if he were speaking in the name of the whole group. No, it was obvious that he knew nothing.

Yet Krekhov believed himself to be very subtle—one who really knew his way around. He even made Lopatkin smile for the first time in many days when he asked him a very tricky question. It was during the lunch hour, after the director had paid his usual visit. The general, accompanied by Lopatkin and Krekhov, had strolled, hands in his pockets, from drawing board to drawing board and then taken himself off. Krekhov returned to his place, took out his bottle of coffee, and sitting with his back to Lopatkin, said:

"It is a pleasant thing to work, when one knows that the project won't be shelved."

"Are you sure it won't be?" Lopatkin asked.

"Oh, my dear Dmitri Alexeyevich, we have seen what we have seen! Even Avdiyev himself was for it. But tell me—now that we in a way belong—what tactics did you use?"

"I asked to be received by the Minister."

"Oh, so you saw the Minister?" Krekhov sang out. "All right. Perhaps it's really better not to tell. But in spite of all your distrust of us you are quite a lad! To force your opponents, all, without exception, to face about at an angle of one hundred and eighty degrees—that is quite a feat, you know!"

For them Lopatkin was a success, one who had triumphed over his enemies.

No man can see himself from the outside, through his neighbor's eyes. It appeared that, unknown to himself, Lopatkin possessed a second personality, which won him the sympathy of the other designers. It had turned out that he was exceptionally gifted. In two or

314

three years he had developed into a good mechanical engineer and in addition had studied the hardening processes of molten metal so thoroughly that he had succeeded in shaking the scientific theories of leading lights such as Fundator and even Avdiyev himself (though the truth was that they simply *had* no theories). The designers held that Lopatkin could not be regarded as a "materialist." In their opinion he could easily have earned four or five thousand roubles a month, he had even been offered such a position, but he had refused. (When he heard of all this gossip, Lopatkin was worried lest Shutikov should take him for a tattler.) It was also told, as an indisputable fact, that Lopatkin had obtained the approval of an exceptionally important person (who remained unnamed). And it was known, too, that the inventor of the pipe-casting machine had been unlucky in his private life, that he was an ascetic, a recluse, and that he had taken his machine for a wife.

All this was gradually disclosed to Lopatkin by Krekhov in the form of questions that were impossible to answer. The July evenings were beautiful, and it happened somehow that every day, on his way home, Lopatkin walked along the boulevard with this designer, who appeared literally to be in love with him.

"Tell me, Dmitri Alexeyevich," Krekhov asked him one day, after assuring himself that no one could overhear, "did *he* receive you in person? Or did you simply send him a letter?"

"Who? Who is it you are asking about?" Lopatkin laughed. "No one higher up than the Minister ever saw me."

"Oh, all right; let's leave it at that. I understand there may be all sorts of considerations. . . . But I am asking for a practical reason. . . . Did you send your letter by post or simply hand it in at the dispatching office?"

"I always try to cut out as many intermediate stages as possible."

"Ah! I get you!" Krekhov fancied himself as a diplomat and liked ambiguous phrases. "By the way, about letters. I heard that you numbered them. You must have used up a lot of notepaper before you . . ."

"Yes, I used up plenty," Lopatkin assented.

"Ah! So it's true!"

"What is true?"

"Oh, nothing. You are an energetic fellow. You've got that something . . ."

"What 'something'? You have a wrong idea of me."

Krekhov hated this kind of answer.

"Do you know," he said one day, "I believe in everything except modesty. This sort of make-believe doesn't suit you. Remember that we realize your merits but yet without forgetting our own. Most of us in this institute are inventors or potential scientists."

Lopatkin bit his lip to suppress a smile and gave him a sidelong glance, which Krekhov interpreted as surprise.

"Nothing to be surprised at. All normal people are born with creative impulses, and most of them are even aware of such possibilities within themselves."

"Then why don't you realize them? Forgive me; perhaps I am mistaken?"

"No, no. You are not mistaken. We, Dmitri Alexeyevich, have gone to seed without noticing it. We get decent salaries, and we have become swine. Who would want to go back to those remarkable times when an unfulfillable hope was one's bread, one's pillow, and one's jacket? It is not possible to meddle with *their* technical policy."

"But there are some people who *do* meddle!"

"That's just why we want to know whom 'some people' succeeded in winning over to their side. We are realists, we would like to try going the same way. As our associate you ought to help us. . . ."

"I give you my word that as soon as . . ." Lopatkin began, but suddenly remembered the professor's "make no vows." "It's all right in general," he said instead. "And what have you invented?"

"Nothing myself," Krekhov said. "But a friend of mine—you don't know him—has invented . . . To some extent he is your rival. He, too, has a casting machine."

Having said this, he looked at Lopatkin, but was disappointed; he was not frightened by the thought of a possible competitor and did not even become more cautious.

"He is only a young lad, and yet he has had the gumption to work it all out. It's a machine for the precision casting of steel under pressure," Krekhov said, after a pause. "We already cast aluminium and zinc, low-melting point metals under pressure. But he casts steel. He has found a completely new way of doing it. A magnetic field creates the pressure, slices off a section of the metal and also heats it. Marvelous! Isn't it?"

"It is," Lopatkin agreed.

"And this infernal thing might already have been working in two five-year plans!"

"Then why . . . ?" Lopatkin began, but stopped himself, then laughed and flapped his hand. He could have answered that question himself.

"Well, you see," Krekhov said softly, "this young lad hasn't yet got the strength to attempt such things. In his ministry there were people who set up obstacles. Not everywhere do you come across such unbiased, right-minded people as Vassily Zakharovich Avdiyev."

Lopatkin could only gasp with surprise. He even stopped in his walk. But he took himself in hand at once and said nothing—let life itself one day speak. It would still have something to say to this man.

After such talks with Krekhov, Lopatkin understood that the designers could not tell him anything about what was being prepared. They were convinced of his success.

He himself was ready to believe in a happy end to the long history of his machine when an unexpected encounter opened his eyes. He was on his way to work one morning, bobbing up and down on a bus seat and looking out into the sunlit street through the open window, as usual seeing nothing but his machine and one recalcitrant section in it. Motorcars were moving along the dusty asphalt at the side, and a gray Pobeda came up to his window.

"Comrade Lopatkin! Inventor Lopatkin!"

Galitsky was sitting in the Pobeda next to the driver. He was leaning half out of the car window, shouting and waving his hands.

"Get out! Get out! At the next stop!"

Lopatkin at once pushed his way to the exit and got off at the next stop. The gray Pobeda was already waiting there and Galitsky's long arm was waving to him. They exchanged a greeting.

"I am in a hurry. Get in and come with me. We'll drive to my Ministry, and afterward the car will take you wherever you want to go. Get in and tell me all about it."

Lopatkin opened the car door, bending his head, and fell on to the soft back seat as the car moved on.

"So you are working in a ministry?" he asked, looking suspiciously at the back of Galitsky's childishly formed head and his black hair that had not been trimmed for a long time.

"I am a member of the directorate," Galitsky said without turning his head. "Did you think a doctor of science couldn't be that? But go on, tell me. Briefly. Remember that I know something about this business. Be quick."

Lopatkin related, all in one breath, everything that had happened to him during the last few months.

"It's obvious," Galitsky said. "Do you trust *them* for an instant! Certain people would be chucked out of their jobs if your project were realized. Didn't you know that? Rest assured that *they* understood and appreciated your idea. This Uriupin will add something of his own to it, to make it appear different. *They* will produce some monstrosity, 'develop' it and 'improve' it in five years or so, and for this they need peace and quiet. But you make a fuss, you write letters. It stands to reason that *they* finally had to give you serious attention."

"But perhaps Shutikov, who has an interest in the matter, has realized that my project is better."

"Shutikov certainly has an interest. But in technical matters he is a babe unborn. He thinks that this machine or that machine is much of a muchness as long as it's a machine. The design, the idea, are trifles in his eyes compared with other tasks that he considers important. He is a great expert in establishing relations between people. That is where the solution must be sought. But we shall see.

318

We shall see-e-e!" Galitsky made the word sound menacing. "It's a pity I haven't time now."

They went silent for a whole minute. During this pause Galitsky was probably going through his timetable, searching for an hour when he would be disengaged.

"No, for the present I can't," he said at last. "I suppose you think, 'Dig up a bit of time out of your private stock! Dig it up, now that you have put your finger in the pie.' Weren't you thinking that, Dmitri Alexeyevich? But no! I have no private stock of time. Let me tell you: I have some fine guns, yet I put off going out shooting from day to day. I don't know whether this is the right line to take. Some people say that the good administrator is the man around whom business is on the boil, but he himself is at leisure. But I haven't learned yet how that is done. And then there are so many gaps still that a good administrator, around whom work is boiling, can always find for himself, too, if he likes work. To the end of my days I shall probably never get a chance to go out shooting." Galitsky spoke with sudden irritation and then said no more, but took out his notebook, angrily scribbled something in it, tore out the page and handed it over his shoulder to Lopatkin.

"My telephone number. If anything breaks, give me a ring. This is where I get out. The driver will take you wherever you want to go. So long."

Lopatkin's days passed in alternate calm and anxiety. The project was rapidly approaching completion and somewhere behind the camouflage the enemy was deploying his troops.

They were deployed in complete silence, and during the last days of July the attack came, in a totally unforeseen sector of the front.

It began with the telephone ringing. Lopatkin picked up the receiver, spoke a few words, and Krekhov saw him appear somehow to sink into himself.

"Just a moment, Vadia," he said. "I don't understand. What pipes?"

"Cast-iron ones," the receiver squeaked ironically.

"So what?"

"Well, congratulations on the solution of the problem."

"But we haven't solved . . ."

"Dmitri Alexeyevich, if the assistant of the Deputy Minister congratulates you, it means that the problem *is* solved. You will be able to convince yourself. The truck will be here soon."

"What truck?"

"I think it's a three-tonner."

"Vadia, tell me plainly what all this is about."

"I am speaking quite plainly," said the receiver in a fading voice. "A report has come from Muzga about the successful testing of the machine and about the first pipes the comrades have produced. . . . Wait a minute, I'll look in the day's draft order . . . made out by Comrades Uriupin and Maxiutenko."

"What order of the day is that?" Lopatkin quietly asked.

"The order not to hang back but to go ahead. Come and see me, Dmitri, and you can see the order at the same time."

"All right, I'll come round," Lopatkin said, putting down the receiver. He remained motionless for a few seconds, with his large fists propped on the table, gazing into the distance as though the yellow wall in front of him did not exist. He could already perceive his enemies' scheme though not yet with absolute clarity. It was something quite new and it appeared watertight.

The designers were all sitting or standing silently at their worktables, their heads bent lower than was necessary. Lopatkin walked past them, and, as he reached the door, said calmly: "I am going to the Ministry for a couple of hours," then left the room.

When he jumped off the bus at the huge Ministry building he at once caught sight of a truck standing at the main entrance. Out of it workers were unloading varnished black cast-iron pipes and carrying them through the entrance. Lopatkin went closer and touched the pipes. Yes, they had been cast by the centrifugal method, and not badly either. "Could I have miscalculated?" he thought, and felt himself sweating.

"Phew, how hot it is!" he said, and again examined the pipes.

320

"If it is not to be me, then, it just isn't," he thought. "But it's certainly a pity that so many years should have been lost."

But no. Nothing was lost. For was not his machine the better one? While this one . . . ? It could not produce more than twenty pipes an hour. And after all, one could cast a good pipe even by hand. That wasn't the point.

And as if in confirmation of his thought one of the workmen accidentally dropped one end of a pipe on the asphalt, and swore. A piece of the pipe had broken off on a slant and on the surface of the break had appeared some silvery-gray crystals.

"That's chill!" Lopatkin thought. "Yes, of course, they use water cooling."

On the second floor the doors of Shutikov's waiting room and office were wide open. The July breeze blew freshly through, and cheerful male voices could be heard talking pleasantly together. Ten engineers in white jackets—young secretaries and assistants— stood around the long table that was used for conferences. On this table, covered with green cloth, five or six pipes lay side by side, looking like gun barrels, smooth and shining, as though they had been turned on a lathe. Shutikov was there, too, of course. He beamed, patted the pipes, crouched down to peer through them, and still found time to reply with a radiant face to the sympathetic speeches of the engineers who had come to congratulate him on a remarkable achievement.

As Lopatkin entered the room, he heard Shutikov's delighted voice exclaiming:

"Yes, it's true they cast pipes like this abroad. But, comrades, we have introduced a novelty: the interchangeability of molds. That gives a colossal result! Simply colossal! Ah, here is Comrade Lopatkin, who has come to rejoice with us!"

Everyone stood aside as Shutikov stepped forward to meet Lopatkin, embracing him and drawing him to the table.

"Here, at last, is the result of our common labors! Look at them, you, who are a specialist. Not bad, eh?"

Lopatkin looked through one of the pipes. He did not know

what to do. Not to rejoice? But here were these people around the table. . . . There were honest men among them. And the workmen had come in, too, and were sincerely rejoicing. If he did not rejoice with them, they would think: "Ah, the rival is annoyed; one can see at a glance that he is thinking only of himself and that he does not care at all about a triumph for the community!"

And yet, in spite of everything, Lopatkin was unable to rejoice, for calamity shone in the black varnish of the pipes, glittered in the gold of the deputy-ministerial spectacles—a subtle deception of all these trusting people who seriously believed that an achievement of national importance had taken place. Shutikov himself, dressed in pale gray, bustled about and beamed even more than was necessary. For no pipes had existed and now some had been produced. The rest didn't matter—Avdiyev would embellish this *result of his investigations*. Shutikov did not even try to conceal his exultation, although those around him could not decipher the reason for it. They all saw an unselfish and indefatigable worker who had proudly refused the tempting offer to participate in the development of the project. Everyone could see the splendid shining pipes. But how much would they cost to produce? Who would bear the burden of this cost? The pipes had noticeably thickened walls; it was obvious that too much cast iron had been used in them! And the chill? How many pipes would break during transit and in storage? And the productivity of labor? There was, after all, a better machine already in existence. Was it permissible to let it perish?

It would have been better to reveal his anger. But he had not realized it in time. Yet all this time his pale face was twitching with the struggle between a smile and a look of despair. And it made the worst possible impression on everyone. Everyone looked attentively at the inventor, exchanging glances.

Shutikov took in the situation. He held Lopatkin's arm and walked up and down the room with him, as though they were discussing the pipes together. But this was what he was saying to him: "I understand, Dmitri Alexeyevich. You must bear it with fortitude. Control yourself. I hope that you will still think of some other new thing."

"Some new thing? What about the machine?"

"The Minister has decided to stop work on it. I shall, of course, give you another five days or so to finish the project, but that will be the end of it. You are young and energetic, you will not perish. You have something here." Shutikov touched his forehead. "But only a miracle could help you now. Unless you could bring your machine here immediately and completely ready for use!—a machine that would produce more pipes, even if only five more."

"I shall write to the Central Committee of the Party," Lopatkin said without hearing Shutikov out.

"So what? Do you imagine that everyone who writes to them gets satisfaction? Well, you are wrong. Only those who are right get any satisfaction. And your problem is an eminently specialized one which cannot be decided without expert advice. The experts' opinion will be taken. And we both know already what that opinion is."

"But I know a more authoritative judgment for such special problems; that is, the testing of a prototype. The machine must be made and tested."

"Well, make it then. Make it! Oh, you have no funds? Well, ask the Ministry for funds. And we shall again ask—"

"Avdiyev?"

"Whom else? Why not? We shall ask him and other scientists whether it is worth while allocating funds. We already have a machine, you know. Why should we need two different ones?"

"But this one happens to be mine," Lopatkin muttered in a low voice. "If they hadn't messed it up, it would produce twice as much."

"Come, come, you're talking nonsense! Calm down! By the way, I haven't forgotten. . . . Do you remember how pleasantly we chatted together on this divan? And I am still prepared to meet you halfway if you will think the matter over. Please ring me—I will see you about this at any time."

After saying all this in a soft voice and squeezing the dismayed inventor's elbow, Shutikov went back to the pipes. Lopatkin found Vadia Nevraev at his side. This time he was looking dignified, one button of his jacket was done up and he was moving with a swagger.

"Dmitri Alexeyevich," he said under his breath, "don't draw your sword against windmills!"

"He suggested to me . . ."

"Don't draw it!" Vadia repeated in a warning tone. "Look over there a minute. Why do you think he is looking through the pipe so often? What does he see there? Don't you know? Dmitri Alexeyevich, what he sees at the other end of that pipe is a certain comfortable armchair. So don't draw that sword. And I advise you to accept the compensation before it is too late."

After saying this, Vadia turned his back on Lopatkin, went up to the table, and putting his arm around the waist of one of the engineers, talked to him, smiling.

That very day and even that very hour Lopatkin was in the Minister's waiting room asking the young man with the arched eyebrows if Afanasy Terentievich could see him. The young man turned to one side and dialed a number. When he had finished dialing, he said: "Is that you, Nikolai? Are you free this evening—Afanasy Terentievich is engaged. No, I wasn't speaking to you, to someone here. . . . Listen, ring me up . . ."

When he had picked the words that concerned himself out of all this, Lopatkin bowed to the back of the young man's head (those bloody good manners!), withdrew, and sat down at an empty table. Here he wrote a letter to the Minister, enumerating in quiet words the losses the State might suffer from the operation of the new pipe-casting machine made in Muzga. He then requested the authorization of further work on his own machine, pointing out that a not inconsiderable amount had already been spent on its projection and the consultations connected with it. He assured the Minister that his, Lopatkin's, machine, would produce at least fifty pipes an hour, apart from the fact that the pipe would be of good quality. He furthermore called the attention of the Minister to a special feature of this machine: that it could also be used for the casting of water pipes.

Here he was assailed by a sudden feeling of despair. He threw down the pen and sat motionless, gazing hopelessly at the pale pink wall and at a sunspot, reflected by a bowl of water, that was floating across it. But in a minute or two he pulled himself together, forcing himself to finish the letter. He also made a copy of it for Nadia's records and then reread it. It was perfectly in order, the word "Minister" written with a capital letter throughout, as was correct. Lopatkin signed his name and handed the sheet of paper to the young man with the arched eyebrows. The young man began reading it at once, returning Lopatkin's cautious greeting without even raising his eyes from it.

As soon as Lopatkin opened the door, the professor saw at once that things had gone wrong. The old man had just prepared dinner and was sitting at the window waiting for his friend. Lopatkin came in, sat down at the table, and began tossing a fifteen-kopeck coin on to the oilcloth.

"When an inventor begins asking questions of fate, things are really bad!" the professor said. "What's the matter?"

Lopatkin handed him the copy of the letter addressed to the Minister. The old man drew the paper slowly across his spectacles from the bottom to the top, and laid the letter on the table.

"Squaring the circle," he said, and a long silence fell in the room. Lopatkin again began tossing the coin on the table.

"Do you know what I was thinking?" he asked with desperate gaiety. "I was wondering whether I ought not to accept Shutikov's offer."

"What offer?"

"To give all this up. He said: 'Accept a good job and a salary to go with it.' "

"As openly as all that? That means that he considers the matter a foregone conclusion. But I see that Diesel was right. You are beginning to lose the habit of hoping."

325

"What do you think? Will my letter get as far as the Minister?"

"It will be submitted to him. This evening. They are no bureaucrats, God forbid! But *how* will it be submitted? The paper will tomorrow then be filed with your dossier, and that boy of yours with the eyebrows will write on it: 'Submitted to Minister So-and-so.' My dear fellow, I wore out not only my trousers, but my knees as well, in those waiting rooms. It's not the Minister who counts!"

"But after all nothing is done without him!"

"You are quite mistaken. Without him no one will stop to punish your *friends*. And without them, you will never get through to him to make a complaint. Without *them,* he will never believe you. So that . . . ! Let's have dinner and then consider what is the best thing to do."

So saying, the professor went over to his bed, where, under the pillow, wrapped in a blanket and some newspaper, a pot of borsch was keeping warm. He set the pot, which Nadia had bought some time ago, on the table, and got two plates out of a cupboard. Then he took the lid off, exclaimed: "Smells good, doesn't it?" and ladled out a plateful of rich dark-red borsch for Lopatkin.

"I might have foretold what has happened to you," the professor said, filling a second plate and beginning to eat. "The same thing happened to me, only my memory failed me. In my view Shutikov's idea is this: that now you cannot complain of him any more. The Ministry has spent a lot of money on you. You were discussed. Your project was twice put in hand, you were given the best designers, you were coddled. And, as the result of a creative competition, it was the other machine that won. Heavens, after all someone must always win. Someone must always have the worst of it. Your complaints will be regarded as a loser's normal reaction. So this is what we have been racking our brains about! Now it's all quite clear."

"Except for one thing," Lopatkin interposed. "What are we to do?"

"I suppose you are right. Now one really begins asking fate questions!"

"In any case I shan't go to work for Shutikov. I have been think-

326

ing, Evgeni Ustinovich! Shall you and I go away somewhere—to Sayan, or to the Yenisei? What do you say? There would be the sky and the earth and children. The really first-class things, Evgeni Ustinovich. You push me and I'll push you, and we will both wake up somewhere far, far away where the clouds sail in the sky!"

"You decide," the professor said. "I'll go with you."

3

Lopatkin spent the whole of the next day telephoning to the Minister from a street telephone booth. He was told the Minister hasn't come in yet, or the Minister is engaged, or the Minister has left. On the second day Lopatkin called at the Ministry, and making use of his permanent pass, got as far as the Minister's waiting room. There was no one there except the Dawn, who, huddled up dreamily, was reading a thick, tattered book.

"Afanasy Terentievich will be back in the evening," the Dawn said, reluctantly tearing herself away from her book. Then she woke up. "Oh, it's you, Comrade Lopatkin!"

Her voice was more lively now, but this time Lopatkin was faced with a different Dawn—not a mournfully sympathetic but a disgusted and angry one.

"He will not see you, Comrade Lopatkin," she said. "I have asked. He gave orders that you were not to be put through. And you . . ." Her face suddenly seemed to grow pinched and she stuck her lower lip out with a hostile expression. "One really cannot be as selfish as all that. After all, machines are not made for your sake, but for the people's, for the community. I could never have behaved as you did. I would have congratulated them. They have made the machine and good luck to them. How *could* you? I should never have believed that you . . . !"

She stopped speaking and in the waiting room, isolated from the world by the sound-insulated walls, fell a heavy silence.

"Afanasy Terentievich said that you were not to come here any more," the Dawn whispered at last in a despondent voice.

"All right. I shall not come." Lopatkin spoke almost inaudibly. "Good-by."

He ran from the room, hardly noticing how he got out of it and into the street. He was overcome with shame. "Enough!" he said to himself, going toward the bus stop. "Enough! Enough!" he whispered to himself in the bus. "So long, comrades! I've had it!"

"Enough!" he said when he reached home. He went quickly into the room, sat down on his bed, and remained there motionless.

The professor was lying on his chest, pretending to be reading a book. Nadia was there, too, wearing a bright summer dress. The summer school holidays had already begun, and now she came to see her friends in the morning.

"*What* is enough?" she asked, cautiously approaching Lopatkin. No doubt she knew it already. "What is enough, Dmitri Alexeyevich?"

"Selfish!" he said, frowning. Tears welled up in his eyes and ran down his cheeks. He covered his face angrily with his hand, wiping them away. "Enough! I won't go anywhere again!"

"Dmitri Alexeyevich." Nadia sat down beside him, putting her hand over his. "Nothing so dreadful has happened, Dmitri Alexeyevich!"

She pressed his large graying head to her bosom and began rocking him gently, as though she were holding an infant in her arms. A minute passed, then another. Lopatkin, breathing in her soothing fragrance, suddenly felt a vernal lightness in his heart. He straightened up and looked at Nadia.

"Yes," he said, remaining motionless, without thought, giving himself up to the feeling of lightness. Everything within him felt as though he had passed through a heavy storm of rain and hail.

"So far as I see, these are the final remnants of naïveté," the professor observed from his place. "Your Shutikov carelessly touched them with his sleeve, and all the little china elephants fell off and were smashed, and a good thing, too! Nothing should get on the nerves of an inventor!"

"I am not to show myself at the Ministry any more," Lopatkin exclaimed. "They regard me there as a selfish, dishonest speculator, a traitor to the common interest! The day before yesterday, in front of them all, I confirmed the axiom that inventors are survivals of a past age and will soon be extinct."

"It would be interesting to know how you did that."

"There was a celebration there, everyone was happy, they all came and congratulated one another on this success. I alone did not show the proper enthusiasm. I don't know myself how it happened. But everyone noticed it. If you had heard the things a girl said to me today—the Minister's secretary. The way she looked at me, the poor thing. It is frightful! It would be a hundred times better to be taken for a lunatic!"

"Never mind," Nadia said softly, looking at him sadly and yet with delight. "Never mind. It will all pass. It will pass very soon. I have something interesting for you here. Shall I show it to you?"

"Another necktie?" He tried to joke.

"No. No necktie and no teacups. Better than that." She went over to the table where her small school bag was lying.

For some time now Nadia had been going to the Lenin Library at Lopatkin's request to read the literature that dealt with centrifugal casting and pipes, and to make abstracts of the articles. It was not an easy task, but Nadia had found a way out. She had copied the articles almost in full into a thick exercise book. It was this that she produced out of her bag.

"Nonsense!" Lopatkin said. "I've done with all that. I am gone! Not here at all!"

"Wait a bit before you go. Look at the pipes that exist in the world. This ought to interest you. Do you see? 'Bimetallisches Rohr.' The pipe consists of two layers. The outer layer is of plain steel, but the inner layer is acid-proof—for the chemical industry."

"What if it is? Oho!" Lopatkin said, but stopped speaking as he turned the pages of the exercise book. "This could be done on my machine," he suddenly boomed in a threatening voice.

"Nadezhda Sergeyevna and I are of the same opinion," the professor said quietly from his place on the chest; he, too, knew all about this.

"What about *them?* It would be interesting to know whether *they* are making them like that."

"Not on your life! They have no such pipes. It says here: 'During the last four years our designers and technicians are seeking ways and means . . .' No, they are racking their brains over it without being able to find a solution."

"Ah, so *they* are not making them yet!"

"That's just the point!" Nadia said, beaming. "They use steel pipes and have to change them every week, because they corrode. They need pipes like this, pipes with a processed internal surface. Shall we offer them some?"

"Offer whom? The Germans?"

"Why the Germans? He still doesn't understand. No, we'll get in first. There are people here, too, who need pipes like that. We'll find out who they are and offer the pipes to them."

"Are you sure we won't come up against another Shutikov? No! I won't go anywhere any more; or write—except to you. I shall live in the forest without any more bothering. Two layers? Oh-ho-ho! what an idea!" he ended unexpectedly.

Nadia glanced at the professor, who winked at her significantly, as if to say: "The man is done for! He will never leave his machine. Look, he is already riding his hobbyhorse again!"

Lopatkin jumped up from his bed and leaned out of the open window as far as possible, lying on the window sill. He lay there about twenty minutes, ruffling up his hair from time to time. Then he stood up, and they saw that he had been scratching something there, with a nail, on a sheet of iron nailed to the other side of the window sill.

"Oh-oh-oh!" he said, looking back at his drawing on the iron. "Whew! What an idea!"

"You see. I told you so!" Nadia, trying to conceal her pleasure, was fanning her face with the exercise book. "Look, comrades, how hot it is!"

331

"Nadezhda Sergeyevna, this is the real thing," Lopatkin said. He sat down, then got up again. He picked a torn envelope up off the floor, took out his fountain pen, and sat down at the table. "You have given me an idea."

"Not I," Nadia protested softly. "It is your own."

"We'll put in an application containing both our signatures."

"I shouldn't if I were you," the professor warned in a deep, booming voice. "Cut out the application."

"But it's settled! There are two of us now!" Lopatkin said.

Nadia blushed and said nothing. In the library, when she had seen the paper on double-layer pipes, she had realized at once that it was an important discovery, one more problem that Lopatkin, without knowing it himself, had solved long ago. Her fingers trembled as she turned the pages. She felt that she could now, for the first time, be a real helpmate to this remarkable man, Dmitri Alexeyevich. "Dmitri Alexeyevich!" she repeated, blushing with happiness.

"I would advise you, nevertheless. . . . Do at least ring up that Galitsky of yours and discuss the matter with him." The professor looked anxiously at Lopatkin. "I have never seen him, but judging by what you have told me about him, he is what I imagine a genuine Party man should be."

"True. That makes sense." Lopatkin stood up, without taking his eyes off Nadia. "Yes, that's right," he thought. "She wants to be given something, some token. Take this, my dear. I can't give you anything more, but this is yours."

"Still, do ring him up," the professor insisted.

Lopatkin took a fifteen-kopeck piece out of his pocket and looked at it.

"Ah!" the old man said. "That's the one you were tossing up with yesterday. Run off and put it into the slot. It's your lucky one!"

Lopatkin left the room, and Nadia ran after him, as light-footed as a child. Now they both felt happy! As they ran downstairs, Nadia, leaning on Lopatkin's shoulder, even risked taking several steps at a single stride. They crossed the courtyard, not holding hands, but with their little fingers crooked together, stepping over the pigeons who tripped daintily along in front of them on their tiny pink feet. Anyone looking at them would have thought: "A happy young couple."

They reached the telephone booth. Lopatkin went in, dropped a coin in the slot, dialed a number, and heard the ringing tone in his ear. Then there was a click and a female voice said: "Hallo."

"Comrade Galitsky, please."

"Comrade Galitsky has been transferred."

"Could you tell me where?"

"Such information is not given over the telephone."

"But is he in Moscow?"

"No."

"Excuse me. . . . Is he expected back soon?"

"I tell you, Comrade, he has been transferred elsewhere, permanently."

Click-click-click. The secretary in the Ministry had hung up.

"Galitsky is not in Moscow," Lopatkin said briefly as he came out of the telephone booth. The world around him was still as bright as it had been before, but he himself felt desiccated; it seemed now as if there were dust in the air, a smell of gasoline fumes, and the honking of motorcars hurrying along the lane appeared more deafening than before.

Nadia did not speak. They entered the courtyard in silence, and the lilac- and chocolate-colored pigeons in their short white trousers again tripped in front of them to the entrance of the house and then flew off in all directions.

"Well?" Lopatkin said, looking at Nadia with a faint smile. "Are the little elephants still being smashed?"

"Dmitri Alexeyevich," Nadia sighed. "I think they were all smashed long ago. And what very small elephants they were!"

"But the big one was still left whole, wasn't it?"

"It was the first to fall down. But I was lucky; I was able to save it. But the others, the smaller ones have all been smashed."

"You had better break the one that is left quickly, Nadezhda Sergeyevna. It would only hurt more if someone else were to."

"You don't understand," Nadia said caressingly, as they walked up the stairs. "On the contrary, I shall take great care of it."

The professor met them on the landing at the top of the stairs. "Well?" his raised eyebrows inquired silently.

"It was an unlucky fifteen-kopeck piece," Lopatkin told him curtly. "Galitsky has left Moscow. For good. He described himself correctly. Always putting things off and never getting anything done."

They moved slowly along the passage in single file, the professor last. He shuffled along, sniffing and muttering to himself:

"Gone. . . . And I had hopes of him, I don't know why. . . . I thought he . . . Aye! . . . How familiar it all is! And how bitter!"

They went into their room and sat down on the chairs and beds. Nobody spoke. Suddenly all three of them realized that life was still going on just as before. Childish voices sounded in the street, the pigeons fluttered their wings, a little boy playing marbles shouted "I'll take the white!" In the distance a phonograph was playing—in this terrible moment someone was learning to dance.

"In a silence like this," the professor said, "one feels how trifling our troubles are measured against time and space. Dmitri Alexeyevich," he added after a pause, "I think this is just the time for a little dinner."

Nadia jumped up at once, picked up the pot from the floor and carried it out to the kitchen. The professor followed her with his eyes, then turned to Lopatkin.

"I also think that it would do no harm if we took stock of our resources and introduced a rationing system."

Later, when Nadia had gone, the two friends made up a budget. It was not too austere. It did not come to cod-liver oil. What was more, funds were even allotted for the purchase of drawing paper for the new project.

The professor was pleased with the result of these calculations. Lopatkin, too, felt cheered, and remarked that the time for his five-mile walks was approaching. All this was familiar to them both.

But somewhere, behind hundreds of stone walls in several houses, other people were sitting and evolving other plans, making telephone calls and dictating letters to typists, in which the name of D. A. Lopatkin was mentioned. And on account of this the inventors' calculations were modified the very next day.

When Lopatkin reached the Institute next morning he noticed first that the group had done no work at all during his absence. They already knew about everything and did not want to work for the files. "They are right! What's the good of wasting paper?" Lopatkin said to himself. He went from worktable to worktable with friendly greetings for everyone. His face was unclouded, and this was so unusual that Krekhov could not contain himself.

"Dmitri Alexeyevich! It's a miracle. You are walking on the waters—like Christ!"

Lopatkin laughed.

"No, but really! Excuse me, but they hit you on the head with a bludgeon! I would have died, upon my word!"

"What did you say?" Lopatkin asked with lighthearted absentmindedness. "That's nonsense. If you knew what an idea I have in my head right now!"

The designers exchanged glances. "Our inventor seems a bit off his rocker!" these glances said. Lopatkin did not notice, but all that day in the group there was low-voiced talk to the effect that "With this inventing business, why certainly you never knew! Here today and tomorrow in the loony bin! Ward Number Six!"

Little work was done that day. The telephone rang again and again at one of the tables and a woman's voice in the receiver asked loudly: "May I speak to Comrade Antonovich?" Antonovich, elderly, clean-shaven, and dandified, with a nervous twitch in his face, came to the telephone. "Have you got an advertisement displayed on the Arbat?" the receiver asked. "Tell me, are you really single?" "Why, yes!" Antonovich replied. "How have you managed it all this time? Do you know, I am looking for a room, too." "So what?" "Couldn't we share a room together? I, too, am single, intelligent . . ."

"Ha-ha-ha!" The group roared with laughter.

"Disgusting!" Antonovich threw down the receiver. "You've put one of the copying girls up to this! Really, it's the limit! You're like children! Can't you find someone else to play with?"

Until that day Lopatkin had not suspected that such serious men as Krekhov could find pleasure in this sort of thing. And yet he had gone out, as if to buy cigarettes, and a few seconds later the telephone had rung. Antonovich had picked up the receiver, had said quite seriously, "I am listening," and in reply the receiver had said, loud enough for the whole room to hear: "I want the single, intelligent engineer . . ."

"I know it's you, Krekhov! Look here!" Antonovich began threateningly, but the receiver did not allow him to finish.

"Wait a minute before you tick me off! I have just read your ad on the street corner here. There are mistakes in it, you know."

"What mistakes?"

"Well, the word 'intelligent' is spelt with one l."

"Impossible!"

"Why impossible? Come and see for yourself."

And Antonovich had gone to see for himself. And of course there had been two l's—for was he not intelligent? But Krekhov, the best designer, a serious man with an old-fashioned ring on his finger, had been delighted with this practical joke. He had sat down at his worktable looking as if he had just eaten an excellent meal. He kept casting grateful glances at the telephone, as though awaiting more unexpected things to come from it.

And the telephone did not keep him waiting. It trembled slightly and rang in a way that echoed through the room. The practical jokers were all on the alert and would have picked up the receiver, but Krekhov was quicker than any of them. One, two, long paces, and he lifted the receiver.

"Yes," he said, and suddenly tightened his lips. "At once. Comrade Lopatkin!"

"What is it now?" Lopatkin thought as he took the receiver.

"Comrade Lopatkin?" asked a slow, stern voice.

"Yes," Lopatkin answered hoarsely, clearing his throat nervously. "Yes, it's I, Lopatkin."

"This call is on behalf of Comrade Galitsky."

"But he is away!"

"That's right. But we have had a technical conference here. Can you come and see us in this office?"

"Of course I can! Excuse me, shall I bring the portfolio or not?"

"Better bring it. Although we know your pipe-casting assembly. Can you come at once? You can? Then I'll send a car for you."

Yes, this really was a jolly day! As he put down the receiver, Lopatkin looked suspiciously at the telephone. Was somebody playing tricks at his expense as well? All the same he went to the open window to wait for the promised car.

Twenty minutes later, as in a fairy tale, a gray car smoothly turned the corner and stopped at the entrance. It was the same gray Pobeda Galitsky had been using.

Lopatkin by now was no longer surprised at any new developments or promising moves, even if they came as unexpectedly as this one. When he encountered them, he behaved with calm, anticipating that all these things would have the same outcome in any case. While he was being driven along in the Pobeda, another three-minute storm blew through his mind, uprooting trees and carrying away roofs, but tightening his lips and closing his eyes, he quickly recovered from it, successfully hiding all the damage. And the man who entered the office on the third floor of an unknown yellowish building with a row of columns in front was the kind of inventor that ministries fear, a man with a special kind of pallor in his face, the dusty pallor of one whose nerves have been racked. His smile betrayed readiness for sharp retorts and derisive hatred for handsome rich drapes, desk sets, and white carpets with blue and red designs.

But those who sat in the expensive armchairs, or stood with inscrutable faces by the handsome curtains, or walked slowly across the white carpet—these departmental heads and engineers, and the dandified general in black, with the blue stripes down his trouser seams and the white civilian shoulder boards—had seen many inventors in their time and had expected Lopatkin to be like this; Lopatkin, the hero of six years of struggle for a pipe-casting machine. No one smiled behind his back when he entered, although there was a short silence. But it was quickly broken. Someone offered Lopatkin an armchair, the general came out from behind his desk, sat down opposite the inventor, and opened his cigarette case to offer it to him. The others moved their chairs closer.

"Dmitri Alexeyevich," the general began softly, snapping open his lighter and offering Lopatkin the little blue flame. Both men were enveloped in a cloud of smoke. "Dmitri Alexeyevich," the general said again, "we know your machine well here. Comrade Galitsky has explained everything to us in detail."

"Excuse me, but where *is* Galitsky?" Lopatkin inquired.

"*This* is what we are interested in," the general went on; he obviously did not like being interrupted. "Could you produce a variation of your machine adapted to the casting of certain hollow rotary bodies? For instance, one in the shape of a pointed arch? Like these, say."

By this time an assistant's nimble hands had very accurately laid four little squares of drawing paper with symmetrical shapes drawn on them in fat lines on the table: a cigar, an acorn, a cone, and a pipe with a diameter increased stepwise.

"The cigar. That's a bit tricky . . ." Lopatkin began, but the general interrupted him:

"Will you undertake the job?"

"Yes," Lopatkin said, feeling a new and joyful storm rising within him. The general nodded to the assistant, who quickly collected the squares of drawing paper.

"You will work in the same institute, with the same group, in the same room,"the general said. "You will get money from the same little window. Your salary will be the same. We will regard the job as an order from us given to the Institute. The work is secret, as you will realize. If your friends—Shutikov, Drozdov, Avdiyev—want to find something out don't tell them anything.

You will get your instructions from Comrade Zakharov, Vladimir Ivanovich. He will represent the customer. Have you anything to add?"

"Yes, I have. The structure of this machine provides us with possibilities. . . . We are, for instance, about to produce double-layer pipes with it, pipes made out of two different metals."

The general stared fixedly at Lopatkin, then looked at one of the engineers, a serious, well-scrubbed man, who up till then had not spoken.

"Or out of two different kinds of steel," Lopatkin added.

The engineer smiled very slightly, stroked the table with his dry fingers, and shook his head.

"We must not dissipate our attention. No. This is still an unsolved problem."

"Have you applied to the Inventions Office?" a little gray-haired old man with a raddled face and bright black eyes—a scientist by the look of him—asked with lively interest. "You haven't? I think for security reasons it ought to be taken up and the application made through our department. For however problematic the thing may be, even the idea alone is a discovery. The way itself promises an interesting solution. We can arrive at a whole complex."

"We have begun work on it," Lopatkin said. "And we, at all events, are convinced of success."

"Who are 'we'?" the general asked.

"I and my partner, Nadezhda Sergeyevna Drozdov. She is informed about every detail."

"Well, if you have a partner, the partner must be included in the order," the general said, and his assistant at once bent over the table and scribbled something with a pencil.

It was decided to include the casting of double-layer pipes in the schedule of work. The general summoned two more departmental heads, and after a short conference it was resolved to give this point preference. A few other details were mentioned—terms, the possible formation of a special designing office consistent with the results obtained. Then everyone stood up and gathered in the middle of the white carpet, and Lopatkin understood that the conference was ended.

"You inquired about Galitsky," the general said. "He is in the Urals, director of our largest factory. I shall be flying out to him tomorrow and can convey a greeting. And now . . ."

He held out his hand, and after him all the others came up to shake hands with the inventor. Lopatkin noticed that in doing so they observed some kind of accustomed seniority. The last to come up was the assistant, who left the room with Lopatkin, and outside in the passage noted Lopatkin's home address and the times when he could be found in.

"The car is waiting," he said.

Lopatkin asked to be driven to Liakhov Lane. All the way there he was smiling or beating a sudden quick tattoo on his knees with his fingers, clearing his throat, and glancing frequently at the driver. In imagination he was already six months into the future, already in the workshop turning the prototypes of his machine. When the car reached his house, he jumped out, ran across the courtyard, frightening the pigeons, leaped up the stairs to the top landing in three bounds, and made the bell on the other side of the door ring wildly, telling everyone how overjoyed he was.

The professor came shuffling hurriedly to open the door, narrowing his eyes suspiciously as he did so. He was dressed in a long white shirt worn outside a pair of linen trousers, loosely caught by a narrow, sagging belt.

"Well, well, well now!" Lopatkin cried out cheerfully from where he was standing. "I told you that I would succeed in handing it over, didn't I? And who was it who prophesied failure?"

Without a word the old man made way for him to come in.

"You were not mistaken in one thing," Lopatkin said. "Galitsky is a very decent sort indeed. He did far more than we could have expected. Now a dozen Shutikovs can't stop me!"

The friends entered their room and, sitting on a stool beside the professor, and bending down to speak into his ear, Lopatkin told the old man about his interview in the other Ministry. He did

340

not mention the shapes sketched on the squares of drawing paper, but Busko, having heard him out, was nevertheless on the alert.

"You say it is secret work? Then why are you entrusting the secret to me?"

"But, Evgeni Ustinovich, I have not entrusted anything to you yet!"

"The most important secret, if you want to know, is that you have been placed on the secret list. True, you had to tell me, seeing that I know all about your affairs. But it would have been better to have carried on this conversation in the street."

He suddenly opened the door, looked out into the passage, sat down again, said nothing for a while, and then began speaking very loudly and distinctly.

"Yes, I told you long ago that that singer has an exceptionally fine voice. When I heard him for the first time he was singing the part of Prince Galitsky. No, my ear has never deceived me yet. Of course you are to be congratulated. This is a turning point in the history of our—musical education. But I am glad of it for you. You despised some of my advice, you know."

"Miraculous!" Lopatkin was not listening to the old man at all. "Shnip-shnap-shnurr!" He danced round the room, clicking his heels.

"I have noticed that with you everything is always either plus or minus," the old man said dejectedly. "It was the same with me. And the pendulum swings wider and wider each time. At the moment a tremendous plus is starting for you. I would like to say: Don't play this game."

"Sorcerer!"

"Child!"

"Sorcerer!"

"Child! And supposing the pendulum were to swing back as far in the minus direction? Do you understand? It would be much better to stop the pendulum swinging at all, as someone with more experience than you has done. If your business were to end in a catastrophe, I could not bear it. Believe me all this means nothing! So stand aside while you can, Dmitri Alexeyevich!"

"I don't believe it," Lopatkin said. "I shall sail away to unknown seas, like Magellan!"

Lopatkin spent the whole of the following day in the Institute, sitting at his table and waiting for things to happen. The sultry heat that precedes a storm silenced all the designers. Their coats hung on the backs of their chairs and the window sills were filled with rows of glasses and empty lemonade bottles. Lopatkin was feverish with joy; he lived from one ringing of the telephone to the next, but when it rang it was never for him.

At five in the afternoon, a little before the end of the working day, Vadia Nevraev floated in through the open door of Lopatkin's office. All his color seemed to have been sucked out by the July sun. His light-gray jacket hung over one shoulder and his light-blue tennis shirt was unbuttoned, showing the raspberry pink of his sunburned body.

"Would a certain Comrade Lopatkin be here?" Nevraev inquired softly. "Might you be Comrade Lopatkin, citizen? May I have the honor of your acquaintance?"

"I made your acquaintance five years ago," Lopatkin said. "Don't you remember?"

"No, I don't seem to. Isn't what you mean that our acquaintance began with those unpleasant documents that I was compelled to write? You are a nurser of grievances, Dmitri; as our Tepikin, doctor of science, says, you are angry *to* me!"

Instead of answering, Lopatkin patted him on the shoulder, and Nevraev fell into a chair. It was impossible to be angry with the man.

"But this hand has been concerned with good works as well." Nevraev justified himself with a deeply contrite air. "Perhaps you are familiar with an article entitled 'Open the gates wider to our inventors!' On that, too, you could have read the name Nevraev. Unfortunately the editor cut it out. And now, too, I have come

342

with serious intentions, Dmitri Alexeyevich. I have come to re-
monstrate with you for having given up working for the public
good and withdrawing from collective proceedings. . . ."

"What proceedings?" Lopatkin asked, again deceived by Vadia's
smile. He had been told more than once that Vadia was the Ministry's barometer, but he could not help it, he enjoyed seeing those
clear eyes that radiated only an artless friendship.

"I wanted to write to the shop newspaper about this," Vadia
went on, looking as though he were dying of the heat, "but I decided
to restrict myself to personal contacts. Dmitri Alexeyevich"—he
lowered his voice—"if you do not come with me this very instant . . ."

"To the corner? No, I won't go there," Lopatkin said, laughing.
"It's too hot, can't you see?"

"No, I can't see any heat," Vadia answered seriously. "That is
why I am inviting you to the beach at Khimki."

"I can't go to Khimki, either. I must stay here for the present.
You know what my position is. Three more days and Shutikov will
close me down."

Lopatkin was being cautious, and saw at once that a mysterious
mechanism had started working in the Ministry's barometer.

"It is dangerous for you to sit by the telephone just now," Vadia
said so softly as to be scarcely audible. "You might be killed suddenly, finished off by an unexpected piece of news."

"Can it be that he knows?" Lopatkin asked himself.

"No piece of news could finish me off," he said. "The devil himself couldn't think up a trick dirty enough to frighten me."

"Why 'frighten'? It might just as well be gladden! You're not
used to that yet, I think. Better come with me, Dmitri."

"No, I'd rather ring you tomorrow and then we can . . ."

"As you like. So you still want to stay near the telephone? Very
well, but if anything happens, remember I warned you!"

He was preparing to go, but Lopatkin grabbed him by the
jacket.

"Come here. Tell me something that makes sense."

"Something that makes sense? I met a very interesting child on the beach. If you come with me, I'll show you."

"No, tell me plainly: what are you warning me about?"

"I don't know anything. You need self-control."

"All right. And how did you learn that I ought to be prepared to hear some news?"

" 'For that purpose one must possess the art of one's craft,' as a doctor of science we both know likes to say."

Vadia took himself off and Lopatkin heard no news of any kind that day. But next morning he was summoned to the director of the Institute, who informed him in a steady voice that the group was to be entrusted with some responsible secret work. The director knew that the other department must already have communicated with the inventor, and that all this must have been preceded by moves behind the scenes about which Lopatkin knew more than anyone else. Knowing quite well that his words were pointless, he nevertheless continued uttering them, saying something to this effect:

"Having discussed the matter, we have decided to recommend your candidacy, taking into account the circumstance that you have sufficient erudition in this sphere. Krekhov knows all about mechanics and so does Antonovich. . . . They will do the spadework. In my opinion it is all right, and there will be good results."

As he spoke he studied Lopatkin's face, but Lopatkin, remembering the caution he had been given, only nodded and said nothing.

"They say that you now have a partner," the director said, and came out from behind his desk sniggering. "What is your partner like? Pretty?"

Later the whole group was summoned to the director and the general repeated the same speech, this time addressing himself to all of them. His words still did not sound quite natural, because the designers and engineers, wise through experience, after the first instant's astonishment, began probing for the roots of this whole business. And it was after this conference that they began ascribing another quality to Lopatkin—that of having penetrating force.

4

AUGUST was over. It was September, and the first chill of the still-distant winter breathed in the clear blue of the cooling sky. Autumn stole in unnoticed and spread itself constantly wider; autumn, the season when lonely, thoughtful, elderly men, carrying their hats in their hands, make their appearance in the parks. The cold, sunny days of September are the best time, too, for any business that takes complete possession of a man, for all work that drives away the futile memories of the irrevocable past.

A sudden terrifying feeling stabbed Lopatkin sharply one day that autumn, when, on his way to his Institute, he decided to take a short cut and walk across Sokolniki Park. He found himself suddenly in a deserted, yellowing avenue of maples. It seemed for a moment as though he were watching his own autumn approaching. He might, perhaps, have hastened to forestall it—clear young eyes had already opened within him—when suddenly one of the ubiquitous outdoor telephone booths rose before him. Yet that would have been nothing—as he entered the booth, he still resembled the Lopatkin who had so much attracted the girls in the ninth form. He decided to ring Krekhov up and find out how things were going.

"Dmitri Alexeyevich," the receiver answered in Krekhov's voice. "Shutikov has been to see us. He condescended to us in person. What impression? I'll tell you my impression when I see you. Everything is quite clear," he added in a lower tone; he was obviously shielding the receiver with his hand. "In my view the comrade was searching for a key. A little key he wanted to pick up. He smiled a lot, but the smile was a bit frosty."

The clear young eyes closed, and the feeling of autumn receded

346

from the man who came hurriedly out of the telephone booth and walked briskly along the avenue, aroused by his struggle, and even beginning to laugh.

"In person! Looking for a little key! Just wait! This time you'll pick up something you could do without."

Another fortnight passed. The October rains came on. The building superintendent decided to test the heating system and, as a result of the test, the room in which Lopatkin's designers worked was flooded. A plumber came, accompanied by the elderly stoker Afontsev, who always seemed sleepy. Having found the break, they started replacing the radiator. But the thread of the coupling must have rusted or scale must have developed and in addition the workmen must have been handling it roughly, for the engineer's heart in Lopatkin's breast felt instinctively that in another minute the ancient pipe would burst all along its seam. He jumped out from behind his desk, removed his jacket, and took charge. He made the men bring a blowtorch, heated the sleeve, or as the plumbers call it, the union, so that it turned on its thread with a squeak. The joint victory led to a joint lighting of cigarettes, and when Lopatkin turned to get a packet from his table, his eyes saw the huge figure of Avdiyev standing in the middle of the room.

The professor was wearing a light-gray pin-stripe suit. His unbuttoned jacket was disproportionately long and wide and dangling, covering his hand, which was weighed down by a heavy brief case. He was listening with a scowl to Krekhov, who had emerged from his combine and was shrugging his shoulders as he told the professor that he, Krekhov, was not empowered to discuss any detail of secret work with an outsider. There was the originator, Dmitri Alexeyevich Lopatkin, if he were to consider it permissible. . . .

How things had changed! Avdiyev apologized and hurriedly stood farther away from the forbidden drawing.

"Quite right, the devil take it!" he said in his hoarse, feminine whisper. "There is even a sign, I see: 'No entry except on business.' What sort of atomic laboratory have they got there? I said to myself. Perhaps I am not a complete outsider, I'll go and have a look. Where is Lopatkin then? . . . Oh, is that you, Dmitri Alexeyevich? Why haven't you got your coat on? Why on earth mess about with all that rust? Flirting with the working class, I see!"

Lopatkin wiped his hands on a newspaper and greeted Avdiyev. The professor, returning the greeting, inquisitively searched his face with his turbid blue eyes. Behind the unreasonable gaiety there was now also a shade of alarm in the expression of those marble eyes.

"What are you working on now?" Avdiyev asked, looking around the room. "You say it's something secret?"

"Nonsense. Nothing of the sort. We are projecting a machine, that's all," Lopatkin replied in a casual tone, taking a folder out of the cabinet with the drawings of the project which was already almost completed when the finished pipes arrived at the Ministry from Muzga.

"Here, you can see, Vassily Zakharovich," he said. "We are doing a bit of projecting—with your blessing."

"Then what's the inscription for: 'No admittance except on business'? And 'Secret.' You never had that before. What do you want it for now?"

"The building superintendent put it up. By order of the general. Why not ask *him*?"

"What a strange one you are." Avdiyev shook his yellow-gray curls. "One asks a simple question. . . . The superintendent, you say?" He shook his head, and stood still for a while, staring at the floor. "Well, all right, carry on."

He went away, swinging his brief case.

But he left behind him in the room an oppressive sense of the seriousness of the situation. Lopatkin realized that nothing he had gone through up till now had yet been a real fight. At all events, not for Avdiyev, Shutikov, or Drozdov. For them it had still been child's play. But now that these people, perhaps for the first time in their lives, were faced with a genuine disaster and genuine hatred —now they, too, at last, would bring their every resource to bear, perhaps for the first time in their lives. His face darkened as he prepared himself to meet this uttermost effort of his enemies.

Krekhov, guessing Lopatkin's thoughts, came up to him, and drawing his finger over the paper, said under his breath:

"They are in a flurry; there will be whistling." He whistled low, exactly as the German mines had whistled.

But it looked almost as though these alarms had been false. The autumn flowed on muddily into November and the work was still making good progress. Two more tables had been set up in the room and copyists were now working at them. The first model was reaching completion.

Nadezhda Sergeyevna, like Lopatkin, had one day during this autumn heard a sad warning in the eternal rustling of the yellow leaves. She felt that Lopatkin's road, marked with innumerable milestones, was nearing its end. Soon the wanderer would throw down his load, and then Nadia would once more quietly attempt to awaken him. Or perhaps he would wake of his own accord—had she not once seen his eyes opening?

She did not force her presence upon him; she would come and go, leaving something very useful behind on the table for him: her latest find, for the sake of which she had no doubt spent more than one evening in the library. Lopatkin would ask her to stay. He even said to her once: "I have no one in the world, except the old man and now—you." But Nadia did not stay—perhaps in order that she might hear these same words again another day. Something obstinate inside her continued to guide her with a sure hand.

In her capacity as co-inventor she now appeared in the designing room and even signed the drawings: first came her signature, and lower down, Lopatkin's. Lopatkin had insisted on this, as an answer to certain hints that had been dropped by one or another curious designer. Not only in this group, but in other sections of the Institute also, people knew of Lopatkin's interesting co-inventor. More than once Lopatkin had been compelled to rebuff some clumsy inquirer by a hard look or a stern word.

Even Antonovich, a meticulous man in such matters, could not refrain one day from cautiously touching on the secret of this partnership. Lopatkin paled and held his breath a moment before answering.

"Once and for all we will not discuss this. In order for you to understand it all, I should have to tell you the whole history of a six-year-old relationship. And that would be a long and not a very amusing story."

Antonovich retired in confusion and asked no more questions.

The procedure of signing the drawings caused Nadia some embarrassment. Before, when Lopatkin had made a drawing of *their* machine for her on a piece of paper, she had understood everything. But now, when she looked at the drawings of the project, where all the details were shown as though they were transparent, and here and there even as if they had been cut open by that skilled anatomist Krekhov—now Nadia could scarcely recognize even the familiar parts of the machine.

"Never mind," Krekhov consoled her one day. "You may sing a tune, and I can write it down and arrange it and put in so many crotchets and quavers that the devil himself could not find his way through them. That is, of course, if he were not a musician! But when it comes to be played, you will see that the tune is the one you sang."

Nadia was grateful to him for these chivalrous words, but the next moment she blushed, wondering if they had not been tinged with familiarity, if they had not been a subtle hint at the relationship between the two partners? Was not this clever old man raising his hat to her in order to express his approval of her partner, "and his respect for him"? She watched Krekhov stealthily, growing pale in anticipation and prepared any moment to stand up, go away, and die of anger. But no, Krekhov was an artless, a truly clean-minded man.

Nevertheless, there was still a trial in store for her. It came from another direction and it came suddenly and roughly. Once when she looked in at the Institute for half an hour, in order to take some instructions from Lopatkin, a much stouter, chubbier Maxiutenko and a muscular, sunburned Uriupin burst suddenly into the room. They had both been holidaying in the Caucasus after Muzga, had acquired a tan, and now, dressed in new jackets of gray gabardine, bright with fresh green facings, they were making the round of the Institute.

"Greetings," Uriupin said briefly, raising his dry brown hand with pale nails, and a huge black watch on the wrist, in a sportsman's salute.

The greetings were addressed to Lopatkin. He stood up, with the unpleasant feeling that he would have to show these outsiders the door. But at that moment Uriupin, his hand still in the air, his brisk gesture unfinished, suddenly caught sight of Nadia sitting at a table close to him. His luxuriant, graying, bristling head of hair moved slowly forward toward his forehead and then quickly receded.

"Nadezhda Sergeyevna! I can't believe my eyes! How on earth? . . ." He put his hand on his breast, took a step backward and bowed. "I am glad to acclaim your entry into these halls."

Nadia looked at him coldly and gave him only the slightest of nods.

"I see that you are firmly established here," Maxiutenko said, reddening, as he glanced at Uriupin.

"Nadezhda Sergeyevna is our originator," Krekhov remarked.

"Ha-ha-ha!" Uriupin laughed loudly but suddenly cut himself short; he had caught sight of a small square of paper with a drawing on it lying under Nadia's hand; she had just signed her name on it in front of his eyes. "Haw!" He turned the laugh into a worried cough, moving his scalp backward and forward again. "Maxiutenko, look at that square of paper. Do you see what it means? She really is an inventor. Nadezhda Sergeyevna, you are an inventor. I see here . . . Don't you think? . . ."

But the old dandy Antonovich interfered unexpectedly at this point.

"By your leave, comrades!" He came out from behind his drawing board. He was dressed in a long jacket with sloping shoulders

351

and buttoned only by one button. "One moment, Comrade Uriupin. Have you permission to examine secret drawings?"

"Ah! Antonovich is here too! Well, how are you off for a room?" Uriupin was saying when Antonovich marched up to him and pointed to the door with his finger.

"Have you read the sign on the door? Read it, comrades, there *is* a sign. Yes, yes, have the goodness to look at it."

And although the guests tried to joke about it, they were forced to go out into the passage.

Again the October days flowed evenly along. They brought no stresses, no threats, they passed with an amazing precision, one like another—peaceful autumn days. Gay, sun-tanned men and women returned from the summer resorts and plunged into the damp, coldly transparent Moscow air.

How could one fail to be convinced of success? There was Krekhov, with his blue satin sleeve protectors, turning his head alternately to right and to left as he transferred to the drawing paper a construction he had devised himself. The day before, he had approached Lopatkin and asked him, as if incidentally, and keeping his voice very low, whether a bit too much space had not been assigned to the frame.

Lopatkin registered extreme amazement. "We must have room for the tilting table, mustn't we?" "Table?" Krekhov replied. "We'll cut it in three and put the parts one above the other . . . like this . . . and this . . . then we shall have conquered space."

The old fellow was in fact able to cut the table into three, and made a contraption with levers and counterweights, after which it was decided to shorten the frame by a whole meter. He was sitting there now, very pleased with himself and even talking to himself aloud.

"One only gets to know a real machine gradually, as one does a human being. At first we are simply struck with the idea and take our hats off to the originator. Later, when we get to know the layout in more detail, it turns out that the thing is full of all sorts of tricks, and not uninteresting ones at that. The designer hasn't fallen down on the job either. That's the sort of machine I like. That's what I call perfection."

It was obvious what machine he was talking about.

Lately it had begun to seem to Lopatkin as though he had been working in this group for many years, with Nadia, Krekhov, and Antonovich. One day he remembered his visits to the Conservatory the year before and during the work-filled quiet of the morning he suddenly said, for no apparent reason:

"Let's organize an outing, comrades! Let's go to the Maly theater, the whole lot of us!"

The group unanimously agreed to this proposition. Nadia was commissioned to get the tickets. But it was then that a little cloud appeared on the horizon: Lopatkin met Vadia Nevraev in the street. Vadia was wearing a gray military overcoat, mincing primly along, pink-faced and zealous, carrying an enormous brief case. He encountered Lopatkin face to face, looked him in the eye with an unfriendly blue glance, and passed on without a sign. Lopatkin laughed and grabbed him by one padded shoulder.

"I can't now. Next time," said Vadia, shrugging himself free and walking on with the same even step. He walked like this to the end of the long street, as if he were walking along a plank, without faltering in his step and without once looking back.

An hour later Lopatkin had already forgotten this strange encounter. But the abrupt change in Vadia Nevraev's behavior had a very serious origin indeed.

Two days before this chance encounter in the street, Shutikov, the Deputy Minister, had been brought a sheaf of secret documents that had made him put everything else aside.

"Pavel Ivanovich," he read, "special circumstances compel me to submit this matter to your consideration. I think prosecution is indicated." The note ended with a crooked flourish that looked like a knout—Drozdov's signature.

After reading it, Shutikov shrugged his shoulders. But when he came to the next document, he settled himself deeper in his chair and his eyes opened in surprise.

"Secret. To the head of the technical section, Comrade Drozdov, L. I.," he read, "I forward herewith a report from engineers Uriupin, A. I., and Maxiutenko, V. O., regarding the criminal infringement of the rules governing procedure in connection with official secrets by Lopatkin, D. A. The facts stated in the report have been confirmed by an investigation conducted by me, which I herewith bring to your notice."

This paper was signed by the director of the projecting Institute.

The third sheet of paper contained a circumstantial report in Maxiutenko's feminine handwriting. Shutikov read it greedily and little drops of sweat formed on his pale forehead.

"Engineer Lopatkin, D. A., head of a group of designers carrying out a secret government work of special importance, has given Citizeness N. S. Drozdov, whom he has caused to be registered as co-inventor, access to all the group's materials. The abovementioned Mrs. Drozdov examines and signs all drawings relating to the secret project, although not only is she no engineer, she does not even understand many of the simplest elements of a mechanical drawing. The majority of the officials know that this Mrs. Drozdov is merely a blind, and not a genuine co-inventor at all. As to the mercenary or other personal motives behind this abuse, the security organs alone are qualified to judge. We merely considered it our duty to bring this fact of the disclosure of official secrets of outstanding importance to your attention. Maxiutenko, Uriupin."

After reading this report, Shutikov pondered for a while, then his face again radiated a golden calm, a scarcely perceptible smile reflecting his secret thoughts. He picked up the receiver and leisurely dialed a number.

"Is that you, Leonid Ivanovich? Yes, I received it. Why didn't you add your authoritative signature to these submissions? What? What? Oh! Oh, oh, oh! Yes, yes. I noticed it, but thought it must be a namesake. Oh dear! Well, all right, I understand you. Very well."

He hung up the receiver, smiled, grunted, and shook his head.

Then he took the receiver from the cradle of a telephone marked MINISTER.

"Afanasy Terentievich? Could you see me for a moment? A very interesting business . . ."

Yes, the Minister could see him, and, putting down the receiver, Shutikov hurried along, almost at a run, wriggling his shoulders, smiling, and giving eager little coughs.

The Minister was sitting at his desk, expecting him. He answered his deputy's greeting with a slight nod, and his whole attitude seemed to express: "Well, what is it? Out with it!"

Shutikov put the papers down in front of him and began his report.

"Pipes again?" the Minister interrupted. "Is this the same engineer Lopatkin who was here before?"

"You are mistaken, Afanasy Terentievich. He is not an engineer, he is a schoolmaster. From the school in Muzga."

"Possibly. I think he is a brainy fellow."

"Very. At the time he spoke to you he already had an arrangement with Galitsky. All the business about pipes is now being treated as a secret order from outside. Your order . . ."

"What? So he was already negotiating with . . . Then why did he come to me? A two-way insurance, eh? It certainly is safer like that in our circumstances." The Minister laughed and winked at Shutikov, who shrugged. "So-o," the Minister drawled, as he read the documents. ". . . Disclosed official secrets of special importance, has he? And who is this woman? Have you made inquiries?"

"It's our Drozdov's wife."

The Minister threw himself back in his chair.

"Are you sure?"

"The source of information is the husband himself."

"What? So he has taken Drozdov's woman away from him?"

"He has."

There was a silence.

"So he is a rogue after all," the Minister finally said, shaking his head thoughtfully. "He has ulterior motives. He picked his co-inventor with a purpose. To work on Drozdov through his wife. Is she young?"

"Twenty-six, I believe."

"Ah! The fellow knows what's what. And Drozdov is an old woman. All of them there are old women. Well, how would you settle the matter? Where is Drozdov's opinion? Yes, of course. . . . He can't very well in the circumstances, seeing that he wears the horns! And what do you say?"

"I think we ought to call in security. This is an abuse of trust, isn't it?"

"Well, put your opinion in writing. You can do it here. And leave it behind for me. I want to think it all over once more."

On October 23, during the daytime, while Lopatkin was at the Institute, there was a very soft knock at Professor Busko's door. The old man opened it. A young soldier in a wet greatcoat was standing on the threshold.

"Does Citizen Lopatkin live here?" And he handed the professor an envelope addressed to Lopatkin.

The old man thought at first that it was a letter from the general, Lopatkin's new chief, about the project. But at that moment he caught sight of a stamped impression on the envelope: "Military Prosecutor's Office." His whiskers twitched as he looked at the soldier again, at his wet blue cap, then signed the receipt book with trembling fingers.

5

CAPTAIN ABROSIMOV, military prosecuting officer, always went to work on foot. He liked Moscow and enjoyed his walk along the Sadovaya boulevard each morning. On this particular day, too, he came out of his house—a huge new block of flats for officers and their families—cast a cursory glance at the mirrorlike polish of his boots, and proceeded at a leisurely pace along the pavement. He was a tall, slim young soldier, pale-faced and spiritual-looking, like a young priest. His mustaches curled, and he trimmed them in such a fashion as to make them look like a stripling's ungroomed down. His luxuriant chestnut hair could not be contained by the blue military cap. He was half a head taller than anyone he met on his way. When he had gone two blocks, the easy, domestic expression of his face gave way to his service thoughtfulness. At home, in the company of his wife, he was one man and in the prosecutor's office a completely different one. He knitted his dark eyebrows and his white forehead seemed to grow even more transparent. The glance of his dark brown eyes receded sternly into the distance, no longer aware of any obstacles. "What sort of man is he, this Lopatkin?" the investigator wondered. "And this woman, what is she?"

A few days earlier he had been summoned to his chief, who had entrusted a fresh case to him, with some papers clipped together and a sprawling scribble on the topmost one: "Comrade Abrosimov, for further proceedings." When he had looked through the papers, he saw at once that this was not one of those utterly definite cases in which there can be only one solution. When it is a case of murder, embezzlement, or robbery, the facts themselves are clear and demand immediate action; the criminals, conscious of their culpability, destroy the evidence and go into hiding, and the investigator has to find and expose them. But Lopatkin's case was different. The chief had said that in this case there was no need to prove anything: the disclosure of official secrets was evident. There was the person to whom the secret had been entrusted. And there was the objective side: that Lopatkin had given access to this secret to someone who had no right to know it. "Even if to one person only," the law said.

And yet Abrosimov still felt uncomfortable. The offense, so precisely defined by the *ukaz,* was in real life always tied up with circumstances which the investigator could not foresee. It lay in that no-man's land between crime and misdemeanor, where a trifling hesitation, the smallest detail, grew to be a decisive factor that could lead to opposite conclusions: in the one eventuality the culprit must be committed, in the other, disciplinary measures alone were required. Such cases held dangers for the investigating officer, and Captain Abrosimov, according to the quarterly reports, had a record of failures. Hence from the start he didn't care for the "monkey puzzler," as he called such indeterminate cases.

"Why are they prosecuting this Lopatkin?" he asked his chief.

"It's tied up with an important official secret. A particularly important one," the chief replied. "The general himself rang up. By the way, he asked that the case should be put into your hands."

These words flattered Abrosimov's vanity. His name had been mentioned several times already in the general's orders, and always in connection with instances of resourceful operative work. "So the secret must really be an important one," he thought. "That makes it easier."

Once the monkey puzzler was Abrosimov's to deal with, it was up to him to consider carefully those features and motives in the case which might tip the scales. They had to be dug up, so that the case should change its quality from indefinite to definite, and so that the prosecutor's reasons for prosecuting should be clear to the judge.

Similarly Abrosimov might dig up other attenuating motives, if the general were to consider it inopportune to take Lopatkin into court. Such was the nature of these indefinite cases. Abrosimov did not like them but for some reason cases of this sort were often assigned to him rather than to someone else.

He took the papers away to his office, and there in the quiet of his room began studying them. After looking through five or six secret enclosures bearing the signatures—in various colors and with various flourishes—of several departmental heads, he saw again with satisfaction that he had been put in charge of a matter of great responsibility. Two of the signatures were familiar—a well-known scientist and a well-known Deputy Minister thought that Lopatkin should be prosecuted for disclosing an important official secret. Abrosimov agreed with them. Then there was Uriupin and Maxiutenko's report. Having read it carefully, he underlined with a red pencil the words: "registered as co-inventor," and laughed. "Clear enough!" The next papers were two testimonies characterizing Lopatkin, one signed by the director of the Institute, and the other, which took up six pages, by a group of doctors and candidates of science. The first of these satisfied Abrosimov completely. Through it he saw that Lopatkin had possessed the government's confidence and had not justified it. But in the second testimonial the captain at once noticed an unpleasant contradiction. This pernickety engineer must have got well under these scientists' skins, if they had decided, even belatedly, to throw a stone at him, and demanded that he should be called to account for the malicious slandering of Soviet science and Soviet scientists. Lopatkin's pipe-casting machine, they declared, was "the fantasy of an ignorant adventurer, who, by a stroke of the pen, wishes to cancel all the results of research both of Soviet and foreign scientists." They described Lopatkin as a sham inventor who had exploited the confidence and incompetence of certain officials to pass off a worthless project for a new idea.

Having read this characteristic document Abrosimov's eye glanced down the long column of names and signatures on the last page with a sardonic smile. All these Tepikins and Fundators had, without knowing it, complicated the investigating officer's work by proving convincingly that there had been no official secret to disclose. Abrosimov reported this to his chief, who instructed him not to add the scientists' letter to the documents belonging to the case, but to pass it on to the secretary as a document that had no direct bearing on the matter in hand and caused unnecessary complications. The chief's argument was that if Lopatkin's actions in fact amounted to the crime called slander—a matter which was still in doubt—such a trifle could be left unheeded in the interest of greater clarity and speed in investigating. Slander would merely entail a fine, a trifling measure compared with the penalty awaiting one who had disclosed an official secret. And besides, this was a matter for a civil lawsuit—let them bring an action against the man before the People's Court.

Abrosimov questioned Uriupin and Maxiutenko that same day and learned certain interesting details about Mrs. Drozdov, who was to be called as a witness. He felt suddenly that there was a large group of people who, for various personal reasons, had an interest in accusing Lopatkin. But these were merely unnecessary touches which could only be a hindrance. Among scientists and officials every affair is overgrown with all kinds of conflicting interests. To rummage among them would merely draw out the investigation, complicate the case, and still lead to the same final conclusions. What must be sought out was the fundamental fact, the disclosure of an official secret and the reason for this disclosure, which was already clear in any case: *Cherchez la femme.* And everything else followed from this one evil. It was this line that the investigator decided to take, and he wrote out subpoenas for Lopatkin for the morning of the twenty-fourth, and for Mrs. Drozdov for October 25.

Now he was walking to his office pondering the questions he should ask Lopatkin.

Lopatkin was sitting in the twilight of the empty passage. He felt an indefinable weakness throughout his body. Now and then he wiped his dry chin and cheeks, as though they were still wet with Nadia's tears. The parting from her had been very hard.

He heard footsteps, and a young officer with a pale face and a curly mustache appeared at the end of the passage. He gave Lopatkin a hard look and did not take his dark, searching eyes off him again the whole time he walked slowly along the passage.

"Lopatkin?" he asked politely, unlocking the door of room number seven, opposite which Lopatkin was sitting. "Just stay where you are, I'll call you later," he said, seeing Lopatkin stand.

The door remained closed for about twenty minutes, then the investigator looked out again and with the same politeness invited Lopatkin in. The investigator sat down at his desk and began to turn the pages of a swollen dossier of about four hundred pages with his blue-white priestly fingers. "My case! What on earth is it all about?" Lopatkin thought in dismay. He did not know that it was precisely in order to achieve this that Abrosimov had put on his desk the documents relating to an old and very muddled case dealing with some theft of fodder—a trick that had been devised by interrogators at least two centuries before.

"Well, let us get acquainted," the investigator said suddenly, pushing away the file and drawing a form headed "Minutes of Interrogation" in front of him. He leisurely entered Lopatkin's name, age, and the official data concerning him on it. Then he gave the usual warning about false statements, made him sign the form, and wrote into the minutes: "Regarding the facts of the case, I have knowledge of the following," then laid down his pen.

"Please tell me in sequence everything relating to your invention."

"May I smoke?" Lopatkin asked, and not waiting for permission, struck a match and inhaled the cigarette smoke deeply. After he had gulped in a few mouthfuls silently and sighed several times, adjusting himself to his new position of suspect, he began a detailed account, from the moment when he had visited the Muzga *kombinat* foundry with a party of schoolchildren. He had told Nadezhda Sergeyevna about all this, about the antiquated methods of casting pipes, the conveyor belt in motorcar manufacture, and the little old man, Ivan Zotych.

The investigator listened to him for about forty minutes. While he did so he drew a female head on a sheet of paper, then added mustaches, spectacles, and a hat. Then he crossed the drawing through with his pen and raised attentive eyes to Lopatkin.

"Good. I understand you. Now tell me, in the same detail, how you came to be assigned to secret work."

Captain Abrosimov had his own method of interrogation, which he had worked out during years of crime detection. He questioned cautiously, without pressure, as one shoos pigeons into a pigeon loft. Circumstantially Lopatkin recounted everything to do with his meeting with his new customers, from the moment when the ash-gray Pobeda car had picked him up; then he passed to the work in the designing group. As he did not mention Nadia's name, Abrosimov thought to himself, "No, that won't come off," and interrupting him softly, asked him to enumerate all the members of the group. Lopatkin named them all, but again said nothing about Nadia.

"You have forgotten one collaborator—Mrs. Drozdov," the captain reminded him quietly.

"She is not on the pay roll," Lopatkin replied.

There was a pause. The investigator wrote something down, his pen scratching on the paper. Then he looked out of the window, lit a cigarette, and gazed at Lopatkin through the smoke as though from a distance.

"You say she is not on the pay roll?" He seemed to wake up suddenly. "Then what is her connection with us? Why does she come and go in the group? Has she a permit?"

"She is my partner."

"Oh, she is? What is she—a specialist in pipe casting?"

"No, she is a teacher of geography. We have known each other for a long time and she has gradually come to know all about things. Now she is quite familiar with it all. It was she who gave me the idea of casting two-layer pipes by the centrifugal method."

"Do you know if she is married?"

"Yes, she was the wife of Drozdov, the head of the technical directorate. I don't know how it is with them now. I believe they have parted."

"And what is the basis of your relationship?"

"I think she is not completely . . . indifferent to me."

"And you to her?"

"My feelings for her are not entirely simple. Sometimes it seems to me that I, too . . . This morning, for instance, when we said good-by . . ."

"Yes." Abrosimov enveloped himself in a cloud of blue smoke, and propping his chin on the hand that held the cigarette, asked, as if incidentally, although he was in fact on tenterhooks: "Have you not had sexual relations with her? Excuse me, but in our work we are sometimes compelled to touch on . . ."

Dmitri drew the smoke of his cigarette in, paused for an instant, then said dryly:

"No."

Abrosimov, his head bent sideways, scratched with his pen.

"What does he want?" thought Lopatkin.

At this moment the door opened and Abrosimov's chief, an elderly, easy-going man with a major's badges of rank and a puffy, yellowish face came in, his hands in his pockets. The major liked taking part in interrogations and always spoiled the captain's hand by frightening his pigeons. So now he went up to Abrosimov and began reading the minutes of the interrogation.

"You are covering up, Lopatkin, covering up!" he said, coming forward from the desk.

Abrosimov grew pale, and his nostrils twitched. Dmitri, narrowing his eyes, looked at the major with cold curiosity and did not reply.

"Yes," the major said, pacing up and down the room, "it won't do, you know, to disclose official secrets. It's just what our enemies are waiting for—that such as you, who set their personal interests above those of the state . . ."

"So that's it!" Lopatkin thought. "But she is my *partner* in the invention!" he shouted at the major.

"Stop playing about, Lopatkin!" the major said. "You gave her a feel up every day, no doubt. Did a little drawing for an hour or so, and then—a feel up! Look, Abrosimov, no need to bother with the fellow, he'll only tell you a pack of lies!"

When the major had gone, Abrosimov remained silent for a while, as if to collect himself. Then he looked at Lopatkin.

"You were warned, were you not, that the work was secret?"

"I was. But I consider that inventors, by virtue of their position, cannot help knowing what they are working on."

"Inventors again. So you still insist that Mrs. Drozdov is your partner in the invention?"

"Perfectly true," Dmitri confirmed.

"And that there was no physical intimacy between you?"

"No, none!" Lopatkin lied.

Although at the first question he had concealed the truth in order to protect Nadia, now he was already defending himself. "If I were to say 'yes,' I should have to add to this brief syllable an analysis of our relationship that might take three hours," he thought, "But the captain wants only these short syllables: 'yes' or 'no.' And so it is better that it should be 'no.'"

Meanwhile the captain had finished the minutes. Putting them in front of him on the table, he took out a fresh cigarette, and began reading them aloud. Everything had been taken down quite accurately, and Lopatkin signed his name at the bottom of each page.

"Can I go now?" he asked.

"Wait in the passage for a minute," the captain said.

He left the room with Dmitri, locked the door, and went to the far end of the passage. In half an hour he returned, holding a white paper in his hand.

"Come in," he said, unlocking the door of his room.

When Lopatkin was again seated in the same place by the desk, the captain, still standing, said:

"We are taking you into custody. Here is the order. Read it!"

Lopatkin took the order and began reading it: "Taking into consideration that the suspect Lopatkin, D. A., if left at liberty, might escape or hinder the discovery of the truth . . ."

"Do you understand it?" the captain asked. "Sign here."

Lopatkin signed obediently. The investigator gazed at him fixedly.

"Not there. Look, here, see, on the dotted line."

Lopatkin obediently signed once again, growing suddenly very quiet, stooping, and growing a little pale. But it was not the thought of prison that frightened him. He seemed to have climbed to the top of a hill and looked right through those walls at new distances suddenly opening before him. And there, leading to fresh horizons, lay the same winding road, seamed with new, far-off milestones.

6

NADIA received her summons the same day as Lopatkin. The envelope was handed to her by the same soldier in the rain-soaked greatcoat, and having read that she was to go to the military prosecutor's office, she decided, for the first time in six months, to speak to her husband without having first been spoken to. When Drozdov came home to dinner and sat down alone at the large dining table (he dined alone now) Nadia came and put the summons down in front of him.

"Do you know what this means?"

"How should I know?" Drozdov's yellow face preserved its calm. He closed his eyes, then slowly opened them, as though just awakening. "For what day? The twenty-fifth? Well, I suppose on the twenty-fifth you will find out everything that concerns you.

"I might, perhaps, have made some sort of guess, but as you do not inform me of your activities, of where you go every day, or what you are up to, as you are now an independent person, why come to me?"

Nadia saw in his dark, shrewd, coldly-sardonic eyes that he knew a great deal, and exclaimed:

"I am convinced that you know everything."

"You tell me nothing." Drozdov went on stroking his face with his hands, and suddenly a laughing eye looked out at her from between his fingers. "You didn't tell me, for instance, that you sold . . ."

"Yes, I sold my fur coat."

"Why?"

"I needed the money. Not for my personal needs."

"For State needs?"

"Yes, if you like, for State needs."

"What was it? A loan? A squadron named after . . . what's the fellow's name?"

"The time will come when you will realize that I did right."

"So we must be patient—till the twenty-fifth."

Drozdov, of course, knew everything. In the first moment Uriupin's and Maxiutenko's report had sounded to him like a shot past his ear. The male in him had been hurt and had screamed with pain. He had suddenly experienced a helpless grief, had felt himself to be an old man unwanted by anyone, and had realized that the most merciless and irremediable symptoms of old age are those one is not aware of oneself. Then he had grown cold at the thought that outside the door of his room, in the innumerable cells of the Ministry honeycomb, satirical gossip at his expense was already going the rounds. When Drozdov heard that the case had been passed on to the military prosecutor, he had at once decided to help Lopatkin and Nadia, so that the matter might be suppressed: he could not allow these two crazy lovers to be questioned in public, in an investigation in the background of which he himself, Drozdov, stood. But Shutikov had told him that the proceedings would be secret, *in camera*. Drozdov had been reassured. Even his good humor had returned; he saw that, with Lopatkin's arrest, the most unpleasant problems of his personal and public life would finally be solved. Everything would fall into place, and he would even keep Nadia—she would never leave her child.

In fact, it was only their son now who was a bond between them, and Drozdov made skillful use of this tie. Nadia could not bring herself to break up the family routine to which Nikolashka was accustomed. Without having agreed to do so, the father and mother from time to time kept up something of the external appearance of their former relationship in the child's presence. But the child realized everything and looked at his parents with his small eyebrows raised in alarm. Now he was in a constant state of alarm. His grandmother spoiled him, stuffing him with sweets. Nadia competed with her jealously, and perhaps this was another reason why the child lost weight and grew more and more capricious.

Drozdov was aware of all this. Nadia's restless eyes, darkened by fear at times, did not escape his notice. Sometimes in his presence she suddenly clenched her fingers as though in pain. He knew that his son's fate, Lopatkin's imminent arrest, and even his own position as the blamelessly suffering husband who understood his wife and never made scenes—that in the final count everything would combine into a single decisive and irresistible force.

This was how Drozdov acted during these days, and this was why he involuntarily smiled when he talked to Nadia.

She picked up the summons and left the room without a word. She gave her lessons at school that day in a state of abstraction; she saw before her constantly the blue envelope from the prosecutor's office, the first summons she had ever received. At dusk she took the subway, and half an hour later was running along Liakhov Lane, under the dismal autumn rain that was invisible in the darkness. She pressed the button of the general bell five times, but no one opened. She rang once more until Tymiansky came shuffling in bedroom slippers and let her in.

"Are they out?" Nadia asked.

"No, they are busy discussing something."

Nadia knocked softly at the door, then knocked once again more loudly, and felt a shock of pleasure when she heard Lopatkin ask angrily, in a loud, sharp, questioning voice:

"Who is it? Come in!"

She loved that voice because it reflected Lopatkin's whole being, and a wave of humility and obedience flooded over her.

"Come in! Who is it?" Dmitri exclaimed in an even sharper tone, throwing the door open.

She entered and at once saw a blue envelope similar to hers on the table, bearing the scarcely perceptible impression of the military prosecutor's rubber stamp.

"What is this?" she asked.

"I have been asked to go there." Lopatkin spread out his hands in a gesture of perplexity. "Tomorrow morning."

368

She sat down on the stool.

"I have been asked to go, too!"

She put her own summons on the table and looked at Lopatkin and the professor, who had suddenly grown silent. The old man took the summons, drew it past his spectacles as though examining the quality of the paper.

"This has to do with the same case. And it is, of course, not Krekhov's or Antonovich's case, but your own. I told you that at once. Remember what I said about the pendulum?" He glanced significantly at Lopatkin, and propping his elbows on the table, began looking around him and blowing into his fist.

"What can it be?" The sharp furrow on Lopatkin's forehead grew deeper and more curved, his unshaven cheeks were sunken.

"Drozdov knows," Nadia remarked, and related briefly her conversation with her husband that morning. "He knows, but he won't tell."

"Come. Let's think it all over, let's remember everything correctly," the old man suggested.

Nadia, her fingers at her forehead, leaned forward and looked at the ground. Lopatkin walked back and forth in the narrow space, or leaned with his shoulder against the door, wrinkling his forehead and gesturing with his hands, as he thought aloud: "If Krekhov . . . No, that cannot be! Antonovich . . . Very improbable. . . ."

They speculated, recalling past events for several hours and getting nowhere. When the loud-speaker came to life at midnight and the carillon of the Kremlin rang out, Lopatkin shrugged his shoulders and said: "Drozdov is right. Tomorrow everything will be clear. One can't foresee everything. And now I am going to bed."

At eight next morning Nadia again knocked at their door. Lopatkin was dressed and shaved, with his hair well brushed, and received Nadia with the clear glance of a man who was prepared for any emergency. The old man, holding on to Lopatkin's sleeve, saw them to the stairs, and there, blowing his nose loudly and wiping his eyes with a dirty handkerchief, said:

"If there should be anything . . . I will take every possible step. I will do all I can. Go. But be careful, weigh every word!"

They walked quickly to the iron railings, where the two-story building with its white columns and cornices stood behind the bushes that surrounded one half of the courtyard. There were still fifty minutes left till ten o'clock. They left the house and walked slowly along the deserted boulevard. There was nothing to say. The world in which words seem so simple receded. Lopatkin gazed about him, at the house porters sweeping the yellow leaves from the pavement, at a woman with a dog. . . . Nadia was gripping his strong elbow with all her strength and looking at him, her eyebrows raised anxiously.

They walked to the end of the boulevard and then turned back. Finally Lopatkin said:

"Why are you looking at me like that, Nadia?" He had seen all the time, it appeared. "In the life of a man chapters like this, too, can occur; and they must be read through patiently. In case anything happens, will you write to me *there?*"

"Oh, do you really think . . . ?"

"Yes, I believe so now. You said that Drozdov was smiling. And that is not all. I ran into Nevraev recently, he passed, looked me in the face, and did not even greet me. Now I understand. He really is a barometer. The devil knows what they may have cooked up for me."

He glanced hurriedly at his watch.

"There are ten minutes left. We must settle a few things. Are you going to school today?"

"No, it's my day off," Nadia lied.

"All right. I am going now. If I haven't come out again by two o'clock, even if only for a moment—I'll ask to be excused—to this seat—if I don't come, it means it's all up with me."

He looked tenderly into her eyes. Without a word Nadia threw herself on his breast, put her arms round his neck, and clung there, motionless, until suddenly her chest began heaving and Lopatkin led her gently to the seat and made her sit down. Nadia held his hand without speaking. He dislodged her cold fingers, kissed her somewhere beside her ear, then walked away quickly, in a straight line, leaving behind house porters and the passers-by he encountered, whose eyes followed him with vague smiles of curiosity.

Nadia, slumped on the seat, as Lopatkin had left her, gazed up into the clear, cold, autumn sky. The morning moon floated there, scarcely visible, like a white feather on water.

At first Nadia believed that Lopatkin would come out to her in an hour, or possibly two. But the hours went by, first one, then another, and there was no sign of him. By one o'clock the sky had turned gray and an autumn rain began rustling sleepily among the yellow leaves. Nadia did not notice it. The hands of her tiny wrist watch were approaching two o'clock. Then they calmly passed that deadline. Another half-hour went by. A group of officers in blue caps and gray gabardine greatcoats appeared behind the iron railings. One of them stood out, a tall, thin-legged, pale one, with a soft, dark mustache. The officers crossed the boulevard in an oblique line; they were arguing animatedly about something and disappeared down a side street. It was obviously their lunch hour, for an hour later they all came back, one by one, from the same side street. By four o'clock the rain stopped; the gray and yellow curtains in the sky gradually parted, revealing a pale-blue dusk. The red clouds and streaks in one part of the sky, above the rooftops, where the sun had disappeared, also split apart. They were lit by a red light and lined up as though on parade. Then everything grew even redder, the echelons of clouds grew darker, lengthening one after another and returning to their quarters to a mauve and purple colored music leaving the greenish firmament empty. Everything grew quieter all about. Below, in the darkness, the tracer lights of cars flitted past, and the beams danced on the wet asphalt. Nadia stood up; her whole body felt heavy and aching. She walked slowly along the boulevard. What had happened? Why hadn't Dmitri Alexeyevich come out before two o'clock? Tomorrow she would know everything. . . .

At nine o'clock next morning she walked down the long passage of the military prosecutor's office and knocked on a door marked seven. Entering a room smelling of tobacco, she saw a clean-shaven, aloof, polite officer with a pale, handsome face, curly mustache and eyebrows, and luxuriant, wavy hair that stood up on his head, spoiling the beauty of his face by giving it a touch of femininity. Nadia was offered a seat and the interrogation began. The interrogator wrote down all her personal data, warned her sternly of her responsibility in case of false statements, then took from a drawer a long strip of paper on which he had put down point by point some kind of plan on each of whose points he began questioning Nadia. After every question he bent his head to one side and wrote for a long time, his pen scratching in the silence.

"You are co-inventor with Lopatkin?" he asked.

Nadia decided to defend Lopatkin to her utmost.

"Nonsense. My part in the creation of his machine is trifling. The true inventor is Dmitri Alexeyevich."

Without a word the officer began to write diligently. Then he glanced at his plan and put another question.

"Tell me, did you personally contribute anything to his machine? Perhaps you devised the principle of the machine and he gave it shape?"

"Oh no!" Nadia replied heatedly. "The idea of the machine was entirely his."

"Just a moment." He stopped Nadia and began writing. "Good," he said, putting the pen down after a minute or two. "Have you any special training that might afford you the possibility at least of competently . . ."

"I am a geographer," Nadia said. "I have no such training. It was Dmitri Alexeyevich who . . ."

She raised her voice proudly, but the officer stopped her and again began to write.

"One more question," he said. "Have you known him long?"

"It seems to me that we have never been strangers to one another."

The interrogator smiled.

372

"We were taught to believe that the soul cannot be eternal."

"I made Dmitri Alexeyevich's acquaintance in forty-four . . . no, forty-three. . . ."

"You love him?"

"It is impossible not to love him," Nadia said with hidden passion.

The interrogator paused and looked at her.

"And does he love you?"

"I don't know. Tell me, did you ask him this question?"

"Now just this," the officer said, without answering Nadia's question. "Was there any physical intimacy between you?"

He asked this question calmly, but Nadia suddenly felt that the officer sitting opposite her was strangely tense, and it frightened her. He repeated his question.

"Answer, please. This question is written down in the minutes." He did not look at her, but examined the buttons on his sleeve.

Nadia read the question. It was formulated with perfect precision. Not understanding the implications, she answered, blushing: "Yes."

The interrogator betrayed himself: he began hurriedly to write the answer down. Coming from his pen, it turned into a long sentence: "Yes, I did, in fact . . ." and so on. And Nadia suddenly realized with horror that by this answer she had sealed Lopatkin's fate. The captain glanced at her and saw that he had made a mistake. He stopped writing, and groped casually for his cigarette case, lit a cigarette, shook his hair out of his face, and started a conversation with Nadia about the school and about co-education, of which he was an opponent. "If they are brought together they begin to think of co-inventorships too early," he said with a laugh.

"Where were we?" He suddenly turned serious again. "Oh yes. Well, I think we have dealt with everything. Here, read it."

While Nadia was reading the minutes, he walked to and fro with long strides, smoking. Everything had been accurately written down in the statement. Nadia signed each page, and the investigator, no longer concealing his satisfaction, put the papers into a folder.

"Tell me," Nadia asked him in a low voice. "Have you arrested him?"

"Yes, he has been arrested."

"What for?"

"I am not empowered to tell you. It is an official secret. There it is, Nadezhda Sergeyevna, I can't tell you! To my regret, it is impossible. Can you find your way out? Straight ahead to the right, and down. Good-by!"

7

ONE morning at the beginning of November, Lopatkin was taken from the prison to the inner courtyard of the familiar pale-green building with the white cornices and columns. The car stopped at the wing in which the hearing was to be held. The prisoner was conducted along several passages to the courtroom, which seemed to him very brightly lit after the darkness of the passages. Lopatkin was wearing the same gray, slightly crumpled suit. His hair, cropped close in prison, had turned white, and the childishly large bulges of his skull showed clearly through the bare scalp. Dmitri sat down; his dark eyes looked silently round, and he caught sight of Nadia sitting on a chair near the door. She seemed to be straining forward in his direction. But at that moment there was a sound of footsteps, and three officers came out of a side door. The judges took their places behind a long table. An old lieutenant colonel with blue-gray hair parted smoothly in the middle, and a stern, bony, clean-shaven face, sat down in the center and at once opened the folder holding the documents of the case. He sat bolt upright, his head in the air. To his right sat a stout captain with a shiny face and hair that was thin on top, to his left a young major with the everyday, inconspicuous features of a redheaded Russian lad, high-cheekboned, short-statured, and heavy-fisted. He would have appeared very broad-shouldered indeed if his coat had been padded in the right places as that of the other judge, the captain's, had been. But there was no padding there, and his powerful shoulders sloped like those of a porter.

Separated from the judges, at the very end of the long table, sat the secretary, a second lieutenant, who at once began writing, holding the pen like a cigarette, between the index and middle finger.

The chairman put on his horn-rimmed spectacles and declared the sitting of the court open. The questioning of the accused began: what was his name, where and when was he born.... The judge took off his spectacles and put them down on the open folder.

"Witness Maxiutenko?"

"Present," answered a somewhat uncertain voice from the back of the almost empty courtroom.

"Witness Mrs. Drozdov?"

"Here," Nadia answered.

The judge called on the witnesses to stand up, and warned them of the legal consequences of false testimony. Nadia and Maxiutenko signed the sheet held by the secretary, and without looking at each other, left the courtroom. After this Nadia sat in semidarkness, listening to the confused, distant sounds in this large, mysterious house.

In the courtroom the proceedings took their usual course. The chairman explained his rights to the prisoner and asked whether he wished for counsel to defend him. Lopatkin shrugged his shoulders, said that his case was clear, and that he needed no defending counsel. Then the chairman, pushing the documents a little farther away, read the indictment, which said that Lopatkin, Dmitri Alexeyevich, while head of a group of designers, was accused of having given access to documents constituting an official secret to a person not entitled to such access—that is to Mrs. Drozdov, Nadezhda Sergeyevna—registering her alleged participation in the work of the group under cover of co-inventorship, although in fact there was no such co-inventorship, whereby he had committed the crime defined in paragraph so-and-so of such and such a date.

Having read to the end, the chairman called on Lopatkin to stand up and asked him whether he admitted his guilt. Lopatkin drew in his chin stubbornly and answered:

"No."

"Tell the court everything you know of this matter."

376

Lopatkin remained silent a few minutes to weigh his words and then began relating in detail the difficulties he had encountered when, to his own surprise, he had turned inventor. He had wanted to go on to say that the continued support Nadezhda Sergeyevna had given him would in itself have been enough to qualify her as co-inventor.

But the chairman gently stopped him.

"You are not keeping to the point."

"On the contrary, I am trying to get to the point, to the essence of the matter," Lopatkin objected.

At this the chairman, in the same inflexibly upright posture, said:

"Answer these questions. Does the work you were doing in the group constitute an official secret?"

"Of course it does," said Dmitri, shrugging his shoulders.

"Take cognizance of an order of the Minister regarding the especially secret character of the information disclosed by the accused, page twenty-eight of the documents of the case," the chairman said, and there was silence behind the table as one after the other the judges quickly examined the document.

"Who was the person chiefly responsible for the non-disclosure of this secret?" the chairman asked.

"I suppose it was I."

"Suppose? And quite *positively*, who was it?"

"It was I."

"Did Nadezhda Sergeyevna Drozdov have any knowledge of this secret?"

"She had."

"She had," the chairman repeated pointedly, looking at the secretary: had he got this down all right? "And who disclosed this secret to her? Who informed her of every detail of the matter?"

"She knew them all long before the machine was put on the secret list."

"Who informed Mrs. Drozdov of the fact that the machine had

been put on the secret list? Who kept her informed of the subsequent changes in the project?"

"I did. But she is registered as my partner. There is an order to that effect."

"We shall examine presently whether there was any foundation for issuing such an order."

"Very good. Then please tell me what I have disclosed? If I have disclosed a secret, it must be known to you."

"Do not put questions to the court!"

"Very well, I won't. I will submit an appeal to the court: I ask the court to establish what I have disclosed."

"The court rejects your appeal, as it is not within its competence to probe into the subject matter of secret information, precisely because it *is* secret. It is known from an official source that according to the enumeration laid down in the order regarding it this information was top secret. That is sufficient. Answer the court's question: who is the originator, the creator of the entire fundamental principle of your machine?"

"I am. But as to the variant for double-layer pipes, it is Mrs. Drozdov and I. It was she who suggested the idea to me."

"Was she able to do so consciously? Does she possess the necessary knowledge for that?"

Lopatkin did not answer. He was thinking hard. Everything pointed to his having in fact disclosed a secret. But why had he felt *at that time* that he was under an obligation to place Nadia's name on a level with his own? Why ask? He would do the same again. But how could he explain this to the court?

"Tell me," the redheaded major asked suddenly, speaking with peasant slowness, and leaning forward eagerly, "why did you attempt to conceal your personal relationship from the investigator?"

"Personal relationship with whom?"

"With Mrs. Drozdov," the major said insistently, repeating it three times, and sounding the o's with a special roundness.

Lopatkin looked at him, trying to understand the purpose of this question, but failing.

"I wished to protect her from the necessity for unpleasant explanations. She is a woman. . . ."

Here the chairman intervened:

"Was it not because you mixed the intimate personal side of your life with the official side, turned your secret government work into a domestic affair, and when an investigation began, tried to conceal this?"

"No, it was not for that reason. I demand the calling of witnesses representing the authority giving the order and of General . . ."

The chairman looked at the men on each side of him, first at the captain, then at the major.

"The court rejects your demand. These persons had been misled by you, and this aspect of the case is perfectly clear."

"One more question," the major said slowly. "How would it be possible, in your opinion, to prove it really was Mrs. Drozdov who gave you the idea?"

"But I tell you . . ."

"Just a moment. Don't be in such a hurry! Could it be proved by an expert examination?"

"The projecting of my machine was begun precisely because it was decided to do without experts; for once the princes of science were by-passed. They were by-passed and the result is a criminal prosecution against me. If you looked through the documents of the case and also my correspondence during the past six years, you would see that my accusers are all the same men who obstructed me during the six years . . ."

The chairman cut him short. "Your correspondence has nothing to do with this case, and as for your accusers, they simply showed vigilance—the vigilance which you failed to show. Yes. Any more questions?"

There were no further questions, and the chairman called the first witness. Maxiutenko came in. Standing to attention, he told the court how he had seen Mrs. Drozdov in the room occupied by the group, and how surprised he had been that she was Lopatkin's co-inventor. Uriupin had attempted to examine her, but after the very first question she had become confused and not known what to say till she was helped out by a member of the group, Antono-vich, who had showed Uriupin the door, as being a stranger. Maxi-utenko went on to say that he had known the accused for a long time and knew that he had always worked at his machine alone, without any partner.

Everything was quite clear, and the witness was dismissed with-out any supplementary questions.

When Nadia entered the courtroom, the chairman took off his spectacles and eyed her with attention, then put them on again and invited her to tell all she knew about the matter in hand.

After these words had been spoken an oppressive silence reigned in the courtroom. Nadia stood saying nothing.

"We are waiting to hear," the chairman said.

Again there was a silence.

"I don't know. . . . I have no knowledge of anything," Nadia finally said in a low voice.

"Do you fully confirm the statement made by you during the preliminary investigation?" the chairman began, turning the pages of the dossier.

"Yes, I confirm it," Nadia said softly.

"Page thirty-two," the chairman said, addressing himself to the secretary.

He read out all the questions that had been put to Nadia by Captain Abrosimov, and all her replies. As he read each answer, the chairman raised his eyes to Nadia and, speaking more and more softly, she answered "Yes."

"So you claim that Lopatkin is the sole inventor of his machine and that no one else, including yourself, contributed any essential elements to the principle of the invention?"

"Yes, of course." She gave Lopatkin a caressing look, as if to encourage him.

"The crucial is not the principle," Lopatkin said suddenly in an incisive tone. "A co-inventor can also contribute the application of the principle . . ."

"You are disorganizing the court's work," the chairman interposed, rising in his seat.

"I ask your pardon. May I ask the witness a question?"

The chairman, who was turning over the pages of the dossier, did not answer, merely raising his eyebrows to indicate: "You may."

Dmitri turned to Nadia.

"Do you know the basic drawings of the project? Do you know where the basic correspondence is kept? I mean the non-secret stuff you filed?"

"Yes, of course I know."

"Ask questions that are to the point," said the chairman.

"Do you know that if I am condemned, they absolutely must be saved?" Lopatkin asked.

The chairman looked at him, shaking his head.

"I understand everything!" Nadia whispered, nodding several times to Lopatkin, and looking in terror, first at him, and then at the chairman.

The chairman again began turning the pages of the dossier. He obviously regarded the case as perfectly clear. Closing the folder, he turned to the captain, who nodded hurriedly. Then the major whispered something in his ear, making slight gestures with his hand, as though trying to persuade him of something. The chairman shrugged his shoulders and again opened the folder. The major turned to Nadia and spoke, stressing his "o's" in a loud, singsong voice.

"You described the accused's work very flatteringly and with great conviction. Tell us, did you personally help him in any way?"

"I did do something."

"Tell us what it is, that something."

"I used to go to the library for him and read the foreign technical literature . . . I typed . . . and dealt with his business correspondence. Sometimes I did a little housework. . . ."

"When I was very broke, an unknown patron sent me six thou-

381

sand roubles," Lopatkin interrupted, "and after that the witness had no fur coat! Let us be frank, Nadezhda Sergeyevna. You have given your signature to the court regarding false statements."

Lopatkin was joking, but his eyes remained stern, as if he had forgotten how to smile.

"Did this happen?" the major asked.

"It did," Nadia confirmed in a low voice.

"And one day she came to me from the library and said: 'I have found an interesting . . .' "

"All these are details concerning your personal relationship," the chairman objected.

"Had there been no Mrs. Drozdov, there would not have been this secret invention either!" Lopatkin exclaimed.

"Order!" The chairman tapped the table loudly with his pencil. "Witness Drozdov, there are no more questions for you. Prisoner, can you add anything to the facts?"

"I shall say nothing more." Lopatkin sat down and shook his white head. "Everything has been said."

There was a long silence. Dmitri sat motionless, staring at the legs of the table.

"We are waiting to hear you, Lopatkin. Do you forgo the right of the last word?"

"I do."

"The court will now withdraw for consultation." The chairman rose.

The judges left the courtroom through the side door. The secretary marked Nadia's and Maxiutenko's passes and remarked severely that the witnesses could go, that it was all over.

The room to which the judges had proceeded had obviously been the former study of some great personage. The large fireplace was still there, and in its dark recess one could see several empty ink bottles. The high ceiling was framed, as it were, in a border of massive stucco ornament. There were two tables in the room, with plastic inkstands standing on them, several chairs, and a divan covered in black rexine, on which the chairman of the tribunal at once threw himself down.

"That Abrosimov is a marvel!" he said, lighting a cigarette. "He arranged the interrogation very well. If he had questioned Mrs. Drozdov first, she would of course have rushed to Lopatkin at once, he would have coached her, and then there would have been difficulties at the hearing. But as it is, her evidence is clearer than holy water. No ulterior thoughts, only the truth, like a babe in arms."

"Ye-es," the major drawled without conviction. He was standing by the window, smoking and looking down into the street.

"I thought the whole time, by the way, that now she would guess what was up and say, 'Yes, I am his partner in his invention,'" the chairman went on, knocking the ash off his cigarette against his boot. "We should have had to send the case back to Abrosimov for further investigation. To have given him a bad mark in the quarterly report, and to have appointed an expert commission. And then another expert opinion on top of the first. . . . It would have been a proper muddle!"

"And now it isn't a muddle, you think?" the major said, still looking out of the window.

"Why a muddle?" The lieutenant colonel blew out a puff of smoke, and flung out a finger to point each argument. "What we have to establish in the first place is whether any action incriminating the accused did or did not take place. No one, I believe, would dispute that such action did take place; that he revealed the secret. The disclosure of documents, verbal information, failure to ensure suitable storage—each of these variants fits the case. Note how the legislator has formulated the point—there is no need even of actual disclosure. A genuine possibility of the secret becoming known to another person is sufficient."

"A representative of the customer should have been called all the same. The order had been given to both of them, not to one only."

"So you are following that line? Didn't you see how he con-

383

ducted himself at the end? He felt you were on his side. Why these concessions, these sops? You say that the customer's representative should have been called. Zakharov perhaps? Very well, let him confirm it. What of it? Lopatkin never should have proposed her as co-inventor; he should have kept everything from her."

"But she already knew the construction and the principle of it."

"Only within non-secret limits. Then something was added—the double-layer pipes. A special assignment. And the designation 'Secret.' That classification changed the whole situation."

"But she had participated in its birth." The major turned to the chairman, and his round "o's" now sounded agitated. "The idea—I'll call it idea number two—is Mrs. Drozdov's. That is perfectly clear, even though it was not investigated. Is she to forget what she already knows, once the designation 'secret' is put on it? Is she to renounce her rights? And why expert opinions, when the facts can be ascertained on the testimony of witnesses? Zakharov for one. Old Busko for another. We did not even take into consideration that foreign journal about pipes—which makes three witnesses. Was the request slip in the library examined? And supposing there is only one signature on it—Mrs. Drozdov's? Then she alone would have read that journal. Which makes four. So we can see already . . ."

"Come, come. I am not a babe in arms. She did carry out certain technical work. You merely took a liking to him; he doesn't look like a criminal. And do you think it is only a bandit with a knife between his teeth who can stand in the dock? Meek incompetents also appear there. And those like Lopatkin, who like combining the agreeable with the useful. And *how!* Ha-ha-ha!" The chairman gave a brief, boyish laugh. "He hasn't picked himself a bad . . . er . . . co-inventor!"

"Listen. Why not let them alone? History shows plenty of instances of a scientist being aided in his work by his wife. And no one besides the two of them knows the essentials of the invention. Comrade Lieutenant Colonel, if we condemn him, it will be an injustice, and we shall not only be depriving him of his liberty but

384

also depriving the state of the services of an inventor who might have been very useful."

"Nonsense. If he had been a genuine inventor and they had really needed him, they would not have let him go; they would have fought for him. No, he is simply an intriguer and a trouble-maker. He has put everyone's back up. You should look at the petition those doctors of science sent to the public prosecutor. They ask that he should be prosecuted for libel."

"I *have* seen it," the major said wearily. "It was that very thing that made me think. They want to cook his goose. Their relations should have been investigated. Why didn't Abrosimov add that petition to the other documents in the case?"

"That was not why I mentioned it. Do we need it in order to get at the truth? We don't. Besides, it would cause a horrible tangle. One can confuse any case if one wants to. A judge ought to see further than his own nose. He should be able to sense the crux of a case, to feel its pulse beat. He should be able to eliminate the element of chance. The sentence is pronounced in the name of the state and not in the name of Major Badyin. For this reason what one has to take into account is the interest of the state, and not the weakness of your nerves. Well, that's that!" The chairman got up from the sofa. "Captain, you write a good hand. Please write: '1st November, 1947 . . . mmm . . . consisting of . . . as chairman . . .'" And he began walking to and fro, turning the descriptive section of the sentence over in his mind.

"I shall submit a dissenting opinion," the major said, lighting a fresh cigarette.

"I knew it!" The chairman stopped his pacing. "Think again before you get yourself into a jam. Listen, Badyin, can't you see? You and I are not scientists; it is difficult for us to grasp and understand completely the importance of this case from the start. But look: scientific public opinion as a whole, including ministers and their deputies, is watching this case. How can we—when the prosecution and the court are expected to deal with the matter quickly and thoroughly—how can we engage in microscopic analysis, examine the water of the accused?"

"We must thoroughly grasp and understand the importance of the case, Comrade Lieutenant Colonel," the major said as slowly as before, having heard out the chairman to the end. "Why are the scientists and the ministers and the deputy ministers all so interested? Until we know this, we cannot pronounce on the case. A judge should not be a prisoner of ready-made conceptions about things. 'Public opinion is watching?' We must examine what sort of public opinion it is and whether it has the right to call itself public opinion. 'Interests of the state?' One should find out first whether the interests really are those of the state. A state official is not the state, and a scientific big shot, or even three scientific big shots, are not science. A judge must verify everything; it is his duty."

"But look: it is impossible to make a serious matter dependent on whether one man can or cannot grasp some thing or other connected with it."

"But if, though not grasping it, he submits to the current, he is no longer a judge, but a mere tool. I don't want to discuss this any more, Comrade Lieutenant Colonel, or you and I may quarrel over it. The matter is one of principle. I cannot be a blind instrument, particularly in a case like this. So you go on with your sentence and I will sit here, at one side, and write a dissenting opinion. Let us refer the difference of opinion to a higher authority."

Lopatkin, of course, knew nothing of this dispute in the council chamber, nor of the dissenting opinion of one of the members of the court. All he heard was the sentence, according to which he was to be imprisoned for a spell of eight years in a reformatory labor camp.

When the sentence had been read, the judges again withdrew to the council chamber. And there, as soon as the door had closed upon them, the chairman and the major, forgetting their differences, admitted to each other that it was not often one met anyone who received a sentence of eight years in a camp as calmly as this prisoner. While the sentence was being read, Lopatkin stood and looked at the wall at one side, as if it were transparent, and as if beyond it he saw measureless distances. He seemed to be calculating how much time and energy he had left, before he set out on a new and distant journey.

THE ROOM belonging to the designer group was sealed on the same day as the investigator had questioned Nadia. That day Nadia learned that the group had ceased to exist, and that the designers had been transferred back to the offices in which they had previously worked. Immediately after the trial Nadia telephoned to Zakharov.

"Comrade Drozdov?" she heard an irresolute voice coming through the receiver. "Yes, we know. What can I say? . . . Most distressing. Words won't cure it. Of course we cannot influence the court in any way; that's impossible. Yes. As for further work on the project, this business of the prosecution will have no effect on it at all. The contract with the Institute remains in force, so you must go to the Institute and start negotiations about it."

"But—excuse me—they have broken up our group."

"Oh, have they? What a pity. It's a nuisance, but there is nothing we can do—they are masters in their own house. But all the same, you should try to negotiate with them. I'll ring up the general."

"All right. Thank you." Nadia realized that all was lost, that Zakharov was simply pretending to be surprised, and manifesting a horrible capacity that some people possess for pointless sympathy. She thanked him once more and hurriedly put an end to a conversation which was so unpleasant to both of them.

There was still half the day left. Something had to be done. Nadia hurried off to see Professor Busko.

She rang the bell five times. Someone opened the door to her and made some remark, but Nadia, without even so much as looking at him, ran to Busko's door and knocked on it impatiently. The door was locked, and behind it something was moving, making a creaking noise. Nadia knocked again. The old man behind the door hurriedly shifted something heavy, then there was silence and, a minute later, he pushed back his ingenious wooden bolt almost without a sound.

Nadia entered. The professor seemed frightened; his hair stood on end. Everything in the room was in its usual place as if nothing had been moved, but it was this that made Nadia surmise that the old man had again changed the hiding place of his precious powder and the notebooks with the formulae and calculations. She sank wearily on to a stool.

"Is the trial over?" the old man asked.

"Yes."

There was a pause.

"At least tell me about it, Nadezhda Sergeyevna. What happened? And how? And what he was tried for at least? What sentence did they give him?"

"I don't know anything. It was a secret trial. I only feel that I played some part in it all. That it was I who finished him off."

She turned away, reddening and biting her lip, then quickly pulled a handkerchief from the pocket of her coat and dabbed at her wet cheeks with it.

The old man stood facing her, staring, his knees twitching impatiently.

"In our circumstances this sort of thing should be reduced to a minimum." The professor disliked feminine tears. "Better go to the Institute and rescue what can be rescued. I told him not to take it. But he took all his correspondence there. He had a safe there, an iron safe! The drawings and this file must be saved at all costs."

Nadia went to the Institute. At the corner of the side street she got her door pass out and looked at it with a doubt in her mind. She entered the lobby and walked resolutely toward the stairs. Her forebodings had not deceived her. The watchman, a disabled ex-serviceman, who was posted there, unfolded the pass, glanced at a note lying under the glass on his little table, and shook his head.

"This pass is not valid."

Nadia turned and stood for a minute or two biting her lip, then she went to the telephone and called Krekhov in the department of basic equipment. He recognized her voice at once and lowered his own. Nadia realized that her name could now be spoken here only in a whisper.

"Can you hear me?" Krekhov said, in a voice that showed he was cupping his mouth with his hand. "I'll ring the watchman at once to let you pass."

So, in spite of everything, he was showing some courage! The telephone on the watchman's table rang loudly. The man picked up the receiver, said: "Yes, I understand," laid the receiver down carefully, and turned to Nadia.

"Pass, little one."

The director was in his office and received her at once. As she walked across the large room, dressed in a gray tailor-made suit, her hair smoothly combed into a large dark-gold bun on the nape of her neck, the general, hiding a smile, watched her expectantly from under his knitted gray brows.

"Sit down, Nadezhda Sergeyevna," he said. "Sit down and we'll have a talk."

Nadia sat down on the edge of an armchair, holding herself very straight.

"Has he been sentenced?" the general asked.

"Yes. I have just come from the trial."

"To what term?"

"I don't know. I was not allowed to stay to the end."

"Never mind. We'll find out in a few days. What can we do for you?"

"I have come about some documents. Dmitri Alexeyevich asked me to take charge of his correspondence. It is all filed in a gray folder with a brown back. And the drawings also."

"I am afraid I shall distress you; you will get nothing. First of all, as you know, the safe has been sealed up by the investigator. Second, even if we could get permission to remove the seals, we should have to treat these documents as secret papers must be treated."

"But Zakharov told me . . ."

"Yes, he rang me up. What can I say? A contract, of course, remains a contract, but we intend to decide about these machines in our own way, as our knowledge and our practical experience dictate. As for your own participation, I should think you yourself would not wish to . . . In what capacity could you work—as a tracer? You could not cope with it, could you?"

"No, for what? If you intend to solve the problem in your own way—and I can guess how that would be—I should be out of place in such a group and among such people. But all the same I ask to be given . . ."

"There can be no question of that. The safe will be opened by a commission consisting of persons admitted to deal with secret papers. If I were to give you these documents, I, like Lopatkin, would be put in prison tomorrow for having disclosed state secrets."

For a moment Nadia was dumfounded—she now heard for the first time of what crime Lopatkin had been accused. In an instant she remembered all the answers she had given to the investigator's questions and in court. She remembered how the handsome investigator's pen had at once began scratching after her confused "Yes." As these memories flashed into her mind, Nadia understood it all and grew pale. The general noticed nothing.

"And even apart from any consequences for myself, I cannot and do not wish to break the law, and I will not do so."

"But it was I myself who typed these papers! Many of them were signed by me."

"And many of them were marked 'secret' by you. That is the position, Nadezhda Sergeyevna. My advice to you is to return to your family and try to forget this unpleasant affair."

"He is right about one thing," Nadia thought, as she left the room and passed through the waiting room into the passage. "The

391

'secret' mark. What can one do? We are not given access to secret material and they all are. Now they will open the safe, do what they like with the papers, and nothing will be left of it all except the case for the prosecution. What shall I do, oh, what shall I do?" she asked herself over and over again.

Immersed in her own problem, to which there was no answer, she walked slowly along the passage, unaware of anything round her. On her way she encountered several young engineers who were anxious to catch sight of the famous Mrs. Drozdov. Without even attempting to appreciate properly all they had been told about Nadia and Lopatkin, they swarmed out of their offices, each suddenly discovering something he had to do in the passage. The person they saw passing was Drozdov's wife, a beauty, a desperate character, the mistress of an adventurer. They walked past her and back again, trying to impress her with their padded shoulders, fluttering around her like moths about a candle, almost prepared to fly into the flame. But this "almost" was still a long way from a headlong leap. The moths fluttered and flew away again, their wings still unharmed, while Nadia walked the length of the passage, quite unaware of it all and reaping undeserved laurels.

Krekhov again showed his fidelity to former friendship, this time in public, by opening his door, inviting Nadia into his office, and offering her a chair.

"Why did you come here?" he asked in a low voice.

Nadia looked about her. Drawing combines stood quietly all round; here and there she saw the top of a man's still head, a pair of motionless protruding elbows, or a pair of feet in yellow shoes. Only Antonovich, sitting beside Krekhov, was wholly visible. When Nadia came in he bowed to her.

"Dmitri Alexeyevich told me today at the trial . . ."

"What, already?" Krekhov asked.

"Yes."

"And the result?"

"I don't know. I was sent out. Secret trial." Nadia gave a faint smile.

"Well, what did he tell you?"

"He said: 'Save the papers!' " Nadia shook her head. "So I came here to do it."

"And what did Dmitri Alexeyevich have in mind?"

"The drawings. And the folder with all the correspondence. The one with a brown back. Do you remember? That must not be lost. If those were lost, we should be back where we started—after six years of struggle."

"Mm . . . yes," Krekhov said vaguely, averting his eyes. The combines stood quietly as before; motionless heads of hair, protruding elbows, and the yellow shoes of some designer revealed themselves here and there. "Well, ring us up now and then." Krekhov raised his voice. "Don't forget us."

Nadia understood all he wanted to say and could not, and took her leave. "Nothing will come of it," she said wearily to herself. Going toward the stairs, she passed the door of the room in which their group had worked only a month ago. Two yellow seals connected by a green thread had been stuck on the door, and silently confirmed: "Nothing will come of it."

While she was pensively descending the stairs, the director of the Institute was already ringing up the chairman of the tribunal.

"Comrade . . . er . . . Lieutenant Colonel? What do you want done with the papers? The whole department has been sealed up, you know. Mrs. Drozdov has already been here and demanded that they should be handed over to her."

"Those not marked 'secret' you can let her have," the chairman answered. "Remove the seals and deal with the documents according to the existing instructions. You want it in writing? Very well, I'll send a written order. Don't worry, I'll send it. You can safely take the seals off."

"And what am I to do with the secret documents?"

"Those that are still required must be preserved in your records, and as for those that are not needed, appoint a commission and destroy them. You must have received instructions."

Nevertheless, the general refrained from tearing the seal of the military prosecutor's office from the door on the strength of a mere telephone conversation. You could never be sure! He decided to wait until official permission was received from the tribunal. Meanwhile, he summoned Uriupin and asked him to form a commission for the examination and sorting of the documents belonging to Lopatkin's former designing group.

Uriupin's short gray hair moved, and he smiled one-sidedly, revealing half his steel teeth.

"I suppose we cannot dispense with the participation of science in this business. Telephone to them, please, and let Avdiyev send someone to help us."

"Yes, I can do that." The general made a note on his calendar: "Phone Avdiyev." Then he remembered: "One of the members of the Lopatkin group must be taken onto the commission. Perhaps Krekhov? What do you think?"

"Krekhov is out of the question. He has begun to take too much notice of certain things recently. He and Lopatkin were great friends, and he might even pull off something. No, it must be the solitary intellectual, even though he did chuck me out of their office!" Uriupin laughed. "Antonovich is a law-abiding citizen. Meticulously so. He will act only according to existing instructions."

"All right. Let it be Antonovich then."

"And Maxiutenko as well, I think."

"Why? Do you want to form a whole platoon? What for?"

The director smiled as though asking: "Afraid of the responsibility, are you?" and Uriupin grinned wordlessly in answer, expressing clearly: "I should say I am! It's a ticklish business!"

"Very well!" said the general. "Take Maxiutenko in. It seems you can't wipe your own noses without each other's help!"

One day soon after this conversation a paper came from the tribunal giving permission to open the two sealed safes containing the documents belonging to Lopatkin's group of designers. At about one o'clock the commission approached the door, which bore the inscription: "No admission except on business." Uriupin, with an important air, pulled the end of the green thread, from left to right, thus cutting both yellow seals. The commission entered the room and the door was closed. A few hours later Avdiyev stamped heavily along the passage, probably in reply to a telephone call. He knocked on the door and was admitted. At about five o'clock Vadia Nevraev arrived from the Ministry, proceeded noiselessly along the passage, and disappeared behind the same door. Soon the director of the Institute also appeared. Then all of them came out and betook themselves, leisurely, talking in loud voices, to the director's office, while the commission remained behind. Krekhov passed the door just as all the high-ups were coming out of it, and succeeded in catching a glimpse of the room. "Antonovich is writing and Uriupin walking up and down and dictating," he said to himself under his breath as he entered his own office.

Next day the commission drew up a report, which was then typed, signed, and sent to the director of the Institute for approval. According to the report, certain drawings and calculations selected by the commission were to be deposited in the archives of the Institute; as for the rest of the documents, these being of no interest, but owing to their contents being of a secret nature, the commission recommended that they be destroyed.

Having read the report, the general picked up a pencil that had been beautifully sharpened by his secretary, passed it across the paper as he read, and finally put a racy flourish in the upper left-hand corner.

In the evening, when the Institute was empty, two workmen from the boiler room came with sacks to the room where Lopatkin's group had once worked and where the commission was now sitting. All the documents, files, and books that lay on the floor in a disorderly heap were stuffed into the sacks. As Uriupin had foreseen, they just filled two sacks. Maxiutenko tied them up and sealed them, and the workmen, each swinging one of the sacks onto his shoulders, took them away, down to the boiler room. The commission remained behind in the room for a smoke.

"Shall we all go?" Maxiutenko asked.

"I should be glad if you would give me permission to go, comrades," a young candidate of science said in a pleasant but resolute voice. He had been delegated to the commission by C.S.I.F.R. "I live in the suburbs. I'll come in tomorrow and sign the report. I should be much obliged . . ."

Uriupin gave him leave to go and returned to the uneasy Maxiutenko and the taciturn Antonovich.

"You carry on, comrades. I'll just go and have a bite. I have not eaten since this morning. I'll be back in twenty minutes."

He, too, disappeared. Maxiutenko and Antonovich went down to the boiler room, their footsteps clattering on the stairs. Antonovich, reeling like a drunken man, stumbled and stared at Maxiutenko out of befuddled eyes.

"What a coward you are!" Maxiutenko said to him.

They descended into the basement, passing under arches gray with dust, under a grimy little lamp that emitted a feeble yellow-tinted light. They went down still lower, into the damp darkness of a cellar where coal was stored, and where their footsteps resounded on the planks laid over the coal. Still in silence, they walked toward a flickering patch of yellow light where they suddenly caught sight of their two sacks, lighted by orange flames that burned with a low-pitched roar behind three furnace doors that were like windows cut into the dark.

"The bulb is burned out, devil take it," the stoker's hoarse voice said slowly.

"What if it has? Want to read, or what?" a second, younger voice replied.

"No, comrades, we absolutely must have some light," Maxiutenko said peevishly.

"Where shall we get one?"

"I'll try to find one at once," Antonovich said suddenly, making a hurried move toward the darkness. Maxiutenko grabbed him by the coattails.

"Never mind. We'll do it in the dark. There's light enough from the furnaces. When the papers catch fire, there will be even more."

"Excuse me, comrades, but this is a responsible business. More light won't hurt us."

So saying, Antonovich, muttering something, freed his coat from Maxiutenko's grasp and set out at a dogtrot along the plank that crossed the coal bin.

"Funny thing," Maxiutenko said, spitting; then he overturned one of the sacks that contained the documents and seated himself on it. "The whole commission has walked out!"

About half an hour later footsteps were heard from the darkness of the cellar; it was Antonovich, coming back.

"You have certainly taken your time." Maxiutenko received him with a question. "Have you got a bulb at least?"

"All the offices are closed, you know. And the one in the basement is protected by a wire cage."

"Well, brother, you are a real brain, I must say!" Maxiutenko jumped up, half-laughing and half-crying. He blinked at the flames, grunted with annoyance, and ran into the cellar.

He went up the stairs to the basement passage, where there was an electric light protected by wire netting. He bent the netting to one side, took out the hot, dusty bulb from its fitting and, dropping one match after the other, went down again to the cellar.

"Took it out in the basement? Right," the hoarse voice boomed. "Give it to me; I'll climb up and screw it in."

The stoker went off into the cellar, scattering the coals, and came back dragging something, obviously a ladder.

"You get on with the job, fellows," he said. "I'll have to fiddle with this bulb for quite a while."

Maxiutenko untied one sack, pulled out an armful of papers, and carried it to the furnace. The paper caught and blazed. He began hastily pushing it deeper into the fire, first with one hand, then with the other, blowing on his fingers to cool them.

"That won't do," the younger worker said, coming up to the furnace. "You hand me the papers and I'll deal with the furnace."

Maxiutenko gave him a few books. The stoker threw first one

then another into the fire. then began turning over the pages of a third.

"Why are you burning these books? This is Lagrange's *Analytical Mechanics*. This costs money. Here it is: nine roubles."

"You had better talk less, comrade, and get on with the job!" Maxiutenko said.

He took the book out of the workman's hands and pushed it into the fire, where it flared up, but the flame died down at once, and only smoke rose from it.

"This bulb won't go on," the other stoker boomed from above. "Don't seem to be no current."

"All right, come down and help us," Maxiutenko told him.

"Here, Antonovich, take this sack, or go and untie the other one."

"All right, I'll finish this one," Antonovich said, with a feverish titter. "The comrade stoker and I . . ."

Maxiutenko and the younger worker moved to the other furnace. They got on rapidly with the work. Armfuls of paper flared up one after another.

"Ow! Hell!" Maxiutenko hissed suddenly, jumping back from the furnace door: a red ember shone, spreading red, on the leg of his trousers. "I wanted to push it farther in with my foot. I've set my pants on fire!" he groaned, spitting on his hands and slapping at his leg to put out the fire that was burning his trousers.

"The fire knows what's what!" the stoker said, peering into the furnace and stirring the fire with a poker. "It won't take books. See how many of them are already smoking, but the fire isn't burning up. I've noticed it always happens like that: books won't burn unless they are torn to shreds. But you"—here the stoker smiled—"it seems the fire was willing to take you straight away!"

"I've burned my trousers, and they are—they are a part of a suit!"

Footsteps were again heard approaching from the cellar: Uriupin was coming.

"Well, how is it going? Will you soon be finished?" he asked briskly.

"It's going all right. We are beginning to burn our own trousers now," said the stoker.

"I have just met the general. I can give you the latest news, comrades. Lopatkin was given eight years."

"What was that for?" the stoker asked.

"For the disclosure of state secrets."

Uriupin lighted a cigarette, took a sheet of drawing paper out of the sack, laid it aside, on a box full of coal, and sat down.

"Well, Antonovich. So we must even play the stoker, eh?" he said good-humoredly.

"Damn it, such a good pair of trousers!" Maxiutenko could not recover his composure.

"We have seen this Lopatkin," the younger workman said thoughtfully. "We were changing the radiators on the second floor and he came and helped us. He said he had worked in an automobile factory."

"We have finished here." Antonovich sighed with relief and stood up. "Comrade chairman, here is the empty sack."

"You will go far, Antonovich. And it was I who discovered your gifts!"

"I don't know what gifts you mean," Antonovich interrupted him with sudden coldness, "but I have definite conceptions of decency. And I let them guide me. Always and in everything."

"And so you well deserve our praise!" Uriupin sang a quotation from *Evgeni Onegin,* then said nothing more.

Then he suddenly jumped up.

"Stop!" he exclaimed, snatching a paper the young workman was reading, bent close to the furnace door. "Put that in the fire, young man! I like your cheek! Reading a paper marked 'secret'!"

"It isn't marked 'secret.'"

"Never mind, my good man, never mind!"

"There was something about you written in it," said the stoker, not without enjoyment. "Pretty hot stuff!"

"Hot stuff, did you say?" Uriupin threw the paper on the fire. "The tribunal can write even hotter stuff! For those who deserve it; who chatter and stick their noses where they aren't wanted!" He sat down and lighted another cigarette. "How are you getting on there, Maxiutenko? Let's get it over with; I have to ring the general, he told me to."

The last armful of papers flared up. The stoker said: "Seems that's the lot," straightened up, and looked pointedly at Uriupin.

"All right then," Uriupin said cheerfully, as though not noticing the stoker's look. "Let's go! Good night, comrades stokers!"

No one answered. Only the savage roar of the furnaces sounded more clearly audible.

As Uriupin, Maxiutenko, and Antonovich reached the staircase it suddenly began rattling and booming from top to bottom.

"Someone is running down here at full speed," Maxiutenko said, listening with his mouth open.

"Hallo!" From above a female voice sprang down the staircase at them. "Who is down there? Is Uriupin there?"

"I'm here!" Uriupin yelled, showing his teeth and looking upward in alarm.

"The general wants you! Hurry up!"

"What is it? Hasn't he gone yet?" Uriupin grasped the banisters and rushed up, taking several steps at each tremendous stride.

He ran up to the second floor and, passing the empty waiting room, burst into the director's office. The general, his coat unbuttoned, was sitting at his desk, sipping tea out of a glass and turning the pages of a file of correspondence.

"Have you burned them all?" he asked.

"Yes, everything."

"Here, read this," said the general, pushing toward Uriupin with his glass a paper that was lying on the green cloth of the table.

"Application," Uriupin read. "I request that a file of non-secret correspondence and non-secret drawings belonging to D. A. Lopatkin, made by him outside the Institute and kept by him in the safe sealed by the public prosecutor for the simple reason that we had no other suitable place, be handed over to me.—N. S. Drozdov."

"Where is the power of attorney?"

"She's got one all right. The tribunal has confirmed it. Here is a copy."

"Too late. It's all burned."

"You answer her then." The general took a brown pencil and wrote across Nadia's application from corner to corner: "To Comrade Uriupin, chairman of the commission. Consider and make a decision on Comrade Mrs. Drozdov's application."

"What's the date?" he asked. Frowning at Uriupin and pressing hard with the pencil, he wrote it down: "4th November, 1949," and signed his name.

"The hour should have been put in, too," Uriupin said to himself, and his scalp moved backward and forward.

"Comrade General, what shall I consider? We have burned it . . ." he began.

"I know nothing. I have not had a report yet." The general looked Uriupin calmly in the eye. "Tomorrow take the paper from my secretary and answer Mrs. Drozdov. Briefly but in detail. Someone has been coaching her—look, she has put her application in through the registry. That is, she has a receipt for it. And only yesterday. You should take this matter seriously."

"Every scrap has been burned, so what is there to be done?" Uriupin laughed, but it was a worried laugh. "The commission found no documents among Lopatkin's papers which might have . . . which had no . . ."

"Oh, I don't know, it's you who are the artist. You deal with this."

As he left the general's office, Uriupin's face darkened. "A general—*a general!*—and how scared he already is!" he thought. "He's afraid of losing his brass hat!"

He at once began sketching out in his mind an answer to Nadia's application: "To Comrade Drozdov. The commission has considered your application and has also examined the documents, drawings, and other materials from the records of the former Lopatkin designer group. The commission has not found it possible to hand over to you the documents as you request, as they all contain information which should not be revealed, still less allowed to pass into private hands. . . .

"That's how I shall answer," he told himself. "Why be frightened? There's nothing to be afraid of!" But, all the same, he grew even more somber.

PART
4

I

A YEAR and a half had gone by. The blow that had been struck at Lopatkin proved to be that final effort of his opponents which he had feared and expected.

The inventor disappeared from sight. It was as though he had been thrown overboard into the sea at night, while the brightly lighted ship, filled with living beings, breathing with the warmth of human passions, had sailed on, leaving him behind.

For a few days after the trial, the Lopatkin case was still being argued in the offices of the Institute. Opinions differed widely. Some said that it had been a clever trick but one which had been no less cleverly foiled. Others regarded the Lopatkin story as being merely an attempt to undermine the authority of Vassily Zakharovich Avdiyev. Someone had dared to wrench the diamond from the idol's forehead and a thunderclap had followed. The majority of the designers said nothing, but sometimes even silence can be weighed in the scales.

But in a month Lopatkin was quite forgotten. After that the newpapers published articles by Shutikov and Drozdov about a fresh victory for Soviet technique: a machine for the casting of pipes by the centrifugal method. The authors of both articles wrote that the new machines were being produced in series, and that two new factories would soon be equipped with them.

So finally Drozdov, too, lived to experience the honor of signing an article that had been written for him by that same Nevraev. But strangely enough, although he was now the author of a newspaper feature, Drozdov could still not rid himself of the emotion that had always brought a faint, contemptuous smile to his face. The reason for it was that the name of Shutikov, the Deputy Minister, at about

405

this time began to figure in the long lists of those present at all kinds of ceremonial receptions. True, Shutikov's name was one of the last in such lists; after his there followed only the names of writers and journalists, but for all that . . . Drozdov smiled his scarcely perceptible smile of disappointment.

Meanwhile, time passed. In the middle of 1950 the newspapers carried a short item of news; that P. I. Shutikov was going abroad with a group of engineers to study the industries of certain other countries and to exchange experiences with them. He spent more than a month abroad, returned from his journey, and for two weeks after, a whole department of the S.I.P.F.E., as well as several specialists who had been summoned from Leningrad and the Urals, were busy writing a report for him, about his impression and opinions of foreign machinery.

Drozdov watched all this calmly but with slightly more intentness perhaps than he should have shown. And the same caustic smile lurked in his eyes. If it had been he who had been delegated to go abroad to look at foreign technical developments, with so many people working on his report, he would at least have given them directives, would have laid down his own reactions to what he had seen, would have noted the weak as well as the strong points of foreign techniques, would have indicated what they were lacking in and what it would be useful for our engineers to learn from them. Some of it he would have written himself. But this fellow simply distributed the catalogues of foreign industrial enterprises he had brought back with him among the specialists from Leningrad and Sverdlovsk, and ordered them to study these and to write about them! Certainly he had picked highly competent men for this, men with brains. But precisely for that reason, which among these lads would welcome such a division of labor? That is to say: I go on my travels abroad, while you do the work instead of me, reading the catalogues with the aid of a dictionary! You write, displaying your erudition and your style, while I sign it with my name! Ought it not to be the other way round?

So Drozdov reasoned. It was the bitter reasoning of an angry man alone with himself. He even exaggerated somewhat. But when the report was written, at Shutikov's request, he readily undertook to check it for errors. The report was voluminous: built up on a scientific and historical foundation and Drozdov found no fault with it. "They certainly know their job, confound them!" he thought, referring to the authors of the report. True, he had doubts about two passages; these should have been checked and cleared up; but to do this, it would have been necessary to look up the literature on the subject, a long and tedious task. After pondering for a while, Drozdov grinned, and told himself that these were trifles, not worth bothering about.

"The report is all right," he told Shutikov, and the latter, dipping his pen in his favorite green ink, signed his name to it; it looked as if the final sheet had been put through a sewing machine.

Soon a series of pipe-casting outfits were issued. They were set up in a number of factories belonging to two ministries and pipes began to be produced in number, the same kind of pipe as the one into which Shutikov had once peered, and at the other end of which, according to Nevraev, had seen a certain comfortable armchair. Perhaps that armchair was in fact waiting for him—who knows? But in another case Shutikov's sharp powers of vision had unexpectedly misled him. He had overlooked one important detail.

This came to light a year and seven months after Lopatkin's arrest—in June 1951.

One of those undistinguished officials of the Ministry who sit in rooms with ten or twelve others and are sometimes shifted, together with their desks, to no better place than a long passage in the Ministry, was checking some documents one day, and discovered that there had been a considerable overconsumption of cast iron for the quarter in a certain factory. This man, whose name remains unknown, raised the alarm in his department. An inquiry was made into the causes of this overconsumption; letters passed to and from the factory; and it was found that they had been working there for the past year with the new machines, and that the pipes had constantly come out showing a slight deviation from standard; if, for instance, according to the state-prescribed standard the pipes should have weighed sixty-four pounds, the pipes the factory was producing, actually weighed sixty-eight.

The alarm grew and filtered through to the higher authorities. The head of the department realized at once what had happened and the menace it constituted. His face grew stern. He took the necessary papers and telephoned to Shutikov, asking to be received over an exceptionally important matter.

Naturally Shutikov received him. After hearing out the short report he asked quietly:

"Have you calculated what it amounts to in all the factories?"

"I have not yet asked. I didn't want to stir up this affair until you gave instructions, Zegor Ivanovich. We have made an approximate calculation. Here it is. . . . We have a figure in the region of forty thousand tons."

"Are you trying to frighten me?"

"No, it is about forty."

"Perhaps the other factories have not . . . Perhaps in this factory they have simply not yet mastered the procedure?"

"The workshop manager in this factory is very competent. I trust him. He says that with the given system of cooling . . ."

"And we have sent four more machines to another ministry!" Shutikov recollected suddenly.

"No doubt the same thing is happening there, too, Zegor Ivanovich! Only they haven't noticed it yet."

"And when they notice it, they will at once blame us, won't they?"

"Of course."

"All right. I'll think it over."

Shutikov was left in his office alone, completely limp, the yellow gold of his spectacles and teeth gleaming as if he were immersed in a bright dream. No one would have imagined that he was suffering deeply at that moment. He smoked his cigarette through steadily, blowing his cheeks out from time to time and exclaiming: "Pf-pf-pf-f-f!" Then he telephoned to Drozdov, who came at once and gazed fixedly at his chief out of his shrewd black eyes.

By now, a year and a half after the Lopatkin affair, Drozdov appeared somewhat changed: he seemed to have grown even smaller, stooping a little, and looking as if he had just come out of hospital. His fifty-six years showed clearly, and it would have been difficult to say where this alarming breakdown had first started—it was as if time had all at once manifested itself throughout his body. The yellow of his face had grown even darker and dryer, the white of his temples gleamed coldly, his lips were withered, and his eyes seemed to suggest an old man's impatient demands. And it was already obvious that this old man would be dried up and tyrannical.

At the beginning of 1951 Drozdov's mother died suddenly, at the age of seventy-seven, and from that moment the tacit agreement between Drozdov and Nadia ceased to exist. Since Granny was no longer there Nikolashka at once forgot his peevishness, went over decisively to his mother's side, and clung to her with all his loving, disturbed little soul. He would even embrace her dress as it hung on the back of a chair, standing motionless and pressing his face to the silk that still held a trace of her scent. He did not understand his father, and feared him. Drozdov spent his evenings walking to and fro in his two empty rooms, trying to solve a problem that was beyond his powers, and finally he gave up. "Let's make an end," he suggested to Nadia in a jocular tone. To the last he cracked jokes and smiled, exchanging only a few words with his wife. Not for a moment did he show the burden that was weighing him down. Quietly, almost in silence, they passed through all the legal formalities and got their divorce. Drozdov moved to a hotel, and into the two rooms next to Nadia's moved a new, unknown family, a newly married couple who were still at the threshold of their lives.

All these events passed unnoticed by those around them, or so Drozdov thought. He carefully kept secret his whole relationship with Nadia. As was to be expected, people soon forgot all that had come to the surface in connection with Lopatkin's trial. Sensational cases are quickly forgotten, if one patiently lives them down. But traces remained for all that. "A wet mark was left in the old cliff's furrows," Drozdov thought, looking at himself in the mirror.

This was the man who entered Shutikov's office; older and yet new, the same yet not the same.

"Leonid Ivanovich," Shutikov began, pausing and blowing out his cheeks. "You understand? What a business! Pf-pf-f-f. They are in a panic here."

"Why? What sort of panic?"

"Someone has deceived us both. The scientists missed it, or possibly they shut their eyes. Or else it was those fellows Maxiutenko and Uriupin. Those pipes are running four pounds heavier. What do you think? How much does that make them out in the course of a year? D'you see the point?"

Drozdov sat down and drummed on the table with this thin yellow fingers.

"They discussed it and discussed it; they praised it over and over again," Shutikov said disgruntledly.

"Mm—ye-es. . . . It's a little find for the State Control people."

"What are you looking at me like that for?" Shutikov shot a sharp glance, full of suspicion, at Drozdov. "After all, we didn't put that cast iron into our own pockets!"

"That will cut no ice with State Control. They will say that we have put something else in our pockets." Drozdov closed his eyes and slowly opened them again, with an ironical smile. "Something equivalent, of a material or a moral nature. . . ."

He was trying to frighten Shutikov. He himself was afraid of nothing. No blow, even if it had been aimed directly at him, had ever landed on Drozdov. He had always managed to dodge so as not to be hit. True, one brick had fallen on his head: Nadia's affair with Lopatkin. It had been an oblique blow, but a hard one. Yet it could not have been avoided. A young wife and an elderly husband —the eternal story.

"Well, what do you suggest?" Shutikov asked uncertainly, and Drozdov came to himself. His thoughts, meanwhile, had been far away, a bitter memory had wafted him back to distant, irrevocable things.

"What do I suggest?" he asked. "We must take advice in spite of everything. I don't think there has been any overconsumption."

He stopped, facing Shutikov, closed his eyes, and then slowly opened them again—those shrewd, forceful, mocking eyes.

"The offspring conceived out of wedlock can be legitimized by lawful marriage. The matter must be put in the hands of the priest."

Shutikov laughed softly: he required no explanation of who these parsons were to be. He pushed a button on the wall behind his back and when the secretary came in noiselessly, he cheerfully ordered her:

"Connect me, please with our archbishop: with Avdiyev."

Next day a private conference took place in the same office between Shutikov, Drozdov, Avdiyev, and Uriupin. The head of the department which had discovered the calamity was summoned, and this time calmly and circumstantially expounded the whole business. During the last twenty-four hours he had been in touch with the factories by telephone and now had accurate information: the overexpenditure of cast iron amounted to sixty thousand tons.

This figure worried Avdiyev; frowning, he grasped the lower part of his face with his enormous fleshy freckled hand that was as wrinkled as an old toad.

"Science is letting us down again," Drozdov said, making a weary face. "One machine brought us a loss of four million roubles. And this other one . . ."

Then he glanced at Uriupin, who returned the look with an understanding one of his own. They had obviously discussed this cast-iron business before.

"In my opinion, Leonid Ivanovich, there is no need to get hot under the collar," Uriupin said. Avdiyev raised his head and listened intently. "The machine is new. Naturally one cannot demand from casting into molds. By hand we could easily make a pipe even it a performance equal to that of the manual method or of machine

411

lighter than the standard. We could machine it on the lathe and save iron. But that would only be a single pipe! While the machine has a productive capacity . . ."

Uriupin waxed enthusiastic and his voice took on a steely quality. Shutikov looked at Drozdov. "You have wound him up well!" his eyes said, screened by his spectacles.

"I think we ought to put in an application for a new standard to be established in place of the existing one," Uriupin went on.

"A new calculation must be made to render this particular marriage legitimate . . ."

"Your definition is not precise," Drozdov interrupted him with a subtle smile. "There are several kinds of marriage." *

"What Comrade Uriupin has in mind, naturally, is the matrimonial one," Avdiyev interjected, an insane hilarity flickering in his blue eyes.

"Does anyone wish to express an opinion?" Shutikov asked.

"I find the argument put forward by Comrade Uriupin perfectly sound," Avdiyev said tonelessly. "In a year or two, when with his help we shall have produced a new model of this machine which will double the output of pipes, we can more than make up for the losses of cast iron by savings on economical production methods. And later we can also reduce the weight of the pipes, so that the change in the standard weight will only be temporary."

"In general I agree," Shutikov said. "I am willing to sign a request to be sent to the Committee on Standards. As long as it is suitably motivated, of course, I believe science will not refuse us assistance."

"We have squandered the metal together," Drozdov interposed, "so we must also bear the responsibility together!"

"What can we do?" Avdiyev gestured gaily. "We cannot cut ourselves off, so to speak, from the practical tasks of public economy."

"And there is no need to dawdle over this business," Shutikov said as he got to his feet and looked at his watch.

* Untranslatable pun. *Brak* means both matrimony and rejects.

"Of course, today Spartak plays Dynamo! * We must get there in time, comrades!" remarked Drozdov.

No one sensed any irony in these words. Drozdov, with the ghost of a smile on his face, looked on as they all began bustling, laying aside their economic and scientific worries. The room emptied almost at once. Without hurrying Drozdov followed in Shutikov's wake, and then turned off to his own room. "What a crew!" he thought, and coughed.

Shutikov ran down the main staircase with a dancer's light step. His new coat, of the same light putty color, revealed a pattern of checks in the movement of its folds. His pale yellow leather shoes, with a perforated design of large holes, flew noiselessly over the carpet which was held to the stairs by brass rods. Smiling at everyone he met, turning his head this way and that, exchanging greetings, but never halting in his energetic forward progress, the Deputy Minister flashed past, emerged onto the wide pavement, looked around, and was about to frown, when the ZIM car, gleaming as though it was wet, slid to the granite curb.

Shutikov got in, slammed the car door, seated himself with one elbow stuck out, and the machine, hissing and emitting a puff of hot air, leaped away instantly.

A minute later they were racing along Gorki Street in the general stream of cars that was rusing toward the Dynamo stadium.

"What on earth was I afraid of?" Shutikov asked himself. "Something in this affair frightened me. What was it? Why did I suddenly lose my head like that? I might have realized that there has been no overexpenditure. That is, there was, of course, but through natural causes. . . . In a couple of days they will send me the prepared calculations and the drawings for my signature, and everything will proceed on its normal way."

All the same Shutikov knew by experience that the alarm one scarcely feels is just the one that should be heeded most. A vague uneasiness, like the feeling one has before a thunderstorm in summer, is always the reflection of some grave danger. Shutikov had long

* Two well-known Moscow soccer teams.

since noticed that if such a feeling is left unheeded, some serious blunder or oversight of one's own is certain to be revealed the next day. For this reason, whenever a faint breath of doubt suddenly blew on him, he at once broke off whatever he was doing, and began to consider and to check up on all his affairs.

For a moment he again unmistakably recognized his old acquaintance, the undefined feeling of something being wrong, and switching off everything else, began turning over all his actions in his mind. But he found everything in order. "The devil with it, it must be some trifle!" he thought, smiling his habitual smile, which resembled that of a tightrope walker engaged in his dangerous trade. "To hell with it!"

He knew that next day that trifle would turn up again of its own accord, taking off its hat and bowing to him: "Here I am! And not such a trifle either!"

All the same the football match diverted and warmed him. When it was over he even loitered close to the stadium, expressly in order to cheer, to butt in on an argument, to listen to what the experts were saying about the play. He was joined by Avdiyev and Tepikin, both flushed and sweating, eyes open wide, looking as though they had just come from a pub.

"Did you see Lapshin?" Tepikin asked. "What did I tell you? Can he kick goals?"

"Yes, my dear fellow, but what passing! Did you watch the left wing? With passing like that anyone could shoot a goal!" Shutikov argued, and the three of them, their eyes shining, began discussing how Lapshin had managed the ball.

Still arguing, they got into Shutikov's car which mingled with the stream of cars that in a cloud of gasoline fumes was now rushing from the stadium toward the center.

In Gorki Street, beyond the Byolorussian Station, they were suddenly jerked forward. Brakes squealed shrilly all down the street. The driver cursed: "Where d'you think you're going? Stupid!" Shutikov looked out and saw in the distance the culprit who had caused all the bother; having darted across the street, he was now

414

striding calmly along the pavement. The man's hair was close-cropped, his face darkly tanned, he was wearing rough boots, a field shirt almost white with sweat and much washing, and carried a small kit bag over his shoulder.

The car moved on, and the man was left behind. Shutikov, grown suddenly silent, turned sharply around, pressing against the back of the seat, in order to see him more easily.

"Last Sunday the Torpedo team made their second goal just like that," Avdiyev began again, thinking that Shutikov had turned in his direction, wishing to continue an interesting conversation.

"Just a moment, comrades. Wait a minute!" Shutikov stopped him. "Didn't you notice anything? Nothing at all? Why, that man was Lopatkin!"

They all suddenly fell silent. Tepikin was the first to recover after a long pause. He smiled craftily.

"I think you must have been mistaken, Pavel Ivanovich. You took, so to speak, the wish for the fact."

"Did you say, 'wish'?" Avdiyev laughed.

"It seemed to me that it was he."

"You mean that fellow who crossed the road? The one in the coat?" Avdiyev stiffened for a moment, then flapped his hand. "That wasn't Lopatkin!"

"Of course it wasn't," Tepikin said. "But there was something like him about the man. I noticed it, too."

"Are you trying to scare us?" Avdiyev winked.

"Why not?" Shutikov smiled with gentle amiability but felt the same alarm as before rising in him. Only now it was more definite.

"I don't believe in apparitions." Laughing, Avdiyev leaned against the soft back of his seat and plunged his fingers into his yellow-white hair. Tepikin and Shutikov laughed loudly also, though somewhat constrainedly.

After that they again fell silent. No one any longer chattered about football, and Shutikov grew aware of it. "Oh ho!" he thought to himself. His eyes seemed to sharpen for an instant, but were immediately veiled again by an expression of amiability.

"By the way, Vassily Zakharovich, you were saying something to-day about a new machine," he began. "What was it—just a poor maiden's far-off dream?"

"It's a plan; nothing to do with any maiden! Who is to prevent us from changing over to channelless casting? Or to conveyor-belt feeding of molds?"

"I think that is now coming into favor abroad. During my last trip I saw something like it. But Florinsky insists that the priority in this belongs to Lopatkin."

"Priority!" Tepikin threw up his hands in pretended astonishment. "After all, comrades, there are no monopolies in our country. The invention has been registered and belongs to the state. And who is the state? We, and you—all of us! The Ministry, the Institute, the factory—all these are the state. The state can surely dispose at will of what rightfully belongs to it?"

"Well, look out, or you may be carrying on research for another two years. You are very fond of general investigations." As Shutikov said this his eyes met Avdiyev's.

"Even when one is on the right road, mistakes can still be made."

"This is the real point, comrades: give us a good machine, the sooner the better. And fewer mistakes, please. If there is anything that makes sense in Lopatkin's stuff, use it creatively. Tepikin is right. Remember that if we have the standard put up four pounds per pipe, we still cannot get away with it for more than a year or eighteen months. No Saratovtsevs of yours will be able to prove that we have to throw away four pounds of cast iron with every pipe. Well, that's the general idea. You work out the details."

Tepikin and Avdiyev got out in Pushkin Square, the car turned into the boulevard circle, and again Shutikov seemed to be dozing, with the usual bright expression on his face. "That is what you were afraid of," an inner voice whispered. "You take a chance passer-by for that inventor! It would be a pretty good mess if it really proved to be he. That is why you were so scared. That's why you took such fright when you heard of those thousands of tons of cast iron wasted. Nonsense!" He spread his fingers out in the wind. "It's all burned. I have a report about that!"

416

2

SHUTIKOV and his companions felt absolutely certain that the man with the close-cropped head and the military coat could not possibly have been Lopatkin. If they had been startled it was simply because the passer-by with the kit bag had resembled him slightly. He had brought to the surface all their vague and hidden anxieties, had made them think that they must hurry on certain unfinished matters. He had roused them thoroughly without knowing it.

But the most important thing in that chance meeting had escaped them: the man with the kit bag had, in fact, been Lopatkin.

Two weeks before, a paper had arrived at the camp in distant Siberia where he had been imprisoned; it was from the Supreme Court and contained the information that the sentence passed by the tribunal had been rescinded and the case dismissed, because of the absence of any criminal action on the part of the accused. Dmitri had at once been summoned from the work sector where he had been welding the iron rods of a support for a great bridge that was under construction. He had been given his discharge papers and money for the journey, and along the deep ruts worn by the heavy dump trucks he had passed through the gate to freedom.

He had arrived in Moscow on the same day as the football match between Spartak and Dynamo was being played in the Dynamo stadium. He saw the enormous poster: "Dynamo-Spartak," and smiled. Nothing had changed; Moscow was still Moscow. Komsomol Square was still as vast as it had been two years before, and the people in it still looked as tiny; there were still as many of them, and they still moved in the same unending stream from railway station to railway station, so that Lopatkin suddenly began to doubt whether he had really been away for a year and a half.

He went down into the subway and got out at Kropotkin Gate; here, too, everything was just as it had been a year and a half ago—the same busses, the same houses, and the same wooden fences around the cavity in which the foundations of the Palace of the Soviets stood. Standing under the colonnade of the subway station, Lopatkin let his glance roam over the square; he felt as if he were spreading his wings and soaring to the sky like a bird released from the cage. Smiling happily, he hurried along, diving into the maze of familiar narrow lanes. How would Evgeni Ustinovich receive him? "Professor, take off your spectacles! I am back!" He prepared a jovially threatening greeting, and turned into Liakhov Lane.

He had never considered the fact that while time might stand still, it might also fly fast. If one looks at a wrist watch, time passes imperceptibly, like the movement of the hands. On a large clock the hands stand still, then, click! they jump ahead and stand still in another position. Lopatkin was about to experience one of these jumps in time.

As he turned into the lane, he raised his head and stiffened. The old wooden house was no longer there; it had vanished. In its place, next to the tall gray house, a large circular flower bed had been made, full of red, orange, and yellow flowers. Four slatted seats had been placed around the flower bed in a semicircle, where nursemaids and mothers were sitting, each with a baby in a perambulator. At their feet children played in the red earth. Farther off was the now-open yard, containing sheds and dovecotes.

Yes, after all those eighteen months had gone by. Lopatkin stood for a while by the flower bed, his eye passing over the neighboring stone houses; then he crossed the pavement, and, still not quite able to believe his eyes, walked along a path strewn with crushed brick, feeling as though he had stepped under an invisible ceiling. He sat down on one of the seats next to a plump, snub-nosed young nursemaid, and looking her in the eye said:

"There was once a house here, I think."

The plump one, obviously thinking that he was trying to make an approach, shrugged her shoulders and turned away

"Yes, there was," an elderly woman on another seat replied. "It burned down last winter."

"What happened? Why did it burn down, do you know?"

"They say there was an old man, a professor, who was doing something with fire, making experiments or something. Maybe he dozed off—it was in his room that the fire started. In an instant the whole house was ablaze. During the night. They only just managed to get their few bits and pieces out."

"What about the old chap?"

"He was brought out. The lodgers remembered in time, or they couldn't have reached him. They pulled him out, that's what they did. He soon came to himself in the fresh air and started rushing back into the fire; he must have had money hidden in there. He was miserly, the old fellow, wore patched clothes, but he had quite a bit of money. People held him back. What was the good? By then the floor was all burned out and had fallen in. 'Under the floor boards,' he kept screaming, and all the time there were no floor boards left."

Lopatkin said nothing. He sat on the seat for a long time, his head bent a little to one side, and the large flower bed glowed in front of him like a heap of dying embers.

At three o'clock he stood up, shouldered his kit bag, and strolled slowly along the street that was no longer a home for him. Leaving Arbat Square behind, he walked along the boulevard to the Nikitski Gate. Here he entered a restaurant where he spent an hour and a half over a meal, sitting at a little table near the window, looking out between the curtains at the bright June street, and slowly turning his affairs over in his mind. "Why were there no letters either from her or from him?" he pondered, slowly stirring his soup with his spoon. "True, I changed my address several times, and then it was a long way away, letters don't get there quickly," he hastened to exonerate Nadia and the professor. "Still, I would like to know if they did write."

Then he considered something else: what to do first? For a moment he was filled with a sweet anticipation of revenge. He decided to go to the Institute without warning. "Good morning, comrades!

419

Can I have my documents, please?" No, that wasn't the way. "I'll ring up Nevraev!" he decided. And he pictured to himself how it would be: he would telephone to Nevraev, Nevraev would not be there and he would leave a message that Lopatkin had called. "No, that wouldn't do." He broke off these pleasant imaginings and his face darkened. "Jokes are not the thing with that lot."

Having eaten, he walked on to Pushkin Square, his head slightly bent, still considering plans. Suddenly he pulled himself up. "What is there to think about, really, when I am already on my way to her?" An inward voice, mistrustful and confused, at once began conjuring up awful possibilities: What if I go there and she has changed her mind . . . after all, she has a family, a child and all that. So what? All I want is to find out. And then: "See you again some time!" That's all.

In Pushkin Square he halted and looked around. It was as if he had been here only yesterday. He turned into Gorki Street and sauntered slowly toward the Leningrad Road. "All right," he said to himself. "First of all I must get hold of the documents and draw-ings. The only point is: where are they? We can get the drawings in any case; if not here, then somewhere else. I can write to Arak-hovski. He would copy them for me. But the correspondence . . . If that were lost, it would be awkward."

Having passed Malakhovski Square, Lopatkin wanted to cross the road to take a bus, but a solid stream of cars was flowing along it from the stadium to the center. "Ah yes, the football match!" he thought, and decided to wait. Several minutes went by. The ava-lanche of cars still rushed along the road and showed no signs of slackening. He chose a suitable moment and running from one nar-row gap between cars to another, boldly forced his way across. A few other pedestrians followed his example, and it was because of this that two or three cars braked sharply and the shrill squealing of brakes ran like a wave all along the road. But Lopatkin did not even glance back. He walked to the bus stop and stood in the line.

Nadia had been working in the morning shift and had been home several hours when she heard shuffling footsteps on the staircase.

Someone outside on the landing groped for the door and irresolutely pressed the bell, which gave an equally irresolute tinkle and buzz. Her fellow lodger ran from the kitchen to the hall, there was the click of the lock, and silence. Then there was a knock on Nadia's door.

"It's for you, Nadezhda Sergeyevna."

Nadia went outside. In the half-light of the hall stood a tall, bony, copper-faced stranger, the whites of his eyes showing bright. His close-cropped hair, which had already grown a little, was like thick gray bristle. He stood motionless, waiting for something, and in that instant Nadia recognized him. From the hall, perhaps for the first time since the house had been built, there came the sound of loud, quick kisses, and the young fellow lodger, who knew about everything and had been peeping out from the kitchen, hurriedly closed the door. Nadia embraced Lopatkin, or rather put her hands on his chest and around his shoulders, and drew in the powerful odor of a working man, the odor of sweat and tobacco that lingered in his coat.

"Dmitri Alexeyevich, I can't," she said, hiding her head on his chest, smiling guiltily and wiping her eyes with her hand.

After the first seconds of joy Nadia regained her self-control. Feeling an uneasy embarrassment, she glanced cautiously at Lopatkin. Yes, it had been only *her* kisses, *her* tears. It was *she* who had rushed to him, almost knocking him over. Nadia switched on the light and holding Dmitri by his shoulder and his hand began examining his weather-beaten face, making light and noncommittal remarks, for a different truth was already dawning in her. Another Nadia, shy, but profoundly loving and deeply hurt, was to be seen behind all the gasps and exclamations that are customary on such occasions. She gazed at him with pain, finding none of the long-expected response on his face and unable to understand what this could mean. They had not seen each other for a year and a half, and here he was standing and yielding himself up patiently to these first minutes of meeting, still keeping in mind the rules of *external life* and fearing to forget a single one of them. But his inner vision was burning with impatience. A different passion, a different expectation had accumulated there. Suddenly Nadia understood. That other loving being within her who by nature's decree could conquer this man prompted her to say the necessary words.

"Let's go in," she said, growing more cheerful. "I have news for you that must not be postponed even for a moment."

Lopatkin's face became even sterner. He was prepared for any kind of news. It was for this that he had come to her. And Nadia, feeling that she was on the right road, took him by the hand and pushed him gently into the room.

A little boy, cleanly dressed in blue shorts with suspenders and a white embroidered shirt, was standing by a chair, building a castle out of green, red, and yellow toy bricks. He had dark eyes and a bright little face; broad at the eyebrows and narrowing toward the chin—his father's face.

"Ah, you rascal!" Lopatkin said. "Good afternoon."

But this, too, was a concession to external rules of conduct. Having said what it was proper to say to the little boy, Lopatkin sat down on a chair and prepared to listen to the news.

"I'm not a rascal," Nikolashka said calmly and precisely. But the strange uncle was no longer listening.

Dmitri had let his eyes wander absent-mindedly round the familiar room and suddenly, standing by the wall, saw his own drawing board, the "combine" given him long ago by the professor.

"Oh ho, an old friend!" He jumped up and went over to the board. Nadia, who was now watching him anxiously, saw that the old Lopatkin was coming to life in him.

"Yes, Busko asked me to keep it for you," she said. "Oh, what a misfortune! . . . I don't know how to tell you!"

"I have been there. Someone told me," he said.

"So you have heard? You know he died?"

The house did not collapse and the day did not darken at this news. Lopatkin met it without a tremor. Just as had happened on the seat by the flower bed, his mind grew numb, refusing to accept this change in his life.

"I brought him here and he lived with me for almost a year," Nadia related pensively. "He restored nothing of his inventions;

422

he did not even try. He was concerned only about the drawing board and asked that it be kept for you. He grew very silent, and very tense; he seemed to be trembling the whole time. At night he slept little. Galitsky came here; he insisted that he should take up his work again and offered to help him. And do you know what Busko said to that? Very clearly, for the first and last time: 'No one has any use either for the inventions nor for your help. The fire forestalled us both and robbed us of the secret of its destruction.' Yes, he could even joke as you see. And then his left side became paralyzed. It happened a few days after Galitsky left. He lay very quiet for three or four days. He mentioned you, and also said several times: 'The man has died completely. Both halves. There is no trace left.' And so the drawing board was left. Niko-lashka and I have dusted it every day. We have kept Grandpa Busko's memory green for Dmitri Alexeyevich."

"Thank you," Lopatkin said softly. His weary, deep-set eyes rested on Nadia, gradually growing warmer. And he put his arms round her. But that was only to thank her for her friendship and for old Busko's sake.

Nadia straightened, went calmly to a shelf on the wall, and from between two books pulled out Jeanne Ganichev's photograph.

"Here is something else I brought away from there for you. As soon as they arrested you. I wonder what made me do it?" she said carelessly, looking at Lopatkin. "It might have been burned if I hadn't."

Lopatkin took the picture.

"Yes . . . Evgeni Ustinovich . . ." he said, giving the picture a cursory glance and laying it down absent-mindedly on top of the cottage piano.

Something in Nadia quivered with joy. But Lopatkin's eyes once more grew stern. The man who a moment before had been animated, and even loving, had again vanished. He had gone far away from Jeanne, but he had also gone far away from Nadia, and was hardly visible in the distance. And in his place sat a stone-hard fulfiller of a duty, who looked through his fingers at life and at death. The long road, flanked by milestones, had swallowed him up and made him an eternal wanderer. He was walking along it even now calmly and stubbornly, and in front of him stretched misty and indifferent distances, even greater than those he had already traversed.

"Yes, so you say there is news," he asked in the tone of a wanderer who looks only at the road ahead, completely absorbed in that accustomed movement.

A light came into the woman's eyes for a moment but was at once extinguished. Now she was quiet and tender.

"Dmitri Alexeyevich!" She came up close to him from behind. "I see you are sitting here and wondering, I am sure, where to begin." As she spoke she pressed his shoulders softly with her hands. "Am I right? Yes, I can see." She hesitated, blushing, then whispered in his ear: "The machine is already working! On my word! And working well! For two or perhaps even three months. A lot of people already know about it. And there are two more being made. *Two more!*"

Lopatkin did not jump up out of his seat or leap into the air. He merely bent his head, as though listening, and said: "Oh, yes?" He had had successes before, more than once; high tides after which he had again been stranded.

"And where do you say the machine is working?"

"In the Urals. In Galitsky's factory."

"Hm. Well, go on. Tell me about it."

It turned out that Galitsky had come to Moscow one day, had heard everything, had telephoned to Nadia, and had then immediately appeared in person at her flat. Nadia took three hours to tell him the whole story and he rumpled his hair untidily, and rolled his eyes. "Like this," and Nadia rolled her eyes, first up toward the ceiling, then toward the door, and then stared at the floor.

"So you say the machine is working?" Lopatkin interrupted her.

"Of course!"

And she went on with her narration, from time to time drawing a deep breath to start a fresh sentence. And he gazed at her as though she were a window through which he could discern the distant Urals. Galitsky, having heard out her detailed story, three hours without once interrupting, had suddenly asked: "And where

424

do they live, this Krekhov and Antonovich?" Nadia had not known, but had given him the telephone number. "We'll try to do something," Galitsky had said. Then he had suddenly jumped up and began saying good-by. Then: "Oh, but you have a telephone here! May I use it?" He had gone outside to the telephone, had dialed the number of the Institute, and had called Krekhov. "Comrade Krekhov? Good. This is a certain Galitsky speaking. Well, if you know me, so much the better. Let us meet. Come to me at the Ministry, with Comrade Antonovich. You have no objection to making a bit of money on the side? No? Then I'll give you and Antonovich a good project on a contract basis. No, just a trifle," he had said. "You can get it done in a week. You can work about three hours every evening. . . . Come to me as soon as you stop work in the office."

"But we already had a complete project," Lopatkin interrupted her. He was already aflame, beaming as he had done in his happiest, hungry, but nevertheless gay days.

"They burned all the drawings," Nadia said. "A commission headed by Uriupin."

"I see!" Lopatkin said, his face darkening. "Go on. I am listening."

Krekhov and Antonovich had understood everything perfectly, and with Galitsky had in twenty days produced a few fundamental sketches of the project. True, they had worked not three but about six hours each day. The three of them had worked every night in Nadia's room. And Nadia had made them tea, and cleared the ash trays of cigarette stubs, while the white-headed, quiet Busko had sat near the central heating radiator in felt boots looking on, but believing in nothing.

Galitsky had taken the drawings, at his own risk had ordered the factory designers to complete the project, and had then constructed the first machine there in the factory. It seemed that Galitsky had made use of the principle embodied in Lopatkin's machine and built an assembly for the casting of one of those "solids of revolution" which had been mentioned long ago at the meeting with the general. Galitsky's factory was gigantic; in two months the machine had already been set up on its foundations in the foundry and tested. It had at once given faultless castings, pushing them out

425

one after the other. A crowd had gathered round and Nadia's hand had been sore from all the handshakes. But the conveyor—or feeder, as they called it—had proved too small and the molds had quickly become overheated. This was an error of calculation on Galitsky's part. In a week they had increased the length of the conveyor, and since then the machine had been working in three shifts without a stop. Galitsky had said that the machine had rendered a whole section in the foundry redundant. He had sent a detailed report to his Minister. All expenditure on it had been retroactively sanctioned, and Krekhov and Antonovich been paid their fee, which, to tell the truth, they had never expected to see.

"They had not, of course, sat and worked all night for the money's sake," Nadia said. "They cracked jokes the whole time about that fee: 'Look out that you don't instead find yourself having to pay a fine, if the machine doesn't work.' And Galitsky had said little but urged them on, himself working like a machine, saying nothing. He had worked on the table here, Krekhov on this drawing board, and Antonovich on a board he had brought with him which he had put on the bed to draw on."

"And what about these—friends of ours? Are they alive and well?" Lopatkin asked.

"Well enough. They are constantly praising their machine in the newspapers. I think they are building a factory. Shutikov has twice already been abroad."

"And do they know about ours?"

"Not yet I don't think. And even if they find out, there's nothing to fear. Our machine is already working."

"You say they are praising their machine in the papers? How can that be? It means they are hiding something. It can't be that everything is going smoothly with those machines. So we can expect some more trouble, Nadezhda Sergeyevna."

"Oh, still more?" Nadia's face fell. She now believed in all Lopatkin's forecasts. "How long is this to go on, Dmitri Alexeyevich?"

"It remains to be seen who will get the upper hand this time," Dmitri said with a menacing look. "But they will certainly fight

They can't do anything else. A working machine—and now, as you say, there will be three of them—with our three machines pitted against their whole factory everything will at once become obvious. Publicity, debates, comparisons—all this means a scandal and a disaster for them. Losses amounting to millions will have to be written off, and one can sometimes get hauled over the coals for things like that, you know. As soon as they find out about our machine, they will start to cook something up at once, there is no doubt about that."

At this moment Nikolashka, who had never taken his eyes from the guest, deserted his building bricks, hesitantly left the chair, came closer, and stood facing Lopatkin.

"Are you Dmitri Alexeyevich?" he asked.

"I am!" Lopatkin said.

The little boy came still closer.

"You have been on a long journey, haven't you?"

"I have. On a very long one."

The boy retreated, touched his castle with his elbow, and the building blocks fell with a clatter and scattered on the floor. While he was crawling about on the floor, picking them up, Nikolashka was thinking something over, and every now and then he glanced at Lopatkin with his shrewd black eyes—Drozdov's eyes.

"Go and play in the yard, Nicky," his mother said.

"When I grow up, I shall go on a long journey, too," the boy said.

"Oh, much better not to go." Nadia looked at Lopatkin with a faint smile.

He answered her with the same sort of smile.

"No need to fear journeys. Anyone who is afraid to travel of course will not go. But in that case he will not get far either!"

Dmitri paused, pondered, and mechanically pulled out of his pocket a tobacco pouch made from the sleeve of an old coat, took out a piece of newspaper folded in the form of a little book, tore off one leaf, suddenly came to himself, and stood up.

"Smoke. Please smoke."

427

"No, I'll go outside."

"No, smoke here. I want to sit and talk to you."

"No, I'll smoke in the passage. And then I'll ring Zakharov. Should I, do you think?"

"They are expecting you. We thought you would get here sooner."

Lopatkin twisted a cigarette with his gnarled and calloused fingers, went out into the passage, struck a match, and standing with his back against the wall, drew in deep lungfuls of smoke several times in succession. Like all true smokers, he betrayed himself by those frequent deep inhalations. Watching him stealthily, Nadia saw, not simply the actions of a smoker, but also those deep sighs hidden from everyone, sighs that had no bottom. Drozdov smoked far more calmly. Nadia had already noticed that in Muzga.

A thick cigarette, its small red end occasionally glowing, burned down to his fingers, whose tips were covered with a brown deposit. Lopatkin wrinkled up his face as he smoked it to the end, extinguished the stub on the sole of his boot, went out into the kitchen, came back, and picked up the telephone receiver. The cigarette had calmed him, like a mother's hand.

But his calm lasted for only half a minute. He dialed a number and heard a bass voice say, "Yes." His hand squeezed the receiver harder and his voice faltered as he said:

"Comrade Zakharov! It's me, Lopatkin, speaking. Lopatkin, who . . ."

"Ah!" The receiver boomed a welcome. "At last! Good day to you, Comrade Lopatkin! Congratulations on your return! We have been expecting you this whole month. How are you?"

"Not too bad, Comrade Zakharov. I hear the machine has been built."

"I'll say it has!" Zakharov answered boisterously. "And how! It has already caused something like a change of our entire industrial financing plan. Come and see us! Come tomorrow morning. I'll order a car. Where are you staying?"

"Nowhere as yet. I'll come on my own."

428

"What does that mean? Ring me in the morning and I'll send a car for you. Is that agreed? Then until tomorrow. Good-by."

After he had hung up, Lopatkin again leaned against the wall and rolled a fresh cigarette. He lighted it and blew the smoke toward the ceiling. Nadia stood in the doorway and said jokingly:

"I see that now you don't bother about norms."

"It's the last one," Lopatkin said.

When he had finished the cigarette, Nadia again took him by the hand and gently pushed him into the room.

"I heard something of your telephone talk. What did you mean by saying that you were not staying anywhere? What about here?"

"I thought it might be inconvenient."

"Are you afraid of compromising me?" Nadia asked gaily. But involuntarily there was something more behind these words—some sorrowful memory, and Lopatkin tried not to notice it.

"You keep looking around," Nadia said. "*He* has not been living here for a long time. So you can make yourself quite at home here, in your co-inventor's house."

In passing, Nadia glanced at herself in the mirror; a thinner, watchful, strangely pale face with great dark eyes looked back at her.

They sat down facing each other. It seemed to Nadia that Lopatkin was observing her stealthily with his burning eyes, and she lowered her eyelids so as not to hinder him. Recently she had often been told that during these last years she had acquired a sad new beauty. "If that really is so, may it help me now," she thought.

Holding her breath, she waited for a while, then glanced at Lopatkin. It seemed that only to her had the room felt close. He, for his part, was already quite at home. He had taken out a notebook, and, biting his lip, was looking at it with the same burning eyes.

"What have you got there?" Nadia asked softly.

"A few ideas. A little sketch." Reddening with pleasure, he put away the notebook in a pocket of his coat.

"Did you work it out *there?*"

"Yes," he answered, smiling. "As you see, the words 'deprivation of liberty' are inaccurate. Whoever has learned to think cannot be completely deprived of liberty."

"And what did you think about out there?"

"Oh, nothing very important. . . . If our machine really gets going . . . To put it in a nutshell, it's an automatic foundry for the production of pipes. Do you know, I convinced myself . . ."

"Of what?"

"That Busko was right. And that Arakhovski was right, too. A thinker cannot refrain from thinking. When a man practices something for a long time, and turns a bunch of problems over and over in his mind, he gradually attains perfection in that sphere. Then something gets loosened up in his brain, and a chain reaction begins: one thought gives birth to the next; it is a whole world. I see tremendous possibilities. What before appeared to me to be only the solution of a partial problem is in reality the key to many important things. I thought this over for the first time when you gave me the idea of the double-layer pipes. Remember? It was then that I first caught a glimpse of a corner of what became completely clear to me *out there*. So that naturally, when a thought like that comes to you, how can you sit and moan about your physical movements being restricted? On the contrary; there, I was free of this idiotic correspondence, of all these accusations of slander, of self-interest, of sham inventorship. You are sitting high up on the girders of a bridge; above you the sky, below the river and rapids. There is no electricity; something has happened to the transformer. There is no point in climbing down. So while things are being put right below, you are thinking. Two hours! Or you are sitting in the evening beside the barracks hut. . . ."

Yes, this was a man in whom the sensitive readiness for battle had become a habit.

"Never mind," Nadia said to herself, gazing tenderly at his back, which was tightly covered by a coat that had faded to white, then went into the kitchen to put the kettle on. There she lingered for a while, and when she came back it could be seen that her lips—with the aid of her fellow lodger's lipstick—were now of a somewhat brighter red, and that her skin was now powdered, although the birthmark on her cheek remained just as charming and velvety.

"Well?" she said, looking at him and blushing slightly.

430

The question came out of a different life and Lopatkin did not hear it.

"What is well?" he asked, laughing. "You have not finished your story yet! First finish it and then it will be my turn."

"Go on," the same voice prompted, and Nadia, seating herself opposite Lopatkin, went on with the story. It was a new chapter in her narrative—about how and why Lopatkin had been released.

Unexpectedly for Lopatkin, Nadia named Antonovich as one of the heroes of this chapter. It seemed that when he and Maxiutenko had gone down into the boiler room to burn the documents, he had not been frightened, as Maxiutenko had imagined at the time. He had, of course, had nothing to fear. It had been Maxiutenko and Uriupin who had been scared. Antonovich's knees had been shaking for another reason: he had heard that Nadia had asked for the file with Lopatkin's non-secret correspondence to be handed over to her, and that this had been refused. While the commission had been at work, he had cautiously referred to this, and Uriupin, laughing loudly, had made fun of him. Antonovich knew that that file held, not only Lopatkin's liberty, but his whole life's work. And besides he had his own opinion about the whole affair, and considered that Lopatkin had been unjustly condemned. When he had gone down into the boiler room to carry out in practice what he had so recently put his signature to, he had felt his knees give way under him. But this had been weakness of a kind. Courage was being born in Antonovich's soul, and it was this that had shaken him and had made him sway from side to side, unprepared as he was for such ordeals.

He himself had not known why he had felt it necessary to fly from the boiler room, but when Maxiutenko had started talking about the electric bulb, something had driven Antonovich, and he had fled, not in order to look for a bulb—his legs had carried him to the gate by the shortest route. He had stamped his feet on the wet asphalt of the narrow street, had then taken a taxi on the street corner, and in five minutes had been at the building with the iron railings, where the military prosecutor's office and the tribunal had their seat. This building appeared to be drowned in

431

night's deepest shadows, and overwhelmed Antonovich by its un-lived-in blackness—it looked as if it had no windows at all. Antonovich had gone up the deserted stairs to the second floor of the section that was occupied by the tribunal. At the entrance, in a half-dark passage, he had been met by a soldier with a rifle. It had turned out that there was no one in the building, office hours were over, and everyone had gone home.

"A telephone, young man, a telephone!" Antonovich had whispered urgently. "The president's home telephone number!"

But the soldier had not been able to help. He had advised Antonovich to wait until the sergeant returned from his supper; it would be not more than forty minutes.

"What shall I do, what *shall* I do?" Antonovich had walked up and down on the landing several times, then had suddenly clattered hastily down the stairs. The taxi was still waiting at the gate.

"To Spassopoklonski Street," he had ordered curtly. "And quickly, please."

When they had begun to burn the papers, Antonovich had felt the sack with his fingers, and had immediately come upon a hard protuberance, which was the thick, heavy file. If he had not found it in this sack, he would have tried the other one. But it had been there. He had stuffed it farther down into the sack, shivering fever-ishly. Later he had pulled the file out, dropped it in the shadows, and put his foot upon it. Then he had pushed it backward with his foot, toward the partition where the coal was kept, and a few min-utes later had thrown it in there, unnoticed, behind the partition wall, and then had quickly buried it in the coal. All at once his whole being had sung with joy, and it was at this moment that Uriupin had arrived, and Antonovich had made his proud, his-torical remarks about common decency.

Next day Antonovich had gone down into the courtyard to the boiler room over and over again, and had walked about there; sometimes he had even looked in on the stokers farther down the passage, for a smoke. The young workmen had had no idea of what was going on, but the old stoker, Afonchev by name, had smelled a rat, and had once silently followed Antonovich outside, and in the courtyard had stared Antonovich silently in the face. The old man had probably decided that it was a matter of earning a little money on the side. He had been even more convinced of this when Antonovich had invited him to the pub on the corner. In the pub they had sat down at a separate corner table, and Antonovich had ordered everything proper to the occasion. Afonchev had had one drink, then another, and the more he drank the more sober he had become and the more cautiously he had stretched out his neck. Finally Antonovich had asked: "Do you trust me?" "How could I distrust you?" Afonchev had answered, still on his guard. Then Antonovich had related the whole story. First he had explained to him who Lopatkin was. Then he told him about his machine and how this machine was needed by the government. "Did you understand?" he asked the stoker. "Only too well!" Afonchev answered. Then Antonovich had tried to explain as best he could the story of Lopatkin's struggle. Here he had become confused, and the stoker had put his honest hand, blackened with coal dust, on Antonovich's sleeve. "Make it shorter. Speak out, don't be afraid, don't beat about the bush." And Antonovich had taken one more look at the stoker's indifferent and therefore frightening face, then had cast caution to the winds and told him about the file. "So that's it!" Afonchev had drawled. Antonovich had become excited, had wanted to make some request of him, but Afonchev had stopped him. "I am at work now. Come and see me at home tomorrow evening. I live a good way off, but never mind—you can get there by the subway, and then a bus. We can talk there." Antonovich had eagerly taken out a pencil and put down the address. They had then finished their drinks, said good-by, and parted.

Next evening Antonovich went to the stoker's warm, narrow little room. Afonchev had washed himself clean, and had brushed his hair well. He had been friendly but cautious. The file which, according to his own expression, he had *capitulated* from the boiler room without any superfluous talk, had been lying on the table. Having read him Lopatkin's many complaints and the answers to them, from various offices, having shown Afonchev Academician Florinsky's and Doctor of Science Galitsky's opinions about the machine, Antonovich had at last felt that something had happened in the old stoker's mind, that he had understood everything and had even taken some decision. But what this decision was had remained uncertain. Afonchev had brought in a teapot from the kitchen, had taken out a quart of something stronger from behind the curtain on the window, and had slapped his palm down on the table: "Enough of business! Let's drink tea." They had drunk many cups of tea, but Afonchev had still not let the cat out of the bag. "I'll do all that's required," he said, "don't you worry."

This was what he had decided: being a cautious old man he would not give the file to Antonovich. "The matter might take a different turn, who knows." But he did not return it to the Institute either, because what this engineer with the tight trousers and a necktie had told him was very likely the truth. He had decided to send the file to the military tribunal, on the grounds that if all that Antonovich had told him was true, Nadia could get it from there if she produced her power of attorney. But since the old stoker was not only cautious, but also knew a thing or two, he had pretended to be an ignorant country bumpkin, and having prepared the file for dispatch to the tribunal, had sent it with this accompanying letter:

To the Revolutionary Tribunal, from Afonchev, Prokhor Vassilyevich, of Flat 2, Wing 6, New Buildings, Khlebozavod settlement. I, Afonchev, Prokhor Vassilyevich, working as a stoker in the boiler room of the C.S.I.F.E. institute, have, in the night of 5th November, when about to fetch coals from the coalbin, found the secret Lopatkin case, he who was tried by the Revolutionary Tribunal. The which I bring to your notice and forward with this same Lopatkin case, which I believe got into the coalbin by error of the commission. Afonchev.

The stoker had carried the package to the tribunal himself. A secretary, having undone the home-made envelope, read Afonchev's "statement" and had at once gone to report it to the president of the tribunal. . . . Afonchev had been told to wait, and, in keeping with the part he was playing, he had obediently sat down on the edge of a chair. Soon he had been summoned to see the president. "You say you have brought the Lopatkin case," the gray-haired lieutenant colonel had exclaimed gaily. "At your orders, Comrade Colonel, sir," Afonchev had replied. "But this isn't a 'case,' it's only some correspondence!" the president had exclaimed even more gaily, and even louder, as though he were talking to a deaf man. "Where did you dig up this 'case?'" "It's all written down in the statement. In the coal." "How did it get into the coal?" "It must have been when they were burning the secret papers." "But this isn't a secret paper. It isn't marked 'secret' anywhere!" the president had shouted. Then he had suddenly jumped up and walked to and fro in front of Afonchev, casting suspicious glances at him. "The question arises," he had suddenly said, "why it was you and no one else who got hold of this file?" "I wouldn't know, Comrade Colonel," the old man said, turning his head all the time in whichever direction the colonel was walking, now right, now left, following him with frightened eyes. "One of the commission must have left it behind." "Wait! Why didn't you give it to the commission? Why did you bring it here?" "I didn't steal it! I didn't hide it! I came to you! It has 'case' written on it, so I thought the Revolutionary Tribunal would know best what to do with her." "Her, did you say?" The president gave the stoker another sharp look, then sat down at his desk and picked up the receiver. He had dialed a number and had spoken to the general—the director of the Institute. It was obvious that he was one of those who is soft in words but hard in deeds. The conversation with the director had begun like this: "Comrade General? You rang me up about Lopatkin's papers. Tell, were they burned? But how about the papers for which a power of attorney? . . . Oh, the commission could not find them! Ye-es! Well, certain papers have been brought to me. . . . I suspect that your commission made an order to burn them and hasn't done so. How? Well like this: the commission scattered them about the boiler room and went off. Someone collected them and brought them to the tribunal. Return them to you? Oh, but I can't find any 'secret' mark on them. In my opinion, those persons decided to burn the papers for which a power of attorney had been delivered. Pardon me, Comrade General, but I am responsible for those papers. Lopatkin will serve his term and come to me, demanding them! I see he has a certificate of authorship for his machine filed here. Have you the right to deprive an inventor of a document issued to him by a government committee? You didn't know. Well, I'll tell you now. I am informing you that as these papers are not subject to your jurisdiction, I shall hand them over to Mrs. Drozdov; she has been here about them more than once. Good-by." Then he had laid the receiver down, looked at Afonchev with an eagle eye, and cried gaily: "You can go, Afonchev!" The stoker had gone out, bowing his head obediently and holding his cap in his hand. Antonovich had been told all about it the same day, and had quickly given Nadia the news. Waiting a few days for form's sake, she had then gone to the secretary of the tribunal and had complained that the director of the Institute had refused to hand over to her Lopatkin's non-secret papers. "Here are your papers," the secretary had said, taking the familiar folder with the brown back out of a drawer. "Sign for them, please, here, over your power of attorney."

"So the folder is here?" Lopatkin asked impatiently.

But Nadia looked at him with a smile. "You will hear everything in a minute," she said, and left the room. Soon she returned carrying a teapot. She opened a cupboard door, put three cups on the table—not those translucent bulbous cups out of which Lopatkin had once drunk, but new, simple, heavy gray earthenware ones with little flowers on them. And Nadia's hands had become rough—nowadays she had to handle potatoes and washing soda. There was a silent pause in the room. Lopatkin looked with stealthy delight at Nadia's blunted fingers and remembered that winter day when he had glanced with hatred at this woman and had whispered: "A pale convolvulus."

But by now the tea was poured out, a pile of books was put on one of the chairs and Nikolashka seated on top of them. He at once put his mouth to the saucer and began blowing bubbles. Nadia seated herself also, and raising tender gray eyes to Lopatkin's face, said:

"The file is not here. You will get it. But listen to this."

And she began the third installment of her story, which now had a new hero, a certain Major Badyin.

"I beg your pardon, I don't know him. Who is he?" Lopatkin asked.

"He is the member of the tribunal who was sitting on the right and spoke with rounded 'o's'."

Lopatkin had never dreamed that during his trial Major Badyin had been on his side the whole time, and had even written a dissenting opinion about the case. The dissenting opinion had made no difference, incidentally, because Lopatkin's case had been "clean," as the president had put it. If the lieutenant colonel had had the slightest doubt about any point, he would of course have analyzed everything connected with it. But as he had no doubts at all, minutes of the court proceedings resulted which were in keeping with the president's view of the case. This was because at the requisite moments the president repeated aloud the accused's answers for the benefit of the secretary who had to write them down. And from old habit he carefully omitted from these answers all sorts of adventitious matter which would only have brought confusion into what was perfectly simple and clear. He loved forms to be clear and brief. So that the materials that were submitted to the higher forum bore a strong resemblance to the Lopatkin case which had been created in the cocksure old man's imagination. Badyin's dissenting opinion was therefore left unregarded.

The major decided to fight. He summoned Evgeni Ustinovich Busko to his office for a talk, but the old man did not come. So the major went to see him; he walked straight in, introduced himself, looked round and, concealing his surprise, began asking the professor questions about Lopatkin and Nadia. He received a fierce reply: "Since it is not often that one sees people who carry out their judicial duties in so strange a manner, permit me not to answer you." The major could not disclose to the old man all the details of his own dispute with the president, nor his own position in relation to the Lopatkin case. He threw out a few semi-transparent hints, which finally frightened the professor, and Badyin left without having achieved anything.

437

"Evgeni Ustinovich would not see him again," Nadia said softly. "He would not even open the door. And then came the fire. The major was busy with other work, and he forgot the case and his own dissenting opinion. It was just then that Galitsky came to Moscow, and we decided that it was only your machine that could get you out of trouble. His idea was that if the machine worked, then the inventor could be rescued."

A year had passed, and one day when Nadia came home she had seen on her kitchen table a letter with the tribunal's rubber stamp. She was asked to come, bringing with her Lopatkin's correspondence which had been handed over to her on the strength of her power of attorney. The letter was typewritten and signed by Major Badyin. Nadia had gone to the tribunal without the file. Major Badyin had raised his hands in disappointment and exclaimed: "You understand, these documents are his salvation!" Nadia had rushed home, jumped into a taxi, and returned with the file. The major began going through the papers in her presence, exclaiming as he did so: "I knew it all the time! It's all as clear as day now! Here, this is even better! What a business, what a sorry business, Nadezhda Sergeyevna! The kind of people there are in this world! And how many blind ones there are about!" He could not contain himself and told her who these people were, and which one had proved himself blind. He himself had obviously not been so, because, when he had been going through certain cases from the previous year in connection with some special task, he had seen certain new documents connected with the Lopatkin case, and had read them with attention. Afonchev's ruse had not escaped him. He had at once realized that Lopatkin's friends had been at work, and his old determination had again been aroused. He had decided to examine the papers in question, suspecting that they must be that very six-year correspondence of which Lopatkin had spoken at his trial.

Badyin had had a talk with Nadia and had given her to understand that she should send in a complaint to the Supreme Court. The same day Nadia had taken to the Supreme Court a long letter with three signatures: her own, Krekhov's, and Antonovich's. Three days later Nadia had been invited to see the deputy president of the Supreme Court. The speed of all this had somewhat surprised her, but it was all explained: Major Badyin's opinion in the Lopatkin case and the documents of the case were already lying on the deputy president's table.

"And what else do you think was there, too?" Nadia interrupted her narrative. "Guess quickly! What a man! There were several letters from Muzga. From two people you know. It seems that Sianov had been searching for you, and that someone wrote to him from C.S.I.F.E. that you had been tried and sentenced. So our uncle Pete wrote a letter, and an aggressive letter it was, too! Straight to the Supreme Court! And Valentina Pavlovna. . . ."

The deputy president had asked Nadia to bring the folder with the documents. But Nadia had taken it out of her shopping bag on the spot. The slow-moving elderly man with the raddled face had talked with her for a long time, often interrupting and demanding that she should keep strictly to the order of sequence. Nadia had told him, among other things, that the machine had already been built in the Urals, that the first tests had produced pipes of good quality, and that it had a productivity almost double that of the C.S.I.F.E. machines. Then a reporter of the case had seen Nadia. He had asked her even more questions about the work on Lopatkin's machine, had gone through the documents in the folder with Nadia for several hours, and had taken notes the whole time.

Soon after this Nadia had received a letter from the Supreme Court, informing her briefly that the sentence had been commuted and the case dismissed.

"And now you are here!" Nadia ended her narration.

Lopatkin spent all the next day on business—he saw Zakharov, the general, by now even more important, with two yellow stars on each silver shoulder board. The nights he spent on Nadia Sergeyevna's divan, getting up early in the morning and going out again. He was given a fresh contract, and on the third day, when Nadia came home from school, she saw a completely changed man in her room. It was Lopatkin, but wearing a new and expensive dark-gray suit. A silk shirt showed under his unbuttoned coat, and he also wore a necktie with a pattern of small checks. Nadia made Lopatkin stand up, examined him from every angle, and of course approved of his taste. But that was not all; he had a hat as well, and on the chair back hung an overcoat of gray gabardine. Lopatkin put on all the things, and Nadia saw a stern and dignified man with soft gray eyes and a sharply-graven line across his forehead.

Lopatkin had also bought a suitcase, which was filled with all sorts of trifles: a towel, soap, underwear, and even bread—three whole loaves.

"What is this, Dmitri Alexeyevich?" Nadia reddened and looked at him with an offended air. "Are we to keep German accounts?"

He gave her a long, tender look from under his hatbrim.

"I forgot to tell you. I am leaving today for the Urals. For Galitsky."

"For long?"

"Perhaps for a fortnight, perhaps for two months."

"Then I'll just run out and do a bit of shopping. I'd like to bake you some pastries at least."

"If you like. And here is some money."

Nadia turned around in order to answer him in a dignified manner, but her voice failed her. He was holding out a fat roll of hundred-rouble notes to her.

"They gave you as much as that?"

"Yes, they have given me a bit. Take them. I don't want them. Take them!"

"What is this? Are you paying me back?" She blushed.

"Oh, no. It's too little for that," he answered with a gentle calm. "I just don't need them. I have already bought everything for myself. You know the saying: 'Beyond a freshly washed shirt, I say it on my conscience, I need nothing.' Here, take them. It's time you and I stopped bothering about such things. I will bring you some more—they are giving me a salary, you know."

Nadia took the money, pushed it into a drawer, and looked around again. Lopatkin had already begun writing something, his notebook on his knee, without even taking off his hat. She went up to him and removed it, and not looking up from his writing, he flapped his hand and said: "Why? I am going in a minute."

That was the kind of man he had become—perhaps he was absent-minded, perhaps overconcentrated, one could not tell. Nadia gazed at him, then she put on an apron and went into the kitchen to make some pastry. She came back in twenty minutes, but Lopatkin had gone.

He had gone especially to visit Liakhov Lane once again, and the flower bed that was like a heap of glowing coals. All his Moscow affairs had been dealt with, and he had taken a taxi, and in twenty minutes got out of the car opposite the flower bed and sat down on the seat, in exactly the place he had sat in three days before.

The summer was only just beginning; the leaves on the crooked poplar that had grown through a hole in the fence from the garden into the street were moist and green. The quiet of the dinner hour surrounded him. There were no nursemaids sitting on the seats, they had not yet pushed their perambulators along here. Everything around him spoke of Evgeni Ustinovich. Lopatkin still thought of the professor as though he were alive. He had made an experiment! Yes, of course, that was how it had been. "My profession is—fire!" From the darkness memory evoked a tiny bottle of white powder in front of Lopatkin. And he suddenly realized that it was not only the constantly fearful little man with the spectacles and white whiskers who had ceased to exist, but that his other half, the creation he had wanted to leave to the people, and so had hidden, sometimes in the chest, sometimes under the floor, was also lost forever. "Human beings consist of two parts: the physical shell, which disappears, and the work of creation which can live on forever," Lopatkin recollected, musing. Yes . . . let anyone now try to describe the blaze that had been extinguished by a wave of the hand; no one would believe it. The man had vanished completely. Without a trace!

He stared with glazed eyes at the red flowers that seemed to glow and flicker in the light breeze. When he came to himself, he was no longer a philosopher but a man of business; he sighed, then jumped up and strode rapidly along the lane, never to return there again.

3

THE train left at one in the morning. Lopatkin spent the whole evening with Nadia. He held Nikolashka on his knee and told the boy all about his distant journey, skating skillfully over the awkward points and stressing the rugged beauty of the Siberian north. Then Nikolashka was put to bed by his mother and fell asleep. The grownups looked into each other's eyes, and went out for a walk along the Leningrad road. The weather was fine, and for a long time they walked quietly in the dark shade of the trees. Lopatkin was silent, thinking perhaps of what was awaiting him in the Urals, while Nadia gazed now up at the sky, holding his elbow firmly with both hands, now at their feet, adapting her step to his. Then she made up her mind and laid her head on his shoulder.

"You have a good name," he said suddenly. "Nadezhda: Hope. It suits you very well."

"No," she wanted to say. "It doesn't. My name is Lyubov: Love." She would have liked to say it, but did not dare.

At half-past eleven they returned home, and Lopatkin took his suitcase and a cardboard box that contained the pastry. Nadia saw him to the Leningrad Road. Here he hailed a taxi, pressed Nadia's elbow, kissed her hair and temple, got into the taxi, and drove away.

When he arrived at the railway station, he stopped at the post office and sent Galitsky a telegram. Then he went out on to the platform, lighted by bright lamps overhead. The train was already standing there, as if it had run into the station building. Lopatkin absent-mindedly presented his ticket, found a car with upholstered seats, and got into a compartment. Someone showed him to a berth, where he put down the box of pastry and his suitcase, took off his overcoat, sat down, and frowned impatiently. He drummed on the little table with his fingers and sat quietly for a few minutes, until he felt a soft jolt and the lights began to float past his window. After this he grew calmer, lay down on his berth, and throughout the two days of the journey was the most silent passenger in the compartment.

Forty-eight hours later the train stopped at the bottom of a valley, between rounded green hills. It was four o'clock, and the cold summer dawn was already breaking. Lopatkin stepped down from the carriage on to the ground, crossed the rails, and walked toward the station building. From a distance he saw a tall figure in a gray-green cloak and gray cap standing by himself in front of a brightly-lighted station window, who turned and came toward Lopatkin with a firm step. It was Galitsky.

"So you have arrived," said a friendly bass voice. Galitsky shook Lopatkin's hand and, without relaxing his pressure, led him to the lighted window.

"Let me see what you look like now." He took off Lopatkin's hat at the window; the close-cropped hair gleamed with silver. "Aye, they have fired you properly," Galitsky said thoughtfully. "They did not spare the fire, and the brick that came out of it is good. I don't think Tepikin will dare to test it for hardness now. He'd break his teeth on it, wouldn't he?"

"I have not yet been able to gather sufficient data about the hardness of the brick," Lopatkin said.

"The brick is Grade A," Galitsky exclaimed.

"I don't know. I haven't seen . . ."

"We'll go to the foundry tomorrow morning and then you shall see!"

"My dear comrade." Lopatkin took both Galitsky's hands and pressed them, a wave of warmth flooding his face. "Excuse me, but I still don't know what to call you."

"They call me Peter, and I am Andreyevich after my father."

"Dear Peter Andreyevich, you can see now what effect the firing has had on me. I can't control my feelings at all now. Look, what

443

is the good of this sort of thing?" Lopatkin was openly wiping his cheeks with his hands.

"Emotion is the most reliable passport!" Galitsky replied, opening his cigarette case. "Let's smoke, Dmitri Alexeyevich. *They* will be afraid of you now: you have no dirt on your conscience, and you have won through. You did not crack in the kiln."

"I don't know. . . . I don't know. . . . But the machine is what matters! If it really works! . . ."

"Would you like to go to the foundry at once? Though why do I ask you? We'll go and have a look at it now. Not in any gala rig, but in the most prosaic circumstances, early in the morning. That will give the most faithful picture."

They passed through the station garden on to the road. A small dark island in the blue-gray haze was the factory director's car. Galitsky opened the door and let Lopatkin get in first, then sat down next to him. The starter made a scraping sound, the engine snorted, and two yellow beams shone out in front of them. The swirling morning mist receded, revealing a bumpy road on which the Pobeda nosed forward.

"So we are going to the foundry?" Lopatkin asked, unable to contain his impatience.

"Yes." Galitsky nodded. "Drive to the fourth entrance," he told the driver.

Silence fell. Lopatkin and Galitsky each followed his own thoughts, and only the small glowing ends of their cigarettes flared up from time to time and died down again in the darkness. Galitsky's little flame glowed brightly for an instant and then was extinguished.

"You took a correct attitude from the very start," Galitsky said. "Of course I don't imagine it was deliberate, of course it was not by design, it could not have been. It was a lucky quality in yourself."

"What do you mean, Peter Andreyevich?"

"I mean that you are a believer. That you have faith and that you fight. You have not turned savage, like some inventors. Like that old man—Busko. Although it would have been possible to go

444

down that path. This was what won you the necessary helpers. There are not so many of them, but as you see they did help. Do you understand what I mean?" Galitsky turned sharply toward Lopatkin. "So-called 'worldly' people often call me an idealist. But the devil only knows what that means. There's one of your judges, Major Badyin—I got to know him very well—until very recently he was regarded as eccentric, and his chief, the lieutenant colonel, once called him 'a political.' That is almost the same as idealist. It was difficult for him to fight on your behalf. But now the time has come for the 'down-to-earth' lieutenant colonel to wrinkle his brows. Badyin proved to him that creative effort exists for a judge as well as for others. Your victory is his victory. Good for both of you! That's just what I'm saying: an idealist here, an idealist there, and in a third place, lo and behold, another so-called idealist! You run into them at every step, but without a conspicuous distinguishing mark, you don't see them, nor they you. But when Lopatkin lighted his steadfast lantern, they all rallied around to help him! And the result has been not a fantasy, not a 'thing in itself,' not a mere hieroglyph, but an addition to the state budget amounting, straight off, to a few dozen millions! How's that? Now I can ask my general: 'Well, and who is the idealist now?' and he laughs and says: 'Fancy remembering that! You don't understand a joke, Peter Andreyevich.' And that's all from him! But before, I could not have answered him in this way: 'What's this you've cooked up now, Comrade General! Some sort of idealism?'"

"Yes." Lopatkin sighed. "I, too, was . . . let me see, what was I? A pipe dreamer, a bogus inventor, a climber . . . even a bit cracked!"

"But once the lantern burns, helpers flock to it like moths! It appears that there are many pipe dreamers in this world! And your lantern, Dmitri Alexeyevich, is very magnetic. Remember in the technical council, in the Institute, how many it attracted at that time."

"Whom else?"

"What about Krekhov? And Antonovich? True, they did not

speak out at the time, but they have done as much for you as your Judge Badyin. But of course the greatest piece of good fortune that flew into the flame was Nadezhda Sergeyevna. Take good care of her. She is the white swan that for your sake who would present its breast to the arrow. In general, I must say . . ."

Galitsky's voice broke and he stopped speaking. There was something he knew but he had obviously decided not to meddle in the intricate problems of other people's lives. Again there was silence in the car, and the small lighted ends of the cigarettes glowed pensively.

On each side of the road bluish-gray pines seemed to rush toward the car. The light of the headlights grew red and everything around took on a cold blue sheen. The deeply rutted road flying backward under the wheels seemed to be endless.

"Where is the factory?" Lopatkin asked.

"Another six miles," the driver replied.

"So you, too, had to fight?" Lopatkin asked Galitsky after a pause.

"No. So far as you were concerned, it was all smooth going. Everyone was interested, including the Minister. He has his work cut out, you know; he has to fulfil his plan. But the position was critical. He narrowly avoided accepting the C.S.I.F.E. machine, and only just refused it in time. A rumor had reached him that a colossal overexpenditure of cast iron was taking place, and that besides the machines were slow, and that the casting was proving expensive. So he greeted your machine with enthusiasm."

"But you did take a risk!"

"What did I risk? Will you please tell me what *you* risked when you gave up your schoolmastering and began making a machine? Did you believe in it?"

"But I . . ."

"And I, too, know just a little about casting. There could be no risk at all on my part, so just you forget it and don't try to make a hero out of me! I am no good as a model; my figure, you know, would not satisfy lovers of the antique."

446

Then he looked at Lopatkin and added suddenly:

"I think you and I are going to be friends."

The car raced along the broad empty main street of the factory estate. Small fenced-in gardens and white one-story houses with high orange-tiled roofs flashed past to right and left. The settlement was asleep. Then a high, endless fence rushed to meet them—this was the factory.

The car stopped at the gatehouse. Lopatkin got out his passport. Galitsky scribbled something in his notebook, tore out the page, and handed it to the watchman with Lopatkin's passport. The gate opened, and the car rolled along an asphalt road flanked by works buildings ablaze with lights.

"To the foundry," Galitsky told the driver.

The car turned into another road, then into yet another, passed five or six buildings, turned one more corner, and stopped. Lopatkin opened the door and jumped out. "This way," Galitsky said. They entered the shop. First they found themselves in the molding department. Here the machines were banging away rhythmically, shaking iron boxes full of black earth; compressed air was hissing and whistling, and completed molds were waiting on trolleys. Everything was covered with a black dust. Galitsky and Lopatkin crossed the hall and passed into the pouring shop. Five cupolas stood here like five mighty columns, and on one side, along the wall, small fires seemed to be dying down—these were molds that had only just been filled with molten iron. "Good morning, Peter Andreyevich!" called a workman wearing blue goggles under an eyeshade. Galitsky waved to him. "This way, this way!" he said to Lopatkin, and they walked on.

Suddenly Lopatkin caught sight of a trolley loaded with a row of stepped cast-iron pipes.

"Those could be cast on my machine!" he cried.

"We know that as well as you do, comrade inventor," Galitsky shouted into Lopatkin's ear. "These have been made on your machine!"

Lopatkin saw a few more trolleys with the same kind of stepped round castings, then he suddenly realized that from the moment they had entered the pouring shop he had been aware of a rose-colored light that flared up for a few seconds, and disappeared, at regular intervals, at the far end of the hall. At first he had paid no attention to this measured play of light and darkness. But now he suddenly felt: this is it! The rosy light appeared again in a far corner, and suddenly something began to sing, as it spun rapidly.

"Have they poured?" Lopatkin exclaimed.

Galitsky turned to him, pointed his finger in the direction of the rosy light, and nodded.

They left a brick enclosure behind, and Lopatkin suddenly saw the whole thing. For seven and a half years he had had a vision of this machine as soon as he closed his eyes. He had started it, had changed one or another detail on it, and now the machine had emerged from the dark depths of his consciousness, as though matured, had moved to this shop, and taken up a firm stand on a concrete foundation. The air began to hiss, an oil-drenched road descended an inch and adjusted the mold. This was that same *normal assembly* of which Arakhovski's friend—the angry tousled Kolia—had spoken. Now the mold stopped and slipped downward. The conveyor shifted, an empty mold took the place of the other, the air hissed, a bright light went on—the measuring ladle tilted, and a stream of fluid fire appeared between it and the mold.

"Get back, comrades, can't you hear!" shouted a workman in a canvas shirt and gloves. "It may splash, and then . . ."

This one man by himself was handling the machine! Lopatkin stepped back obediently and drew Galitsky with him.

"Peter Andreyevich, why only one man? I provided for two. . . ."

"We arranged it like that, we kicked over the traces a bit," Galitsky said. "Here, you know, we are everything in ourselves. My chiefs are a bit timid, too. If one tells them anything, they start taking advice, gather together all the mammoths and mastodons from C.S.I.F.E., and they trample it to death."

They were silent again. Galitsky took out his watch. Lopatkin's hand also stole to his pocket, to his watch strap. "Four-twenty," Galitsky said. The factory director and the inventor stood at the machine for ten minutes. Then Galitsky solemnly winked a dark eye at Lopatkin. In ten minutes the machine had made eight batches—it worked nearly twice as fast as the C.S.I.F.E.'s revolving machine.

Lopatkin stood in front of the machine, and, strange to say, what he saw in front of him was not a machine, but a trench in Gorki Street, and workmen laying a black varnished pipe down in it.

"Wake up, inventor!" Galitsky shouted. "Well, have you seen the machine?"

"Yes, I have."

"Is it the one?"

"It is."

"Are you satisfied?"

"I am."

"Have you got it off your chest?"

"I have." Lopatkin laughed.

"Now that it weighs twelve tons, now that it is shooting out these gadgets day and night"—Galitsky strode to a trolley full of castings and put his foot on it—"now it would not be so easy to put it in one's pocket and walk off with it, eh? Avdiyev does not yet know it! If he finds out, he'll go sour at once. And on top of everything else you and I will write an article and publish comparative figures!"

Lopatkin flapped his hand.

"To hell with them! I don't want them. You know, Peter Andreyevich, I saw the machine and went soft all over. When I look at it, there is nothing else I want. Yesterday, in the train, I was still imagining how I would jeer at them, what intrigues I would set on foot against them. But now I have all at once lost all desire to fight them."

"Well, I haven't. If you pack up, I shall have a go at them myself. No, friend! While this gang sits round the fleshpots, I shall have no peace. Now they have arranged to write a new textbook.

449

To stuff all sorts of nonsense into the students' heads. 'Avdiyev, Tepikin, and other prominent scientists!' Oh, no, friend! I'll pull these Saracens off their high horse!"

Having said all this, Galitsky coughed belligerently several times, then gradually cooled down and said:

"There is a more important question involved than the adoption of your machine. Just a moment, you'll yet become a politician too. Well, let's go; we can still sleep for a few hours."

The Pobeda was waiting for them. The early morning was clear. A rosy dawn was lighting up the sky behind the foundry building. They drove out of the factory and turned into a wide avenue flanked by two-story houses. After one more turn, the car stopped at a gap between two eight-story buildings. Lopatkin followed Galitsky through the gateway and ran up the stairs to the third floor. "Sh-sh!" Galitsky said, opening a door. "Better take our boots off."

They took their boots off in the hall and noiselessly entered the room, one wall of which was tinted a bright rose color by the dawn. The first thing Lopatkin saw was a large oval table and on it a knife and a large loaf of wheaten bread, cut at both ends. Along the sunny rose-colored wall two completely naked children were sleeping soundly in their cots. One was a boy of seven, the other of twelve. Both lay in the posture of a runner, and the blankets of both were crumpled at their feet and hanging down to the floor.

"Yours?" Lopatkin asked in a whisper.

"Whose else? And these are only two out of five." He nodded toward a door. "Three more in there. You lie down here." Galitsky went around the table and stopped at a divan that was already made up as a bed, with clean sheets and a large pillow in a lace-edged pillow slip. He beat the pillow and gave it a final prod with his fist to make sure. "Come on."

While Lopatkin was undressing, Galitsky carefully covered up his sons, and whispered to them soothingly. Then he returned to Lopatkin and sat down beside him.

"Well, get a good night's sleep, and tomorrow morning early we'll go to the factory."

"Peter Andreyevich, I would like to know what induced you . . ."

"What induced me?" Galitsky asked back. "To do what?"

"I mean, what induced you to take up my case?"

"But I've told you that already."

"No. I know you were concerned not only about my machines, but about me and those—Saracens."

"You know, I will tell you. One's heart boils up, that is why! That is the most accurate answer. Take that Badyin, for instance. A genuine party man cannot tolerate an injustice. He can sense it, however carefully it is hidden. And he cannot tolerate it!" Galitsky brought out these words in a toneless roar, and it was clear at once that he could be something else as well as a friend. "No lies! No falsehood!"

He said no more, staring at the wall, rosy with the dawn, then he put his hand inside his collar under his shirt, and sniffed—he was sleepy.

"And Antonovich," he suddenly spoke again. "The man did a heroic deed! He risked being prosecuted. Formally, he committed a crime. Try to dig down into his soul! You have reason to know that not all judges like to rummage in people's souls! This man was skating on thin ice—and why? Because his heart, too, boiled over."

"But Antonovich is non-party, so far as I know."

Galitsky stretched himself and stood up.

"I would be the first to give him a recommendation. Well, go to sleep. . . . And someday I shall give him a recommendation. The party needs people like that."

In Galitsky's home and family everything was permeated by a particular kind of lovable simplicity which cannot be imitated or faked, and therefore is not often met with. It was a family where there were many children, where everything was clean but lying

451

about untidily, where the furniture was simple and inexpensive, and where generous helpings are served at table.

Lopatkin observed all this next morning. He woke suddenly and for a few moments watched a desperate battle between the two Galitsky boys, the seven and the twelve-year-old. Slaps in the face sounded naturally and honestly. Both combatants were savage and tried to hit the other in the face. The elder finally succeeded in pushing his opponent out of the room, and with a vengeful smile barricaded the door with a chair; it shook with the blows, but the elder boy calmly went about his business; he had decided to cut up a tin can with the scissors. Then the younger left the door and began yelling angrily, with indescribable malice: "You Khunkhuz! Khunkhuz!" then stopped and listened. Lopatkin could not help laughing. There was, in fact, something Mongol or Japanese in the elder Galitsky boy's face. For some time there was silence in the passage, then through the keyhole came a caressing: "Khunkhu-uza! Dear little Khunkhuza!" The elder boy threw the tin can on the floor, snatched the chair away from the door, and then the sound of blows came from the hall. The defeated, but not yet broken, younger warrior howled so loudly that it could be heard all over the house. Soon Galitsky's sleepy, homely bass coming from the next room put a stop to the riot: "Lyoshka, leave him alone!" Then there was an affectionate: "Come here! Why does he touch you?" The younger, snivelling, whined: "Why won't he let me cut?"

The sounds of a domestic court of law came from the next room. Lopatkin got up and began dressing. But now his attention was attracted by the pattering of tiny bare feet. A small, naked, chubby boy toddled into the room from the hall. He had long fair hair, as soft as corn silk. This was the youngest Galitsky. He had obviously only recently learned to walk, and now, having escaped from somebody, was laughing happily until he caught sight of the strange uncle, when he at once grew serious and pointed to him with his finger. Then, treading shakily, he toddled round the table, bent down and pointed his finger first at the bookcase, then at the rubber plant, then at the boys' beds. "Oh, here you are!" said a girl of about fourteen with a thick fair pigtail and the same Mongol features as Lyoshka, whose entrance made Lopatkin dive under the bedclothes. Paying no attention to the guest, the girl picked up the baby, kissed it, and carried it away.

The whole family had breakfast in the kitchen, sitting on benches around a large table covered with oilcloth. On one side the children sat in a row: the girl with the pigtail, the two pugilists, and another little girl. A deep-voiced old woman, somewhat bent with age, whom Galitsky called "Ma," held the youngest child on her knee and fed it with *kasha*. Galitsky's wife, a plump calm woman, put a dish with thick slices of bread and a large frying pan on to the table in which was a mountain of potatoes, appetizingly fried in large flat chips. These were at once distributed, the spoons began clattering on the plates, and the eldest girl instantly cried: "Stop that noise!" The frying pan was taken away, and in its place came a high saucepan filled with cocoa, and about a dozen enamel mugs.

"Sashok, what is all this here?" Galitsky asked, sweeping his hands wide apart, as though to embrace the whole table.

"Meine familie," the younger pugilist answered.

"My family," Galitsky confirmed, eying his brood. "All right, we're going somewhere. But where shall we get to?"

"Where I have taken you," the old woman said gaily in her deep voice. "We shall all get there, we shan't leave the rails, not we! We shall all get there!" She kissed her little grandchild. "You, too, Dmitri Alexeyevich, ought to get yourself such a family. What's the good of remaining a bachelor? It's time to produce a few like these fat handsome ones."

"Dmitri Alexeyevich," Galitsky's wife said suddenly, "we have had an argument with Peter here. About your Antonovich. Perhaps it would have been better if he had waited for the sergeant?"

"His position was somewhat precarious . . ." Lopatkin began cautiously, in order to put his point of view forward as tactfully as possible.

"She likes everything to be done quietly, in the proper order," Galitsky boomed gaily. "One writes to the superior authority or to a newspaper—was that what you would have preferred? And in the meantime Uriupin and Maxiutenko would wait."

"What if I do? He could have made a mistake . . ."

"Listen, Nina. That is what was so fine about it—that in a complicated situation, like a surgeon, he quickly found the only right way to save Dmitri Alexeyevich. And what's more, a lawful way; the law protects the substance, not the letter. I would say Antonovich showed courage of the Suvorov type. And yet, what a little runt of a man to look at!"

Turning to Lopatkin, Galitsky added:

"She is always moderate, my wife is."

"And he is always fighting other people's battles, my husband is!" Mrs. Galitsky turned a forgiving look on Galitsky. "Just like my two boxers here. Chasing after other people's bruises. It's time for him to have a rest."

"We'll rest when the time comes." Galitsky laughed. He sat at the table, his hand on his hip, his shaven chin thrust out, wearing lilac suspenders and a white silk shirt unbuttoned, that showed his chest on which hair grew thickly up to the collarbones, drinking cocoa out of a tall mug—"Dad's mug." "Rest does not run away!" he said, laughing. "Now Granny will tell us whether I am right or not."

"We shall all rest in time," the old woman replied gaily, pushing a spoonful of *kasha* deftly into the baby's mouth. "If one rests when one is young, when does one live?"

"Dmitri Alexeyevich," Galitsky said, taking a sip out of his mug, "I did a little statistical work here recently. Those who worked on our machine were you, Krekhov, Antonovich, and, to a lesser degree, myself. Out of forty-eight assemblies only one did not work. We gasped—that was less than two per cent. You put ninety-eight in the bull's eye. And an entire Institute worked on the C.S.I.F.E. machine! Two institutes. An academician, three doctors of science, two candidates for that degree, and a whole department full of engineers! When the first Avdiyev machine was made, half a million was spent, and the pipes turned out dearer than the ones made by manual methods! The accounts of the factory balanced with a loss of two million roubles. The second time, a million and a half was spent on the attempt, and again it was no good! Overexpenditure of cast iron! And yet they work it all out, and hold conferences and discussions, everything is well founded, with a bow to the address of the great experts. Thirty-three warriors solve the problem, while we have only the four of us—and yet we win! There's a theme for a thesis if you like: what is the nature of a monopoly, and why does it make a mess of everything it undertakes, and in what respect does it differ from a genuine collective?"

"One lad, a young engineer, said to me three years ago: 'This is not Avdiyev's colonial empire here!' "

"Yes, a few people here and there are beginning to see through them. But there are far more who remain blind. If Avdiyev were to come to grief suddenly, it would be like a bolt from the blue for many of your colleagues in C.S.I.F.E."

"The invisible City of Kitezh," Lopatkin said.

"And yet with what assurance they talk of the collective! Do you remember your first technical council conference? It would be interesting to ask Tepikin what he means by the word 'collective.' "

"Tepikin understands everything. He knows what 'collective' means, and he knows what its chief characteristic is, something which I fully understood only when they pointed their fingers at me and exclaimed: 'There he is, the individualist, the self-seeker!' Now I know what a collective is. If one were to take the very largest or the very smallest unit of the Avdiyev set, and look into its soul, one would find a boundless solitude whistling through it like the wind over the open steppe. Although there is a whole gang of them, they form no collective. And for how many years did I knock at their door, trying to get in under their roof! With a palm frond in my hand! I knew nothing then!"

"And I! I used to work in Avdiyev's institute, you know. I believed in him! I admired him like an idolator, and he strutted in front of me like a peacock. Patted me on the back: 'Never mind, my lad, just study . . . All this is attainable . . . Work, only work is required!' I didn't yet even know myself, but he had already taken out insurance. He sensed there was something in me. He sent me up for a doctor's degree—an old trick that! And in my eyes he did, in fact, gain three years over this. Then I saw: he had given me a theme for my thesis that was as far away as possible from his own fertile pastures."

"But how firmly ensconced he is!"

"There was nothing one could do. Alone I was helpless. Mere talk could do no good. They can say that black is white, and carry it, every one of them. And Saratovtsev will confirm it. A fact such as your machine was required here. And a factory that was—like ours—not subordinate to Shutikov. They would never have allowed your machine to be built in any of theirs. You ask why I took up your case? Because you did everything that one man could do—for all of us. You did it for me, too. You put in my hands the possibility of freeing C.S.I.F.E. from these pirates. I am glad that you happened to come along. Drink, drink some more!" Galitsky poured out a full mug of cocoa for Lopatkin from the saucepan. "Drink! Refresh yourself! The armistice won't last long!"

"You fighter! So they are frightened of you, are they?" Galitsky's wife said, and Lopatkin felt that she loved her husband for just this quality of his. "Take yourself off, you warrior!" She prodded her husband's back gently. "Go. It's time you were at the factory."

"Yes," Galitsky said, getting up. "Yes, we must go. Dmitri Alexeyevich and I have a job to do. A new job." And looking at Lopatkin, he stuck up his thumb.

4

P AVEL IVANOVICH SHUTIKOV was going through some strenuous days. First, the working out of the new standard for pipes
dragged on for a suspiciously long time. Finally, all the drawings and calculations together with an explanatory note arrived
from C.S.I.F.E. With it were enclosed the specialists' conclusions,
and even an opinion of Academician Saratovtsev's, who agreed with
the calculations, and considered it possible to increase the weight
of the pipes as a temporary measure, in view of the prospect of a
further improvement of the casting machine.

"Splendid!" Shutikov said gaily, signing in green ink the paper
Tepikin had pushed ready to his hand. It was he who was reporting
on this whole affair.

But these documents were not fated to travel beyond the registry
of the Ministry. The day had only begun, and Shutikov had summoned Vadia Nevraev for an interview over a personal matter.
Vadia was in the waiting room, and came in at once. His gray
jacket was buttoned all the way down, his necktie was accurately
centered, and his blue eyes held an incomprehensible and controlled
anguish. With his hands pressed to his trouser seams, Vadia swam
across the office like a gray duck, and stopped. Shutikov took his
request to be allowed to leave his job out of the desk drawer.

"What is this?" he asked, reading the paper which he had read
more than once already, and beaming with surprise and friendliness. "What does this mean, Comrade Nevraev? Do you want a
change of climate? Are you striking your tents?"

"It is because of the state of my health. I wish to get medical
treatment and then to study. Here are the medical certificates."

"Certificates, pshaw!" Still smiling, Shutikov looked fixedly into

Vadia's eyes. The same quiet anguish was still there. "All right," Shutikov said. "When are you going?"

"I thought of going on leave at once. And I would prefer not to come back here."

Shutikov silently wrote: *For the order of the day. To be discharged at his own request.* Vadia took the paper silently, turned around, and swam out of the room again with the same idiotic expression on his face.

"What is it driving you away?" Shutikov wondered as he followed Nevraev with his eyes. "There seems to be no storm in the offing. Why are you so depressed and excited?" Then he laughed, thinking that even the most sensitive weathervane is sometimes mistaken. The wind blows from the south, and it trembles and points directly to the north. "But what is it he senses? Even if it is a southern wind, what is it?"

If Drozdov had been in Moscow, Shutikov would have called him, and together they would have found out what the matter was. But Drozdov was not in Moscow. Since he had separated from his wife, he was everlastingly away on missions in the factories—he was engaged up to his ears with problems of the new equipment.

Shortly before noon one of the telephones buzzed. Shutikov picked up the receiver and at once showed his teeth, with all the shining yellow gold they contained. It was Avdiyev who was calling and who asked that the material relating to the new standard should be kept back at all costs.

"What's this? I've already sent it on!" Shutikov said, pressing a bell. "So what is it, Vassily Zakharovich, tell me?"

"There are certain considerations," Avdiyev's toneless voice answered. "Oh, by the way, did you know Lopatkin had been released? That is one thing."

"Bring back the material I gave you this morning," Shutikov said to the secretary who answered the bell. "Find out about it in the registry and bring it to me at once. What?" he shouted into the telephone. "Say that again, please!"

"He arrived in Moscow, and has left again. He is building a machine. Or has already built one."

"In what factory, do you know? And which Ministry? Don't you know that, either?"

"One can easily guess the Ministry," Avdiyev answered. "In my opinion, they have a contract. They are already working. I believe the basic assemblies are already in the metal."

"How do you know all this?"

"From a reliable source."

"Very pleasant!" Shutikov said.

"I find it so, too," Avdiyev answered. "We had better have a chat, Pavel Ivanovich."

"Drozdov ought to be back tomorrow, then we'll discuss it. Ring me again tomorrow morning."

He put the receiver down and rang for his secretary. A minute passed, then another—but no one came. He went out to the waiting room—there was no one there. He beamed mildly—which was this time an expression of confusion on his part—and returned to his office. A few minutes later the secretary came in with some papers in a folder.

"They were not sent on, because Leonid Ivanovich wanted to see them when he got back."

"Good. Leave them here."

When the secretary had left the room, Shutikov opened the folder. The documents, set out neatly and precisely which only that morning had filled him with such an agreeable sense of relief, now terrified him by their clarity, by the open and carefully contrived fabrications they contained. They were beautiful, with the beauty of a toadstool. Shutikov shuffled them together, and then returned to the first sheet, which carried his own careless signature, written aslant across the page.

"And I might have sent this claptrap to the committee!" he thought. He took the paper bearing his own signature, and laid it apart on the table. "All right. Now suppose we had had the news too late, and all this had been dispatched to the committee, Drozdov would have reported on it. And say the new standard would have been confirmed. What then?" The answer came pat to his mind: "Then it would become known that there is in existence a machine invented by Lopatkin, which is casting pipes accurately in accordance with the old standard. And the committee would say: Rescind the conformation. Why throw away four pounds of metal with each pipe? But that is not all. Lopatkin will of course raise a stink, will remind people wherever possible that he offered his machine to us eight years ago and that we outrageously, disgustingly, in unprecedented fashion . . . and however else the newspapers put it on such occasions! . . ." Shutikov smiled, but it was not a very gay smile and, his eyes wandering, groped on the table. He suddenly felt the need for a cigarette.

"Stop!" A new thought struck him abruptly. "And the sixty thousand tons of cast iron? What about those now?"

He felt a growing burning in his heart which turned into a violent stab. He groaned and pressed the bell, then went quickly over to the divan, and sank heavily on to it.

He lay with his hand pressed to his chest and smiled, showing his shining yellow crowns. The secretary came in and instantly realized, from this smile, that Pavel Ivanovich was suffering; he had had attacks of this sort before, and had always grinned with pain in this way. She hurried to the telephone and rang through to the polyclinic, and a few minutes later a woman in a white uniform came in, carrying a doctor's bag. She touched Shutikov's forehead, felt his pulse, turned up his silk shirt, and baring his white fat chest, cautiously pressed the membrane of the stethoscope to it.

"Lie quiet for an hour," she said, after listening to Shutikov's heartbeat. "When the pain stops, go straight home, please, and to bed."

She poured out half a glass of water from the bottle, put some drops into it out of a little phial, and gave it to Shutikov, who drank it and lay down again. But when the woman in white had gone, he sat up on the divan and beckoned to the secretary.

"Get me a car."

She called the garage at once.

"Put all these papers in my brief case," Shutikov said, and, frowning, stuffed his shirt back into the top of his trousers, "I am taking them with me."

And he went off home.

Next day he drove to the Ministry in the middle of the day. The high main entrance looked to him like a trap. Twenty-four hours had passed—a tremendous time. Shutikov well knew how precious a day could be at such times. He went quickly up to the second floor and along a private passage, to his own office, where he at once made a telephone call. As soon as the door of the waiting room opened in the distance, he asked: "Has Drozdov arrived?" and sighed with relief when the secretary said, "He has already inquired about you."

Drozdov had returned from his mission during the night. At ten in the morning he was already in his office in the Ministry, picking up telephone receivers. Telephone calls had begun to come in quite early. In twenty minutes he knew all that had frightened Shutikov so much the day before, and a bit more that Shutikov did not as yet know. He was informed that all Lopatkin's correspondence had come to life again, and had got into the hands of the Supreme Court and from there to the district prosecutor's office, to Deputy Prosecutor Titov, who was manifesting a particular interest in the case. This information was given to Drozdov over the telephone by a frightened old man of over sixty, who was the head of the Ministry's inventions office and who, the day before, had been forced to give explanations to Titov.

"Apparently you haven't yet lived long enough in this world!" Drozdov said to him with irritation closing his eyes. "Panic-monger! What has scared you so? That is what prosecutors are for—to dig in our dark places and try to discover our weak spots. You talk about documents! We, too, have documents. We, too, keep records. Bring me all our outgoing documents in this case, and we'll have a look at them straight away."

"Yes," Drozdov thought to himself as he came out from behind

461

his desk and walked up and down the room. "I have underrated Comrade Lopatkin. . . . And why? All because of that politician [that was Drozdov's name for Shutikov]. He sets big things on foot, but as to knowing his way about—he knows nothing at all. What does he understand? The branch has long been rotten and he still sits on it, understanding nothing, only smiling! He should have shifted to another one long ago. But in any case, sooner or later he would have crashed! What a mess he has got himself into! And now he wants to drag others in, too!"

Here it must be noted that Drozdov had been thinking about *the truth in the Lopatkin case* ever since early that morning. He considered the fact that it would have been possible to give support to this inventor as long ago as 1946, to take a slight risk himself, with him to have struck a blow at the opponents—including Shutikov. "No, no, no!" he told himself at once. "At that time such a course would have been beyond the bounds of common sense. It was impossible. We should both have lost. Then—no! But now! . . ."

At that moment the director of the inventions office came in, carrying seven files. He closed the door with his foot, and put the files down on a table that stood by the writing desk. Drozdov put on his horn-rimmed spectacles, and with his hands in his pockets, and one knee on a chair, closed his eyes and gave a violent sniff.

"Well, come on. What have you got there?"

The old man took out his spectacles, cleaned them with his handkerchief, and perching them on his nose, opened a folder with the figure 1945 written large on the cover. The required page was marked by a slip of paper.

"Well, what is that?" Drozdov asked.

"We, the Ministry, answer you, Leonid Ivanovich. You were still in Muzga. To your number . . ."

"Ah yes, I remember. He had put in his declaration through us! Yes, yes, I sent it up to the Ministry. Find it, please. It will be needed. Next. Or, no, let's do it like this—take it to the typists and let them copy all the outgoing papers and my letter from Muzga. Three copies. Get it done as quickly as you can."

In an hour copies of all the relevant papers were brought to Drozdov. It appeared that the Ministry had written more than once to C.S.I.F.E., pointing out the necessity of getting on with the projecting of Lopatkin's machine with the greatest urgency.

"Now question me if you like! I'm at your service!" Drozdov thought, pressing the bell. "We hold enough trumps. Here we wrote on such and such a date. Here we sent a reminder. Here is the Minister's order."

To the secretary who entered he said: "Please ask to come to me here . . . Er'm . . . ah, yes . . . Bocharov, and Grafov, and—who shall we have for the third? Let it be Sevruk. And have five bottles of mineral water brought here for me."

Bocharov was the section head who had reported the over-expenditure of cast iron to the caucus sitting. This quiet official had outlived several complete sets of ministerial top rankers. The other two were rank-and-file young engineers. They were not often summoned to the presence of such a high superior. And so, as soon as they entered Drozdov's office, they at once reverted to the state of students.

"Sit down, comrades," Drozdov said, and all three sat down. "Excuse me, it is getting very hot." He indicated his unbuttoned coat and the open window beyond which glared a hectically bright day, noisy with the hooting of cars. "How are you off for time, Sergei Sergeyevich? Are you free?" he asked, getting sterner each minute and even appearing to grow older. "I want to ask you to head a commission which is to investigate certain facts. . . . Do you know anything about Lopatkin's invention?"

"I have heard something about it," Sevruk answered hastily. "In which department does he work?"

"No, that is another Lopatkin you mean. I have asked you here specially, as being neutral. Incidentally, you must know about the Lopatkin centrifugal machine, Sergei Sergeyevich?"

"Yes, I do know something in general . . . but I have only seen one machine, designed by C.S.I.F.E., which we discussed. . . ."

"Very good. In that case I will give you the necessary information. About eight years ago, Engineer Lopatkin proposed to us the construction of a new machine for the centrifugal casting of pipes. I at once sent his application to the Ministry—this was while I was still in Muzga. For eight years he struggled to get this machine accepted, and all the time some invisible agency prevented him."

The door opened and a waitress brought in five bottles of lemonade and five glasses on a tray. She opened the bottles, poured out a glass for each of them, and quietly went away. Drozdov drank a glassful, then poured out another and drank that. The engineers modestly sipped from their glasses.

"Four times the technical council of the Ministry decided to make this machine," Drozdov continued in a refreshed voice. "The Minister issued two orders about it. Comrade Shutikov and myself repeatedly sent reminders in writing and by word of mouth. But it's no good talking—here are a few documents which we have put out. Study them. Your task will be to find out who is to blame for this unprecedented red tape." Here Drozdov left his desk and began walking up and down. "Now about the C.S.I.F.E. machine." He walked to the other end of the room and stopped there. "While this institute was obstructing Lopatkin's invention in every way, a number of officials in it, together with our scientific bigwigs, hurriedly pushed through a machine of their own, the same one, Sergei Sergeyevich, that has given you so much trouble. They managed to put it through. They misled responsible people in the Ministry by giving a false evaluation of the Lopatkin machine, praising their own exaggerately wherever they could, and concealing its one essential drawback. Now, as a result of all this we are faced with an overexpenditure of metal in the neighborhood of sixty thousand tons."

Drozdov approached the members of the commission, and stood before them—a tired man courageously disclosing the hard truth.

"But this is not all, comrades! The inventors of the Institute machine, Uriupin, Maxiutenko, and the C.S.I.F.R. officials, in order to conceal this overexpenditure, for which they would have had to answer seriously to the state, cooked up—what do you think? They proposed nothing more nor less than to change the state standard

464

for pipes! To add four pounds of metal to each pipe! And in this way to write off the whole overexpenditure! They prepared excellent scientific arguments and even involved old Saratovtsev in the dirty business. They pushed some recommendation under his hand, and he signed it. So they misled me and Shutikov, and even the Minister to whom it was all reported. Do you see to what lengths they have gone!"

"Ye-es," said Sevruk. Grafov was writing something in his notebook. Bocharov bent his head uncertainly.

Drozdov silently walked the length of the room and back again and sat down at his table.

"You will have to draw up a plan for the work. Parcel out the duties. You can invite others to help you—for instance, that honest fellow who discovered the cast-iron business. Certainly take him. In C.S.I.F.E. there is an efficient engineer by the name of Krekhov whom I can recommend. He is well up in technical problems. Remember that you will have to dig into things. Perhaps you may even have to look in at the tribunal and ask a few questions there, since Lopatkin was under arrest. True I don't know all the details of that, the trial was in secret. On account of certain secret matters. But there again the accusation arose in C.S.I.F.R. and C.S.I.F.E. It started there—from the authors of the revolving machine! So, get to work. All the records are at your disposal. I think you should be able to get it done in about six or at most eight days."

When he had seen the commission out to the waiting room, Drozdov came back and sat down in one of the easy chairs in front of his desk.

"So Lopatkin is free," he thought. "And on top of that I am helping him. And of course *they* will already have met. . . ."

He felt a dejection he could not speak of to anyone. Was it possible that all his life he had never experienced a genuine emotion such as *theirs?* He began calling up the past. Yes . . . *that* had eluded him. But he had been close to it more than once. Judging by *her*, it must be something extraordinary. How feverish she had been, how she had bustled about, how she had been forever washing her hair! "No one ever sighed like that for Drozdov!" he told himself with a bitter grin. "There was no reason to, properly speaking. . . ." It was terrible for him imagining how Nadia might have looked at *that man*. Probably just as she had looked at herself in the mirror—as he had once seen her do. "And she sold the fur coat!" he sneered. "She's just a cat! Nothing more!"

Then he suddenly understood quite clearly that feelings do exist —he himself had seen how Nikolashka had hugged her dress. The little boy had been alone in the room and Drozdov had watched him from the doorway. No doubt it was different between those two, a little different. But it all came from the deadly emotion of love, without which that little being, also, would have died. And she, too. "But I did not die. . . ."

Fighting off a paralyzing numbness, he picked up the receiver and dialed a number. "Is the boss in?" he asked softly. The secretary answered that Shutikov would hardly be coming in that day: he had had a heart attack the day before. "That is easy to understand!" Drozdov said, and hung up, repeating: "Easy to understand!"

After dinner he again telephoned to Shutikov. This time he was there and Drozdov went in to see him.

"I have appointed a commission," he said affably, as he entered Shutikov's spacious office.

"What kind of a commission?" Shutikov fidgeted in his chair, with a cheerful expression on his face. "Sit down, Leonid Ivanovich. What sort of commission?"

"What kind of a commission?" Drozdov said, sinking into an armchair. "Lord! A commission to find out who is to blame for the disgusting red tape and delay in connection with Lopatkin's machine, for the overexpenditure of metal, and the tampering with the state standard, of course!"

"Wha-at?" Shutikov wanted to yell, but controlled himself and instead emitted a subdued groan. "What . . . What on earth are you doing? To take a step like that and not tell . . ."

466

"In cases of this sort delay is fatal," Drozdov said, stressing every word, and slapping his yellow hand on the upholstered arm of the chair. "Did you know that Lopatkin's papers were not burned, and are now lying in Prosecutor Titov's safe? Oh, you didn't? In my opinion every department chief ought to investigate any scandalous fact that becomes known to him, without waiting to be reproached with doing nothing about it. The job is done, and there is no more to be said about it. But the chief ought to be given some preparation. He knows nothing yet, does he?"

"No," Shutikov said absent-mindedly; he was thinking about something else and not looking at Drozdov.

"He is thinking of that receding ministerial armchair!" Drozdov thought to himself.

"You must warn the Minister." He gave Shutikov a searching look and dropped his eyes.

"So there's a commission," Shutikov said, still thinking of something else. "Well, that's all right. I think it's the right thing to do."

Twenty days after this conversation every department in the Ministry received the Minister's printed order of the day; it bore the number 222, or "triple failure," as it was afterward called for a whole year. The descriptive section of the order took up four pages and was fully in accord with the commission's findings. True, the commission had refrained from mentioning Academician Saratovtsev by name. They had taken into account that the academician would soon be celebrating his eightieth birthday, and had decided not to spoil the old man's anniversary. Avdiyev, too, got off lightly. An analysis of various documents and correspondence covering the past seven years showed that the professor had only twice expressed an opinion on the machine. The first time he had queried certain details of the project, and had later given a favorable opinion. The names of Drozdov and Shutikov were not mentioned in the order, but there was an oblique reference to them in a passage which said that: "In their unlawful practices Uriupin and Maxiutenko, as well as certain officials of C.S.I.F.R. even went so far as

467

deliberately to deceive the Ministry's leading officials." In addition the commission had calculated the amount of financial loss, and the enormous overexpenditure of cast iron caused by the Uriupin-Maxiutenko machine. But this paragraph had been deleted by the Minister himself, who said that there was no point in making such facts public. People were often unreasonable and might interpret them incorrectly.

For all that, in the Ministry, and in the smoking rooms of both institutes, when the question arose of why Maxiutenko and Uriupin had caught it, people in the know said at once, "Because of the cast iron." Had there been no overexpenditure, the order would have been quite different in tenor.

As it was, the order said: "The engineers Maxiutenko and Uriupin, who concealed the defects of the machine designed by them, which led to serious losses, to be dismissed from their posts. The proposal put before the leadership of the Central State Institute of Foundry Research, is that the scientific officials, Tepikin and Fundator, who, by giving dishonest expert opinions, have for several years prevented the introduction into industry of Lopatkin's centrifugal machine, and have, on the contrary, actively assisted in the adoption of the worthless revolving machine, be called to account."

Next followed several more paragraphs, this, for instance: "The head of the technical section will establish the strictest check on the furtherance and adoption of valuable suggestions made by inventors and rationalizers." This paragraph was familiar to everyone; it was known as "the hardy perennial"; the commission had copied it from another order issued two or three years before.

5

I n September Lopatkin arrived in Moscow from the Urals to take part in an important conference. The representatives of several ministries were to discuss the need for a designing office for the projecting of centrifugal machines, which would be able to serve several departments at the same time. Lopatkin gave a report on the possibilities of the principle he had suggested. After this many unknown worthies spoke, and all supported this beneficial and timely initiative. It turned out that the oil industry and the chemical industry, the building-materials industry, not to speak of the engineering industry, were all interested in getting hold of a high-speed automatic centrifugal machine.

The conference went on for six or seven hours. Lopatkin sat at a long table between deputy ministers and other leading officials, and all these serious and businesslike men vied with one another to secure their share of the working schedule of the bureau which was as yet nonexistent. They fumbled restlessly with their papers, and jumped up, demanding to be heard. Lopatkin's person, his story, and the fact that he was sitting there watching them all with interest, concerned them not at all. They gave the inventor a cursory glance, but all they saw was the machine which would enable them to solve some acute problem—and they all wanted to get a machine of this sort for themselves first, and as quickly as possible.

During the interval a dignified man in a dark-blue suit, heavily built, and broad-faced, with his black hair brushed smoothly back, went up to Lopatkin and took him by the arm. This was the second deputy minister, temporarily exercising Shutikov's functions.

"What? Is Shutikov being shifted at last?" Lopatkin could not refrain from asking.

"Yes, he is now with another minister, Faddei Gavrilovich. As a member of the collegium, I think."

"Still a member of the collegium?"

"Well, you can't deny that he is a valuable worker. And the fact that he made a mess of it where you were concerned— Listen, what do you expect of him? After all, he is a concrete specialist! With Faddei Gavrilovich he will be exactly in the right place!"

"That is not for us to judge," Lopatkin said.

"That's true. Come, why don't you move to Moscow? Why stick there in the Urals? After all, you have a roof over your head here!" This was undoubtedly an allusion, but Shutikov's black-haired successor was serious. "Come to Moscow!"

"When the question of the designing office is decided, I shall be obliged to."

"And when will that be? Not before the New Year. Do come at once! Have some sense! You have condemned one machine and given us nothing in exchange for it. Am I now to wait and then order a machine from your office? No, settle down here with your group, with Krekhov and Antonovich, and finish what you began. Do you need living quarters? We'll find you some. As for having a spoke put in your wheels, don't be afraid! No one would dare. We'd cut their heads off if they did! Between ourselves, the proposal comes from the Minister."

How everything had changed! After the conference, toward evening, he went out into the street, and from old habit Lopatkin started out rapidly and walked briskly for a few paces. "Where am I going in such a hurry?" Laughing, he stopped to consider the question, his head bowed. No, he had nowhere to hurry to!

Suddenly a silence seemed to fall upon the world. He had passed the thundering rapids, and now it remained for him to take off his cap and to make the sign of the cross over the quietly-flowing water and the silent autumn woods. The woods were beautiful but he had not raised his eyes to look at them for at least eight years.

And something had happened to him because of the currents and dangerous rocks that had flashed past endlessly, because of the constant anxiety about the raft on which he had been floating, because of that endless road he had been traveling.

The war was over and he had won! The victor smiled, and felt a sense of triumph, but he had also received a wound. He himself felt it. Suddenly two things came back to him: first he thought of his former love. He remembered it, he did not *feel* it! How strange! The girl remained the same, but the love itself was gone. "I wonder what happened to her?" he thought with lively curiosity. "Did she marry her captain?" Of course she did. The years had gone by and it was time to take some sensible action. Should he go and see them or should he not? Should he frighten the young couple?

There was something else he remembered also. Or rather that he had never forgotten. Now, in the silence, there was no one to disturb him any longer and he again clearly recalled the moment when the examining officer had announced to him that the investigation was over, and had given into his hands, as the law prescribed, all the documents of the case for his information. Among the papers Lopatkin had found the minutes of the evidence Nadia had given. From beginning to end it had demonstrated her love for him. All her answers—cautious and full of unconscious self-sacrifice—spoke of love. Emotion, not thought, radiated even from the lines written by a stranger's hand: "Question: Witness, tell me what your relations are to the accused, Lopatkin? Answer: I love him."

In those days Lopatkin had thought of his machine, not of any woman.

Now it was possible to stop for a moment and think of a woman as well. And Lopatkin began to think. "Do I love her or is it merely that I am used to her? Was it not cruel to go away like that, endlessly pursuing my own affairs alone, paying no attention to her feelings? After all, she is my wife; she has the right to call herself that! But can I deceive her by pretending to be a young man in love? What sort of lover am I if I can sit whole days over a drawing in her presence, as I did yesterday and the day before? And what sort of young man am I? Why, I ought to have abandoned everything else and rushed to her! Yes, yes!" he said to himself. "She is young, she needs flowers, and I am an old gray-haired bachelor like Antonovich. Treason a lot and I have forgotten what feelings are like!"

He stood in the middle of the pavement, smiling. "It would have been possible, of course, not to forget this," he thought, and sighed. But the philosopher in him took over again: "If it *had* been possible for it not to have happened like this, it would not have happened. Sianov was right when he said that happiness does not knock twice at the same door. Very well. But isn't there a miscalculation somewhere? Perhaps the emotions of youth, the green forest, the call of the aspens, are the most precious? No! No! Of course I am happy with my machine. And if it were necessary, I would follow the same path again from the beginning. I could float along for twenty-five years if necessary, as Busko did."

"What is the essence of this happiness?" the philosopher again inquired. "Your machine is made, and is working successfully. An invisible hand was stretched out from the depths of society and I put a pipe into it. And the hand accepted it, did not throw it away. That is the main thing: that I delivered what had to be delivered. And now? What next?" Lopatkin could not answer this question and thought with surprise: "What is this? Am I at a stopping point?"

After thinking this he looked at his watch and suddenly decided to go to Mestrostroyevski Street. Then he hesitated again, although he already knew that he would go there in the end. And he did go. "She has probably got married and moved away from that room, so that I am sure to be going there all for nothing," he pretended to himself. And immediately realizing this self-deception, he thought that it was in this way that a criminal was attracted back to the spot where he had once committed a crime. In such cases they always no doubt invented some justification for themselves. "But have I really done any wrong in this?" he thought. And immediately heard clearly from the depths of his conscience the answer: "The young girl was seventeen when you began to turn her

472

head with your talk about man's high vocation. You shone in every color of the rainbow leading her on. And where did you lead her?"

When the familiar side streets came into sight, Lopatkin felt that he was not yet prepared to meet Jeanne. Yet he still walked on along the street to the tall house she lived in, found the right entrance, and for the first time in his life entered it, climbing to the fourth floor. He at once saw the high oak door with the little round plate: "26." She had lived in that flat with some relatives of hers on her father's side. Lopatkin raised his hand to the bone bell button. The calm, distant tinkle of the bell was the final decisive signal: now he could no longer draw back!

"I'll go in," Lopatkin thought. "What is there so extraordinary about doing this? It is my duty to. She might hear that I had been in Moscow. She would think: that is all a man is worth; as soon as his affairs have begun to prosper, he no longer can spare any time for old acquaintances. After all, we are still friends. So I must see her! And then all my endless promises—let her see that I was right. Let her see!"

When he heard the sliding click of the lock, Lopatkin straightened up, raised his head, and took off his hat—then put it on again. The door was already ajar. Someone was standing there, behind the crack of the door, in semi-darkness, someone who exclaimed in a whisper: "Dmitri!" The door slowly began to open wider and Lopatkin saw Jeanne. He recognized her eyes, slanting slightly toward the temples, and— But what was this? She had cut off her maidenly pigtails, and her head was framed in a heavy, dark chestnut-colored roll—a coil of skillfully arranged and lustrous hair. She was wearing a brown gold-embroidered dressing gown caught into a belt at the waist. On the whole she looked the same, but now she lacked the youthful radiance which had always surrounded her before. Lopatkin did not know that in *those days* the radiance had come from his own soul.

There was no one near. But as now he would have suffered more than ever from the slightest falsehood, he did not kiss her.

473

And she did not take her eyes off his gray hat and expensive over-coat; they held a look of childish amazement, and were filled with a peculiar envy and delight.

So there it was. And, too, the captain was there. He had just come through the farther door and was slowly approaching. He had grown perceptively stouter, and his shoulders had grown round. Lopatkin greeted him, and the captain came closer and stretched out a soft hand. Yes, he had grown very much stouter, as people do whom nature has destined to be lean. His nose and chin were as sharp as ever, his lips thin, and his forehead bony. But swelling cushions of fat bulged in his cheeks and around the ears.

"This is Lopatkin," Jeanne said, standing between them as though to shield Lopatkin. The officer bowed; he had obviously heard something of Lopatkin.

"Glad to meet you, Comrade Captain." The moment he had said this Lopatkin felt uncomfortable: on the former captain's rounded shoulders the shoulder boards bore three stripes. But the officer was not the man to notice such trifles.

"Major Devyatov," he introduced himself.

"This is my friend," Jeanne said softly to Lopatkin. This time she stood as though to shield the major.

The two men, feeling a mutual aversion, stared at each other with quiet curiosity. They went into a room that contained a divan, a small table, and Jeanne's white bed. Through the window was a view of housetops and a turbulent violet sunset.

The major sat down on the divan and lighted a cigarette. Lopatkin took off his hat and stood in the middle of the room looking about him, then sat down, his arm thrown along the back of a chair. Jeanne stood and stared at him wide-eyed. The man who sat there before her was the one Lopatkin had sworn to her he would become. No, here was someone even greater, someone strong, austere, and exceptionally steadfast and tenacious.

"Permit me to ask, Dmitri . . . er . . . Nikolayevich," the major began, "You have been absent for some years, have you not?"

"I was in prison," Lopatkin answered.

The major lowered his eyes and looked at his cigarette.

"I did not want to write to you about it," Lopatkin said, glancing at Jeanne.

"Why not? You could have written . . ." she whispered.

Quite naturally they had somehow dropped the familiar mode of address.

"Excuse me, Dmitri Nikolayevich," the major said, yielding to curiosity. "For what did you . . . er . . . get into trouble?"

"It's a long story. Too long to tell you."

"You got off lightly. Two years?"

"One and a half. I had been wrongfully sentenced."

"How—wrongfully?" The major reddened. "Is such a thing possible?"

"Where are you working?"

"I am adjutant to the commander."

"Well, is the commander always pleased with you? Has he never once ticked you off for some mistake?"

"Perhaps he has!" The major cheered up. "That depends on the mood he is in."

"You see! Even the commander turns out to be no saint. I was sentenced to eight years. And the Supreme Court quashed it."

"Ah!" The major again looked at his cigarette. "And what do you intend to do now?"

"How do you mean 'what'? Work."

"I was told that you had some sort of invention," the major said in the tone of an older person speaking to a younger, although he could not have been more than twenty-seven. He looked at Jeanne as he spoke, and she blushed scarlet.

"I can guess what you heard about me here!" Lopatkin thought.

"So, Dmitri Nikolayevich—I believe that is your name? What is the position with reference to all that? I am asking because I have certain possibilities . . ."

Lopatkin smiled broadly, but suppressed the smile at once; he did not wish to hurt the major's feelings.

"Thank you," he said. "It's a bit late in the day for that. I myself also have certain possibilities at present." His eyes shone with amusement. "If anything . . . I might help . . ."

"Do you mean to say that you have brought it off?" Jeanne intervened, reddening feverishly. "You want . . ." She cleared her throat. "Is that what you mean?"

Lopatkin thought: "Perhaps I ought not to announce my victory to her so abruptly. Why should I take revenge? She will remember things, begin rereading old letters, and have regrets. . . ."

"Why don't you answer?" Jeanne's eyes burned with an unaccountable ecstasy and she insisted obstinately on a reply. "Did you do what you said you were going to?"

"Almost."

"Almost—you had already got as far as that—you remember when?"

"Now things have advanced considerably. Now it really is— 'almost.' "

"Still, you might tell me something about it."

"Fair words butter no parsnips," Lopatkin said, laughing. "I have learned that pretty thoroughly by now."

"Hm. . . ." The major coughed and stood up. "Oh, you go on. Do go on! Unfortunately I must leave you. Jeanne, this business . . ." he spoke under his breath ". . . at eight o'clock . . . the general staff . . ."

"I must go, too." Lopatkin also stood up.

"No, you must stay!" Jeanne ordered him angrily, and he sat down again.

"Well, I was very glad . . ." The major shook hands with Lopatkin, put on his cap, turned to Jeanne, said something to her with his eyes, and walking softly, she followed him out. At the outer door they stopped, and there was a rapid, low-voiced conversation. Finally the door banged.

Lopatkin prepared himself for a decisive explanation. But Jeanne did not return. The sunset outside the window had faded, and now the sky seemed to be covered with dark ashes. Sitting there in his chair, Lopatkin looked round him; the clean little room seemed to be praying for mercy. Everything had been so pleasant here, all these two years. There was a photograph of Major Devyatov in a frame; he looked all hunched up, like a little crab. The twilight and the silence also seemed to have been sent especially to put Lopatkin into a peaceful mood.

Suddenly a switch clicked on sharply like a rattle above his head, and he was dazzled by a bright light.

"Just a minute, I have put the kettle on." Jeanne approached timidly, stood for a moment fidgeting, then sat down on the divan. Suddenly she raised her eyes to Lopatkin, dark-brown eyes brimming with tears. "I was wrong, you may condemn me!" her challenging glance expressed.

"No, no, nothing of the sort!" Lopatkin's kind but startled eyes replied.

"Was it very hard?" she asked.

"Yes. Especially during the year when you and I last . . ."

"What was it?" Jeanne asked so softly as to be scarcely audible. "The conditions or the men?"

"Men." All the wrongs he had suffered could be heard in his voice.

"And I knew nothing. Why didn't you write to me from there?"

"From there?"

She discerned in this word all that Lopatkin had attempted hardest to conceal. Silence fell in the little room.

"If I had written to you from there, the letters would have been like my disagreeable Muzga letters."

"Tell me about it, Dmitri, please tell me!" she whispered.

Lopatkin glanced at her and at once became cooler. He said nothing.

"All right," her voice was sharp. "Perhaps I know what you ought to tell me. If you can't, at least tell me this: has your machine been accepted? Is it in existence?"

She could not look straight at Lopatkin. Her sidelong, jealous glance frightened him. "Supposing I say 'yes'?" he thought.

"No, Jeanne. First tell me about yourself."

"The kettle is boiling!" a voice announced from the hall.

Jeanne went out hurriedly, and soon returned with a teapot. She put two cups and a little vase of pierced china containing a sweet made of fruit on the table. Lopatkin hung his overcoat on the back of his chair which he pulled up to the table.

"What can I tell you about myself?" Jeanne began, as she poured out the tea. "I don't want to talk about myself. You have seen for yourself: everything is all right. I graduated from the university. I spent the summer in the Caucasus, and then I stayed in Muzga for a time. What else is there? My mother gave me a fur coat as a graduation present."

"What fur coat?" Lopatkin asked, bending over his teacup and looking hard into it.

"An expensive one. Mink. But that is really about all. I really have nothing to tell you, except about the fur coat!" She laughed, but it was not a gay laugh. "Soon I shall be leaving for Kemerovo, to work in a chemical and coke factory."

"Why should you have to go there, when this captain, or major, could surely arrange for you to stay in Moscow?"

"He has promised to do so." Jeanne blushed. "But you haven't told me yet whether your dreams are coming true."

"Today I can say nothing definite."

Again there was silence.

"Why are you looking at me like that?" she asked.

"For no particular reason," he answered, smiling as though out of a sad dream. "I haven't seen you for a long time."

And he went on gazing at her.

"You are hiding something from me. I think now that you have won, you have come to pay me back. Well, why don't you?"

"So you did believe in me a bit?" He smiled. "Or perhaps you have been misled by my hat. Don't look at it. It is the hat of a commonplace official. I have taken a job—an established, respectable job, with a salary that allows a lonely bachelor to possess a hat like this."

"Don't try to confuse me." She stared at Lopatkin fixedly. "It seems to me that we are losing sight of one another. Can you even see me?"

"Very dimly."

"And I can't see you at all. Why don't you tell me the truth?"

"Don't get excited." Half-heartedly he went on deceiving her but was already thinking of going away. "On the whole, you were right. I am glad that you did not have to share a lot of unpleasantness with me."

"So you are sorry for me!" she exclaimed.

"Ah!" he said, feeling tired suddenly, and deciding to end it all. "Why should I lie? Yes, of course, I have done everything and now I am a big shot. Soon I shall be writing resolutions on documents: 'Comrade Petrov, deal with this.'" He laughed.

Jeanne, too, laughed so much that red patches appeared in her cheeks. "Drink your tea! Drink!" she said gaily.

"It's time for me to go." He stood up. "I see that everyone on the whole is alive and well, has graduated, and has a fur coat. Let me look at that fur coat."

The fur coat was hanging on the wall, covered with a muslin curtain, and Lopatkin saw what he had expected to see: the familiar pale brown fur.

"Not bad," he said, burying his fingers in the fur and looking thoughtfully at Jeanne. "A nice present. And expensive, surely."

He took the edge of the muslin curtain from her hand and slowly covered up the fur coat. He put on his hat, threw his overcoat over his arm, and went to the door. All at once he felt very far away. And he stopped and gazed for a whole minute, from afar, at Jeanne's tiny figure. Then he came closer once more and slowly opened the door.

"Well then, let's go!" All this ceremony amused Jeanne even more.

At the exit she took Lopatkin's hand and shook it repeatedly.

"And now go away, quickly!" She was laughing through her tears. "Go! Go!" and she pushed him through the door.

Lopatkin had realized earlier that she was crying. The tears had for some time been falling inwardly, while her visible face had been laughing, radiant with feverish rosy patches. And now, when all her true feelings had broken through to the surface, he tried to stop the door from closing; to go back and soothe her. He pushed against it. But in response Jeanne pressed against it from the inside. Her uncertain, expectant pressure told him that he ought to push at the door more forcefully. But he felt unable to lie to her and so he submitted to her feeble resistance, giving way, and allowing the door slowly to close. The lock clicked.

"Why did she close the door?" he thought, as he walked down the stairs. "Why did she push me out?" The answer was: because she was waiting for a decisive movement from you. A yes or a no! If you loved her, you should have forced your way in; that was how she looked at it. She needed tenderness—that was the state of affairs. "The state of affairs!" he thought, with sudden disgust. "What an expression!"

Now he was on the pavement. He looked around and then walked off with his habitual long stride.

"Yes, I felt quite calm the whole time," he thought. "It is a good thing that I did not force the door. 'No' has after all been said. It all turned out to be a sad business—first I led her on, tried to tear her away from the Ganichevs, and now I repulse her."

But he soon put it all out of his mind. First he was diverted by a militiaman, who blew his whistle as soon as Lopatkin left the pavement to cross the street, and went on blowing it in the distance until the culprit realized that this was all to do with him. Then he found himself in a narrow side street and saw that night had fallen and echoes were waking among the stones. Then he thought that he would have to go and see that fellow—the one with the black hair—before the Minister forgot that the old machine had been condemned and that there was no new one yet! "We must build as many machines as possible," he said to himself. "We must consolidate the achievement!" He rode in something or other, crossed something, rode in something else, then walked again and finally, opening the last door, found himself in a room full of a

480

warm twilight. Nadia was lying in bed. Beside her, on the blanket, there was an electric reading light. She was reading a book, and when Lopatkin came in, gazed at him with dark eyes full of sorrowful, almost maternal tenderness.

"Do have something to eat. It's there on the table," she said in a soft, caressing voice. At the same time her maternal instinct told her that Nikolashka had kicked off his blanket. Stretching her white hand out toward his cot, she readjusted the bedclothes and then again gazed at Lopatkin.

"Everything has been decided in our favor," he said, referring to that day's conference. "Everyone says that the question of the designing office will be favorably received."

"Splendid!" Nadia said, in the same soft caressing voice. "There are your favorite baked apples with sugar."

He took off his jacket, washed himself, and a few minutes later, sitting on his bed on the other side of the table, told Nadia all the day's events.

"By the way," he said, "I also went—you know where—today? To Mestrostroyevski Street."

"And then?"

"There were a lot of tears."

"On both sides?" Nadia smiled gently.

"No, only on one. But I, too, was on the brink. But on the other side—well, I said a lot of superfluous things to her. She had already mapped out a definite road for herself, and then I came and trampled on it with my boots in the hall!"

"You are trampling on something with your clumsy boots again at this minute!" a sharp inner voice suddenly pulled him up. So dipping his spoon into the sweet-sour apple, he switched to another subject as smoothly as possible.

"While they are discussing the designing office here I have made up my mind to complete the machine we started projecting in C.S.I.F.E. Especially as I have had a message about it from the Minister."

6

AT midday, one Sunday at the end of October, Nadia was at home, playing with Nikolashka. The boy had just eaten and was sitting on the table dangling his legs. Nadia was standing in front of him, snarling and pretending that she would grab him and eat him up. Nikolashka laughed, squealed, kicked up his legs, and waved his arms, but Nadia grabbed him all the same, and then from a horrid wolf, she turned into a dear kind mother. Nadia had forgotten that the little boy ought to sleep during the daytime, and the game had been going on for an hour. It was a monotonous game, but the little boy enjoyed it, and his mother found a particular pleasure in it, as if trying in this way to fill some bottomless and aching void.

Lopatkin had only stamped his boots incautiously once or twice —allowing something about Jeanne to escape his lips—and his friend had at once begun to ail and pine away. Lopatkin noticed this and was worried. Almost every day he approached Nadia and inquired anxiously and tenderly about her health. But such small attentions had an even worse effect on her. Nadia would take Lopatkin by the hand, gaze at him as though saying good-by, and once, suddenly forgetting everything, they had again jumped out of the train, as they had done one night in Busko's little room. But even after this, Nadia had felt no more confident. And then there had been one more plunge, and then another, and nothing was left behind except a defenseless love and the little son whom she now held in endless bitter embraces.

There was snow on the ground and on all the roofs. It had fallen early that year and gone on falling, day after day. Someone rang the front-door bell, but Nadia paid no attention to it. She only looked up when a breath of outdoor cold blew upon her from the door. She turned quickly and saw a young girl wearing a coat of pale brown fur standing in the doorway. The fur coat was too wide at the shoulders for her, and had slipped to one side; that was what Nadia noticed first. Then she recognized her own fur coat, for which Mrs. Ganichev had given her six thousand roubles. Mrs. Ganichev had forgotten to pay the rest. But it was not this that alarmed and angered Nadia. This fur coat, which she had given up in order secretly to help Lopatkin, and because of which she had suffered torments every time she saw Drozdov—this fur coat was now being worn by Jeanne Ganichev. This woman, who resembled her schoolgirl sister with the eyes that made one think of binoculars, had calmly come here in order to take Lopatkin away forever. Now, of all times, when everything was finished, when all the tears had dried up, and Drozdov himself had beaten a retreat.

"Well, let us talk," Nadia thought.

She looked at Jeanne again and saw a roll of chestnut hair coming down low over her forehead. It looked as if it had been put on at the same time as the little soft shell of red felt she wore on her head.

Jeanne was obviously feeling somewhat uncomfortable; Nadia had been examining her for a little too long.

"I want to see Dmitri Alexeyevich Lopatkin," she said.

"He is not in," Nadia replied. "Take off your things; he ought to be coming soon."

Jeanne took off the fur coat and Nadia put it on a wooden hanger—the same wooden hanger that had been specially bought for it—and hung it in a closet in the hall. As she passed Jeanne, she gave her a sideways glance. Or rather *that other,* who had once appeared to Nadia in the mirror, suddenly stirred, anxiously and angrily, on seeing another one like herself here beside her. Yes, just the same sort of being was looking boldly and hotly out of Jeanne's eyes. She had powdered her face and penciled her eyebrows for the meeting with Lopatkin.

"Please sit down," Nadia said, coming back.

Jeanne sat down, looked out of the window at the snow, then stretched out her hand toward Nikolashka.

"Is he your son? What a sweet little boy!"

But Nikolashka sidled away to his mother.

"To tell the truth, what interests me is . . ." Jeanne said, feeling that an explanation was expected of her. "The reason I have come is that I have graduated from the Institute and am about to be appointed to work in Kemerovo. But I would very much like to . . ."

"Stay in Moscow?" Nadia asked.

"Not exactly that. I could stay in Moscow anyway. I have been offered . . ." Jeanne stopped and bent her head, then made up her mind to speak out. "I would like to work with Dmitri Alexeyevich. We have known each other a very long time; he was my teacher while I was still at school."

"Why not? He is just recruiting staff for his office."

"Excuse me, I have not even introduced myself. My name is Anya."

"What?" Nadia raised an eyebrow.

"Anya . . ."

"I believe your name is Jeanne"—Nadia's eyes sparkled merrily —"and I know you very well."

"True, in my passport I am called Jeanne, but recently I have been trying not to use it. I like Anya better, it is more Russian. And how is it you know me?"

"I even saved your photo out of a fire." And Nadia got Jeanne's picture out of a drawer—the same one that had been pinned up on the wall in Muzga, in the Sianovs' hut.

"Really? Out of a fire!" Jeanne took the picture, and rosy patches gradually began to appear on her face. She looked at herself for a long time. Then with a proud, unnatural gesture she threw her head back so that the heavy sausage of chestnut hair bounced on her forehead.

"Give it to me. I had better put it away," Nadia said, taking the photograph out of Jeanne's hand. "Although it is your picture, it does not belong to you."

"Does he rent a corner here from you?" Jeanne asked.

"Yes, he is staying with me," Nadia said evasively. "He is bound to be here soon."

"You don't happen to know how his affairs are going?"

"Why, don't you know?"

"He has told me nothing, almost nothing."

"One can say that his affairs are going very well *now*. Better than ever before. He has achieved a great deal. His machines are already working in one factory, and soon they will be working in hundreds more. Surely you know that he has been appointed head of a designing office? First, no one wanted him, and now, suddenly, no one can do without him."

Nadia said this without intention. She said it, not thinking that Jeanne might take it as a reference to herself. And Jeanne, of course, pretended to have understood it as referring to those to whom Lopatkin had addressed his applications and complaints.

"Yes, it was dreadful," she said. "I believe he was even put in prison."

"Prison was not the worst of it," Nadia said softly and thoughtfully. "What came before he went to prison was much worse."

"I can imagine. But do you know, he himself told me nothing of all this. He did write, but he did not mention it. 'Everything is all right' was all one heard from him. He concealed it from everyone."

"He concealed it from everyone," Nadia said even more softly and sadly. "He did indeed. But one cannot conceal anything from true friends."

"And had he such friends?" Jeanne asked, then caught herself up and reddened.

"Of course he had!" Nadia looked at her son, who was embracing her knees, stroked his hair, smiled, and scratched him behind the ear. "Yes, he had friends. He had and still has."

"And who are they?"

"Who? All sorts, old men and young ones, but mostly old."

"And women?"

"Naturally. Nothing serious ever happens without us women taking a hand. Nothing at all. One woman loved him very much. But don't worry, Anya, she was unable to take him away from you."

"And who is she, do you know?"

"I do. He could hide nothing from her. She saw everything and began helping. And she could hide a great deal from him. Much of it he has not guessed to this day."

Nadia said these words proudly, but there was a low note of pain underlying them. As she spoke, she looked beyond Jeanne. And it was instantly clear who that woman was. Jeanne asked with a smile:

"The woman is you, no doubt."

"Oh, no! How could I? . . . I have my only darling, here." She kissed her son again and again. "My only care, my worry, my golden dearest one. *That* woman thought only of Dmitri Alexeyevich and sometimes even forgot her own child, as if it did not exist. *That one* was quite different from me; she was a crazy, silly creature. I don't know where you could find anyone else like her! She sold her own things for his sake."

Here Nadia checked herself, feeling that she was talking to herself and not to Jeanne. She lowered her tone.

"Altogether, Dmitri Alexeyevich is the kind of man whom anyone he meets will either at once side with and help in every way—or oppose as his enemy. Once he met a little old man, a professor. They talked for only an hour and the professor gave him this as a present." Nadia showed Jeanne Evgeni Ustinovich's drawing board. "And at that time the professor himself was living on bread and nothing else!"

"You know, I still think it is you," Jeanne said in a low, piteous voice.

"No-o," Nadia drawled calmly. "How could it be? I'll show you who it is. Here." She pulled out a drawer in the table, rummaged among the papers, took out a torn envelope, and from it a folded piece of paper, which she gave to Jeanne without unfolding it. "This is who it is. Read it."

Jeanne unfolded the letter and began reading it in the middle.

I have done my small part [the unknown woman wrote], *and the memory of it will always be a sufficient reward for me. This is a kindness on your part, dear Dmitri Alexeyevich, which only I can fully appreciate and for which I cannot thank you enough. You write that the work is interesting and you even mention the salary. But you and I understand that it is not the salary that matters. I will not come to you, because you know my relationship to you, just as I know your relationship to me. I must not see you any more. I also know that there is a woman who has made greater sacrifices than I have and who no doubt loves you more dearly than I do. Although I cannot easily imagine that. . . .*

The last lines told Jeanne everything. She was shrewd enough—after all, she was a Ganichev—and so, as she put the letter down, she pretended that it had fully explained everything to her. But Nadia, too, was on her guard. She, too, had noticed, and wanted to mend matters.

"She is my friend. Dmitri Alexeyevich wrote to her, inviting her to come and work with him—she is a good linguist. And of course she would have come like a shot, but she knew that you were in Moscow. She is a funny creature. One of the best, though."

"So you have been in Muzga? Excuse me, what is your name?"

"Nadezhda Sergeyevna."

"Drozdov?"

"Drozdov. Nadezhda Sergeyevna." Nadia looked at the girl with innocent candor. "Come what way," she thought, "if she knows

487

something, let her know. If she knows nothing, why should she get mixed up in all this?"

But Jeanne did know something. Perhaps her mother had told her, perhaps her sister had written. The name Nadezhda Sergeyevna was the clue that linked it all together and explained it instantly.

Jeanne, never taking her fascinated eyes from the heroine sitting there in front of her, at once stood up and began to say good-by.

"I have taken up too much of your time already. I won't wait for him now. I'd better come some other time or telephone him."

"I'll tell him you were here," Nadia said as she saw the girl out.

She followed Jeanne out into the street and on to the pavement, swept clear of snow. Standing there was a new, sand-colored Pobeda, shining like glass. In the car sat a stoutish officer, the major, no doubt. When he caught sight of Jeanne, he pressed the horn and the Pobeda hooted lustily.

Jeanne said good-by once more and got into the car. The fur coat still hung somewhat lopsidedly; it had not even been altered to fit her.

"That girl is a riddle," thought Nadia.

Dmitri came in the evening, having spent the whole day with Krekhov examining a machine for the pressure casting of steel, which Krekhov and the inventor had been pushing in vain for many years. The expression on Lopatkin's face showed that the invention had proved very interesting. He noticed nothing, smiled absent-mindedly, and wrinkled his nose, while his mind continued to be preoccupied with the machine. For a long time his eyes still gazed at something beyond the walls of the room. Then slowly he cooled down—Nadia saw it in his face, which took on the soft, tired expression she loved most of all. In such moments it was as though he had relaxed the strict guard he kept over himself; as if she could enter his soul and wander quietly for hours in its labyrinth, occasionally coming upon some tightly closed, unknown door—a door only seemingly closed—behind which lay unexpected gifts.

They sat down at the table together to drink tea. Nadia plucked up her courage and said, as casually as she could:

"Jeanne came to see you today. She was here for an hour and a half."

"What did she want?" Lopatkin looked at Nadia.

"She wants to ask you to give her a job in your office."

"There isn't any office yet. And then it seems we have already said all there was to say to each other. She closed the door herself. She said: 'Go away!' and slammed it."

"That means she loves you. And you must take it seriously and do everything you can. I think you ought to go to her, soothe her, and fix her up with a job."

"Well, she is a chemist. In the foundry, perhaps? It's true, there is a metallurgical slant there. Ought I really?"

"Of course you ought."

Nadia did not mention the major to Lopatkin. She also kept silent about Jeanne's fur coat. Why talk about it? The girl was not to blame.

"If she says I ought to . . ." Lopatkin said to himself, and next morning went to see Jeanne. The door was opened by a woman he did not know.

He walked along the passage, knocked twice on the white door, waited, and knocked a second time. Jeanne opened the door quickly and retreated a step when she saw who it was.

She recovered her composure at once and offered him a chair. Dmitri sat down and looked round. On the bed and on the divan lay all sorts of bundles and silk underclothes, some pink, some delicate lilac or pale pistachio-green, edged with dark lace.

"I am just sorting out my things." Jeanne was embarrassed and threw a newspaper over the things on the bed.

"Why didn't you wait for me?" he asked good-humoredly. "Why did you go away?"

"Oh, I did wait for a bit."

"If you were after a job," he joked, "you should have waited for the boss. What sort of job could you do?"

"None, I suppose. I am a chemist, you know."

"An analytical chemist? That's what you are, aren't you? Then you will work in the foundry on the composition and properties of metals. A whole group in our outfit will be concerned with that."

"What a pity," Jeanne drawled. "No, it's impossible. I am afraid I couldn't do it."

"Is there anything else?"

"I just thought . . ." She turned her face to him and looked at him with her heart in her eyes, as though asking: "Well?" and prompting: "Come! Come on!"

Then she wandered about the room, picked up her handbag, opened it, and began rummaging among some papers it contained.

"I'll give you my answer," she said firmly. "Do you know when? Let me see. On the second of November. That is, in three days. Come here at nine in the evening, on the second of November. All right? Good. I'll give you an answer then."

"On the second, did you say? I don't think I can come on the second. That is Saturday. I couldn't make it at nine. I have to go to Academician Saratovtsev's jubilee ceremony. He is eighty. I have been asked to go and sit on the platform."

"Then at eight?"

"Eight won't do, either. I'll look in at seven-thirty. And take you with me. Would you like to come and have a look at our little assembly?"

"I don't mind. At seven-thirty then. Don't come any earlier, I shall not be in. Please remember that."

"What is there to remember? If I happen to drop in twenty minutes earlier, I'll just wait, that's all. Is it a date? Then *au revoir.*"

He turned and walked along the passage with his usual long strides.

"Dmitri!" Jeanne called to him.

He stopped. Jeanne came so close that her shoulder touched him. She took his hand and pressed it hard.

"We must say good-by! I wish you every happiness, Dmitri Alexeyevich."

He went away. All through the three days he worked at C.S.I.F.E.

490

on his new project, the one that Shutikov had once rejected. This project had been almost completed even then. But now new ideas had occurred to Lopatkin, Krekhov, and Antonovich, and the project to some extent had to be "restyled" in connection with them.

On the morning of November 2 Lopatkin went to the public baths, shaved, and dressed himself in his *Fundator,* as he called his new black suit. In this array he betook himself to C.S.I.F.E., to the room where his group was working. He was met by Krekhov and Antonovich, in new coats with green facings. Until five o'clock the group worked evenly and with concentration, as usual. At five o'clock Krekhov and Antonovich went out and came back again in forty minutes. Lopatkin could hear their loud, cheerful voices while they were still quite a long way off; this forty minutes' absence, they explained, was connected with the program of celebrations in honor of the academican.

At six o'clock a large red-and-yellow bus drew up at the entrance to the Institute. It was intended for the lower ranks of the Institute staff, and as others beside Krekhov and Antonovich had already begun honoring the academician, the bus was soon buzzing with loud exchanges between young and old wits and thunderous bursts of laughter. The bus got under way, and the cars belonging to the higher officials, covered with fresh snow, came sliding noiselessly to a halt at the entrance.

Lopatkin telephoned to Nadia, asked her to hurry, looked at his watch, came out through the entrance at a run, and stopped a taxi. He was due to see Jeanne at seven-thirty.

On the way there Lopatkin realized for the first time that Jeanne had sounded rather strange when she had said: "I will see you at eight, on the second of November."

On Mestrostroyevski Street he jumped out of the taxi, told the driver to wait, and bounded through the arch and across the yard full of violet-colored snow. He reached the stairs and stopped. As he passed under the arch he had already noticed a trail of narrow footprints in the snow. They stopped at the stairs. The trail led from the house to the street. "It can't be. Nonsense!" he thought, and opened the heavy door. The stairs creaked and shuddered under his resolute stride.

He rang the bell and an unknown woman in a soiled apron opened the door. Lopatkin thanked her and walked to Jeanne's room. It was locked.

"Comrade!" he heard from behind him. "Comrade, I tell you she has left."

"Where has she gone? She told me to come at seven-thirty."

"She went to the station. She is leaving for Kemerovo today."

"Oh, so that's it!" he said, and frowned. "Did she leave no message? Did she say anything?"

"Are you Dmitri Alexeyevich? She left a letter for you. Here it is."

Lopatkin went closer to the feeble lamp, tore open the white envelope, and read the whole letter in a couple of seconds.

I have gone to Kemerovo. You will understand everything in a minute. There is a woman who has sacrificed more for you than I have. She loves you more, too: I realized only quite recently that this was possible. I could not live beside you and your friends and comrades, every one of whom is better than I am and has proved it in practice. I perfectly understand that looking at me and Nadezhda Sergeyevna you would involuntarily compare us with one another, because the difference is obvious. She loves you; treasure her and your happiness. I must hurry to catch my train. My dear teacher, Dmitri Alexeyevich . . .

Here she must have realized that she had no more time, she had started to sign *Jeanne,* then had angrily struck the name out and written beside it: *Anya.*

"When does the train leave?" Lopatkin asked.

"She said at seven-thirty."

Lopatkin glanced at his watch. "Five to eight. It has all been correctly calculated. Good for her! Firm, as she always has been "

He did not know how he had got out of the house. Jeanne's letter had touched something in him very deeply, perhaps it was because he saw that her soul had not yet drawn forth those forces which are needed for one to love passionately and to weep bitterly. A riddle? No; no riddle, everything was clear. Her eyes had been opened by something.

At that moment his glance again fell on the row of small impressions in the snow. He looked around, hesitated, then scooped up a handful of snow out of the nearest footprint and watched it until it melted away. Then he regained control of himself and hurried out into the street. The taxi with the chessboard stripe round the body stood where he had left it.

On the road to Taganka, to the industrial institute where the jubilee celebration was to take place, Lopatkin thought that perhaps everything was for the best as it was. All in all, of course, things had not turned out too happily; on the contrary, one might even say rather sadly. He even said it aloud: "Sad," and at the same time looked at his watch to see whether he was very late. He realized at once how absurd this petty worry was at a time when he was faced with something which, he felt, would never fade from his memory. He pondered: "Why this down-to-earth glance at my watch?" But at that moment his taxi pulled up at the Institute gate. Lopatkin hurriedly paid the cabman, ran into the cloakroom, passed a comb through his hair, and greeting friends on the way he ran up the broad stairs, past the old-fashioned mirrors, to the gaily buzzing assembly hall on the top floor.

The academician had not yet arrived. The presidium, the members of which had been chosen and invited in advance, had gathered behind the scenes—a crowd of new coats and black suits. Here was the general, director of C.S.I.F.E.; in a corner Lopatkin discerned Drozdov's shrewd yellow face and new coat. Vadia Nevraev, with only one of his coat buttons fastened, moved from group to group. He came up to Lopatkin, shook his hand most cordially, and remarked: "I say, old Florinsky hasn't turned up!"

Presently there was a lively movement in the hall. Everyone

493

stood up. The academician had arrived. He walked slowly along the central aisle to the stage, followed by an escort of generals with broad red stripes down their trousers and scientists in black suits. Among them was Avdiyev, a black mountain with a yellowish-white peak. The escort trailed along behind the academician like a band of musicians, smiling, moving their lips in inaudible speech, and inaudibly clapping their hands. The academician himself, a chubby, stalwart old man with a little bald patch on the top of his head and mustaches with ends twisted sharply upward, bowed and smiled right and left.

The presidium seated themselves on the platform. Lopatkin sat on the end of the third row. Someone far in front declared the assembly in honor of Academician Peter Benedictovich Saratovtsev open. Someone even farther from Lopatkin stood up, walked to the rostrum at the other end of the stage, and began to make a speech about the services rendered to science by the academician. It appeared that Academician Saratovtsev had written many books and, as long ago as 1928, had worked out a number of important problems which had not lost their value to that day. In addition he had laid the foundations of the theory which had later rendered possible the solution of . . .

Lopatkin was not destined to hear the end of the speech. A man he did not know touched him cautiously on the shoulder, beckoned him to come behind the scenes, and led him on, along twists and turns, to a passage and a narrow staircase. Here, Dmitri found Major Devyatov, pale, and with his teeth tightly clenched, standing against the wall.

"I have come from Anya," he said. "She wants you to come to the station."

"What?" Lopatkin stared incredulously at the major. "But didn't she leave at seven-thirty?"

"She only said that at her lodgings. The train leaves at twenty-one oh two. Anya asked me to bring you."

"All right, I'll go." Lopatkin walked down the stairs to the exit.

A round clock hung above the stairs. It was twenty-three minutes to nine.

"The train leaves in twenty-five minutes," the major said. "We must hurry, Dmitri Alexeyevich. She has to see you."

Dmitri did not stop for his overcoat. They emerged into the street. Exactly opposite the exit a pale sand-colored Pobeda gleamed against the background of the night.

"If you please," said the major, "this is my car."

"You drive on." Lopatkin stepped aside into the darkness, where a long line of motorcars seemed to be dozing. "I'll go by myself."

The major closed the car door without a word. The starter buzzed, the engine came to life, gasped, snorted, and the shiny new Pobeda rolled on.

Lopatkin looked around. There was no taxi in sight. He turned the corner to the main entrance and stopped there. He had only two or three minutes to spare.

"Hi, mister! Jump in! Where to?" several drivers called out to him from the sleepy row of cars.

But Lopatkin asked himself suddenly: "What for? She has her ticket, she is going to Kemerovo, she is on the right road. . . ."

Not answering the drivers' cheerful invitations, he walked slowly back along the pavement. "But do I love Nadia? There was a time when I almost hated her! Yes, I must have got used to her. But is that the right thing? *That* was different. One cannot even remember properly what it was like . . . just as if one was trying to remember one's youth!"

Lopatkin tried to remember his youth. Something of it did come back: a feeling of good health in his whole body; looking involuntarily at every girl in the subway, in the bus, in the street, and his ears listening, of their own accord, to everything they said. And that they had all been lovely. Even those who were not obviously pretty, even they had had a curious tender beauty for him. Where were they all now? And the scents? And the permanent expectation of some unknown happiness? The readiness to burst out laughing

495

on the slightest pretext? Now people thought him ten years older than he was, and it was not surprising.

"It should be possible to bring it all back," he thought. And he seemed to hear the distant sound of Siberian poplars, the call he had once heard so close to him. "You are free, take a shotgun and go away to the ends of the world and become a savage!" Should he not heed that call, while he could still hear it? But why? The oak may grow a thousand years, because it cares nothing about time. Ten years or a thousand years make no difference to it! "But for me, time is everything! I won't waste a minute of it. I want them all for my work!" He laughed as he caught himself in this thought. "Yes, my good fellow, you are developing a hobby! And that means, dear comrade, that we are growing old."

He turned into the side street, went in through the entrance, and climbed the stairs. The little door leading to the stage was ajar, revealing a plywood partition.

"Peter Benedictovich, our respected celebrant . . ." someone on the platform, beyond the partition, was reading in a tremulous gabble, "constantly showed us . . . mm . . . yes, a noble example of scientific objectivity and fidelity to principle. He can understand the mistakes of the young and in correcting them he generously distributes the pure gold of his precious experience. . . ."

Somewhere in the hall Nadia, too, would be listening to these words. She would certainly have arrived by now. "How can I get into the hall?" Lopatkin thought.

At that moment from somewhere higher up Vadia Nevraev came tripping softly down the stairs. He was chewing something and his face was redder than usual. When he caught sight of Lopatkin, he seemed somewhat embarrassed, then he held up a sandwich and pointed silently upstairs with his thumb several times.

"I am telling only you. For old friendship's sake. Hurry up!" And he slipped through the partition on to the platform.

Dmitri went up to the third floor. Here, too, there was a small door, slightly ajar, but beyond it there was no plywood partition. Glass and nickel glittered here, white damask covered the two very long tables laid for the jubilee banquet. Men in white jackets were busy bringing and putting on the tables, one after the other, bowls full of oranges, rather as if they were lighting street lamps one after the other.

"Can one go through here?" Lopatkin asked one of the men. Having been given permission, he quickly walked along the length of the tables to the other end of the hall and from there to the main staircase. From above he could see the three entrances to the assembly hall, with the doors wide open. "Dear Peter Benedicto-vich," a ringing voice came up to him on waves of warm, stale air. "On your eightieth birthday we, the scientific officers and other officials of this Institute, with profound gratitude, send . . ."

Lopatkin walked noiselessly down the stairs, approached the middle door, and at once saw Nadia. Leaning against the shiny painted frame of the door, holding her handbag under her arm, she was listening to the speaker. She was wearing a dark-gray dress shot with lilac—a dress that was no longer new. Her dark hair, streaked with copper, was twisted into a long, tight bun on the nape of her neck; around it, as always, a rebellious golden cloud of hair stood out.

Lopatkin approached her and gently took her arm. She did not start or turn round, only blushed a little, and pressed his hand to her side. A whole minute passed, then she slowly turned her face toward him. Her expression was sad and in her eyes Lopatkin read the familiar ever-present question.

There was no one near them. He calmly handed Jeanne's letter to Nadia. She read it and raised her eyes to Lopatkin's face.

"Has she gone?"

"Yes, she's gone."

They said nothing more. They looked toward the stage. There, on the platform, Vadia Nevraev was reading, not loudly, but very precisely, a letter of greeting from the Minister. He glanced frequently at the academician as he did so. The celebrant was standing while the address was being read. The Minister himself was sitting motionless in the center of the platform, and at this moment looked more than ever like a portrait of Beethoven.

Vadia finished reading, left the rostrum, handed the portfolio containing the address to the academician, and was about to shake him by the hand and even to kiss him when he suddenly found himself facing that worthy's somewhat rounded but still fairly powerful back. The academician, having received the red-and-gold portfolio, had ceremoniously approached the Minister. Space for the meeting of the two great men was cleared on the platform as if by magic. They met, kissed each other three times, the flash of a photographer flared up unexpectedly, and the whole hall resounded with cheers and applause. "Very good! Very, very good!" someone said, not far from Lopatkin.

"I have been thinking of something," Dmitri said amid all the noise, and drew Nadia's soft, yielding elbow closer to him, but said no more.

"What is it?" she asked, looking round at him.

"I have been thinking. . . . You and I. . . . Oughtn't we to get married?"

She said nothing.

"Nadezhda, I am speaking seriously. Offering my hand and heart." He smiled awkwardly.

She closed her eyes and her lips quivered slightly, then she took a deep breath and looked gravely at Lopatkin.

"Do you know what occurs to me? It occurs to me that you have only just now thought of this. *She* is gone and so—it came into your head. Remember: I demand nothing, I ask for nothing. You are not bound by anything. Not by anything at all! Only, always tell me the truth, as you have told it up to now. Am I not your wife as it is? And I know that you . . . that you love me, but not in *that* way. . . ."

She drew back into the corner between Lopatkin and the wall.

"Nadia!" he whispered. "Nadia! Be calm, dearest! Why all this?"

"It's nothing," she whispered, burying her fingers in his coat sleeve.

At this moment on the distant stage a delegation of three men appeared, carrying a model of some machine mounted on a polished wooden base. The model was placed on the table on the platform, in front of the academician. One of the delegates bent over it and touched something; at that the levers of the machine slowly began to move and its wheels began to revolve.

The hall responded to this by a burst of applause. At that moment Dmitri seemed transformed into another man. His hand hardened, he stiffened with amazement, as though his eyes had suddenly been opened.

"Look at that!" he whispered to Nadia. "Don't you see?"

What was Nadia to see? Far away, on the platform table, something glittered and revolved, and the whole assembly applauded together.

"The machine! It is the revolving one! They have presented a six-barreled one to the academician! Uriupin's machine! Millions, can't you see? The millions have come back to that table from another world. The squandered millions!"

Some unsuspecting director of a distant factory had zealously prepared this gift. The news of Lopatkin's machine had not yet reached him from Moscow, and he had probably not read the Minister's "triple failure" order. And so he had presented to the academician the very thing which was to have been passed over in silence that day!

The model carried on with its work; it turned the drum and aimed each of its six barrels at the platform in turn. The academician grew crimson, looked askance at the machine, then gave Avdiyev a glance full of venom, the tips of his mustache quivering with emotion. Drozdov smiled faintly, but applauded. Avdiyev clapped his bulky hands, leaned toward his neighbor, and said something to him, nodding angrily in the direction of the glittering little model and shaking his yellow-white curls. But in general very few people, perhaps only eight or nine, understood what was going on. Another twenty may have guessed that the director had dropped a brick, but pretended to notice nothing, and applauded zealously. The whole hall thundered with ovations. They grew louder and louder each second, because the academician's name was known to everyone. The moment was a solemn one, and the little machine on the table worked automatically, without external assistance, and thus represented technical progress. Hardly anyone in the hall was aware of the unpleasant background behind the solemnity.

"What about me?" Lopatkin thought. "Am I, too, to close my eyes? Now at last I see the 'invisible empire' of bureaucracy. Besides myself only those who are its citizens can see it. If I were to stand up now and tell these people the truth about that little machine, no one would listen to me! They would look at me just as that girl I called Russian Dawn looked at me once." He felt the blood rush to his face. "So it appears that, after all, I have won this long struggle for myself alone. Is it true, then, that I am self-centered? Have I really been unable to dispel the fog, to open the eyes of any of these people sitting here tonight?"

Nadia looked at him and shook her head, then took him cautiously by the hand and led him away from the "invisible empire."

"Perhaps we might return to the first question," she said, laughing softly.

"Which was that?" Lopatkin was startled.

"Have you forgotten it already? You offered me your heart and hand. The hand I am holding in mine now, but where is the heart?"

"Here!" Lopatkin said, drawing her hand to his chest. "Here it is. Can't you hear it hammering?"

"Yes," Nadia said pensively. "I shall have to accept that heart. We are that sort of person, both of us. 'Cracked' as Drozdov says. It was he who cracked us both. There is no place where we can hide from one another."

"Cra-acked?" Lopatkin asked suddenly and angrily. "Oh, no! He only tuned us up, like two strings. He brought us together and showed us to one another. It's thanks to him that we . . ."

500

"Is this true?"

"Of course it is. And somehow the romantic hero in me is tired or sick. . . . I am not at all like the young Des Grieux. Only the inventor and the fighter is left in me now."

"Oh, you misfortune of mine! Very well then, as long as I can be certain that you will not deceive me. Dearest Dmitri Alexeyevich, will *I* be allowed to love you?"

Thinking that he would not notice it, she quickly touched his sleeve with her lips. But he did see it. Tears rose in his throat and welled up in his eyes. He grasped her by the elbow, drew her out of the hall, and pressed his cheek to her wet one. She laughed.

"Let's go," she said and, holding his hand, she led him downstairs.

At the foot of the stairs he put her coat on for her, then put on his own, and feeling strangely light, they ran out into the street, holding on to each other by one linked finger.

7

ONCE more they wandered together along narrow little streets, under trees that rose and disappeared into the dark winter heights, as they had done that night on the Leningrad Highway. Nadia, holding Lopatkin's elbow with both hands, looked down and compared his steps with her own. The unaccustomed momentary lightness had left them and they were both immersed in their own thoughts. "Where do we go from here?" Lopatkin wondered. He was beginning to detest the quiet, peaceful raft on which he was now floating. He detested it precisely because of the unruffled calm of the future it promised. Earlier, in his fighting days, he had been, if not happier, at least younger. And today, looking round him from the position of rest he had attained, he suddenly felt that he loved the old endless, austere road, with its milestones—a road along which he had unfortunately already traveled; it lay behind him.

Nadia was turning over similar thoughts. She glanced at Lopatkin every now and then and told herself that now he would have a respite at last. Her restless man would settle down; his nervous alertness, his readiness to do battle—all this was no longer needed. Perhaps there was a shade of regret in these thoughts of hers; that awakening in the misty dawn would never be repeated.

So they made their way through the center of the city, first at random through a warren of Moscow alleys, then across three squares, as if they were crossing the Azov, the Black Sea, and the Mediterranean. Somewhere near the Riding School they remembered that the celebration was not yet over: in Lopatkin's pocket lay two tickets for the jubilee banquet. It was already after ten.

"We are a little late. Shall we go there and have a look?" Lopatkin said.

"Take me wherever you like," Nadia's eyes answered. "But let
me glance at our tomorrow first, if only for an instant."

A gray cab with a checkerboard stripe brought them to the Institute gates. They entered the deserted lobby and at once heard
from above the triumphant blare of a trumpet and, light as a breeze,
the rustle of a waltz. They leisurely took off their coats and went
out to the marble staircase and the mirrors. Here Nadia suddenly
stopped and gripped Dmitri's arm.

In front of them, somewhat higher up, a black shadow passed
to and fro on the landing. One might have imagined that an ape
had escaped from its cage and was hurling itself at the mirrors in
its search for a way out. But in fact it was Drozdov. He was walking round and round the landing, smoking a cigarette, and his
circles were more than usually crooked and devious. He paid no
attention to Nadia, not even when she passed quite close to him
with proudly averted eyes. He did notice her, however, for he
looked after her a moment with narrowed eyes before he continued
his gyrations.

Nadia at once recognized those crooked circles; they meant that
Drozdov was in a high state of excitement. But why? What passion
had prompted him to withdraw to this landing?

Suddenly Nadia remembered: "Of course! I saw our friends
from Muzga here today! What was it they said? Oh, yes, that the
grapevine telegraph had transmitted some news today: Drozdov was
to be Deputy Minister in place of Shutikov. There is no official statement yet, but they said it seemed decided. He himself has probably
only just heard of it."

They both glanced back to where the black shadow was still
wandering among the mirrors below. And until they came to the
entrance of the assembly hall, Drozdov was in both their thoughts.
Beyond the tall wide-open doors a dance band blared with ex-
uberant gaiety. Beyond the threshold a tightly packed, heated merry-
go-round of dancers was turning and flowing in one direction; black

suits, velvet dresses, bare arms, parted hair, bald heads, and the golden nests of feminine coiffures constantly emerged from the heat of the crowd to its edge.

After standing in the doorway for a while, Lopatkin and Nadia climbed the stairs to a hall on the third floor that was smaller in dimensions but to many people more attractive. Here two tables still glittered with glass and nickel, still dazzled with fine white linen, but the orderly arrangement of the tables was completely destroyed, the bowls, emptied of oranges, stood like extinguished lamps, and hardly anyone was sitting at the tables. Men in black suits and gray coats were promenading in groups or in pairs in the hall, or standing in the window recesses and at the wide-open doors, smoking and filling the hall with a monotonous murmur.

But some people were still sitting at one of the tables. A little group was gathered at the upper end, where the two tables were connected by a third. Academician Saratovtsev was sitting in the center of the group with Avdiyev's head appearing over his shoulder. The general, director of C.S.I.F.E., Shutikov's temporary successor in the office of Deputy Minister, Vadia Nevraev with round crimson face, the solid Fundator, and the sharp-nosed, pallid Tepikin were standing round them. There were also a few others important enough to join the company without a special invitation, and, with the more famous personalities, listen to the academician and laugh at what he said. Farther off a few slim young men, not yet sufficiently important, were gathered in another group. They looked on from a distance and smiled, probably knowing the subject of the academician's remarks. But none of them dared to step across the no-man's-land; it was not so easy to cross that gap of fifteen paces.

The academician, red in the face after a great number of toasts, was holding in his outstretched hand a fork with its prongs pointing forward. His left hand was slightly raised, and drawn back, as it would be in fencing. His mustaches pointed threateningly upward. He was telling a story about the defeat of a certain baron—not the well-known defeat inflicted on him by the Red Army, but about another, earlier one, that had been witnessed only by two seconds.

"Dmitri Alexeyevich! Comrade Lopatkin!" someone shouted from the opposite end of the hall. "Come over here to us! This way!"

There, in an embrasure, a knot of slightly tipsy designers from C.S.I.F.E. had gathered. Krekhov and Antonovich were the life of this group.

Lopatkin and Nadia went up to them. The circle opened for them and Krekhov took Lopatkin's hand and drew him closer.

"What a business!" He lowered his voice but not too much, so that the whole group could still hear him. "The presentation didn't turn out very well! That little machine! Oh-oh-oh! Did you see their faces?"

"Especially your favorite's!" Lopatkin remarked gaily.

"Who is that?"

"Who indeed! The one who arrived in sandals, butted with his head, and broke through every obstacle!"

"True, I really . . . Yes, that was a mistake! . . . But I have no regrets! The longer deception has a hold on you, the clearer and firmer is your new awareness."

"It had a hold on you, not on us!" Antonovich remarked.

"All right, on me. Correct. Yes, you are right. I looked at the platform today and scourged the silly fifty-year-old boy in myself, who for so long worshiped that idiotic wooden idol."

"Well, let the idol go," Antonovich said. "We absolve you from your sins. Dmitri Alexeyevich, we have been arguing. Will you confirm what these comrades won't believe, that Galitsky has refused a decoration?"

"I know he has," Nadia said. "He explained that he would soon be getting a decoration anyway, for his long service. I have seen his letter. He wrote: *'I did what any decent person would have done, and still more, any Communist. If I were to take this other decoration as well, it would appear that in concerning myself with Lopatkin's affairs I was trying to get something out of it for myself.'*"

"Nonsense," Lopatkin said. "There he exaggerates."

"But altogether it is an original way of reasoning," Antonovich observed. "One doesn't hear it very often. It is not the custom with us to let the spoon pass the mouth."

"He has deserved both honors," Lopatkin said. "Both the one and the other."

"I am inclined to agree with him," Antonovich went on obstinately. "Honors should not be devalued. Our Russia, comrades, is not so poor in honest men that we should search for them in daytime with a lantern and decorate them merely because they have served honorably and have not been guilty of dereliction of duty. No, if there are to be honors, they should be awarded for outstanding work or for many years of service during which you conduct yourself every day as Galitsky did. You remember how that was?" He addressed himself to Krekhov and Nadia.

"Saratovtsev is being put to bed!" Krekhov said, turning and clapping his hands loudly.

The whole hall vibrated with a storm of applause, which spread to the stairs. On the floor below the music stopped. The academician, standing in the middle of the hall, repeatedly placed his hand on his chest, bowed in every direction, proceeded to the stairs, and descended, accompanied by an applauding escort. The band jerkily played a cheerful flourish, then everything slowly began to calm down.

When the storm had subsided, Krekhov invited the whole company to the table with the sweeping gesture of a leader to continue what had been begun.

"Otherwise the table will be taken by others," he explained, when everyone had sat down. Then he knocked on a glass with his gold ring. "All those who wish to drink with us, please come here."

"Or here!" a voice said behind Lopatkin's back. He turned and saw Tepikin's bony neck almost at his elbow. He was sitting at the next table. And behind Tepikin's sloping shoulders, from the other side of the table, Shutikov's eye looked fixedly at Lopatkin.

That eye, slightly diminished by the lens of the spectacles, gleamed with good humor.

"The salmon's health!" Shutikov exclaimed, and raised a small glass of vodka. "Comrade Lopatkin! A health to the mightly salmon!"

Lopatkin thanked him and nodded, but Shutikov drank alone, wiped his mouth with a napkin, and whispered something in the ear of Fundator, who was sitting next to him. Almost the whole "invisible empire" was gathered there, to right and left of Shutikov.

"Ah! Look who our neighbor is!" Tepikin shouted, turning around with a friendly air and throwing his arm round the back of his chair. "Haven't seen you for a long time. Congratulations, Dmitri Alexeyevich! You got us into a pretty mess!"

"Never mind, our descendants will mop it up," Fundator put in amiably, chewing the whole time.

"Why our descendants?" Shutikov asked, beaming slyly. "There is a chunk of good meat in this mess, comrades: Dmitri Alexeyevich's machine. It is this chunk of meat that will be left to our descendants."

"Quite right, Comrade Shutikov," one of the young engineers in Krekhov's party said quietly yet audibly. "And the rest will be cleaned up by the contemporaries, not the descendants. They'll eat it all! They are long-suffering folk."

"No-ot ve-ery," Shutikov drawled. "Take Dmitri Alexeyevich here. You can't say that of him. He won't eat what he doesn't like the taste of. No-ho-ho, comrades, that cock won't fight! You just kindly clear up your mess yourselves."

Here the "invisible empire," the whole lot of them, laughed loudly.

"He-he-he! Eat it, eat it!"

"It wo-hon't cho-hoke you!"

As if someone else, not themselves, were to eat all the mess down to the last crumb!

"Listen, Comrade Lopatkin," Tepikin suddenly said in a loud

507

voice. "Today you are the victor. And we are all amazed at the way you went through hell and high water. But your nature, dear comrade, is selfish. You are a lone wolf. Before I met you I would have said that in our country it was impossible to fight alone. I still say it is difficult. The collective helps you, defends you, takes care of you, and gives you material support at the right time. But you kept out of the collective. Yet we are always ready to extend to you . . ."

"It looks as if you were not such a simple piece after all," Lopatkin thought, surveying the company. The circle had widened even more by now, there were shining eyes; some were young lads, still almost students. Eight years before, when the outlines of Lopatkin's machine had first been put on paper, these young people had probably been at the school-leaving age.

Lopatkin pondered for a moment. He remembered Arakhovski and the young man who had invented a casting machine with magnetic fields. Their game could be regarded as won—Lopatkin had long since taken the required measures. But now, from the most secret depths of his memory there emerged Professor Busko with his little glass phials. Busko's invention had vanished without a trace. And Lopatkin thought of the unknown lucky fellow, as young as these lads sitting here, who would, perhaps tomorrow, rediscover that lost idea, and hand it over to the people. He would run along the beckoning road on his young feet and would find it all too short! He would wave to his seventeen-year-old girl, surrounded by a radiance, and would tell her: "Wait for me, I'll only run to that little milestone there!" But would he ever get there? Or would he go on, from milestone to milestone, for eight long years? Or even disappear, like Busko?

He thought of all this and suddenly felt anger rapidly rising in him. Then memories came crowding—memories of Sianov, the workman who had helped with his machine in the Urals, of the unknown benefactor who had put twenty potatoes into the haversack. These people were still working, each in his sphere, and knew nothing of the existence of Tepikin, Avdiyev, Drozdov. . . .

Suddenly Lopatkin realized that his peaceful raft had been seized by the current and was being driven over the rapids.

"We are not going to stretch out our hands for your material support—we are going to fight you!" he said, and it was impossible to make out whether the fire that burned in his eyes was mockery or concealed hatred. "Now we will tease each other, as the fighters did in old days: I will provoke you, and you me, and the more maliciously the better."

"We can give you bruises enough!"

"Today it is not we who may need a lotion," Antonovich remarked.

"What do you want, you intelligent engineer?" Tepikin glanced amiably at him and turned back to Lopatkin. "And you, Comrade Lopatkin, it's a pity you . . . Let us drink a draught of peace instead. For the sake of old friendship. It's time for us to rest, to coddle our old bones, to heal our wounds. Buy yourself a Pobeda. A weekend cottage."

"A television set," one of the youngsters prompted.

"Why not? Let it be a television set, then. Not a bad thing to have."

"Man lives not by bread alone, if he is honest." Lopatkin's voice rang out in the silence.

"Now that you've got what you wanted," Tepikin went on, as though he had not heard, "let the youngsters do the fighting."

"Do you know, Tepikin, what *FRI* is?" Lopatkin asked suddenly with an expression of mockery and hatred on his face.

"What?" Tepikin opened his mouth, then recollected himself and flapped his hand. "Instead, answer the question which I'm going to ask you." Noisily he drew his chair closer to Lopatkin. "You, Comrade Lopatkin, will now be His Nibs, the head of the designing office. And imagine that one of your subordinates, Krekhov here, thinks up something better than you . . ."

"You think this question is a difficult one?" Lopatkin said.

"Wait a little . . . I am convinced that if Krekhov were to give birth to such a thing, you would at once begin to tie up the public

509

interest with your personal interests. You know, it is . . . er . . . harmonious that way."

"Ha-ha-ha!" the whole "invisible empire" laughed in unison.

"You would, of course, work out this project as well, but with your own label," Fundator put in good-humoredly. "With the label, 'KB Lopatkin'! The machine would be called the 'L2'!"

"I look at you and Tepikin," Lopatkin said, "and come to the conclusion that unfortunately it is impossible to offend you."

"Say it more plainly!" Fundator exclaimed.

"What is there to say? You have a tremendous advantage! You disgrace yourself abominably—and never feel it! Wait, I'll explain. I have a friend, an engineer-mechanic, Sianov, Uncle Pete. If you were to praise him for a part someone else had made, he would at once disclaim it—he has his own craftsman's pride and honor. He would have spat and gone away, if he had heard your talk of 'L2.' But I see you still don't understand me."

"All right, don't bring up old scores," Tepikin said. "The Minister has fully squared accounts with us over all that."

"It wasn't that I meant. But thank you for reminding me; *we* have not squared accounts with you yet. The Minister gave you a mild ticking off, but we shall give you quite different treatment. As prescribed by *FRI*."

"And what is *FRI*?" Fundator asked amiably.

"*Field Regulations, Infantry*. If you can get hold of it, read it. It would tell you what we intend to do with you. I used to be described there by the words 'single combatant.' But now we are 'a section in action.'"

"Well, well. If you are such a fighting cock, if you want it that way, stick out your chin. You won't take my words amiss, of course? When I get tight, I get devil may care." Tepikin waved his hand and looked at Lopatkin with unclouded eyes. "I love to talk and joke with a bunch of good fellows over a drink."

Behind his ingenuous smile the tremendous self-control, the training of a hardened fighter, showed for an instant.

"I, too, like that sort of thing," Lopatkin answered seriously.

"We shall crack many a joke together yet! Vassily Zakharovich is joining us, and he, too, as I see, is in a good humor."

Avdiyev, a huge figure in black, was moving toward their end of the table. He caught sight of Lopatkin from a distance and his freckled, puffy face twisted into a smile. He halted, opened his arms, as though for an embrace, and began singing in a pleasant chesty bass:

"I seem to see a happy ri-ival!"

He approached Dmitri, and would have embraced him, pushing aside chairs and people, but at that moment Vadia Nevraev came rushing at him from one side, crimson in the face as though fresh from a Turkish bath, and with an incomprehensible tenderness in his evil little blue eyes.

"Friends!" Vadia's voice was hoarse with drink and came jerkily out of his throat. "Friends! This is a splendid song. Let's sing it!"

Looking at Avdiyev and pushing one shoulder forward, he sang:

"And secretly and maliciously," here he shook a menacing finger at Avdiyev, "my hands grope for a weapon. . . ."

Avdiyev shuddered. There was a silence. "That was a bull's-eye!" someone whispered. "He croaked like a raven!" The great scientist was unable to recover his composure. He looked at the ground, shook his head, stepped over to the other table, and sat down beside Fundator and Tepikin.

"There's trouble brewing for him," Krekhov said. "That raven does not croak without good cause."

At one o'clock, when the guests began to disperse, Lopatkin and Nadia went out of the stuffy hall on to a balcony, white with freshly fallen snow. Leaving black footprints on the delicate snow, they walked over to the stone balustrade. Below them, as though they were seeing it from an airplane by night, the earth lay dark, dotted with a multitude of lights. Lopatkin swept the powdered snow from the gray granite, and leaning on it, lost himself in thought, gazing into the dark distance.

"What is it?" Nadia asked.

"Thinking of all sorts of things. Of all this . . ." Lopatkin nodded toward the darkness. "Aren't you tired? If I were to say to you: 'Let us go further' . . ."

Nadia said nothing. She only moved closer—and disappeared; she was not there at all; there was only a clear little stream from which he might drink and refresh himself on his hard road. All this he realized, leaning even more heavily on the granite slab, twitching his shoulder as though adjusting a load to make it lie easier before setting out. His shoulder had grown more powerful now, but the load was heavier, too. It was a load of new care—care for human beings.

"You'll yet become also a politician!" He remembered Galitsky's words. And perhaps now, for the first time, he really understood the man who had recently become something like an elder brother to him. And although Lopatkin's machine was already made and *delivered,* he again suddenly saw before him the road that lost itself in the distance, the road that certainly had no end. This road awaited him, stretched in front of him, luring him on with its mysterious curves and with its stern responsibility.